"How about the boys ranch for Corey?" Darcy asked.

"I know they have room for one more boy," Nick said, "and I'd much rather see Corey there, but I'm not sure it'll happen. I volunteer at the boys ranch, and it would be great for Corey."

Darcy wasn't surprised that Nick would volunteer there. In the short time she'd been with him, she'd seen a man of action and heart. "Then I'll pray that something is done for Corey."

Nick looked away. "In my experience, He hasn't helped much."

There was something in Nick's voice that touched Darcy. Who did he turn to when he was in trouble or upset?

She started to say something, but the tense set of his jaw and rigid posture indicated this wasn't a good time. He wouldn't hear her.

She didn't want to leave Haven until something was done for Corey. How could she walk away from a child in need?

And how could she walk away from Nick McGarrett?

Margaret Daley, an award-winning author of ninety books (five million sold worldwide), has been married for over forty years and is a firm believer in romance and love. When she isn't traveling, she's writing love stories, often with a suspense thread, and corralling her three cats, who think they rule her household. To find out more about Margaret, visit her website at margaretdaley.com.

A *Publishers Weekly* bestselling and award-winning author with over 1.5 million books in print, **Deb Kastner** writes stories of faith, family and community in a small-town Western setting. She lives in Colorado with her husband and a pack of miscreant mutts, and is blessed with three daughters and two grandchildren. She enjoys spoiling her grandkids, movies, music (The Texas Tenors!), singing in the church choir and exploring Colorado on horseback.

Texas Haven

Margaret Daley

&

Deb Kastner

Previously published as
The Cowboy's Texas Family and
The Doctor's Texas Baby

HARLEQUIN® LOVE INSPIRED®

Special thanks and acknowledgment are given to Margaret Daley and Deb Kastner for their contributions to the Lone Star Cowboy League: Boys Ranch miniseries.

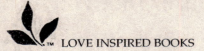 ™ LOVE INSPIRED BOOKS

Recycling programs for this product may not exist in your area.

ISBN-13: 978-1-335-00780-3

Texas Haven

Copyright © 2019 by Harlequin Books S.A.

The publisher acknowledges the copyright holder of the individual works as follows:

The Cowboy's Texas Family
Copyright © 2016 by Harlequin Books S.A.

The Doctor's Texas Baby
Copyright © 2017 by Harlequin Books S.A.

www.Harlequin.com

Printed in U.S.A.

CONTENTS

THE COWBOY'S TEXAS FAMILY

Margaret Daley

To my editor, Melissa Endlich. Thank you.

For if you forgive men their trespasses,
your heavenly Father will also forgive you.
—*Matthew* 6:14

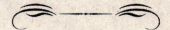

Chapter One

Nick McGarrett marched into Fletcher Snowden Phillips's law office in Haven, Texas. It was time the man stepped up and helped a member of his family. Fletcher's secretary looked up and frowned. As Nick crossed to her desk, he glanced at his mud-splattered jeans and boots. When he'd received a tearful call from Corey Phillips, a ten-year-old second cousin of Fletcher's, Nick had come straight from replacing a section of a fence on his ranch.

Nick owed Corey's older brother, Doug. When they'd gone on their last mission together, Nick had promised his combat buddy that after he left the service he would watch out for Corey until Doug could. At the time Nick had thought it would be only a few months until Doug returned home. His friend was killed in that mission by a sniper. Young Corey looked like Doug, who'd always had Nick's back when they had gone on assignments together.

Nick fixed his gaze on Nancy Collins, hoping it would convey his determination. "I need to see Fletcher *now.*" He'd lost all patience with the man.

Both of the secretary's eyebrows rose, and her chin came up a notch. "Do you have an appointment?"

He peered at the closed door to Fletcher's inner office—shut tightly like the lawyer's heart. Although she probably knew the answer, Nick said, "No."

"I can schedule one for next week. He's leaving soon."

"That's okay." Nick tipped the brim of his brown Stetson and then pivoted and strode into the corridor.

He planted himself against the wall, reclining back with his arms crossed. He was going to talk to the man one way or another. It was in times like this that Nick wished he had enough money to help Fletcher's cousin financially. All he could do was be there for the ten-year-old who lived twenty miles away in a small town on the other side of Waco.

Today Corey had thought his dad was dead. Nick tried to go over to the small, dilapidated house whenever the boy called. If he couldn't, Nick would call Mrs. Scott, who lived next door, to help. Today he'd been worried he wouldn't make it in time if something worse had happened to Ned Phillips than drinking too much alcohol. Thankfully the older woman had stayed with Corey, assuring the child that his father would wake up, which he finally did. Truth be told, Corey shouldn't even be living with his alcoholic father, who left the child practically to raise himself. Nick had been there as a kid and knew how hard that was.

The door to the office opened, and Fletcher came out.

Nick pushed himself off the wall and stepped in the man's path. "We need to talk."

"I don't have time."

Fletcher, tall with an imposing paunch, tried to skirt

around Nick. He didn't weigh as much as the lawyer, but his body was muscular from hard work. Fletcher's idea of exercise was walking to and from his luxury car. Nick blocked his path. "Make time."

Fletcher scowled. "Is this about Corey again?"

"Yes. You're his closest relative. If you don't want to take the boy and raise him, then at least help Ned buy food and clothing." Nick nearly choked on the first part of the sentence. Fletcher wasn't good father material either.

"I'm not giving Ned a cent. All he would do is buy more liquor. I'm a bachelor. I always have been. I wouldn't know the first thing about raising a child. Check with Family and Protective Services. That's their job." Fletcher quickly sidestepped and charged down the hall, leaving Nick fuming.

As if he hadn't tried contacting the authorities. The underfunded and overworked Family and Protective Services had more urgent cases to deal with.

Nick took several deep, calming breaths and then followed Fletcher outside to the parking lot. The wind held a fierce chill even for early January. As the lawyer drove away, Nick hurried his pace and welcomed what warmth still lingered in the cab of his old truck.

When Nick had first returned to Haven after being in the army, serving overseas in a war zone, Fletcher had said the same thing—that it was the county's problem, not Fletcher's.

Painful memories from the war zone inundated Nick. It had been over a year since he'd returned home to Haven. Too many comrades had died. He didn't understand why there was so much death and hatred. At first he had prayed, but when he lost one friend while

Nick was trying to save his life, he'd stopped talking to God. The Lord obviously wasn't listening.

As Nick left Main Street and the small downtown area, he passed Fletcher parking his car in front of his large antebellum home a few miles outside of Haven. The large three-story house overshadowed everyone else's place nearby. Although he came from a family with a long ranching history, Fletcher didn't live on more than two acres of land. According to Fletcher, ranching was manual labor and beneath him.

The sun near the western horizon sent up streaks of yellow, orange and rose through the darkening blue sky. Even though sunset was less than a half hour away, Nick wore his sunglasses to keep the glare from impeding his driving. Through the last burst of brightness, he glimpsed a car coming toward him. The driver maneuvered it to the shoulder of the two-lane highway and then came to a stop.

As Nick approached, he eased up on the gas. The other car's emergency lights began flashing. A blond-haired woman opened the car door, swung her long legs around and stood. Standing partially on the road in four-inch heels, she glanced at him as he passed her. He made a U-turn and parked not a yard behind her. The chilly wind blew even stronger than before. The moisture-laden air would produce snow later tonight.

Nick climbed from his truck and strolled toward the lady using her expensive sports car as a shield from the cold northern blast.

"Not for two hours? It's getting dark." Her throaty voice with a Southern drawl rose in panic. "I'm in the middle of nowhere." She paused while the person on the other end said something and then she sighed heavily. "Fine. Seven thirty or eight." She disconnected and jammed her phone into her leather coat's pocket.

Her gaze clashed with his, and she backed up against her car door. "I know how to defend myself, mister."

"Against what? The cold? That short leather jacket won't keep you warm." His look skimmed her length, taking in her bare legs and the skirt that came to her knees. She had to be passing through. She had *city gal* stamped all over and, by the looks of her Corvette, was rich too. It wasn't that he thought anyone would harm her, but he couldn't leave her stranded for two hours waiting for a ride from whomever she was talking to.

"When I left Mobile this morning, it was a balmy sixty-five degrees and climbing to eighty until I began heading north in Houston."

"A cold front is pushing through. If you don't want to wait, I can drive you to Haven, the nearest town. I know Slim, who owns the garage. Or if you ran out of gas, I can bring you back some. You're only five miles from Haven."

She straightened. "I didn't run out of gas. I have over half a tank. My check-engine light came on when I left Interstate 45. I was praying I could make it to Haven without a problem."

"Haven?" Why? Who was she visiting? She'd fit in about as well as a fox in a hen house.

"I like a small town. Waco is too big."

"And you're from Mobile?" The last time he checked, Mobile was classified as a city.

"South at Gulf Shores. The pace is a little quieter. I noticed you were heading out of town. I'd hate to take you out of your way." The woman hugged her arms close to her body while she pretended she wasn't freezing.

"I don't live too far from here. A few extra miles won't make any difference." His horses could wait, and after he dropped her off, he'd call Corey and decide if he needed to see him in person tonight or if he could wait until tomorrow.

"I hate to be a bother."

In a short time darkness had totally blanketed the landscape, the only illumination coming from his headlights. He didn't want to leave her alone on the road. There was little crime in the area, but if something happened to her, he'd have a hard time forgiving himself. "It's up to you. But after sundown, it's going to get a lot colder fast." He held out his hand. "By the way, I'm Nick McGarrett."

The woman shook it. "I'm Darcy Hill. And if you're sure you have the time to go back into town, then I'd appreciate a ride to the garage. I have a reservation at the Blue Bonnet Inn."

Reservations? The inn was more of a bed-and-breakfast and did a brisk business in the spring, summer and fall. It was well-known in the state for its hospitality and luxurious accommodations, but in the winter it might be half full at its best. "It's not far from Slim's, right off the main street. You might want to get your luggage. Slim will have to tow your car to Haven, and since it's close to quitting time, he probably won't take a look under the hood till morning."

"After being on the road eleven hours, all I want to do is eat and sleep. I can call my auto service back and cancel if you're sure."

"Yes, ma'am. I'll put your luggage in the back of my truck."

She withdrew her key fob from her pocket and

clicked it. The trunk popped open. "I also have some pieces in the passenger seat."

Nick stared at the back area of her sports car, every inch crammed with her belongings. While he emptied the trunk—two suitcases and some soft bags—Darcy took out a couple more pieces from the front seat. "How long are you staying?"

"Not sure yet. For a while."

Nick carried the luggage to his truck. *Who makes plans to come to Haven for an undetermined amount of time in the winter?* The last *city gal* who came to Haven a while back was now buddy-buddy with Fletcher. They didn't need another troublemaker like Avery Culpepper in town, even if Darcy Hill was pretty and sure to turn men's heads.

Darcy settled herself in the passenger seat of the man's beat-up truck, called her auto service and then put her cell phone in her purse. She patted the soft leather, reassuring herself that her handgun was still inside. Her dad had insisted she bring it on the long road trip. She was twenty-seven and lived in her own house not far from her parents' estate in Alabama, but they still worried about her. She was their only child, adopted when she was a few weeks old. In her heart, Mom and Dad were her true parents. They had even supported her trip to Haven.

"Do you know anyone around here?" the cowboy asked as he started his pickup and pulled onto the highway.

"No." Which was true, but she was hoping to get to know her biological father. She wasn't sure whether she would approach him or not—especially since her birth mother had made it clear that she didn't want to meet Darcy. Being rejected by her twice had been a blow. She didn't want another rejection.

"Most people have a reason to visit Haven."

She warmed her hands near a heat vent in the dashboard that put out an inadequate stream of hot air. "I'm not most people. When I was a child, I wanted to visit every state. I've been in Texas before, but it's so big I felt I needed to divide it into sections to do it justice." All technically true. As they neared Haven, she stared out the side window at the lights from a large antebellum house she knew belonged to her biological father. The private investigator who had located Fletcher Phillips had given her a photo of the man's house, along with other pictures of him. She swung her gaze to Nick, the dim interior lights casting his ruggedly handsome features into the shadows but not concealing the strong slope of his jawline and the broad width of his shoulders. "Now that place makes me feel right at home. Who lives there?"

Nick tensed, his shoulders squaring. "Fletcher Phillips."

His stern tone sent up red flags. "I get the impression you don't care for the man. What does he do for a living?" She already knew that but didn't want to appear suspicious.

"A lawyer," he spat out as though it were a dirty word.

"You don't like lawyers or just Fletcher Phillips?" A hard edge entered her words. She'd met her share of people who didn't like any attorney until they needed one. She worked as one for Legal Aid.

"Not this one. He butts his nose in a situation he shouldn't but ignores family members he should take care of."

Darcy swallowed hard, her hand curling around the door handle. Had she made a mistake looking for Fletcher Phillips? Or catching a ride with Nick McGarrett? "Family members?"

Nick slid a glance at her. "You caught me at the wrong time. I just had a run-in with the man over helping his cousins."

Although she couldn't see his face completely, she sensed a softness in his expression. "Cousins?" Before coming to Haven, she'd investigated only her biological father, not anyone else who might be kin to her in this area. Now she wished she had dug a little deeper. She was curious about these other relatives. "Why do they need help?"

"Ned Phillips, Fletcher's cousin, has no business being a father, especially to a young boy."

Her curiosity grew. "Why?" Maybe she should leave now. No, she hadn't come all this way to leave because of Nick's opinion of Fletcher. There were always two sides to a situation. But she made a note to be more cautious about approaching Fletcher.

"Ned has a son, who he neglects—even leaves him alone, usually to go out to drink. Corey is only ten and shouldn't have to take care of himself. I've tried to get Fletcher to at least help the boy."

"And this Fletcher won't?" Obviously it had been a good choice to come to town and scout the situation out first before she said anything to Fletcher Phillips—if she ever did. She wanted information, not a father. She already had a wonderful dad who loved her.

"It's not his problem, according to Fletcher."

So Fletcher doesn't care about family? Darcy's stomach tightened into a knot. She'd known from an early age that she was adopted but always felt as if she were Mom and Dad's real daughter. They had never treated her any other way. So why set herself up for another disappointment by her birth parents?

"But Corey is your problem?" A lump lodged in her throat as she said the boy's name. She'd dealt with enough legal cases that involved children, and she always fought for what was right for them. One day she hoped to have her own kids, and she wouldn't abandon them the way her biological parents had. Although she had had a wonderful childhood with a loving, caring mom and dad, it looked like it could have been just as easily the opposite if she hadn't been put up for adoption.

For a long moment silence reigned in the truck. Then the blare of a country and western song resounded through the cab.

Nick glanced down to see who was calling, and then he pulled over to the side of the road and answered it. "Mrs. Scott, is something wrong?"

The worry in his voice drew Darcy's full attention. As he listened to the person who had called him, his features slashed into a frown. Something bad had happened. Who was Mrs. Scott?

"I'll be right there. I'm glad the police are at Ned's."

When he disconnected, Darcy asked, "What's wrong?"

"Corey is missing. I need to go and help look for him."

Her cousin was missing! She couldn't walk away from an opportunity to meet and help a relative, especially a ten-year-old boy. And it didn't hurt that she would be with Nick McGarrett, an attractive—and caring—cowboy. "Let's go. I'll help."

Chapter Two

"**W**hy do you want to help?" This was the last thing he thought Darcy Hill would offer. "I'm only ten minutes away from the Blue Bonnet Inn. You said you were tired and hungry." Nick gripped the steering wheel and stared at Darcy in the dim light from his dashboard. He couldn't believe he'd told her so much about Corey's situation, but after his meeting with Fletcher today, frustration churned his gut.

"Because a child is missing on a cold winter's night. You'll need everyone you can get to search for him. I couldn't go to the inn without trying to help."

The worry in her expression lured Nick. She showed more feelings toward an unknown kid than Ned did toward his son. Her caring nature appealed to him and made it easy to talk to her. "Corey lives in Dry Gulch. It might take a long time if we can't find him right away."

"I don't care. A child is in trouble."

Her words touched a cold place in Nick's heart, forged from years living with an alcoholic father like Corey's, and calmed his earlier anger at Fletcher. "You can't go looking for him in what you're wearing." He couldn't believe he was arguing with her about helping

Corey. She was right. In the dark, it would be doubly hard to find the child. Did he have a coat on? Did he run away or had something else happened?

"I have some boots in one of my bags. It won't take me long to change into them." She gave him a smile. "I should have when I stopped in Houston and heard the weather report about the cold front moving through this part of Texas."

"Fine. I can't guarantee how long this will take." Nick made another U-turn and headed out of town. He handed her his cell phone. "Slim's number is in my contact list. You can call him and have him tow your car to his garage, and then you can check with him tomorrow morning about what's wrong with it." He shot her another look before pressing on the accelerator. "That way your car will be moved off the shoulder of the highway."

"Thanks. Do you have the number for the Blue Bonnet Inn? I'd like to tell the owner I'll be late."

"Under Carol Thornton. I've got to warn you, she'll ask a ton of questions about why you'll be late."

"I guess she'll think it's strange I'm helping out."

"No. She's one who will jump in when someone is in trouble, whether she knows the person or not. If I had the time, I would recruit her and a few others. Most townspeople are like family." He increased his speed outside of Haven, pushing the limit.

"Except for Fletcher Phillips?"

"You pick up fast. I won't bother calling him to let him know Corey is missing." Nick tossed a glance at Darcy as a car came toward his truck. Her blond hair hung in thick waves about her shoulders while her blue eyes held a frown. "I hope you have a hat to wear."

"A cowboy one like yours?"

"Nope. A warm one like a beanie."

"Yes, I do, and gloves." She studied the list of contacts on his phone and then connected with one of them.

While she called Slim and Carol, Nick focused on the last twelve miles to Corey's house. The unknown ate at Nick the whole way to Dry Gulch. Nick kept replaying his promise to Doug to keep his little brother safe. When he made a promise, he kept it. What if he couldn't now?

When Darcy finished talking to Carol, she gave him his phone back. "You're right. She drilled me with questions, most of which I couldn't answer. I have a feeling when I finally show up at the inn, I'll have to tell her everything we did."

"I guarantee you will. Carol is like a mother hen."

"Does she have children of her own?"

"No, but not from want of trying. It's a shame. She would have been a great mother."

"I'm assuming Corey doesn't have a mother around since you've only mentioned his dad. Do you know what happened to her?"

"She died years ago."

"That's sad." Her voice caught on her words, and Nick chanced another look at Darcy. Her forehead knit into a thoughtful expression. "Did Mrs. Scott tell you the details of Corey's disappearance?" she finally asked, her tone still emotion-filled.

"Not a lot. Usually Corey will call me, and we'll talk. Mrs. Scott lives next door to Corey and keeps an eye out for the child. All I really know is that Corey is gone and a deputy sheriff is at Ned's house." No doubt Ned had gone out to get some more liquor.

"So he was staying home alone?"

"Most likely." His own feelings warred inside him—

from anger at himself for not going earlier, to fear. Apprehension won out. Why didn't Corey call him again instead of running away? What if he couldn't find the boy? "I don't know anything else. Mrs. Scott didn't go into a lot of details. The neighbors are forming a search party to help the deputy. We can join them." Hopefully he'd find out more when he arrived in Dry Gulch. Better yet, maybe Corey was already home and safe.

Nearing the town, Nick slanted another glance toward Darcy, her hands clasped together as though she were praying. It wouldn't help. He'd tried that. Nick had given up on the Lord answering his prayers. At least Ned so far hadn't physically harmed Corey, but neglect of a child was a form of abuse. Corey hungered for love and acceptance.

"We're almost there. Ned and I have exchanged a few words concerning Corey, but nothing will keep me away. I promised Doug, Corey's older brother, that I would watch out for him. I just wanted to let you know things could get tense."

"Does Ned know about what Doug asked you to do?"

Nick turned down a street on the outskirts of Dry Gulch, a town about the size of Haven. "Yes, and he isn't too happy about that." He pulled behind a long line of cars crammed into every parking spot available. A few floodlights illuminated the area as though it were daytime. "It looks like a lot of people are here. Good. Corey could be in town somewhere, in the woods or on a ranch nearby. Lots of hiding places, and with the darkness he'll be harder to find."

"So you think he's hiding, not taken by someone?" Darcy asked as she opened the passenger door.

"More likely hiding or running away." He hoped. The alternative was even worse. When he hopped down and looked over the hood of his truck at Darcy, he was glad she'd come with him. Although he barely knew Darcy, her presence comforted him. Her immediate response to his news earlier had been to help. There was more to her than too many clothes and shoes. She might come from money, but she didn't act like a spoiled socialite.

He waited for her to join him and then he made his way toward the group of people on the front lawn of Corey's home. Mrs. Scott stood near Ned, talking to him as more neighbors joined the throng. The furious expression on Ned's face alerted Nick that the man probably hadn't been the one who'd called the sheriff's office.

Mrs. Scott saw him and came toward Nick. "We've searched the neighborhood and there wasn't any sign of Corey. We're reorganizing to cover the areas away from here. The sheriff is arriving soon and some more deputies. They're bringing in a couple of tracking dogs too. Five to six inches of snow are predicted tonight. We need to find him before he freezes."

"What happened?" Nick stared at Ned.

"After you called me earlier to check on Ned and Corey, which I did, I left Corey's house because Ned woke up and assured me he was fine. He practically kicked me out. I decided then to make some cookies to share with Corey and Ned as an excuse to check on them after an hour and a half. When I went over to the house, Ned finally opened the door. He looked like he had just woken up, so he'd probably continued to drink after I left. At least that's how he smelled. He invited me in while he called Corey. The boy never came. I helped Ned search his house to make sure Corey wasn't hiding. That man was getting madder by the second.

I discovered just a few minutes ago Ned went to the store not long after I left the first time."

Nick swung his attention to Mrs. Scott. "The liquor store?"

Mrs. Scott nodded.

"Are you the one who called the sheriff?"

"Yes. Ned didn't want to. He was sure Corey would show up. By that time it was getting dark. I went home and called."

Nick nodded toward Darcy. "Mrs. Scott, this is Darcy—a friend who heard about Corey and wanted to help."

Darcy shook Mrs. Scott's hand. "I wish we were meeting under better circumstances. Where do you think Corey would have gone?"

"He isn't at any of his friends' houses. The deputy checked those first, so I don't know." Mrs. Scott patted Nick's arm. "If anyone can find him, it's you. I don't know any of his favorite haunts and neither does his father." Anger infused the last sentence. "I declare I haven't seen a man quite like that one."

A conversation Nick had had with Corey last month came to the foreground of his thoughts. The child had been so mad at his father for forgetting to pick him up at his friend's house. He'd ended up walking home. Since it was getting dark, he had used the woods as a shortcut and stumbled upon a thicket—a great hiding place, according to Corey. "There are a few places that Corey and I have talked about. A couple we've been to. But one he said was his secret fort. He told me the general location in the woods. I think we should look there first." Nick didn't want to stand around while the deputies organized the search.

Mrs. Scott's mouth pinched into a frown. "But it's

so dark at this time of night. How are you going to look there?"

"I have some flashlights, one in my glove compartment and another in my toolbox. That's all I need." He turned to Darcy and added, "But you might want to stay here—"

"I'm game. It's getting colder." Darcy shivered. "I won't be surprised if there's snow in the next hour or two. We need to find Corey."

"Mrs. Scott, please tell the deputy where we're going and that we could use more people. It's the wooded area behind the elementary school." It would be better if Nick didn't go near Ned at the moment. He threw one last look at the man, who was still frowning as if this whole affair was an inconvenience. Although Nick's and Corey's situations were different, Nick knew the emotional whirlwind the boy was going through and how alone the child must feel.

"Will do, but, dearie," Mrs. Scott said, peering at Darcy's high heels, "you can't go in those shoes."

Darcy grinned. "I'm going to change."

As Nick and Darcy headed for his pickup, she said, "I think you and Mrs. Scott are right—Corey's dad has been drinking a lot. His eyes are bloodshot, his hands are shaking and his skin is pasty. In my job I've encountered enough alcoholics to know when I see one."

Nick opened the passenger door. "It's been getting worse. That may be what made Corey leave." When his own dad drank, all Nick had wanted to do as a child was hide. He shut the truck door, made his way to the driver's side and switched on the engine, throwing a glance at Darcy. "What's your job?"

For a long moment Darcy didn't answer. Nick turned

the truck around and headed the way they had come. Still no reply.

He was about to tell her to forget the question when she murmured, "I'm a lawyer—for Legal Aid."

Surprise flitted through him. He wasn't sure what he'd pictured her doing. When he thought about it, the fact that she was a lawyer wasn't what astonished him—it was that she worked for Legal Aid. The clothes she wore and the car she drove didn't fit his image of the belongings of someone working for the poor. And yet, she'd quickly volunteered to search for a child she didn't know. He was discovering there was a lot under the cool, composed facade she presented to the world.

"You can close your mouth now. I've been working at the office in Mobile since I got out of law school a few years ago. My father comes from old money. Giving back to the community is very important to both my parents. When I was young, no more than five, he had me volunteering right alongside him or my mother. By the time I went to college I knew I was going to fight for people who often can't fight for themselves."

"You need to give Fletcher Phillips a lesson in how to give back. Instead, he pushes his own agenda to make more money."

"Are you talking about Ned and Corey?"

"Yes, that's one example, but the boys ranch is another."

"What boys ranch?"

"We have a Lone Star Cowboy League Boys Ranch here in Haven, founded in 1947 by Luella Snowden Phillips. She used her own ranch as a place for troubled boys around the state to receive support and care and to learn a better way to deal with their problems."

"Any relative to Fletcher Phillips?"

"Yes, his grandmother. But he wants to close the place down."

"Why would he want to shut down something his grandmother started and supported?"

"Good question. Now you see why he isn't one of my favorite people. He says it devalues the property around the boys ranch and hurts Haven's economy. All he sees is a bunch of troublemakers, not young children and teens who have problems. His father, Tucker, was actively involved in the ranch. He isn't alive, but if he were he would be so disappointed in his son."

"I can see why you feel that way about Fletcher, but has anyone invited him to the ranch to see first-hand what's going on? Maybe even volunteer and get to know the children?"

Had they? Nick didn't know. "The townspeople are always welcomed at the boys ranch."

"Sometimes the obvious has to be pointed out to some people."

Nick chuckled. "That would be Fletcher, but I can't see even a grand tour of the boys ranch changing that man's mind. And I certainly can't see him volunteering there." He pulled into a parking space at the elementary school. "I met my share of people in the army who had to have it their way or no way. They were rigid and never wanted to compromise."

"There are people like that in every facet of life. I try to look at things from their perspective."

Nick climbed from the truck, paused and asked over the hood, "How's that working for you?"

"Actually pretty well, but I'll admit there are some who can make it hard for a person."

Nick studied her profile as she stared at the woods across the field. Was he one of those people? The thought didn't sit well with him. "So why do you think Ned drinks himself into a stupor and ignores his son?"

"I imagine the second part comes because of the first—Ned's drinking problem. Most people drink to excess because they aren't happy and don't know how to make it better. What happened to Corey's mother?"

Nick walked to the back of the truck and let the tailgate down. "I don't know. Corey was a toddler when she died. He said his dad wouldn't talk about her." And that topic never came up with his army buddy, Corey's older brother. Her question brought thoughts up about Nick's own mother, who died when he was seven. Was that what led to his father's drinking problem? Even so, that didn't give him the right to hit Nick whenever he felt like it. He was thankful that by the time he was fifteen his dad had backed off. Probably because Nick was stronger and bigger than his father.

He gestured to her multiple bags. "Which one do you need?"

Darcy pointed to two of them, and Nick slid them to her. "Maybe Corey running away will shake up his dad," she said as she changed her shoes and found her hat and gloves.

Nick shut the tailgate, handed her a flashlight and then started across the school playground toward the woods. "Probably not. This isn't the first time he's gone missing, but usually the sheriff isn't involved. No doubt he is this time because Mrs. Scott knew something was wrong and called them. Ned never would have. I don't know what would have happened if Mrs. Scott didn't help me out by keeping an eye on the boy. If she hadn't come back with cookies, Ned would have resumed drinking and still might have been oblivious to the fact that Corey could be freezing to death."

"Did you know Doug before y'all were in the army?"

He switched on his flashlight, the crunch of fallen leaves sounding in the quiet. "Yes, the family lived in Haven for a while when I was a freshman in high school. That's when Doug and I became friends. Then his family left and went to Dry Gulch. When I enlisted, I met up with Doug again at boot camp. He was escaping his father like I was." The last sentence came out before he could censor himself. Darcy was too easy to talk to.

"You were?"

He didn't share his past with anyone. Even he and Uncle Howard didn't talk much about what had happened as Nick grew up. It just brought up hard feelings toward his dad, and Nick had enough to deal with keeping the ranch afloat due to his father's mismanagement. Nick had used all his savings to bail the Flying Eagle out of debt, but he didn't have enough left to do much else. "I was a teenage boy who thought he knew what was best for him."

"Where is Doug now?"

"He was killed on a mission."

Darcy slowed her step. "I'm sorry to hear that. I see why you're trying to help Corey."

Frustration at his inability to help Corey as much as the kid needed plagued Nick. It brought back all the helplessness he'd felt as a child.

As they moved deeper into the stand of trees, Darcy followed a step or two behind, sweeping her flashlight over the left area while Nick searched the right side.

She'd never imagined she would be spending her first night in Haven looking for a lost child. But there was no way she would have stayed away. Corey and she were kin.

Family had always been important to her—something she didn't take for granted. What if her mom and dad hadn't adopted her? Then where would she be? Until she'd begun the search for her biological parents, she hadn't really thought much about where she'd come from. When her birth mother rejected the offer to meet with her, it had devastated her more than she thought possible. And after hearing about Fletcher, she didn't think meeting her birth father would be any different. The thought saddened her.

She shouldn't unpack. Instead, she should just leave when her car was fixed. She should forget the father who had never cared for her—and, from what she was discovering about the man, would never care in the future. He'd turned his back on a ten-year-old cousin. She always tried to look for the good in others, but with each bit of information she found out about her father, it was becoming more difficult. *Lord, how could Fletcher Phillips do that to a child—in fact, to a whole ranch full of boys in need?*

She didn't realize she had slowed her step until suddenly Nick was several yards in front of her. She hurried her pace and the toe of her boot caught on a root, throwing her off balance. She floundered and nearly fell.

But Nick grabbed her, halting her ungraceful descent. "You okay?" He steadied her, close enough that she got a good whiff of his citrus-scented aftershave.

Her heartbeat picked up speed. "I tripped. That's all." She needed to keep her thoughts centered on finding Corey, not why she came to Haven—or the man she was with. There was something about Nick—the way he talked about Corey—that attracted her.

Her breathing shortened. He was too close for her peace of mind. "Thanks." She stepped back and inhaled deeply. "Are we near the place Corey was talking about?" she asked, wanting to focus on the child, not the racing of her heartbeat. "I noticed a few snowflakes falling."

"I know. His fort should be up ahead. I just hope he's there. If not, I'll call Mrs. Scott and see if Corey has been found."

"What if he hasn't been?"

"Then I think we really need to comb these woods. He uses it as a shortcut from school as well as to his friend's house. It'll be harder in the dark. We'll need a lot more people. I'm glad they're using some tracking dogs. In the meantime, we can at least rule out his fort and this part of the forest."

Darcy scanned the towering trees, some leafless, others evergreens or ones that retain their dead leaves until spring. A black veil dominated the area beyond the glow of their flashlights. She quaked. "I guess for a boy this would be a great place to play in during the daytime." *But not at night*.

"But not for a girl?" Nick continued forward, glancing back to make sure she was behind him. Even from a distance she sensed the concern that gripped him.

"No, for some it would be. Not for me though. I wasn't much of a tomboy, except when it came to fishing. I love to go fishing. My dad owned a boat, and we often went out in the Gulf of Mexico. So much fun. What did you do for fun growing up?" Maybe concentrating on something other than Corey's predicament would reduce Nick's stress. She'd learned in her work that tension only made a situation worse, sometimes leading to bad decisions.

"I played football and baseball. I was also part of the junior rodeo."

"I took ballet and played the violin. I did learn to ride a horse English-style." As a teen she gave up the other two interests to focus on her mare and going to horse shows.

"We come from different worlds."

The more she was around him, the more she realized that, and yet there was something about Nick that intrigued her. He'd made a promise to a comrade to take care of his little brother, and he was determined to keep it. Like her, he fought for the underdog. She admired him for that. For that matter, he'd stopped to help her when her car died even though he was going the other way.

Finally Nick halted and pointed to a large thicket of bushes up ahead. "That's the fort," he said and then he called out loudly, "Corey, it's Nick."

Darcy held her breath. *Please, Lord, let him be here and okay.*

Nothing but the sound of the wind blowing through the woods.

Nick closed the distance between them and the dense undergrowth. "Corey, I want to help."

"I'm glad it's cold enough that things like snakes are hibernating," Darcy said as they approached.

"So am I."

"Are you scared of snakes?"

"Nope. But we have a lot of rattlers around here, and I don't want Corey to encounter one. Oh, and by the way, snakes don't hibernate. I've seen some in the winter." He winked and then started to the side. "You stay here. I'm gonna circle this brush and see if there's an easy way in."

Oh, good. He'd said that bit about the snakes on purpose and then left. She scowled at his back. As Nick moved farther away, Darcy hugged her chest and tried to see through the green-and-brown barrier in front of her where she was shining her flashlight. What if a rattlesnake was keeping warm under the thicket—and Corey had been bitten by it? What if...

Darcy quickly shut down those thoughts. She liked frills and lace. She liked girly things, and a snake wasn't one of those. She and Nick were definitely opposites and that was fine by her. And yet, she remembered his quick reflexes when he caught her before she could hit the ground. Okay, they might be opposites, but there was an appeal to the cowboy who dropped everything to look for a child.

Whoa. Where were these thoughts coming from? Exhaustion after driving all day? She wasn't in Haven for anything but gathering information about her birth father. She was going to be here only a short time. The more she heard about Fletcher the less she wanted to talk to him, but it wouldn't be right to pass up discovering what she could about her biological family since she wanted children of her own.

To her left Nick shouted, "Stop, Corey!"

The next thing Darcy saw was the boy rounding the end of the undergrowth, coming to a halt when he spied her and then darting to the side to avoid her. Nick closed in on him from behind. Darcy shot forward, trying to block his escape. When she was within a few feet of him, she took a flying leap and tackled Corey to the ground.

"Get off me! Get off me!" the child yelled.

Still clutching her flashlight, Darcy threw her body across his stomach while Corey wiggled and twisted. Was this what riding a wild bronco felt like?

Through her strands of blond hair she saw two cowboy boots planted near Corey's shoulder, a pool of light coming no doubt from Nick's flashlight. She thought it was safe for her to sit up, but the second she did, the boy jumped to his feet and tried to race away.

With lightning speed Nick grasped the child's upper arms and held him still. "What's going on with you, Corey?"

"I don't want to go back. I'll run away again if you make me go."

The anger in the boy's voice made Darcy forget about the dead leaves clinging to her coat and the bruises she was sure to develop from stopping him. Beneath his fury was desperation. She'd heard it enough in her job at Legal Aid. Not long after desperation came hopelessness. She tried to stop that from being someone's reality. Who was going to give Corey hope? His father? Not unless something changed.

Corey tried to yank his arms away from Nick, tears running down his face now.

All Darcy wanted to do was hold the boy until he calmed down, but she couldn't, even though he was her cousin—family. Besides Fletcher, she was probably his closest relative in the area. But no one knew that but her.

"Let me go. Dad doesn't care." A sob caught in Corey's throat.

Nick still held Corey, but when he knelt in front of the boy, his expression softened. "But I care about you. It's gonna snow and get really cold tonight. Did you think about that?"

Corey looked to the side. His blue gaze—so much like Darcy's—landed on her. "Who are you?"

The words *I'm your cousin* almost slipped out. Instead she smiled and said, "I want to help you."

"You can't. No one can."

The hopelessness leaked into his words and broke her heart. Coming to Haven was so much harder than Darcy had ever thought it would be.

"That's not going to stop me from trying. I don't know about you, Corey, but Miss Hill and I are cold. Let's settle this somewhere warm."

Her cousin stuck out his lower lip. "Fine. Nothing's gonna change."

"There are a lot of people searching for you and worried about you. Mrs. Scott was beside herself. She called the sheriff." Nick kept his hand clamped on Corey's shoulder and started back toward the elementary school parking lot.

"Dad will be mad about that."

"What did you think was going to happen if you ran away?" Darcy boxed the boy in on the other side and prepared to go after him if he broke loose from Nick's hold.

"Somethin' better. Anywhere would be better than here," Corey mumbled and dropped his head as he shuffled his feet toward the edge of the woods.

When Darcy returned to Mobile, the first thing she would do was hug her parents. She knew raising kids was difficult, but seeing someone like Corey only made her want to have her own children more than before. She had so much love to give a child.

She'd been blessed to have a wonderful mother and father. But others, like Corey, hadn't been. Maybe while she stayed in Haven, she would check out the boys ranch. Her biological father might not want to have anything to do with the place, but she did.

The minute they returned to Nick's truck, he settled Corey inside. While the boy sat sandwiched between them, Nick called Mrs. Scott to let her know they had found Corey.

The child folded his arms over his chest and hunched his shoulders farther down as Nick drove closer to Corey's house. In that moment Darcy felt like a fish in the Gulf taking the bait and being caught. It would be hard to drive home to Mobile without making sure something long term was done for Corey. The question was what. Nick, one of the few people who cared for the child and the person who had stopped to help her tonight, might be able to assist her with that.

Chapter Three

Darcy didn't even know Corey, and still she wanted to do everything she could to take care of him. Make sure he was warm and fed a proper meal. There was something about the child that drew her—more than family ties. There was a lot of anger in Corey, but beneath it she sensed a need to be loved, or maybe she was just putting herself in Corey's situation and projecting her emotions onto him.

As they drove away from Dry Gulch, where they'd left Corey with the neighbor, Darcy turned to Nick. "Where I live, I volunteer at a shelter and work with children to find solutions for their situations. I've seen families deal with a member who is an alcoholic and the toll it puts on them, especially the children. Some of the kids have to grow up so fast because they are left to fend for themselves. It breaks my heart."

Nick waited at a stoplight to turn onto the highway that would return them to Haven. He slid a look at her, his expression still full of worry. "Me too." Unspoken emotions dripped from those brief words.

"What do you think will happen to Ned?" Darcy asked the question she was sure was on both their minds. They had left Dry Gulch after the sheriff arrested Ned and hauled him to jail.

"He'll probably only get a slap on the wrist. I'm more concerned about Corey. At least he's with Mrs. Scott for the night."

"Are you upset that Ned wouldn't let you take Corey home?"

Nick gave her a tired smile. "Am I that transparent?"

"Well…yes."

"Ned doesn't want to be the father he should, but he feels threatened by my relationship with Corey. I'm glad Ned let Mrs. Scott take Corey without much of a fight. She'll take good care of the child, and I'll go to her house tomorrow morning."

"But you wanted to take him home."

"Yes, I feel responsible for him," Nick said, although she hadn't asked a question.

"Because of the promise to Doug?"

"Yep. When I give my word, I mean it. But it's more than…" Nick's voice trailed off in silence. "He'll be all right. I'm glad she called the sheriff earlier. All Corey had with him was a thin blanket. He could have frozen tonight."

There was something Nick wasn't saying. What? "Ned could be looking at child endangerment and neglect. The state could step in."

"I hope they do something this time."

"What do you mean, *this time*?"

"I have reported Ned's behavior before, but nothing was done. He left Corey alone overnight. Corey called me afraid because he heard a noise outside. I came over to be with him until his dad showed up in the morning. That's when my precarious relationship with Ned turned from bad to worse. Thankfully Mrs. Scott has been able to step in more, but she's had health issues. She's a temporary solution but not a permanent one."

"How about the boys ranch for Corey?"

"I know they have room for one more boy, and I'd much rather see Corey there, but Ned would never go for it."

"Unless this time the state does something about it."

"I volunteer at the boys ranch, and it's done a lot for the kids who live there. I'm there several times a week. It would be so much better for Corey than living with Ned. The boys ranch isn't like what Fletcher says. They aren't hooligans but kids who need extra help."

She wasn't surprised that Nick would volunteer at the boys ranch. In the short time she'd been with him, she'd seen a man of action and heart. "Then I'll pray to the Lord something is done for Corey."

"In my experience He hasn't helped much."

There was something in Nick's voice—pain—that touched her. Who did he turn to when he was in trouble or upset? She started to say something in reply to Nick's last statement, but the tense set of his jaw and rigid posture indicated this wasn't a good time. He wouldn't hear her.

She didn't want to leave Haven until something was done for Corey. How could she walk away from a child in need, a child she was related to?

She relished the silence as Nick drove toward Haven. Exhaustion weaved through her body, and she had to fight to keep her eyes open. But she perked up when he neared the place where her car had stalled. "Good. Slim must have towed my car."

"He'll be able to give you an estimate for fixing the car early tomorrow morning."

"I hope he can fix it right away." She only had a few

weeks to discover what she'd come for, and after what Nick had told her about Fletcher trying to shut down the boys ranch, she wanted to see it too.

"At least the Blue Bonnet Inn is near downtown and within walking distance of most places, but Slim is gifted when repairing anything with a motor. The only thing that will hold him back is if he has to order a part. We don't have too many suppliers in this area, but Waco will."

Nick parked in front of a three-story Victorian house with a sign saying Blue Bonnet Inn. Lights illuminated the long, partial-wraparound porch and its white wicker furniture. Darcy's first thought was that it looked inviting, homey and peaceful. A perfect place to take her long-overdue, four-week vacation. She hadn't realized how much she needed to take a break until this moment. She sighed.

"Ready? Knowing Carol, she'll be up waiting for you." Nick assessed her.

And usually when someone did, it made Darcy uncomfortable, but she must be too tired to even feel that. "It's eleven. A lot has happened today."

"More than you bargained for, but I appreciate your help."

"Anytime. I hope you'll let me know what happens with Corey."

"Yes, ma'am, just as soon as I know." Nick tipped the brim of his cowboy hat and then climbed from his truck.

Darcy did the same and grabbed some of the luggage he'd put on the ground near the tailgate. When he hefted the two bigger suitcases as well as her duffel bag, he looked loaded down but strong enough to manage. Yesterday when she'd packed, she hadn't known what she would do once she came to Haven, so she'd planned for everything she could think of. Now she realized it appeared she was moving in rather than staying for a short vacation.

Darcy started for the entrance to the inn with her hands full too. "When I was trying to figure out what to bring, I read that the weather here can be spring-like one day and full winter the next."

"So you brought all your clothes?" He paused on the porch, the bright light allowing her a good look at Nick McGarrett.

He was mighty attractive. "No, I left more than half my wardrobe behind."

"You're kidding?"

"I'm afraid not. I like clothes but especially shoes. The duffel bag is full of them."

He shook his head and moved toward the front door. "I own a pair of tennis shoes and dress boots as well as work ones. That's all."

Over six foot three, he commanded a confident presence. His chestnut-brown hair peeked out from under his cowboy hat. She would have been able to tell his build was muscular even if she hadn't known one suitcase was full of books she'd wanted to read but had been too busy to this past year. The angular planes of his face complemented his firm mouth, but what drew her full attention were his piercing blue eyes, reminding her of the Gulf on a sunny day.

"Men don't have all the choices women have," she finally said when she realized she was staring at him and he'd noticed.

"Don't see a need for so many choices. Makes getting dressed much easier."

The heat of a blush flooded her face. She opened

the door and stepped into the inn, the scent of lavender filling the air and welcoming her in from the cold. Ah, someone who understood the importance of essential oils. Already she was letting go of her stress.

Darcy scanned the large foyer, glimpsing into a dining room on one side and a large living room on the other. Antiques, such as a bookcase, desk and end tables, were sprinkled among the elegant but comfortable-looking couches and chairs. She took a step toward what must be the heart of the inn, enthralled by the beautifully carved mahogany coffee table between two cream-colored sofas.

A middle-aged woman with auburn hair pulled into a bun came from the back of the house. "You must be Darcy Hill. I'm so glad you're here. I'm Carol Thornton, the owner of the Blue Bonnet Inn." Her eyes crinkled at the corners when she smiled.

Darcy immediately felt at home. "Yes, I am. You have a beautiful place."

"It's been in my family for years." Carol turned to Nick. "How's Corey?"

"Safe and staying with Mrs. Scott, his neighbor. The sheriff arrested Ned."

"It's about time they did something about that man's neglect and drinking. If I can help, let me know, Nick," Carol said, then shifted her gaze back to Darcy. "I called Slim, and he has your car. He'll look at it first thing in the morning."

"That'll be great. Nick told me I could walk to the garage."

Carol waved her hand. "It's only a few blocks away, but then a lot of places are here in Haven. If you need a ride, I can help or my husband, Clarence, can. Speaking of my husband, he fell asleep an hour ago. He's been fighting a migraine all day. Will you please—"

"Say no more, Carol. Where do you want me to take these suitcases?" Nick, still loaded down with Darcy's bags, walked to the staircase. "Then I need to leave. Tomorrow will be here soon enough."

"The second room on the right. Thank you, Nick. I knew I could count on you."

"And I can take care of these." Darcy gestured to the few she'd set on the floor. Before Carol could say anything, Darcy picked up the bags and mounted the stairs behind Nick.

"Are you hungry?"

Darcy paused halfway up and looked down at Carol. "Starving."

"When you're settled, come down to the kitchen. I'll fix you and Nick bowls of vegetable soup to tide you over until morning."

"Thanks. It sounds delicious." If she had the energy even to eat.

Darcy continued to trudge up the stairs, her body protesting with each step. When she reached the second floor, she noticed the door to the second room on the right was open. Nick came out of the entrance and retrieved two pieces of luggage from her.

"You look like you're on your last leg." He disappeared into her room.

How did he still have so much energy? She'd left hers back in Dry Gulch after getting Corey into Nick's truck. Once they'd found the child, what she'd been functioning on drained from her quickly.

The second she moved into her suite all she wanted to do was go to sleep. Suddenly, not even food was enough to motivate her to go back downstairs.

"Will you please tell Carol that I've changed my mind? If I made it downstairs, I know I wouldn't make it up here again. And I doubt she would want a guest sleeping on a couch in her living room."

He stopped in front of her and removed the remaining bags from her grasp. His eyes locked with hers. "I know how you feel. I've been running on adrenaline the past few hours, and now I don't have any left. I'll tell her and let you know when I hear something about Corey."

Fighting the urge to lose herself in his blue gaze, she was surprised she had the energy even to smile, but she managed somehow. She didn't look away. "I appreciate that."

For a long moment he remained in front of her. She couldn't move. Nick attracted her. She didn't know a lot about him personally, but she'd seen him in action tonight, trying to find a child. Too bad she wouldn't be here more than three or four weeks before she returned to Alabama and her life there.

For the past two years, she'd been dating a guy who worked with her at the Legal Aid office in Mobile. They had so much in common—helping others, the same career—and she'd known him for years, but right before the holidays, they had mutually decided to be only friends. There was no spark between them, and she was beginning to believe there never would be.

She needed to focus on what she came to do, not a cowboy who made her start questioning her love life—or lack of one. She was just passing through Haven, here to learn about Fletcher and now any other family members. Then she would leave.

Nick strolled past Darcy and out into the hall. He gave her one nod. His actions dragged her away from her perfectly happy life in Alabama. Their gazes connected one last time. Her pulse sped while her lungs held her breath.

"Again, thanks for your help this evening. Good night." His deep, husky voice wrapped around her, chasing away any lingering chill from earlier and confusing her even more.

The sound of his footsteps going down the stairs echoed through her mind until she finally shook herself out of her daze, plodded to the four-poster bed and collapsed on it. Her last thought as sleep descended was of Nick holding Corey as he tried to console the boy. He would make a great father.

After feeding the animals the next morning, Nick entered his house through the back door, stomping off the snow that had fallen lightly throughout the night. At least Darcy was comfortable at the inn and Corey was with Mrs. Scott. Nick would drive over to Dry Gulch after he ate breakfast. Then he could hopefully let Darcy know what would happen with Corey.

The events of the day before only reconfirmed he wouldn't be a good father. Yes, he had found Corey, but he should have been there in the first place and stopped the child before he ran away.

Nick hung his overcoat and Stetson on a peg, noticing a beige hat and a black jacket on the remaining two hooks. The ever-present scent of coffee peppered the air. He loved that smell. The sound of shuffling footsteps coming toward the kitchen alerted him to his uncle's presence.

"I didn't hear you come in last night or get up this morning. I tried to stay up, but obviously I fell asleep in my lounge chair. You should have awakened me. How's Corey?"

"We found him." Nick went on to tell his uncle about Ned's arrest and Mrs. Scott taking the boy.

"I figured he was okay or you wouldn't have come home. What's this about you picking up a stranger?" His uncle, a tall, thin man with graying hair, ambled to the refrigerator, removed a mixing bowl and poured its contents into a black skillet on the stove.

"How did you hear about Darcy?"

"Carol called me to let me know what was happening in case you forgot to. Of course, she knows you would have filled me in eventually. It was just an excuse to gossip, although she didn't tell me a lot about this woman you rescued on the highway."

"I don't know a lot. She's about my age. She's a lawyer." He wouldn't tell his uncle how pretty Darcy was or he would make more of it. Uncle Howard was determined Nick would marry one day. Nick was just as resolved to stay single. Even when his mother was alive, his parents' marriage had been volatile—not something he would want.

"Carol told me Darcy has the room booked for three weeks with a possibility of staying a fourth one." Uncle Howard's curiosity came to the forefront of their conversation as he scrambled the eggs and then popped some bread into the toaster. "Why would a young woman come here and stay? We don't have too many coming through here, besides that Avery gal. And Avery has her own agenda."

Nick chuckled. "Don't know why."

His uncle shook his head. "Did you find out anything else about her?"

"I figure Carol and Clarence will get the lowdown

and tell you. You three are such gossipers. Darcy is probably being drilled right now by Carol."

Uncle Howard propped one hand on his waist. "I do not gossip. I'm genuinely interested in the people around me."

"And yet you haven't discovered who is sabotaging the boys ranch or, for that matter, who messed with our fence a while back."

"I'm working on it, but I ain't no detective." When two pieces of bread popped up lightly toasted, Howard buttered each slice and set it on a plate. "I don't see why anyone would steal children's saddles, especially from a home for troubled boys."

"I could think of one—Fletcher. And the way the man feels about me bothering him about Corey, he could have sabotaged our fence too."

"I've considered him, but he would just use his influence and money to shut down the ranch, not soil his hands taking the saddles or letting the calves loose. Don't quite know why he's so against the ranch when his dad did a lot for it. I'm glad Tucker isn't alive to know what his son is doing. Now, our ranch might be another story. Fletcher ain't too happy with you. When are you going to the boys ranch next?"

"Tomorrow for sure. Flint said there are two horses I need to look at." Nick volunteered as a farrier when they needed one.

"I'm so glad he's found someone. Lana is perfect for him and will be a great mother for Logan."

"Married life will agree with Flint." Left unsaid was that marriage wouldn't work for Nick, especially with someone who wanted children. Seeing what Corey was going through only reinforced that notion.

"It's good for a lot of men. Look at Heath and Josie."

"Stop right there. Flint is the foreman at the boys ranch, and Heath is a Texas Ranger—they do all right for themselves. I'm struggling to make this ranch viable, and I don't know how I could support a wife when this place needs so much. So quit trying to fix me up. I don't have the time."

"There's always Avery Culpepper," Uncle Howard said with a chuckle, while dishing up the scrambled eggs.

Several months ago, Cyrus Culpepper, one of the boys ranch's earliest residents, had died and bequeathed his family place to the Lone Star Cowboy League. The larger property allowed the boys ranch to take in more kids. The only hitch to the inheritance was that the town had to find the four other original residents of the ranch, besides Cyrus. Also Avery Culpepper, Cyrus's granddaughter, needed to be located. And she had been, but Lana didn't think the woman who claimed to be Avery was the real one.

"Do you think she is for real?" Nick asked. If she wasn't, the boys ranch wouldn't meet all the terms of Cyrus's will, and the ranch would be sold to a developer to build a strip mall. The boys would have to be moved again. If that wasn't motivation to find everyone listed in the old man's will, Nick didn't know what was.

"I sure hope she is."

"Avery has been cozy with Fletcher, and he wants the land to be sold."

"I don't see him behind what has been going on at the boys ranch." Uncle Howard placed a plate in front of Nick and then went back and brought the coffeepot to the kitchen table.

"I agree. Stealing a therapy horse and saddles and letting out calves doesn't make sense unless Fletcher has really stooped low and is resorting to these tactics to shut down the boys ranch. He's a lawyer. He'll seek a legal way if he can."

"Fletcher has blinders on to the good the place does for kids who need help. But then the man doesn't have any children." Uncle Howard poured some coffee into his mug and then handed the pot to Nick.

"Neither do I, but I see the benefits of the ranch. He's just plain mean-spirited."

"He never used to bother you so much until you came home and began looking out for Corey."

"How can someone who has plenty of money turn his back on family? Ned Phillips has no business being a father. No wonder Doug was concerned about Corey." And no wonder Nick never wanted to be a father himself. He didn't have the skills needed to be responsible for someone else.

"You've done what you can. Sometimes we just have to leave it in the Lord's hands."

"And look how well that has worked out," Nick mumbled and drank a mouthful of his coffee.

"I wish I could have done more for you with your father, but I lived so far away. I failed you. I'm sorry."

"You didn't know. He was good at hiding his abusive behavior. Once I tried telling someone, and I learned the hard way to keep my mouth shut. As far as I know, Ned hasn't physically abused Corey, but verbally he tears the boy down all the time. It breaks my heart." Nick's stomach roiled with thoughts of the boy's situation and the reminders of what he had gone through when his father drank.

"That's why I think you'd be a good father. You know what not to do." Then before Nick could reply,

Uncle Howard bowed his head and said grace. When he looked up at Nick, he said, "I'm not giving up on you."

"I don't need—"

The ringtone on Nick's cell phone distracted him. Quickly Nick answered, noting it was Mrs. Scott. "Is something wrong with Corey?"

"The state is sending him to the boys ranch. They just came and took him. Corey threatened he would run away again."

Chapter Four

The morning of her second day in Haven, Darcy stood at the inn's front picture window in the living room, holding a warm cup of coffee and staring at the snow-covered street. The snowfall had only been a couple of inches, but for a Southern gal like herself, driving even in a small accumulation made her so nervous she was afraid she would cause an accident. She would stay at the inn or walk to where she wanted to go until the car part came in and Slim installed it, hopefully later this afternoon.

Still, sitting around waiting today made her antsy. Her time here was limited, and after Corey running away last night, she wanted to make sure he would be all right before she left Haven at the end of the month.

She took a sip of her coffee as footfalls sounded on the hardwood floor. When she glanced over her shoulder, Avery Culpepper entered the room. She had long, bouncy blond hair and wore a baby blue wool dress that matched her big eyes and spiked heels, as well as more makeup than Darcy put on in a week. Darcy had met her briefly earlier that morning.

Darcy smiled. "Good morning. Carol will have

breakfast ready in five minutes. There's coffee in the dining room."

"I'll get some later." Avery joined Darcy at the window. "Thankfully there wasn't too much snow. I'm meeting Fletcher this morning."

"Fletcher Phillips?"

Avery brushed her hair away from her face. "He's the only Fletcher in this town. He's a lawyer who's been giving me some advice for when I get my inheritance."

"Inheritance?"

"From my grandfather, Cyrus Culpepper."

"The one who bequeathed his land to the boys ranch?"

"Yes." Avery glanced out the window. "I've got to go. See you around."

Darcy watched as Avery headed toward Fletcher's Lexus. He climbed out of the car and rounded the hood to open the passenger door for Avery. Darcy's biological father wore a Stetson, a black suit and boots. She must have gotten her height from him because her birth mother was only five foot two.

He turned his head toward the bed-and-breakfast, and their gazes met and held for a few seconds. Because she was looking for it, she saw a resemblance between them in the eyes and chin. He had a cleft in it like she did. She pivoted away and moved from the window. Her heartbeat thudded against her rib cage.

What was Fletcher Phillips doing with a woman half his age?

She felt as though she'd stepped into the middle of a story and didn't know what had already happened.

"I hope you're hungry. Breakfast is ready," Carol said from the living room entrance.

Darcy blinked and pushed thoughts of Fletcher from

her mind. Besides Avery and her, there was only another couple staying at the inn. The husband and wife
weren't in the dining room. She was curious about the
people of Haven, and from what she'd seen so far, Carol
would be a great person to talk to.

"Will you sit and join me? I hate eating alone."
Darcy sat at a table for four with a coffeepot and a
bread basket already on it.

Carol smiled. "I'd love to. Be right back with our
breakfast."

When she disappeared through the door into the
kitchen, Darcy poured herself a cup of coffee and
dumped several scoops of sugar into the brew. Carol
returned with two plates, placed one in front of Darcy
and then took the chair across from her.

Darcy peered at her omelet and the slices of melon
on the side. "This looks delicious. I usually don't have
much time to eat a big breakfast."

"I have some blueberry and bran muffins in the basket."

"This omelet and fruit is perfect. I stay away from
breads."

"You have to watch your weight? You're thin."

"I have celiac disease and have to avoid all foods
with gluten in them." When she was diagnosed six
months ago, Darcy had begun her search for her biological parents. Celiac was a genetic disorder. Was
there anything else she needed to be aware of in her
family history?

"Are you all right now?"

Darcy didn't like talking about that time of uncertainty when she didn't know why she was tired all the
time, losing weight and getting sick after eating certain

foods. "Yes, so long as I follow my diet." She bowed her head and blessed the food.

When she looked up, Carol was studying her. "If you're still here on Sunday, you're welcome to attend the Haven Community Church with me and Clarence."

"I'd love to. What few people I've met so far have been friendly."

"Most are in Haven. There isn't much that goes on in our town that others don't know about."

"Nick mentioned someone called Fletcher Phillips. Do you know him?"

"I imagine Nick wasn't too happy with Fletcher when he talked about him. Nick volunteers at the Lone Star Cowboy League Boys Ranch, and Fletcher is trying to get it shut down."

"Why?" Darcy wanted Carol's take on the boys ranch.

"He thinks having a boys ranch here is bringing down the value of the property around town. All he sees is troublemaking kids. That's really not the case. The children need love and care, but he won't listen to reason."

"How do the people in Haven feel about it?" Darcy ate her first bite of omelet, the taste tempting her to take cooking lessons from Carol.

"Some go along with Fletcher, but there are many who don't."

"What would happen to the boys staying there if he got his way?"

"That would be the state's problem. The ranch is licensed by the Texas Department of Family and Protective Services for their residential needs and for programs to help the boys."

First from Nick and now from Carol, Darcy wasn't

getting a good feeling about her biological father. "Which side of the argument do you support?"

"One hundred percent for the boys ranch. My husband was there for a few years as a kid when his dad died and his mother couldn't manage him. Fletcher thinks of the boys as juvenile delinquents. They are troubled but still children."

As Darcy ate her omelet, she decided she would drive out there and look into the ranch. Without seeing it, she couldn't form an opinion. Did Fletcher have a legitimate concern? "I'd like to see the place, maybe later today if I get my car back. How would the people running it feel if I went to see the ranch?"

"I'm sure Bea Brewster, the director, would welcome you." Carol rose and stacked their plates. "I'll make a map for you. And I'll call her to let her know you're coming by."

As Carol hurried away, Darcy finished the last of her coffee, pleased she had something to do. When she'd planned to come here, she hadn't thought of how she would spend her time other than catching up on her reading. She liked to keep busy, and looking into the boys ranch was a good way to have something to do— and possibly see Nick when he volunteered.

A minute after the phone rang, Carol reappeared in the living room. "Nick's on the phone for you."

"He is?" Darcy followed Carol to the phone in the hallway, surprised to be hearing from him, especially after she had just been thinking of him. When she answered, she asked, "Is Corey okay?"

"Not exactly. I'm at Mrs. Scott's house. The state is taking Corey to the boys ranch, and he's locked himself in the bathroom, screaming he won't go there. Mrs. Scott is looking for the skeleton key."

Her first urge was to drive to Mrs. Scott's house and do…what? She was a relative stranger to Corey. "I wish I could help. My car won't be repaired until late this afternoon or possibly tomorrow. Will he go to the ranch today?"

"Yes. I just wanted to let you know because of your concern last night."

"Thanks. I appreciate it. If I get my car fixed later today, could I visit Corey at the ranch?"

"Seeing someone familiar would be great."

"We don't know each other well, but I'm glad to come as soon as I can."

When Darcy hung up, Carol came over to her. "I couldn't help overhearing that Nick's friend is going to the boys ranch. If you don't get your car back, I'll drive you."

"I couldn't ask you to do that."

"It would be a good reason for me to pay a visit to my friend Bea. I could take you after I do a few things around here."

"Thanks. I'll let you know about my car."

An hour and a half later, Carol drove Darcy to the boys ranch. Carol had called and discovered Corey was there at the barn with Nick. Darcy dressed in jeans, a white blouse and tennis shoes. As she strolled to the porch with Carol, she noticed Nick's beat-up pickup parked next to the barn. Before she had a chance to ring the bell, the front door swung open and an older woman with brown hair and brown eyes appeared in the entrance.

The lady hugged Carol and then turned to Darcy. "It's nice to meet you, Darcy." She stood to the side. "Come in. I understand you're staying at the inn for a few weeks. What has brought you here to Haven?"

"A forced vacation."

Bea's eyebrows rose. "Forced?"

"My parents, who fund a legal-aid office in Mobile, insisted I finally use my vacation days. It's their way of telling me I work too much."

"Why Haven?"

"Texas interests me, but I don't want to go to a large city. I'm here for rest, not sightseeing. I thought I could help out while I was visiting. It's hard to go from working ten-hour days to no hours." When she'd been diagnosed six months ago with celiac disease, her parents were convinced the stress of her job had made her symptoms worse.

"She's met Nick and even helped with locating Corey last night," Carol said as Bea closed the front door.

The manager of the boys ranch grinned. "My, you've jumped right in. So you're familiar with ranches or, in your area, farms?"

"Well, no. But I'm a quick learner. I help out in my church's nursery as well as in a shelter for families. I love animals and children."

"Good. We have both," Bea said with a chuckle. "C'mon. I'll show you the house while Katie, our receptionist, calls down to the barn to have one of the other volunteers show you what we do there."

"I'd show you," Carol said with a chuckle, "but I'm a displaced city gal who can barely tell the difference between a cow and horse."

Bea laughed. "She isn't quite that bad, but I can attest to my friend being out of her element when she comes here."

"Give me another year, and I'll get the hang of it. Darcy, you're young and probably not as set in your ways as I am."

As Bea escorted Darcy and Carol through the three different wings of the home that each housed up to eight residents, Darcy glimpsed the various ages of the children, often seeing older boys helping younger ones. In addition, she met some of the houseparents, their ages a wide span too. The home was large but had a warm, comfortable feel to it. She could see why Nick thought this place would be better for Corey than where he had been.

When Bea and Darcy returned to the director's office, she met Katie Ellis, who was talking with Nick. He swung his attention to Darcy as she entered the room.

"You have your car back already? What was wrong with it?" he asked in a Texan drawl.

"No, Carol brought me. Slim told me it was a glitch in the electrical system. Thanks for recommending him. He should have it done later this afternoon."

"He's the only one in town, but he's a good mechanic. Saves us having to go into Waco." Nick looked at Bea. "I finished taking care of trimming the horses' hooves. I can show Darcy the barn and some of the corrals before I need to leave. And Carol, I have to go into town. I can bring Darcy back to your place."

"I appreciate that. Clarence just texted me that he forgot to tell me about a dental appointment I have in half an hour and we have a new guest coming right after lunch." Carol glanced at Darcy. "You can go with me now or have the grand tour of the barn."

"I understand Corey is at the barn."

Nick nodded.

"I'd like to see how he's doing after last night and this morning at Mrs. Scott's."

Bea shook Darcy's hand. "Katie will give you the application to fill out, and we'll get the necessary information so you can start as soon as possible. We have all our volunteers do that. I hope to see you around even if your stay is temporary."

After Bea left, Katie gave Darcy a sheet of paper. "I'll take it after you fill it out. You won't regret volunteering here."

Darcy grinned. Based on what she had seen of the house, she had to agree with the receptionist. This would be perfect for her while she became acquainted with her biological father and made the decision whether to approach him or not. But, even more, she would have a chance to get to know Corey and possibly help him, even if he never knew she was his cousin.

And see Nick occasionally. The words sneaked into her mind and made her grin. She didn't understand why she responded to him. Maybe it was because he was so different from the men she knew at home.

Darcy turned to Nick, whose neutral expression told her nothing. "I'm ready. I'll fill out the form later."

As she walked in the direction of the barn, Nick pointed to her feet. "I'm glad you decided not to wear those heels you had on last night."

She chuckled. She'd probably looked as though she was going to her office rather than driving across country for eleven hours. Even working at Legal Aid, she always dressed as she would have if she'd worked for a big law firm. Her professionalism helped ease her clients' fear they wouldn't get good representation in court.

She slanted a look at Nick. "I still haven't gotten into vacation mode."

"How often do you take a vacation?"

"This will be my first in three years, since I finished law school. I'm not even sure I know how to slow down."

"Volunteering here won't necessarily be restful, but nothing beats helping these boys." He held the barn door open for her to enter first. "I'll introduce you to the ranch foreman. When I left, he was in the tack room showing Corey around."

A tall, rugged man stepped out of a room off to the right, accompanied by a black Lab. He smiled, deep creases at the sides of his blue eyes. "You must be the new volunteer Katie told me about. I'm Flint Rawlings."

News spread at sonic speed here. She shook his hand. "I'm Darcy Hill, and yes, I'm that person."

Corey came out of the tack room but hung back by the door.

"Do you want to help with the animals?" Flint asked Darcy.

When the black Lab sniffed her fingers, she petted him. "I love animals like dogs and cats, but I have to confess I haven't been around cattle, and the last time I was on a horse was several years ago." When her mare had died, she had walked away from riding. The memories of her horse robbed her of the pleasure she'd always gotten from riding. "But if you need help, I'm willing to learn."

"Flint, we could always use someone to clean out the stalls," Nick said next to her. "I can show her what to do." One corner of his mouth tilted up.

She got the impression Nick thought she didn't know how to get her hands dirty. She'd changed enough diapers while in the church nursery and cleaned Beauty's stall the ten years she had her. Their bond had gone beyond horse and rider. "Is it much different from cleaning out cages at an animal shelter? I used to volunteer there as a teenager." She decided she'd keep quiet about having her own horse.

Nick's face lit with a smile. "Not quite. On second thought, you'd fit in better at the house, maybe helping with homework or something like that."

"It's been nice to meet you, Darcy. I'm leaving to have lunch with Lana. She tutors the boys after school and has said on a few occasions they could always use more volunteers doing that."

"So what will it be? Mucking stalls or teaching kids?" Nick asked in a light tone.

But she also heard the challenge in Nick's voice. He thought she was a pampered socialite and couldn't do either task. Yes, she came from a wealthy family, but her father and mother always believed in working for what you wanted. As much as she would like to prove she was capable of mucking out a stall and doing much more with horses, she said to Flint, "I look forward to meeting Lana then. Tutoring the kids would be perfect for me." In that area she could help Corey, and that was the reason she'd come to the boys ranch.

"I'll tell her. C'mon, Cowboy." With his dog beside him, the ranch foreman left the barn.

"I think that's a wise choice," Nick murmured close to her ear, a dare still lingering. "Less messy."

She looked at Corey, his shoulders hunched, his head down. "What do you think, Corey? Mucking stalls or homework?"

The ten-year-old shrugged, his stare focused on the ground by his feet.

Nick walked to Corey and clasped his shoulder. "Let's give Darcy the grand tour."

The boy didn't reply but followed a step behind

them. First Nick and then Darcy tried to include him, but they could only get one-word responses from him.

When Nick paused by the fence of one of the paddocks, he rested one booted foot on the bottom slat. "These are some of the horses the kids get to ride. They see to them. Several children are assigned to each horse and rotate duties every week."

Darcy paused next to Corey. "Which horse do you like the best?"

"Dunno," the boy mumbled.

"I think that's smart to check each one out before you commit to a horse." The urge to hug the child and tell him things would get better inundated her, but she wasn't even sure that was true. His dad could get Corey back and everything could remain the same as it had been before he was taken into state custody. She'd seen that happen working in her job.

Nick locked gazes with her for a brief moment and then shifted his attention to Corey. "C'mon, partner. I have to get you back to the house. Miss Bea still needs to show you the house."

As Nick settled behind the steering wheel and started his truck, he slanted a look at Darcy. "So what do you think about the boys ranch?"

"Corey is much better off here than with his dad. He's not happy right now, but then he wasn't happy at home."

"He's scared." That was why Bea had brought him to the barn first to see Nick. "In Dry Gulch, he had friends and knew some of the people, like Mrs. Scott. He'll feel better after he meets some of the other boys his age."

"What if he doesn't?"

"He's confused. He wants to be with his dad, and

yet not if he's always being left alone. He doesn't know what to expect from day to day and certainly doesn't feel safe." Those same feelings used to plague Nick while he was growing up.

"I've dealt with kids like that."

"In a perfect world, Ned wouldn't drink and would love Corey unconditionally. But that isn't going to happen. Ned isn't going to change." He knew firsthand the mindset of an alcoholic and remembered the times his dad promised to stop drinking and reform. He never did; in fact he got worse.

"People can change. I've seen some turn their lives around."

Nick shook his head as he pulled away from the barn. "Ned is too far gone."

"How do you know that for sure?"

"I just do." He didn't share his past with anyone. It was a part of his life he wanted to wipe from his mind, but it was always there in the background. He never wanted to see a child grow up the way he had.

"Then I'll pray for the best for Corey."

"The best scenario would be the state taking Corey away from Ned and a family adopting him. I wish I was in a position to do it." The second he said that last sentence he wanted to snatch it back. He had no business being anyone's father.

"Because you're single? That might not matter in certain cases."

"I'm not dad material." How could he explain that he was struggling to erase the debt that his father had accumulated? If he lost the ranch, he would lose his home and job. But, more important, what if he wasn't a good father to Corey? It was one thing to be there to help when needed, but it was very different to be totally responsible for raising a child.

In the silence Darcy's stomach rumbled. She chuckled. "I guess I'm hungry. I've wanted to do something for you for helping me yesterday. I'd like to treat you to lunch."

"I don't—"

"You have to eat, and we don't have to take long. I know you said you had something to do in town. We could meet after that."

He'd been toying with the idea of talking to Fletcher again about Corey's situation, especially now that he had been moved to the boys ranch. Instead of paying Fletcher a visit at his office, Nick would eat lunch at Lila's Café, where the man often indulged in some of the best food in Haven.

"You're right. I do need to eat. I still have a long afternoon ahead at my ranch, but no work could keep me from being there for Corey when he arrived at his new home. When he gets scared, he clams up and sulks."

"Then he must have been really scared. He hardly said a word. I'm glad you were there for him. Do you think Ned will cause trouble for Corey?"

A vision of his own dad coming drunk to one of his baseball games and making a scene in the stands popped into his mind. Nick gripped the steering wheel so tightly his hands hurt. He had dropped the ball and the game had gone into extra innings. All he'd wanted to do was crawl into a hole and hide.

"Nick, are you okay?"

The concern in Darcy's voice pulled him away from the past, but the anger the memory produced lingered. "I'm fine."

"You're worried about Ned, but sometimes having a

child taken away finally leads a parent to making the changes needed to reunite the family."

"And often it doesn't. And even if Ned stopped drinking in order to get Corey back, would it last? It's not easy to walk away from a habit that is so in-grained in you."

"But not impossible."

Nick pulled into a parking space near Lila's Café, switched off the engine and twisted toward her. "You want Ned to take Corey home." Anger laced each word.

She didn't flinch or turn away. Instead, she shifted to face him. "I want what's best for Corey. The same as you. The boys ranch is nice and a good temporary situation for Corey, but it isn't a home with a family."

"You grew up with a mother and father always there for you?"

She nodded. "Family is everything."

"That's nice and I agree—when it's available. But this isn't a perfect world where all children grow up with a loving family."

"You don't think I know that? I work with dysfunc-tional families all the time in my job. But we can't give up on the family. That's the fabric of our society. When the family goes, everyone is hurt."

She was right about the importance of family, but she looked at life through rose-colored glasses. "Are you one of those do-gooders who thinks all you have to do is throw a little money at a problem or breeze in and out of a person's life and it will change?"

Her blue eyes narrowed to diamond-hard chips. "You don't know me or what I've been through. I'm sorry you didn't have a family—"

"Hold it right there. Who said I didn't?"

"You did. If you had, you wouldn't feel the way you do."

The truth in her words deflated his anger. This whole affair with Ned had brought back painful memories he had tried to forget. "You're right. I didn't have the perfect family with loving parents. My father was just like Ned and my mother died when I was seven."

"I'm sorry."

"I didn't tell you to get your sympathy. I've dealt with it and moved on."

"Have you?"

He looked long and hard into her eyes. "Yes. My dad died eighteen months back, and the world is a better place now. Nothing else I can do about it."

"Yes, there is. You can forgive him."

He glared at her. Forgive his father? No way! "If you're hungry, I suggest we go inside. I've worked up quite an appetite."

"For what, rattlesnake meat?"

He paused in opening the truck door and glanced over his shoulder at the twinkle in her eye.

"I couldn't resist saying that," Darcy said with a smile and climbed down from the pickup.

How in the world did the conversation end up on subjects he never talked to others about—even his uncle? What was so different about Darcy that he let himself be baited? He shook off the feelings she'd stirred about his past and smiled back. "If you want, we could go rattlesnake hunting while you're here. I know people who do."

"I'll pass on that."

He winked. "You have an open invitation if you change your mind."

She laughed. At the entrance to the café, Nick

opened the door for her. As he entered behind her, he spied one empty table in the back corner, not far from where Fletcher was eating with the mayor, Elsa Wells. No doubt Fletcher was trying to sway her to his way of thinking about the boys ranch.

While passing their table, Nick slowed and tipped the brim of his cowboy hat toward Elsa before stopping next to Fletcher and staring down at him. "I thought you should know, since you're related to Corey Phillips, he's now residing at the boys ranch—in case you want to visit your cousin there." He couldn't resist that last dig.

Then Nick continued toward the vacant table and held the chair out for Darcy. As she settled, he took his seat across from her, facing Fletcher. The older man's gaze stabbed through him.

"Who was that?"

"That's Fletcher Phillips and Elsa Wells, our mayor."

"I saw him this morning picking up Avery Culpepper. She's staying at the Blue Bonnet Inn."

After the waitress filled their glasses with water and handed them a menu, he opened it, saying, "What do you think about Avery?"

"She's a bit young for Fletcher."

He stared at her for a few seconds and then laughed. "She's made it clear she isn't happy that her grandfather left his place to the boys ranch. She has said that she won't hire a lawyer and take the Lone Star Cowboy League and the boys ranch to court if she receives a hundred thousand dollars. The league turned her down."

"So has she hired Fletcher Phillips to represent her?"

"Not sure, although they have been chummy."

Darcy studied her menu and then lifted her head. "Is the lawyer the reason we came to eat here?"

"I was going to pay him another visit at his office, but you're right that I do have to eat, so why not do both at the same time?"

"I like the way you think. What are you getting for lunch?"

"Chicken-fried steak. They make the best in the county."

"With mashed potatoes and gravy?"

He nodded.

"Sounds delicious, but I'm on a gluten-free diet. I have to be careful what I eat. I'll order a salad instead."

Surprise flitted through him, and yet it shouldn't have. Darcy was thin and probably constantly watching what she ate and dieting. She seemed so out of place here.

So many things about Darcy just didn't seem to add up. Her desire to help with the search for Corey and to volunteer at the boys ranch was astonishing for someone who was here on vacation. There was something else going on here. He felt it in his gut. Just what was Darcy's real story?

Chapter Five

The following Monday afternoon, Darcy entered the library at the boys ranch and scanned the room for Lana Alvarez. She spied the school teacher/volunteer at a table with two boys.

As Darcy approached, Lana lifted her head and smiled, her dark brown eyes fixed on Darcy.

"I'm Darcy Hill. I'm hoping I can help you with tutoring." She held out her hand.

Lana shook it. "We always need extra tutors." Lana rose and moved away from the boys. "Flint told me you helped Nick find Corey."

"Yes, and I was hoping I could work with him especially. I want to help him adjust to his new situation." Darcy searched the library for Corey and found him at a table alone.

"That can certainly be arranged. This is all so new. I think he feels a bit overwhelmed."

"I agree. He's staring at that book, but I don't think he's reading."

"Today was his first day at school. I don't know a lot about him yet. I was going to finish with Danny and Mikey, and then see what he needs to do."

Darcy looked around the room. "I can see why you need help. There are only a few volunteers."

"It varies from day to day. I hear you'll only be here for the rest of this month."

"Right, but while I'm in Haven, I can be here every day to help out." Seeing Corey sitting by himself bothered Darcy. "I hate to see him alone."

"Aiden asked him to sit with him, but Corey didn't want to. Aiden hasn't been here long, and he lives in the same wing as Corey. I think he'll be good for Corey."

"Which one is Aiden?"

"The table to the left, brown hair. If you can help Corey, that would be great. Sometimes it takes a new boy a little time to fit in, but Corey isn't even trying."

"Thanks. I'll see what I can do."

Darcy made her way to Corey and took the chair next to the boy. He stiffened, but he slid a glance her way. "How was the first day of school?" she asked him.

He shrugged.

"Did you meet any friends?"

He shook his head.

"Have you seen Nick today?"

He nodded.

Darcy touched the corner of his book titled *The Adventures of Shaun*. "This isn't a textbook. Did you get it at school?"

His head bobbed up and down.

She'd dealt before with children who occasionally would give her the silent treatment. She decided to ask him a question he couldn't answer with a yes or no. "Who's your new teacher?"

He didn't say anything for a long moment and then murmured, "Mrs. Harris."

"What are some of the things you did today at school?"

"Work."

"What do you have to do for homework? Math? Reading?"

"A report on the library book that I checked out."

Darcy peered at the page he was on. He'd read only two pages. "You haven't read much. When is the report due?"

"End of the week."

"Why did you pick it?"

"It was the last one left on the book cart for the class."

She picked it up and read the back-cover copy. "This sounds really interesting. Shaun and his friends find a secret cave with a treasure in it. I'd love for you to read some of it to me."

His head dropped and his shoulders hunched.

"This isn't the best place to read a story. Let's go into the house and find a quiet area."

He mumbled something she couldn't hear.

Darcy leaned closer. "What did you say?"

He slammed the book closed and leaped to his feet. Darcy stood and grabbed *The Adventures of Shaun* while Corey hurried from the library.

As she passed Lana, she said, "I've got this." She prayed she did.

Then Darcy rushed across the short distance to the house. Walking down a hallway, she looked right and left. Which way did Corey go?

Darcy checked the living room but didn't find Corey. When she left, she glimpsed him sitting on a step near the top of the staircase. Corey tensed and then started to stand.

She slowly ascended the stairs. "Relax, Corey. You don't have to read if you don't want to."

Corey's eyes widened as though he felt trapped.

"I'm only here to help you." She sat beside him. "Coming to a new place can be scary. I remember the first time I went to summer camp. I was eight and didn't know anyone. A lot of kids knew each other from the summer before. The first day I hid a lot. I had such a good hiding place that I didn't realize the whole camp was looking for me. I missed dinner."

"Where did you hide?"

"Under the porch."

"What about the bugs and critters?"

"I was fine until a snake slithered in front of me. I got out of there so fast, I fell and rolled down the hill. I landed at my counselor's feet."

Corey giggled. "Was she mad at you?"

"She wasn't happy, but the other campers couldn't believe I crawled under there and stayed. Now, I don't recommend doing this, but after that, I had a lot of kids who wanted to talk to me."

"I don't mind snakes."

"I never thought about it until I encountered one under the porch, but now they're one of my least favorite animals. I have several pets at home. My parents are watching them while I'm here."

Corey twisted toward her. "I've never had a pet. What kind do you have?"

"A cat named Calico and a dog named Arnold."

"They get along?"

"Best buddies."

"Do you miss them?"

"Yup. If you could have a pet, what would you get?"

"A dog. I liked meeting Cowboy at the barn."

"How about the horses?"

"Yes!"

Maybe Nick would be at the barn. "Well, then, let's go to the barn. I'll let Lana know we're going for a walk."

"But I'm supposed to do my homework."

"You will afterward."

He turned forward and lowered his head. "I can't."

"I'll help you."

"You don't understand. I can't read real good."

His behavior made sense. Did the school and boys ranch know he had a problem? "Tell you what. Let's go find a quiet spot and I'll read the first page if you'll try the second one. That's all for today. Then we can both go to the barn and see the animals for the rest of the time."

"Only a page?"

She nodded.

Corey jumped to his feet and hurried down the stairs. More slowly, Darcy followed. She'd just found something that might motivate the boy. She couldn't wait to tell Nick.

As the sun set, Nick brushed down Laredo after riding him along the perimeter of his ranch to check the fences. He did that more frequently since the one along his northern boundary had been sabotaged. Finally they all appeared to be in good condition. His dad must not have fixed any in years. That went for a lot of things around the place, but after sixteen months of hard work he was beginning to see daylight.

The barn door opened behind him. Weary from a long day that had started at five in the morning, he looked over his shoulder, brushed his gelding's flank

one last time and then rotated toward Darcy. The sight
of her lifted his spirits. "What brings you to the Flying Eagle?"

Her smile lit the dimness in the cavernous barn. "I
came to see you. Your uncle told me you were here."

He held the halter and led Laredo in the direction of
the back door. "I'm gonna put him out to pasture and
then I'll be right back."

Why was she here? Over the weekend he'd hoped
she would be at the boys ranch when he was there. Lana
had told him she'd dropped by after church yesterday to
set up times for her to volunteer, but he'd arrived in the
late afternoon and missed her. He'd felt disappointed
and knew he needed to stop thinking about her. Easy
to say, hard to do. There was something captivating
about her—fragile and yet not.

After reentering the barn, he crossed to the tack
room and hung up the halter. He knew the exact second
she stood in the doorway, although she didn't make a
sound. Her presence was almost tangible.

Slowly he faced her. Her shoulder-length blond hair
framed her beautiful features. Her blue gaze held his
for a long moment. As he crossed to her, breathing in
her flowery scent, which chased away the smells of the
barn, his look dropped to her full lips. They were covered in a light pink gloss. He balled his hand to suppress the urge to touch them. *To kiss them.*

A whinny destroyed the moment. Darcy stepped
back, and he skirted around her, needing to put some
space between them. If he was smart, he would remember to keep his distance, but clear across the town
wasn't far enough to stop him from wanting to cup her
face and…

He refused to complete the thought. "So why are

you here?" Nick asked as he strolled toward a stall containing a pregnant mare. Before he left he wanted to check on her.

"I came to talk about Corey."

He opened the door and went inside to assess Morning Star, running his hand over her. "I took Bea and him to school this morning. I'd promised him I would for his first day. He was quiet, but he seemed all right. One of the boys on his wing is in the same class—Aiden. When I left just before the bell rang, they were talking together."

"That's good. But he was sullen when he came home."

Nick gave Morning Star a carrot. "It won't be long, girl. I'll see you before I go to bed." After rubbing her nose, he left the stall, closing the door.

"She looks pregnant. Is that why she's in the barn? Most of the stalls are empty."

"Yes. The first foal she had last year died not long after she gave birth. I want to keep an eye on her this time."

"That would be something Corey would get a kick out of."

"You've been with him a few days, and you think you know him."

"Today he told me he never had a pet but would love a dog. When we went to the barn, he said he wanted to learn to ride. Horses were his second favorite animal."

How had she discovered so much about Corey in such a short time? He didn't know about the child wanting a dog. Things like this only confirmed to Nick that he wasn't father material. "I promised him I would teach him to ride, but then Ned wouldn't let me bring him to my ranch."

"Flint told Corey he would be put in a group to care for one of the horses. He smiled all the way back to the house."

Nick gestured toward a hay bale. "Have a seat."

"I probably shouldn't stay long."

As she sat, he leaned one shoulder against the wall of the barn. "How did you find me?"

"Bea told me where you live. Just down the road from the boys ranch."

"Yes, it's convenient for me to pop over there when I can, even for half an hour or so. How did it go with Corey today? Lana told me you were volunteering to help with homework after school." And he'd purposely stayed away. He needed to get her out of his head.

"Today there were only four of us for twenty-four kids. Thankfully the younger ones didn't have that much homework. Corey took up my whole time."

"Why?"

"He wouldn't do his work. Just sat there staring at the page. He finally told me he has trouble reading. The book he had to read was too hard for him."

"I've helped him with math, but he never asked for any help with reading. He's good at math and really didn't need much assistance." Nick sank onto the hay bale next to Darcy. Yet another thing Darcy had discovered about Corey that he hadn't known.

"He didn't admit it easily, but at least now I know how to work with him. I let Lana know. She'll talk with his teacher tomorrow."

"How was his reading?"

"Slow. He retained what he read, but he struggled with quite a few words that someone his age should know. I told him I would make flash cards of the ones he had trouble with and we'd review them."

"It sounds like you'll be spending most of your time with Corey."

She grinned. "I enjoyed this afternoon. Lana and I decided I would work primarily with Corey. Tomorrow there will be more volunteers. Monday seems to have the least number of people. Maybe you could help out with the homework."

"Me?" He pointed at his chest. "I think I'll stick with helping in other ways. The extent of my higher education was one year at a junior college before I joined the army. The only teaching I'm gonna do is how to ride a horse." Another thing they didn't have in common. She'd gone to law school after four years of college. They were so different, and he needed to remember that. He stood and held out his hand for her. "I appreciate you letting me know."

She allowed him to help her to her feet, which brought her within inches of him. Again her light, sweet scent teased his senses. "I'd love to be there when you give him his first riding lesson. I hope you'll let me know. I have a lot of spare time on my hands."

"And that bothers you?"

"*Bother* isn't quite the word I would pick. I'm used to being busy. By the time I adjust to this leisure, my vacation will be over."

"Uncle Howard is preparing stew tonight. He makes it from scratch with tons of vegetables and beef and always fixes a big pot of it. Why don't you join us before you head back to the inn? That is, unless you have something else to do."

Her smile encompassed her whole face. "I got a whiff of it when I was up at your house. It smelled great. So yes, I'd love to."

He automatically reacted to her grin with one of his

own. The weariness he'd felt earlier vanished as though her presence charged his energy. "Good. Let's go. I'm starving. Forgot to eat lunch."

"I didn't, and I'm still starving."

Nick shut the barn door behind him as they left. "You might like the temperature for the rest of the week. It'll be in the sixties."

"Now, that's getting closer to what I'm used to in January."

"Did Corey say much about his first day at school?"

"Not much except that his teacher was nice."

"I hope this works for him. Did he mention his dad?"

"No. We mostly talked about the animals. Why?"

Nick paused on the back-door stoop. "Because I got a call from Mrs. Scott this morning. Since Ned was released on bail, he hasn't left his house. He came home not long after Corey was taken to the ranch, went inside and stayed."

"Do you think something is wrong?"

He let her go into the house first. "I imagine he's holed up, drinking. I asked Mrs. Scott to go check on him and to call me. She tried, but no one answered the door."

"Are you going to visit him?"

"I might." He felt he owed Corey that, but being around Ned always left Nick stuck in the past.

"I can go with you. I don't think you should go alone."

"Go alone where?" Uncle Howard entered the kitchen.

"To see if Corey's dad is all right." Nick strolled across the room. "I need to wash up. I'll be back in ten minutes or so. Ask my uncle if he's used anything with gluten in the stew."

Nick headed for a quick shower after a hard day of labor. He didn't want her to think he was making a big deal that she was here sharing dinner with him.

He rubbed the steam off the mirror and stared at himself, his beard a day old. He hadn't shaved this morning because he was running late to take Corey to school.

What are you doing? She'll be gone from Haven at the end of the month, if she even stays that long.

Five minutes later, he hastened back to the kitchen, the sound of laughter drifting to him.

Uncle Howard raised both eyebrows when Nick entered. He sent his uncle a narrowed look that he hoped conveyed Howard better not say a word about his showering and cleaning up.

"So what's so funny?" Nick approached the table, not sure where to sit, across from Darcy or catty-cornered.

"Howard was telling me about when you came to visit him in Galveston."

"About the time I sneaked up into the attic and fell partway through the ceiling?"

"Yes. I can just picture you swinging your legs around, trying not to fall all the way through." Darcy took a sip of her iced tea.

Her teasing look mesmerized him for a few seconds. "I was trying to pull myself up through the hole before Uncle Howard found out what I'd done."

"You didn't think the hole in the ceiling would clue him in?"

"I was eight. I wasn't thinking that far ahead." He didn't tell her he'd been in the attic hiding so he didn't have to return to Haven later that day.

Darcy chuckled. "I don't want you to ever talk to

my parents. My curiosity got me into a lot of trouble. But I have to admit they took it in stride."

Whereas his dad hadn't. At least his problems with his father helped him to relate to Corey. "Now you've stirred my curiosity. What kind of trouble?"

A twinkle danced in her blue eyes, brightening the sparkle in them. "I used to open all my Christmas gifts and then seal them back up so my parents didn't know. I couldn't stand the waiting. They got wise to me and didn't put anything out until after I went to bed Christmas Eve."

He'd rarely received a present from his dad, but this topic was bringing back too many memories he was determined not to remember. Ever since he'd begun watching out for Corey, he'd relived his past over and over, and now his conversation with Darcy was having the same effect.

"What time will you be finished working with Corey tomorrow? I want him to choose his horse and start learning how to take care of it," Nick said, changing the subject.

"If Corey has his way, as soon as he comes back to the boys ranch after school. I can bring him to the barn after he completes his homework. He usually doesn't have much."

"I think I'll hitch a ride with you, Nick. I haven't seen Corey since Ned stop letting him come to our ranch." Uncle Howard bowed his head. "Let's say grace and eat this beef stew before it gets cold."

After grace, his uncle started passing the food. "Darcy, how in the world did you end up here in Haven? Did you throw a dart at the map of Texas?"

"The name was what sold me on this town. I had a difficult case right before I came here. A custody battle between a husband and wife with two children caught in the middle. The two had a tug of war with the children."

"Did it end okay?" Nick wasn't surprised the parents were using their children as pawns.

"Yes, because the judge was firm but patient. He came up with a decision that made the two parents agree to a friendlier solution."

Uncle Howard broke a piece of bread and dunked part of it into his stew. "Something like Solomon when the two women claimed the same child?"

"Yes, neither parent wanted to give up seeing one of their children. They both were fighting for full-time custody. The hate in the courtroom was palpable. Each night when I left them, it was hard to decompress. I needed a break, and my boss insisted I take it."

Those poor children would have to deal with each parent's hostility against the other. What he'd seen of families only reinforced he didn't want to have kids. "Do you work with families a lot?" Nick dipped his spoon into the beef stew.

"At least a third of my clients. But enough about me. What do y'all do on the ranch? I've seen some horses and a pasture full of cattle." Darcy shifted her gaze between Nick and his uncle.

"The Flying Eagle has two thousand acres, considered small compared to other Texan cattle ranches. We have one hundred and twenty head of cattle and about ten horses. I'd love to acquire more horses to train, but with a staff of only myself, Uncle Howard and hired hands during the busy times, that's not possible." One day Nick hoped he could. Cattle were his business, but his interest and love were horses.

As his uncle expounded on some of the everyday

duties, Nick watched Darcy focus her total attention on him. She seemed genuinely interested in the ranch, and yet, even dressed in her more casual clothes, she had *expensive taste* stamped all over her, from her Ray-Ban sunglasses to her Louis Vuitton purse.

When dinner was over, Uncle Howard waved them out of the kitchen. "You're a guest. I can handle the dinner dishes."

In the hallway that led to the front of the house, Darcy sighed. "His beef stew was delicious. And the bread smelled so wonderful that my mouth watered, but I can't eat bread made with wheat."

With his gaze fixed on the aforementioned mouth, Nick grappled for something to say. Between the exhaustion creeping through his body and his losing battle to keep himself from staring at her, his mind went blank.

"Are you okay?" Darcy asked in the entry hall.

Yeah, as soon as you leave. "I'm fine. I'm just tired from riding around those two thousand acres checking fences, cattle and the land itself."

"At least the snow melted and the temperature was above freezing." At the front door, she turned toward him, not a foot away.

All the reasons he should stay away from her raced through his mind, but all he wanted to think about was how it would feel to kiss her. She was the breath of fresh air he'd needed ever since coming home to Haven last year.

He reached around her, brushing against her arm, and grasped the door handle. "Good night. I'll see you tomorrow after Corey finishes his homework." He opened the door and quickly put some room between them.

She smiled at him, her crystalline blue eyes enticing him to come closer. To taste her lips.

He stepped back. "Bye."

Then, he remained in the doorway watching her—until her taillights vanished in the dark.

He had to stay away from her. She was here temporarily and they had nothing in common. End of story.

But one word seeped into his thoughts: *Corey.*

Chapter Six

"That's correct, Corey." Darcy sat next to the ten-year-old as he finished his reading homework in the living room the next afternoon.

He slammed the book closed and hopped up, grabbing his school backpack. "Let's go. It's time to meet Nick. Aiden is comin' when he gets through his homework."

Corey had worked twice as hard as he had the day before. She needed him to have an incentive every afternoon. Maybe she could talk Nick into coming to work this time every day. She smiled at the thought. She would get to see Nick as well as Corey. She liked that plan.

Corey stopped at the living room entrance and looked back at her. "C'mon. I don't wanna be late."

"What do we do with your books?"

"In here." He took them from her and stuffed them in his backpack, then he started for the front door.

"Corey, you need to put on your jacket."

"Oh, yeah. Forgot." After shrugging into his coat, he added. "Now can we go?"

"Yes."

He shot outside so fast she'd have to jog to keep up with him. Corey's attitude today had improved so much. One reason was the lesson with Nick, but also today Aiden and Corey had played at recess.

She allowed him to race ahead of her. The chill in the wind cut through her. She was used to a breeze from the Gulf, but this wasn't like that. She began to wonder if it would snow again.

She'd been looking forward to seeing Nick herself, but she didn't want to seem too eager. She liked that they were different. She'd dated plenty of men who were from a similar background and career, but no one had stayed in her thoughts as much as Nick did. She wanted to attribute it to their mutual interest in Corey. But that wasn't it. Nick kept himself closed off from others. Last night with his uncle was the first time she'd seen him really relax, especially as they talked about the Flying Eagle.

When she entered the barn, Corey had already left his backpack near the tack room and was hurrying toward Nick at the far end. Nick smiled when he spied the boy. Then he scanned the area, and his gaze latched onto her. Her heartbeat sped as she approached the pair, Nick's eyes still locked with hers as though she was roped and he was drawing her to him.

"Corey said he got all his homework done."

She nodded. "He really buckled down and did a great job."

Corey beamed. "I already know which horse I want. Ginger. Aiden said they needed another person on his team."

"Sounds good to me," Nick said. "You'll make the third one in Aiden and Ben Turner's group."

Corey's forehead creased. "I've seen him but haven't talked to him. He's in wing one."

"Each team has at least one older boy. Let's go get Ginger in the paddock and bring her in here. I'm going to teach you how to saddle her."

"When do I get to ride her?"

"When you know how to care for her and can do every step that leads up to riding her."

"I'll stay back while y'all get Ginger." Darcy stood at the back door as they left. Sheltered by the barn, she watched them enter a corral, a halter in Nick's hand. Corey seemed to listen intently to every word Nick said.

So did Darcy. His slow Texan drawl reminded her of warm butter dripping from a freshly baked biscuit. Forbidden to her.

As Nick showed Corey what to do, a loud voice boomed through the cavernous barn. "Where's...my son?"

Darcy turned toward the man who was slurring his words as though he'd been drinking. At the other end of the barn stood Ned Phillips, his face set in anger. She looked around for anyone else in the barn. No one was there but her and her cousin.

Ned stormed toward Darcy, pointing at her. "I've seen you. Where's Corey? I'm bringing him home. Ain't no one taking my son away from me."

Darcy shut the door behind her and braced herself in front of it. "He's not here, as you can see. You need to leave."

Ned cursed. "I saw him come in here. He's hidin' again. Corey, come out here. Now!" He shouted the last word so loudly that his voice rang through her head. She hoped Nick had heard and would keep the child away.

Instead, the back door banged open, and Nick filled the entrance with his large presence. His arms stiff at his side, he curled and uncurled his hands. "You don't belong here. You need to leave. Now." His emphasis on the same word Ned had used was so different—it was quietly spoken with a commanding tone.

Ned cut the distance between him and Nick. "And you do?"

"I help take care of the horses." Nick's voice dropped even quieter.

Ned thrust his face even closer to Nick's. "Where is *my* son?"

"You reek of alcohol. Someone will drive you home. Then, if you want to see Corey, call the boys ranch office to find out the procedure."

"What? He's mine, not yours."

"He's not a piece of property."

Ned whirled around and stumbled forward. He headed for the stall nearest him. "Corey?" Then he searched the next one.

Darcy moved quickly to Nick and whispered, "I'll take Corey up to the house and let them know what's happening down here."

"He's right out back, holding the reins to Ginger. Tie the mare to the fence and go. I'll keep Ned in here while you do."

"But—"

He bent forward and murmured into her ear, "Go."

She hurried out the back as she heard a stall door slamming closed. "Let's go to the house."

Fear seemed to freeze the child against the barn, his eyes huge.

Darcy stepped to his side and took his free hand. "I'll be with you the whole way."

"But—but Dad's…" He choked on his tears. "I don't want to go home."

"You aren't going to." All she wanted to do was hold him and keep him safe. "Come on." With her arm around Corey's shoulder, she guided him to the nearest fence and helped his trembling fingers tie the reins.

"Get out of my way," Ned yelled from inside the barn.

Darcy grabbed Corey's hand and started for the house. Her cousin kept glancing over his shoulder.

She caught his attention. "I'm not going to let anything happen to you, Corey. Neither is Nick."

He looked up at her, tears filling his eyes. "He must be drinkin'. He usually yells like that when he is."

As they mounted the steps to the porch, the door swung open and a boy about Corey's age with brown hair and eyes came outside. "I was just coming to the barn. What happened?"

"Let's all go inside. Can you go find Miss Bea?" she asked the other kid.

He nodded and raced toward the back of the house.

"That's my new friend, Aiden." Corey's face reddened. "I don't want him to see my dad drunk."

"He won't." She guided him to the living room couch. It was in front of the window that looked out onto the porch. "We'll wait here for Miss Bea." After settling, Darcy put her arm around Corey and drew him close.

Corey's trembling body stirred maternal instincts in Darcy to protect this child at any cost. He stared down, eyes glued to his lap. Even when Bea hastened into the room, he didn't look up but only curled closer to Darcy.

"Aiden told me you needed to see me."

"Where's Aiden?"

"He's worried about Corey. I told him to go to his wing and let one of their houseparents know I need to see them." She closed the distance between them and sat on the other side of Corey.

"His dad showed up in the barn. I think he'd been watching. He'd seen Corey going in." Darcy lowered her voice. "He was drunk. Nick's taking care of him."

Bea withdrew her cell phone from her pocket and placed a call. "Flint, I need you to go to the barn. Corey's dad is there. He's been drinking."

When the boys ranch's director disconnected the call, Corey yanked his head up and said, sobbing, "He isn't a bad man. Only when he's drinking." Then he buried his face against Darcy.

No child should have to deal with that. Darcy wrapped her arms about him, sheltering him the only way she could.

Standing in front of the barn door, Nick held his palm out. "Ned, I'm driving you home. Give me your keys," he said in a commanding voice.

Red-faced, Ned glared at him. "You have no right to keep me from Corey." He stepped back and swayed.

"If you want to see him, I told you to go through the proper channels."

"I—I dunno…" Ned latched on to a post nearby. "I need a drink."

"No." Nick prepared himself for a fight as he came toward the man with bloodshot eyes, who was frantically looking around. "Give me your car keys. You're going home."

"You can't—" Ned paused, blinking rapidly "—make me."

The barn door behind Ned flew open, and Flint

rushed inside. Nick was relieved to have help. He'd seen Ned go off, much like his dad used to.

Ned peered at Nick, his arms falling from the post. His hands fisted. He took one step toward Nick, rocked from side to side and then collapsed to the ground.

As Nick knelt by Ned and checked for a pulse, Flint hurried to them. "Is he alive?"

"Yes. Just passed out, which will make getting him into his car a little easier."

"Thank the Lord. It looked like he was going after you." Flint squatted near Ned's legs. "I saw an old Chevy outside next to your truck. Is that his car?"

"Yep." Nick patted Ned's pockets until he found the keys. "I'm gonna drive him back to his house. Can you follow me and bring me back here for my truck?"

"I wish I could. I have to attend a parents' meeting about the baseball league. I'm going to coach Logan's team. I could try to get out—"

"No, don't. I'll see if Darcy is available. I didn't get the impression that she had plans this evening." For a second Nick was surprised that the person he'd thought of immediately was Darcy—not his uncle or someone else at the boys ranch.

Flint gripped Ned's legs, while Nick took his arms. The smell of alcohol was nauseating. "Are you sure?"

"I can always get Uncle Howard to help if Darcy can't. Ned might not be my friend, but I can't let him stay here and sleep it off or drive somewhere else."

"You could call the sheriff to deal with the man."

A blast of cold air blew through the barn's front entrance as Nick maneuvered through it. "He's in enough trouble with the sheriff after what he did last week with Corey. Let's put him in his backseat."

Flint dropped Ned's legs and opened the car door. "Did Corey see his dad?"

"No. I had him stay outside with Ginger." After Nick and Flint wrestled to get Ned inside the Chevy, Nick climbed into the front. "Thanks for the help. I'll drive up to the house and see if Darcy can follow me."

"There's always the sheriff," Flint said and jogged toward his place on the ranch.

Even if Darcy couldn't drive to Dry Gulch, Nick wanted to stop by the main house to see how Corey was feeling about his father being at the boys ranch.

He left Ned sleeping his drunken stupor off in the back of the beat-up Chevy while Nick climbed the steps to the porch. The door opened before he could ring the bell.

His gaze fixed onto Darcy's concerned face. "How's Corey?"

"He went to his wing with his friend a couple of minutes ago. Where's Ned?"

Nick jerked his thumb toward the car parked next to Darcy's Corvette. "In the backseat, passed out. I'm driving him home. Could you follow me and bring me back here for my truck?"

"Sure. Let me get my coat and tell Bea I'm leaving."

Nick returned to the Chevy to make sure Ned was still asleep. He waited to get into Ned's car until Darcy appeared a few minutes later and got into hers. He pulled away from the house, contemplating rolling down his window. The stench of alcohol brought back memories of taking care of his father after he would finally pass out, much to his relief. Now, Nick's stomach roiled.

The thirty-minute drive was thirty minutes longer

than Nick wanted. Visions of his dad yelling like Ned just had paraded across his mind.

When Nick drove into Ned's driveway, all he wanted to do was get him inside and leave. As he climbed out and drew in a deep breath of fresh air, Darcy parked behind him.

Approaching him, she asked, "Do you need help getting him out of the car?"

"I can manage. It's not far to his house. If you can unlock the door and hold it open, I'll get him inside." He gave her the set of keys. "I don't know which one fits the lock."

While Darcy began working on opening the front door, Nick put his arms under Ned's armpits and pulled him from the back. Then, clasping Ned's upper body, Nick dragged him into the house and, with Darcy's help, laid him on the couch.

She picked up a blanket from the floor and covered Ned with it. Then she backed away and scanned the living room. "Was the place this bad when Corey was here?"

"Yes." He swept his gaze over the piles of clothes on the floor, the half-eaten food sitting on the table and two almost-empty bottles of liquor.

He grabbed them, headed for the kitchen and poured the alcohol down the drain. Then he tossed them into the overflowing trash can.

"Wow. What died in here?" Darcy asked from the doorway.

"Probably more than one thing. Let's get out of here before this smell is permanently ingrained into my mind."

She held up the keys on a chain. "What do you want to do with these?"

"Hide them. Then he can call me to find out where they are." Nick took them from Darcy, strode to the couch and stuck them under a cushion Ned slept on.

A few minutes later, settled in Darcy's Corvette, Nick finally relaxed his tensed muscles. "I hope that's the last time I have to do that, but I wouldn't be surprised if he showed up at the boys ranch again."

"Unless something drastic happens, I doubt Corey's dad will change. In my job I've dealt with alcoholics on more occasions than I liked. They said they wanted help, but I never had but one follow through with what I arranged for them."

"They have to hit rock bottom before it really has a chance to work, and even then it's a hard road." Nick's father never did reach this point. He lived in denial his whole life.

He took out his cell phone. "Maybe you really don't believe that as much as you think." Then he called his uncle and told him the reason he was running late was Ned's unexpected visit to the boys ranch. He needed to check on Corey.

"I can save dinner," Howard said. "I just started. I was with Morning Star. I think she'll have her foal tonight. I'm going back and forth to the barn."

Probably, which meant a long night for him. "She's due."

"If Darcy wants to come to eat with us again, I have more than enough for her."

What was his uncle up to? He would have to talk to Uncle Howard about the fact that Darcy was only in town temporarily and had a good life in Alabama. "We'll see." Nick hung up.

"How's your uncle doing?" Darcy asked.

"Fine. He thinks Morning Star will deliver tonight."

"Really? How exciting. When I was a child, I was there when my dog had puppies and for a few days I dreamed of being a veterinarian. But Dad was a lawyer, so I went that route. You probably understand with your family ranch."

Love for the Flying Eagle was one thing his father hadn't managed to destroy—at least he hoped so. "I wanted to be a cowboy ever since I can remember." At first he'd been trying to please his dad, but later it became about much more. He was going to prove he could make it alone. "My roots are deep here. When I served in the army, I longed for Haven."

"I love where I grew up. That's how I feel." She slid a glance toward him and then turned into the boys ranch.

He knew she did volunteer work in Alabama, but why had she become attached to Corey so quickly? Her first encounter with the boy was when he ran away from home. Maybe it was because she was used to dealing with people in trouble in her job. She had a big heart.

"See, we have something in common. I knew we would."

"Why?"

"Because we both care for Corey. Before you called your uncle, you said something about how I really don't think people can change. I think they can or I would have given up on the one person I dealt with who was an alcoholic and did become sober. Still is."

"Who?"

"My college roommate." Darcy pulled up to the main house and parked. "You said something to your uncle about checking on Corey before you went home. I'd also like to. I'm hoping he won't be so distressed now since we made sure his father got home okay."

"Sure. I'm glad you are. He's feeling pretty alone right now. I know Bea and the staff will do what they can, but no matter how upset he was before he came to the ranch, his home in Dry Gulch was familiar to him, at least." In his childhood, Nick had clung to that fact. He'd disappear for hours on the ranch when his dad was angry or drinking.

"You think Corey should have stayed with his dad?"

"No, but his emotions will be all over the place. However, the staff at the boys ranch has dealt with that before. And the place can give him one of the things he needs—to feel safe."

"That can really help him adjust more quickly. His close relationship with you will help too. You're good with him."

"Thanks," he mumbled, the compliment taking him by surprise. Her words touched a part of his heart he'd kept from others for years. He'd always wanted to make a difference in someone's life and had thought being a soldier was the answer. Instead, all the death and destruction had isolated him even more.

They both exited the Corvette and headed to the front entrance. Lana answered the door and let them inside.

"I was just about to leave. I'm glad I waited. How is Corey's dad? Flint told me he helped you get the man into his car."

"We left him on his couch sleeping it off." Nick took his cowboy hat off and hung it on a peg.

"Good, because Corey has been asking about him."

"We wanted to check on him. Where is he?" Darcy asked.

"In the rec room with some of the boys. There's a ping-pong tournament going on."

"Thanks, Lana. See you tomorrow for study hall."

Nick led the way to the rec room, a large open space with tables and chairs. Boys crowded at one end where two were playing ping-pong. He searched for Corey and found him leaning against the wall, not really paying attention to the game.

"It'll be hard to talk privately with him in here. Do you know where we could go with Corey? I noticed when we passed the living room there were several groups in there." Darcy walked with Nick toward Corey.

"There's a small room near Bea's office. She uses it for counseling and as a place where parents can meet with their child."

As they approached Corey, he stared at a spot on the floor between him and the group of boys. Nick remembered often retreating—if not physically, at least emotionally—from what was going on around him.

He cleared his throat and gave Corey time to look up at him. "Let's go talk."

Corey didn't say anything until he'd left the rec room. In the hallway, he asked, "How's Dad?"

"He's home safe and sleeping." Nick clasped his shoulder.

"It's all my fault."

Nick waited to reply until they stepped into the small counseling room. "The only one at fault for what happened at the barn was your father. He chose to come here. He chose to get drunk."

Corey plopped down on a couch with Darcy sitting beside him and Nick across from him. "I ran away and he got into trouble for that."

"The state doesn't take a child away from his parents because he ran away. Your dad wasn't caring for you. Ten-year-olds aren't meant to fend for themselves."

"But I can take care of myself. I know how."

And yet Nick had received various calls from Corey because he was afraid to be there by himself. "Do you feel safe being alone there at night?"

"He never…" Corey dropped his gaze. "He was working to take care of me."

"The whole night?" Darcy asked.

"Well, maybe." Corey hunched his shoulders.

There were so many times Nick had made up excuses for his father. "Corey, not from when you came home from school to the next morning."

The boy bent over even more as though he was trying to curl up into a ball. Darcy put her arm around Corey. "You're a child. A parent has certain responsibilities that your father wasn't living up to. He needs to get help."

"I tried to help him. He doesn't want it. I asked him to stop drinking. He stormed out of the house and was gone for a day. I never said anything else about it after that."

Nick rose from his chair and stooped in front of Corey. "You can't fix him. He has to do that himself. You're here where you'll be safe, have three square meals a day and guidance if you run into a problem. I'm gonna be here almost every day, and you can always call me if you want to talk. Even when I'm working at the ranch, I have my cell phone with me."

"I understand that this Saturday Nick is going to give you your first riding lesson. I can remember my first time on a horse at summer camp. I was so excited to be the first one to ride into the ring that when I reached to open the gate—" she paused and waited while Corey lifted his head and peered at her "—I didn't let go while my horse went on inside. Much to my embarrassment, I was left hanging from the fence."

Corey's eyes grew round. "Did you get hurt?"

"Nope. I was just taken down a notch. So remember, when you're going through a gate, make sure you let go of it."

Corey giggled. "I know that."

"Good, because I'm going to be here to see you ride for the first time. I'll be watching. No pressure there." She ruffled his hair and hugged him.

Corey's cheeks turned beet red.

Nick stood. "We need to go, but I'm just a phone call away. Okay?"

Corey nodded.

Darcy rose at the same time Corey did. "Looking forward to seeing you tomorrow."

Corey closed the short space between him and Nick and threw his arms around him. Nick's heart swelled in his chest. "We'll continue the lesson on taking care of your horse tomorrow." Nick gave him a quick hug and stepped back, his throat tight with emotions he didn't allow himself to feel.

A few minutes later Nick stopped next to Darcy's car, tired but pleased that Corey had left them with a grin on his face. "Uncle Howard will have dinner ready at the ranch, and he wanted you to know you have an invitation to join us again tonight. I think he's taken a liking to you."

"Just your uncle?"

The heat of a blush, much like Corey's, suffused Nick's face. "I'd like you to come too. You helped me tonight, and the least I can do is give you dinner."

"Then, yes. I'll follow you to your house."

While she started her Corvette, Nick hopped into his truck and turned toward the highway. On the drive to his place he couldn't quit berating himself for prolonging the evening with Darcy. He did want to thank her for going to Dry Gulch to pick him up, but a simple thank-you would have been enough. No, he had to invite her to dinner two nights in a row.

His restless sleep last night was playing havoc with his good judgment.

As he drove onto the road that led to his house, he decided to park at his barn and check on the pregnant mare before eating. Darcy pulled up next to him.

"I'm going to see how Morning Star is doing."

"I'll come with you."

In the large foaling stall, Morning Star settled down on the straw, then immediately got back up, walked in a circle and then went down again. She did that several times. Finally on her feet, she began to push while he ran his hands over her flank.

"What's wrong?" Darcy asked him from the stall door.

"I think she's ready to deliver, but something is wrong. She's in distress. Most horses lay down to deliver." Nick retrieved his cell phone from his pocket. "I'm calling the vet."

Chapter Seven

Darcy leaned against the half door of the foaling stall as Dr. Wyatt Harrow, the veterinarian, and Nick fought to save the foal's life. Nick calmed the mare while the vet inserted his hand to reposition the foal's legs, hooves first, so it could move through the birth canal safely.

Wyatt glanced at Nick. "Okay, she should be able to push the foal out now."

Morning Star lifted her head and immediately dropped it back to the hay, her big brown eyes sliding partially closed.

His brow crinkled, Nick looked at the vet while continuing to soothe the mare. "She's exhausted. I'm not sure she can." Nick tried to coax her with a soft touch and calm words. But Morning Star didn't move while her labored breathing resonated through the stall.

"Can I help?" Darcy asked, feeling helpless and wanting to do something for the chestnut mare.

"I need some rope to pull the foal out," Wyatt said.

"Rope?" She peered at Nick.

"In the tack room on the wall."

Darcy swung around and hurried toward the front of the barn. She grabbed what the vet had requested and hoped this would work. Morning Star had been in labor to the point where she had exhausted herself. When Darcy returned, the vet quickly took the rope and began tying the foal's front hooves.

Darcy couldn't stay outside the stall watching any longer. Kneeling by Nick, she ran her hand along the horse's neck. "You're going to be okay."

At the sound of Darcy's voice close to her, Morning Star's dilated eyes shifted to Darcy. She continued her gentle stroking. Touching and comforting the mare brought back so many memories of Beauty. "If you want to help Wyatt, I can do this."

Nick moved to the vet while Darcy took over the job of consoling the mare. The last time she'd done this was when her horse had an accident while jumping a fence and died from it. She'd stayed by Beauty's side while the vet eased her death. As the memory surfaced, Darcy's throat closed. At the age of twenty-three, she'd walked away from riding. For ten years, since the horse was born, Beauty had been hers. She didn't want to see another horse die, but the foal had to come *now*.

Darcy bent closer to the mare and whispered encouraging words over and over while Wyatt and Nick struggled to pull the foal from Morning Star.

Finally it slipped free and landed in the straw. Wyatt hurriedly checked the newborn before cutting the cord while Nick wiped the afterbirth off the foal, putting it in a bucket.

"It's a filly," Wyatt said, snatching a towel to dry her off.

"You did it, Morning Star. You've got a baby girl.

Way to go!" Darcy rubbed the mare that was still breathing hard.

Slowly Morning Star calmed down as Wyatt and Nick took care of the foal. She lifted her head and glanced back at her baby.

The next hour was devoted to cleaning up the mess and seeing to mother and child, both horses standing by the end, although the foal wobbled.

Wyatt gathered his black bag and stood by the stall door watching the two animals. "She's a beauty, Nick."

He grinned. "I think so too. I'm gonna call her Evening Star."

When Wyatt said *beauty*, a shaft of regret pierced Darcy's heart. If only she hadn't practiced jumping fences that day, Beauty might be alive today.

"Nice meeting you, Darcy. I'm heading home. Call me if you need me, Nick."

Pulled back to the present, Darcy erased the memory of Beauty's death and forced a grin. For years she'd loved riding horses. It was time to reclaim that love.

Nick shook the vet's hand. "I'm glad you got here so fast. I don't know how long Morning Star was in labor before we arrived."

After Wyatt left, Nick looked at her for a long moment before asking, "Okay?"

"Yes, this ended happily."

"Are you still hungry? I am. That was a lot of work."

"And you weren't even the mare in labor."

He chuckled. "Uncle Howard said he would dish up plates of food for both of us and we could warm them in the microwave."

"I'm surprised he isn't down here."

"I told him one of us needed to sleep since we're expecting a bull delivered early this morning in—" Nick checked his watch "—three hours. Besides, you were here to help if I needed it."

"Three hours?" She'd been so engrossed with the mare she'd lost track of how long she'd been here. "What time is it?"

"Four thirty in the morning."

"Really? That went by fast."

"So are you hungry for a late dinner or early breakfast, whichever you want to call it?"

"Now that I think about it, yes, but I'll just grab a quick bite and some coffee, and then I'll head back to the Blue Bonnet Inn. Thankfully I have the luxury of sleeping in all morning."

"I'm glad one of us does." Nick strolled from the barn with Darcy beside him. As they covered the distance to the house, he took her hand.

The warmth of his palm against hers in the chill of night made her realize how much she cherished being here to help him and Morning Star.

The porch light shined, beckoning them inside where it was toasty. In the kitchen Nick microwaved each plate of baked chicken, wild rice and green beans while Darcy switched on the coffeepot.

She hoped the caffeine would keep her awake long enough to drive back to the inn. Now that the excitement of the birth was over, exhaustion was slowly weaving through her. She yawned. "Maybe I'll just take a cup with me and go before I fall asleep."

"Drink and eat some. If you don't feel awake enough to drive, I have a spare bedroom you can use."

"I appreciate the invitation, but I'll be fine after a cup of coffee."

Twenty minutes later, after eating every bite of her tasty meal, she relaxed back in the chair. "That was delicious. Thank Howard for me." With a sigh, she rose, took her dishes to the sink and then held up the mug. "Can I top this off and take it with me? I'll bring it back to you later today."

"Yes. I'll walk you to your car."

"It's only a hundred yards away. There's no reason for both of us getting cold."

"True, but besides escorting you to your car, I'm going to check on Morning Star and her foal before I catch some shut-eye."

"Well, in that case, you can."

After putting on her overcoat, she hooked her arm through Nick's and proceeded out the back door. When she left to come to Haven, she'd never imagined that she'd be volunteering at a boys ranch because she'd discovered a cousin needed her help. Nor had she imagined someone like Nick.

At her car, she turned around to face the cowboy. "Thank you for an…interesting day."

"That's an…interesting word to describe today." He inched closer, cupping her face, and dipped his head toward hers.

She should pull away; she was here only for a short time. But she stood her ground and met his lips with hers. He slid one hand behind her neck and held her as he deepened the kiss. A flutter in her stomach spread outward and encompassed her whole body.

When he leaned back, he smiled and then stepped away. As she drove away, he waited outside the barn, watching her leave. After going through the gate to the ranch, she stopped and looked both ways on the road into town.

The memory of his kiss swept through her as if it were happening again. Against her better judgment, she wished it could.

As she climbed out of the Corvette at the Blue Bonnet Inn, it was still dark but almost six in the morning. She used the key she'd been given to enter the large Victorian house after ten at night and came face-to-face with Carol, descending the staircase.

"I wondered where you were, but Bea told me about the problem with Corey's dad and I figured you were helping Nick out. Although there's little crime in Haven, I worry about my guests. Avery is still out, but she usually is several times a week."

"I'm sorry, Carol. I should have called to let you know. Actually Ned passed out, and we left him on his couch. I got caught up with a mare giving birth in the middle of the night."

"I'm gonna make coffee. Would you like some to take up to your room?"

"I'd love a cup. You make the best coffee I've had in a long time."

"Now, that makes my day, and it's barely started."

Darcy followed Carol to the kitchen, anticipating the aroma that saturated the house every morning. As she made the coffee, Darcy asked, "What in the world would Avery do a couple of times a week? I can't say Haven is teeming with nighttime activities." Could Avery be with Fletcher?

"Your guess is as good as mine. I suppose she could be going to Waco for more nightlife." Carol sat across from Darcy at the table. "Lana doesn't think she's the real Avery. If that's the case, we only have two months to find the real one."

"Why does she think Avery is an impostor?"

"Lana has a gut feeling something isn't right. She has observed Avery and believes she only says what she thinks we want to hear. Lana overheard that the only thing Avery worships is money. That wasn't too long after she'd told Lana that she wondered if a church service would help her deal with all the things she missed out on because she didn't know her grandfather. All she wanted to do was honor him."

"And yet she's close to Fletcher, who doesn't want to honor Cyrus's wish to give his land to the boys ranch."

"Yeah, that's what I've been wondering too. What if she's working behind the scenes to find a way to break the will? It sure would be easier if she wasn't the real Avery. Dealing with Fletcher is one thing. Dealing with Cyrus's closest living relative is more complicated." Carol walked to the coffeepot and filled two mugs.

Interesting. Maybe she could see if Lana needed any help proving whether or not Avery was the real one. "I've seen the good the boys ranch does. I'd hate to see that change." And if she was the real Avery, maybe she could be persuaded to legally fight whatever Fletcher was doing to ruin the provisions of the will.

Carol handed her a mug. "You and me both. A strip mall isn't what Cyrus really wanted the ranch to be used for."

Darcy rose. "I'll be seeing Lana this afternoon at the boys ranch. But if I don't want to miss working with Corey, I'd better catch some z's."

Darcy sipped the coffee and headed for the staircase. In the entry hall she spied Avery mounting the steps to the second floor. Had she been with Fletcher? Were they scheming to take the boys ranch away? The idea that her biological father could do something like that sickened her.

On Saturday Nick stood in the middle of the corral as three boys rode for the first time—Corey, Mikey and Miguel, all only a few years apart in age, relatively new to the ranch and living in the second wing. Corey on Ginger led the group.

"Mikey, you're holding the rein too tight." When the blond-headed boy adjusted his grip, Nick added, "That's right. If you all keep this up, I'll take you on a trail ride." He moved to the side and lounged against the fence.

Corey pumped his arm in the air while Mikey grinned, displaying the gap where his two front teeth used to be, and Miguel cheered.

"I hoped I'd get here before Corey started his riding lesson." Darcy's soft voice floated to him from behind.

He shot her a glance over his shoulder. "I wondered if you were coming."

"You wouldn't believe it. I had two flat tires when I came out of the inn."

"Who changed them?"

"Me with some help from Clarence and Slim. My car hasn't given me any trouble until this trip." She opened the gate and entered the corral. "What I don't under-stand is two at once unless someone did it deliberately."

Lately so many things had happened to people in-volved with the boys ranch. Could it be the saboteur who had messed with her tires? Why? She didn't live here. But then, she'd been at the ranch every day this past week.

"What did I miss?" Darcy asked.

"About nineteen laps around the perimeter. All three are naturals, especially Corey."

"He's a sharp learner. Each day I work with him reading, he's a little better than the day before. I think all he needed was someone to listen to him and practice."

He was glad to see her. He'd missed her the last two days at the boys ranch and when he had spotted her before that, he'd felt awkward after the kiss they shared. He shouldn't have kissed her. She would be leaving at the end of the month, but her presence that night had been like returning to the fortified base after a skirmish. "So what have you been up to since we last talked?"

"Besides tutoring, I've been helping Lana track down information on Avery Culpepper. Lana told me on Wednesday that Avery doesn't have any of the Culpepper family coloring."

"You don't think the one in town is the right Avery?"

"If she isn't, then that might hurt the boys ranch because of the provision in the will."

His gaze still trained on the riders, Nick straightened. "What if Fletcher recruited a fake Avery in order to mess up the stipulations that have to be met by March?"

"Just a sec." Darcy came into the paddock. "I found out a few details, like the fact that Avery was born on February 2. Since she is staying at the Blue Bonnet Inn, I'm going to try to get to know her and test her on the facts I've discovered."

"And she won't get suspicious?"

"I'm a lawyer. I know how to interview a person to get what I want."

"I'll have to remember that. Do you want to go on a trail ride with us?"

She grinned, her blue eyes twinkling. "I would love to. I haven't ridden in years. I need to start again."

"Do I need to give you a lesson?" Nick asked with a chuckle.

"I think I'll be okay. How are Morning Star and Evening Star doing?"

"Great. Morning Star is a natural mother. I'm glad this foal lived." Nick approached the circling riders. "Stop by the gate. We're gonna go for a trail ride. I want to show Darcy the ranch. Okay?"

Cheers rose from the boys. Corey grinned from ear to ear—its sight infectious. This past week he had lived at the barn in his spare time, doing whatever Flint or Nick would let him. Corey had even told Nick that he wanted to be a farrier like he was. For a moment Nick had thrust back his shoulders and stood up tall, as though he were a proud dad and his son had declared he wanted to follow in his footsteps. Then reality swept the thought out of his mind. His life wasn't an example for a child to follow. He was barely making a living and he was filled with anger at his father that he'd never been able to shake.

"Nick, are you okay?" Darcy's soft Southern voice pulled him back to the present, where three boys were staring at him.

"I'm fine. I'll be right back with our horses." Nick had already selected the horses he would use. There was a creek he wanted to show her.

In ten minutes he returned to the paddock, lead-

ing two mares. He loved seeing the grins on the boys'
faces, especially Corey's. Each day he saw signs that
Corey was fitting right in and starting to relax and
enjoy himself. At least now Nick didn't have to worry
about the child. He could be near him and keep an eye
on him—be the big brother Doug had been for Corey.

After giving Darcy a leg up, he swung into the saddle. "I have a special place I want to show y'all. I'll be
in the lead. Darcy will be in the rear."

For January the day was beautiful, not a cloud in
the sky, the temperature in the mid-fifties. Corey rode
next to Nick, smiling the whole time.

"How's school going, partner?"

"Okay. Aiden's in my class, and he's been showing
me around."

"I'm glad you're making friends. Any problems?"

For a long moment Corey didn't reply.

"You can tell me. It'll remain between us if that's
what you want."

"There's one boy in wing three. Jasper. I saw him
hide Billy's backpack the other day right before we
were supposed to get on the school bus. Billy was
freaking out."

"What did you do?"

"I found the backpack. I don't think Jasper liked that."

"He can be the class clown at times. Usually he
plays pranks, most of the time in fun. Sometimes he
goes too far."

"Why?"

"I don't know for sure. Maybe for attention."

Corey sat up even straighter in the saddle. "Then
I'll make friends with him. We had a kid like that at
my old school. That's what I did there. Doug told me

when I started school I should look out for the ones who need a friend."

"He's younger. You'll be a good role model for Jasper. Doug's advice is right on." Helping others would also give Corey something to do to take his mind off his own problems.

"Yeah, Doug was a great big brother. I miss him."

"So do I, Corey."

Twenty minutes later, the group arrived at the stream, which was partially shaded by trees that retained their leaves in the winter.

Nick dismounted and turned to the boys. "You saw how I got off my horse. Y'all do the same thing and then tie the reins to a bush or small tree so the animals can graze while you look around."

"How long can we explore?" Corey slid off his mount.

"You can't go too far. Keep me in sight. I'll give a shout when I want you to come back."

As the boys moved away, sticking together, Darcy stopped at Nick's side. "Mikey had a little trouble keeping his horse from wanting to eat as he walked, but otherwise they all did great."

"Riding is good for both them and the horses. This ranch is big and has a lot of places they can explore."

She looked around. "This would be a fun place to have a picnic."

"That's something we could do when the weather permits."

Shielding her eyes, she shifted her attention to him. "You'll be able to. A cold front is coming through tomorrow, and I won't be here after the end of the month."

Yeah, he had to remember that. He was attracted to

her, and there was no future for them. She'd made it
clear she loved her home. Long-distance relationships
didn't work. Too many barriers. "Who knows? Weather
can change rapidly here in the winter. The other ranch
site wasn't nearly as big and didn't have the opportu-
nities this one has, like the ability to have a picnic in a
place like this. I'm going to talk to Flint about having
trail rides on the weekend. Not a bad way to keep an
eye on what's happening on the ranch too."

Darcy tilted her head. "You know, back in Mobile I
was good at organizing fund-raisers. I've been thinking the past few days, it would be fun to do a small one
for the boys ranch. If I were staying longer, I'd go all
out. The money could go to equipment and other items
this place needs."

"Sounds good. You need to talk to Bea—"

"Nick, come quick," Corey shouted, about two hundred yards away.

Nick ran toward the boys, who were staring down
an incline. It looked like they were all right, but the
urgency in Corey's voice had been clear. Something
was wrong.

He halted with Darcy right beside him. "What's
wrong?"

Corey pointed a shaky hand down the slope.

Nick stepped forward. Below, a cow was down on
the ground, trying to get up but not able to. "Darcy, can
you take the boys back to the ranch, wait for Wyatt to
come and then show him here?"

"Yes."

He started down the incline. "I'll call the vet and
stay with the cow."

"I don't wanna leave. I found her. You might need me." Corey stood his ground.

Darcy put her hand on his shoulder. "C'mon. I might get lost going back to the barn. I need y'all to guide me."

"Oh, o-kay."

Darcy waved at him as Nick knelt next to the cow and saw that it had a broken leg. If Wyatt had to put the animal down, he didn't want the boys to see it. And once again Darcy had been here to help him. He didn't want to get too used to that. She was leaving soon.

Chapter Eight

Darcy rode back to the barn for the second time that day to let the boys know that Wyatt would be able to cast the cow's leg and save her.

With Flint's assistance, the cow had been moved to a board and then loaded on a trailer. Wyatt and Nick were coming back with the animal, hoping to keep her calm. It was Darcy's job to put the boys' fears to rest. She arrived at the barn a few minutes before the men.

The second Corey saw her he ran toward her and met her at the back door. "What happened? Is she okay?"

"Yes, Wyatt will be putting a cast on her leg. They're coming right behind me," she said as the other two boys skidded to a stop next to Corey.

Relief transformed each child's serious expression into joy.

When Bea and Lana approached, they interrupted the boys' plans to help the cow.

Bea directed her look at Corey. "Y'all will not do anything unless the vet says so. You three can fix up a stall for the cow with Johnny." She waved for the older teenager to join them. "Johnny, these guys are going to help you clean out the big stall so Wyatt can use it to work on the cow."

He nodded and waited for the trio to follow him. The teen stuttered as he told the boys what they needed to get, but the young ones were oblivious to it.

Bea watched the group head to the stall with tools. "Johnny has been such a big help to Wyatt. He'd rather spend his time at the barn than at the house. If I let him, he'd sleep down here."

"A lot of them would," Lana said. "There's something about animals that allow the kids to heal. That's why this place is so important to the boys and has to stay open."

Darcy waited until the children disappeared inside the stall. "Speaking of the ranch, I've discovered a couple of pieces of information about Avery after doing some digging. If I can catch her in a lie about one of them, that might prove she's an imposter. But you need to be prepared. It's possible she is the real Avery."

Lana sighed. "I hope not. This ranch is too important for the boys to lose it at the last minute. We still have a couple of people to track down, like Gabe Everett's grandfather. Then there's Morton Mason—"

Darcy spied Wyatt entering the barn right behind Bea.

Bea interrupted Lana. "With everything happening today, I haven't had a chance to tell you, Lana, that I found an address for Carolina Mason, though no phone number or email. So I'll be writing her a letter about the boys ranch's anniversary party. Hopefully she knows where her great-uncle is. If so, we'll be set with that original resident."

Wyatt began to open the other half of the front entrance, but he halted, the color washing from his face as he stared at Bea's. Then, before Bea had a chance to say anything, he pivoted and hurriedly unlatched the door. But Darcy had seen his look of regret—and something else. A flash of anger?

Darcy spent the next hour keeping the boys quiet as they watched Nick, Johnny and Wyatt put a cast on the back leg of the cow. Flint kept her down and as calm as possible.

"Boys, it's lunchtime," Bea announced to the three younger ones.

Corey turned to the director. "We want to stay and make sure she's okay. Please."

Bea exchanged a look with Lana and Darcy. "Wyatt is almost finished. Come up to the house and eat and then you can return and assist Nick and Flint."

Flint stuck his head out of the open top half of the stall door. "I'll let you three take turns keeping an eye on the cow with Johnny. She's going to have a calf in about a month. We want to make sure they are both all right. Is that a deal?"

Corey's eyes popped wide. All three kids happily agreed. "Do you want to join us?" Bea asked Darcy.

She peeked into the large stall. Like the boys, she wanted to stay and help, but Nick had already put the last of the plaster on the cast.

"Bring us back something to eat. Wyatt and I will be with old Bessie until you get back from lunch," Nick said to Darcy.

"Bessie?" Did they name the cows in their herd?

"Yup. My name for her." He gave her a grin and a wink. "Aren't all cows named Bessie?"

"I think there's a Flossie and Elsie."

He laughed. "I've worked up quite an appetite. Lifting a cow ain't easy work."

"I'll remember that." Darcy gathered up the boys, and the group left the barn.

Once the kids were outside, they sprinted toward the house, leaving Lana, Bea and Darcy in their dust.

Lana chuckled. "I can't believe they don't want to walk with us."

"Next they'll be calling us old fogies," Bea muttered, "and at the moment I feel that way."

"Why?" Darcy asked.

"Did you see Wyatt's face when he heard about me writing a letter to Carolina Mason?"

Lana's forehead crinkled. "Yes. Didn't those two date?"

"Yes, and she abruptly left town three years ago. I'm not sure why, and I don't think Wyatt knows either."

"If anyone should know, it would be you or Carol." Lana mounted the steps to the front porch.

"I'm discovering that while staying at the Blue Bonnet Inn," Darcy said. "I feel like I know a lot of people in this town, and I haven't even met them. Carol knows everyone." And through it all, what Darcy had discovered about her biological father wasn't good.

After eating lunch, Darcy made up a plate of food for Nick while Lana did the same for Flint and Logan, who had joined his dad. Johnny and Corey had already headed down to the barn while Mikey and Miguel finished their hamburgers.

As the group left the house, Mikey tripped on the stairs and cut his leg. Lana handed Darcy one plate and gave the other to Miguel.

Lana knelt next to Mikey, tears running down the seven-year-old's face, and examined the injury. "We'll be down after I clean this and get a bandage for him."

Darcy and Miguel continued their trek. Inside the

barn, Flint stood at the entrance of the tack room while Cowboy barked over and over at the closed back door.

She passed Flint his food. "Miguel has Logan's. Y'all eat. I'll see what Cowboy is upset about."

"Thanks. If he doesn't stop, I'll take him home." He held up their plates. "After we eat. We're starving."

"Is Nick with the cow?"

"Yeah."

"Are Corey and Johnny there too?"

Flint nodded as he took a bite.

"Miguel, please give this to Nick while I see about Cowboy."

When she neared the black Lab, he scratched at the door, looked back at her and then barked again. Maybe all he wanted to do was pee. He never ran off, so he should be all right. She exited with the dog. Cowboy charged around the side. She hurried after him in case she'd been wrong and he was escaping.

The scents of gasoline and smoke laced the air. Her steps quickened as she rounded the corner, the black Lab yelping at the gray smoke and flames eating their way up the barn.

For one, two seconds she stared at the fire. Then her gaze fell on a gasoline can nearby, cap off and knocked over.

As she dug for her cell phone, she whirled around and raced to get the people and animals out before it was too late.

Nick leaned against the stall door while Corey stroked the cow. Johnny had gone to get Bessie something to eat. Unlike a horse, a cow could be content lying on the ground, resting and munching on grass.

They rarely ran around, which meant the leg should heal fine.

"Get out! There's a fire!" Darcy's warning instantly invaded the tranquil moment.

Nick jerked upright and swung around. "Where?"

She hastened to him and pointed. "That side of the barn in the middle. I smelled gasoline and checked it out."

Flint ran out of the tack room with Logan and Miguel, gesturing for the boys to leave and saying, "Go get help at the house." Then Flint asked Darcy, "Have you called 911?"

Darcy took deep breaths, her chest rising and falling rapidly. "Yes, but I didn't let anyone at the main house know about the fire yet."

"Nick, get everyone out. I'm calling Bea and shutting the front doors." Flint pulled out his cell phone and strode away.

"Darcy, open the stall doors on that side and wave your arms to get the horses to run out the back." Nick turned to Corey and Johnny. "Y'all try to direct the horses into the corral where you were riding this morning. Don't worry if any of them get away. We'll find them later."

Already on his feet, Johnny rushed out of the stall, but Corey, hand still on the cow, didn't move. "What about Bessie?"

"You don't worry about her. I will. Go. Get out. Now."

Nick stared at the cow. The cast was hard. Maybe she would walk out okay. He needed rope and possibly someone to hoist Bessie to her feet and move her outside. First, he had to see to the mare stabled on this side.

Smoke began to fill the barn, its insidious smell invading every crevice. Flames ate at the outside of the wooden wall.

Nick opened the stall door and tried to coax Ginger out. Her eyes wild-looking, she backed away from the exit, her nose flaring. "Easy, girl. You'll be all right," Nick said in a soft, calm tone.

After a long thirty seconds, Ginger finally shot out of the stall and raced for the back door. Nick glanced out to make sure all the horses were accounted for in the corral. He was missing one—a black gelding.

Flint was occupied with organizing the staff and teenage boys to hose down what they could until the fire department arrived. Nick would have to take care of Bessie and check to see if the gelding had gone toward the front because his stall door was opened wide.

As Nick hurried back in for Bessie, the big black horse charged toward him. He dove to the side and the gelding ran outside.

Darcy quickened her step to him. "He was the last one. The stalls are empty except for the cow's. What do you need me to do?"

"Hold the rope while I get her to stand and then we'll walk her out."

After securing Bessie with the rope, he gave it to Darcy. As she stood in front, trying to coax the cow, he urged Bessie to stand, no mean feat with a cast on. Once Bessie was up, Darcy led her toward the exit.

Nick pivoted one last time to make sure the barn was clear, but the smoke had grown denser. He could hardly see the other end. A beam crashed down, flames engulfing it.

"Nick, get out," Darcy shouted from the back door.

He hastened out the exit as the sound of the building beginning to collapse drowned out the crackling of the fire. Grabbing Darcy's hand, he put distance between them and the barn, the blaze quickly spreading up one side and across the roof.

Two fire trucks barreled down the gravel road toward them.

"It's too late to save the barn, but at least they can keep the fire from getting out of control and destroying more of the ranch," Flint said to Nick when he reached him.

The loud whinnies from the nearest corral vied with the noise of the fire. The scent of smoke hung heavily, and the staff began steering the boys to the house. Some of them were crying, others stunned.

When Corey didn't want to leave, Darcy walked to him and said something that Nick couldn't hear, but Corey nodded and trailed after the others.

Nick glanced at the paddock twenty yards away. "Should we move the horses farther away?"

Flint nodded. "Just in case the wind picks up. Let's put them in the pasture on the other side of the main house for the time being."

Nick stared at the nearest ranch structure, his eyes watering, his throat burning from the smell. "Are there any halters and reins in the storage barn?"

"No, because we're using this one as our primary barn for horses."

"Then I'll head to my ranch and bring enough back to move the horses. I need to park my truck farther away anyway. It shouldn't take me too long."

"Go. There isn't anything we can do now but pray."

"I'll help you, Nick," Darcy said beside him.

For the first time in years, Nick sent up a silent prayer that no one was hurt and nothing was damaged except for the barn. It could be rebuilt with the insurance money.

Darcy hopped into the cab of his pickup with two bottles of water, and they pulled away from the chaos at the boys ranch. He let out a long breath, clasped the drink and downed half of it. "Thanks. That's what I needed."

"That's the first fire I've been in, and I never want to repeat that experience. I had trouble with that black gelding. All I could do was pray he found his way outside the barn. I opened his stall and barely jumped out of his way."

"I noticed even in the corral he was more agitated than the other horse."

"I'm glad we were able to get Bessie out. Corey was so worried about her."

Nick drove through the gates of his ranch. "What did you say to him to get him to leave with the others?"

"I promised him I would make sure the barn was rebuilt even better than the one that burned."

Nick frowned. "How can you make him that promise? You'll be leaving in three weeks."

"I'll get the town behind it. As I told you earlier, I've had a lot of experience with fund-raisers. When the people see what the boys lost, they'll help. Instead of using what we raise for equipment, we can use it to rebuild the barn. A fund-raiser could also show Fletcher Phillips that Haven supports the ranch."

"He's probably the one behind the fire."

Darcy gasped. "You really think that?"

"If gasoline was used, it was arson. It has to be someone who doesn't like the boys ranch. That fits Fletcher."

"How about Ned? He was furious that Corey was taken away from him."

Nick parked by his barn. "That was the alcohol talking. If Ned ever stopped drinking, he might be the father Corey needs. I know that's most likely not going to happen, but I can hope it does."

"You knew him when he wasn't an alcoholic?"

"Years ago, when they lived in Haven." According to Uncle Howard, Nick's father had been a better man too, before Nick's mother died. "Believe me, I know that if he doesn't stop drinking, he'll keep doing what he's been doing."

"Are you talking about your father? I got the impression that he had a drinking problem based on something you said before."

For a moment, he considered telling her everything about his father, but the words wouldn't come. Confiding in Darcy was a risk he didn't dare take.

Chapter Nine

Darcy slipped into Lila's Café to meet Avery for coffee before going to the church to discuss the fund-raiser. The fire department had confirmed it was arson, which didn't surprise her. Gasoline cans didn't just lie around the boys ranch.

She was so glad she'd started thinking about doing a fund-raiser because the boys would need something positive to focus on and to look forward to. She'd talked to Bea about the idea and the director had encouraged her. Any money they received helped. She paused by the entrance and scanned the restaurant for Avery. Darcy spotted the young woman sitting at a table— with Fletcher. The two seemed deep in a conversation. Good time to break up the pair. She threaded her way through the crowded café and slid into a chair.

"I'm sorry I'm late. Carol stopped me right before I left the inn." Darcy swung her attention from Avery to Fletcher.

"I'm Darcy Hill, visiting Haven for the month." She held out her hand to her birth father.

Fletcher shook it. "I'm Fletcher Phillips. I'm not staying. Avery told me she was meeting you for coffee. I understand you were at the fire yesterday at the boys ranch."

Darcy nodded. "It was arson."

"I heard that this morning at church."

"I told Fletcher how ragged you looked when you returned to the inn last night. I would have been hysterical if I'd been caught in a fire," Avery said.

"Thankfully we had plenty of time to get the animals and people out of there."

"I've been saying ever since the ranch was set up for this purpose that something bad like this would happen. I wouldn't be surprised if it was one of those *boys*. We're fortunate that the wind wasn't too strong or it could have spread—possibly even caused a major wildfire affecting the whole town."

Darcy gritted her teeth, trying not to say anything she would regret, but she couldn't keep quiet. "But it didn't, and it wasn't one of the kids."

"How do you know that?"

Disappointed in her biological father, Darcy asked, "How do you know it was one of them?"

His sharp gaze cut through her as he rose. "It's been interesting talking to you, Ms. Hill. Avery, we'll talk some more later."

She giggled. "I'd like that, Fletcher. I want to move forward."

Move forward doing what? Upsetting the plans for the Culpepper ranch?

Each morning, when Avery came down for breakfast, Darcy made a point of speaking to her. Nothing Avery had said so far had sent up a red flag suggesting she wasn't the real Avery Culpepper, but Darcy hoped she could discover something. "I've seen him pick you up a couple of times this week. Are you two serious?"

For a few seconds, the woman's pupils dilated. "Like dating?"

"That's what I've heard."

Avery tossed back her head and laughed. "He's the lawyer for my grandfather's inheritance. Haven has a nest of gossipers spreading untruths."

"Then why do you stay here? Aren't you from—Dallas?"

"To honor my grandfather's wishes. I may not have known him, but family is important to me."

While the waitress took their order, Darcy clenched her fists so tightly that her fingernails dug into her palms. Talking to Avery would require all her restraint. "It is for me too. I understand you were a foster child. Do you remember your real parents?"

"Vaguely. My mother died when I was really young and my father, John, Cyrus's son, followed a few years later. That's when I became part of the foster care system, but I had a nice set of foster parents."

"I was adopted when I was a baby. When I found out, I asked my parents if my birthday was really in April. They assured me it was. Did your foster parents know when your real one was?"

"Of course."

"When's your birthday? Anytime around mine?"

"Mine isn't until M—" Avery glanced down at her watch. "Look at the time. I have another appointment, and I'm gonna be late." She pushed to her feet. "We'll talk another time."

Avery scurried toward the exit, leaving Darcy with her bill when their drinks came. Whether Avery had been about to say March or May didn't make any difference since the real Avery Culpepper was born on February 2. Darcy didn't even get a chance to ask her what her biological mother's name was. Maybe she'd find another time to quiz her, but today at the fund-raising meeting at the church, she would let Lana know what the fake "Avery" said. Evidence was piling up against the women who claimed she was the grand-daughter of Cyrus Culpepper.

When the waitress arrived with coffee to go, Darcy paid the bill and left so she wouldn't be late for the meeting.

Ten minutes later she entered the large classroom at the Haven Community Church. Only a few people—Nick, Flint and Lana—were there, but it was still early. She would need all the help she could get to pull off this fund-raiser in another week. She wanted to be in town for it.

Darcy sat between Lana and Nick. "Do y'all know if anyone else is coming? Carol will be here." Sitting next to Nick gave her the confidence she would be able to successfully make the fund-raiser work.

"My uncle Howard is, but he may be a little late."

"Bea and Katie are coming and Pastor Andrew will be here after he returns a phone call. Also Heath and Josie." Flint grinned. "They're getting married in a few weeks and meeting with the pastor afterward."

"That's great. I know this is rushed, but when I dis-cussed this with Nick—" she paused, her glance falling on him "—my extensive background in fund-raising seemed the best way to help. If this is successful, hope-fully you can have more of them."

"That's what I'm hoping." A petite, very pregnant woman with long, auburn hair and brown eyes stood at the doorway with a tall man wearing a Texas Ranger star pinned to his shirt.

"Come in." Darcy rose and faced the couple. "I'm

Darcy Hill. You must be Josie Markham and Heath Grayson." She shook hands with both of them.

"Yes," Josie said and took a chair across from Darcy.

"I understand congratulations are in order. I really appreciate y'all helping when you're also planning your wedding and having a baby."

"Well, the baby's not due for eight more weeks unless it decides to come early. I especially want to see what you do because I'm hoping the Lone Star Cowboy League will start a ranch for girls."

As Lana asked Josie about the wedding, which was going to be small, Bea, Katie, Carol and the pastor came into the room. Katie slid a glance at Pastor Andrew as she sat next to him. When he looked at Katie, her cheeks reddened. Darcy had heard rumors about Katie having a crush on Pastor Andrew.

Nick bent toward her and whispered, "We should go ahead and start. I'll fill in my uncle on the plans."

The brush of air along her neck sent goose bumps down her arms. The memory of his kiss instantly flooded her mind. "Okay," she managed to say while her heartbeat accelerated.

"When Carol, Bea and I started talking about a fund-raiser, we thought it would be fun for the kids to show off some of their riding skills. I know that some are practicing their showmanship. We could also have competitions like barrel racing and roping. I was hoping I could leave that up to Nick, Flint and Howard since y'all work with the boys. We could have food for sale, charge an admission fee and also give tours of the new ranch."

"We can use the arena between the burnt barn and the storage one. But where will people sit? And, although the arena is covered, we'll have to consider the weather for stuff like the food," Flint said.

Pastor Andrew waved his hand. "I have a solution for where people will sit. I know a church in Waco that has portable bleachers we can borrow. A friend is the pastor there."

"We can set up big tents where the food will be served. If it's colder than predicted, we can possibly get some heaters," Darcy said.

Flint looked at Nick. "Didn't you ride in the rodeo as a teen? Could you demonstrate roping and tying a calf? Maybe invite members of the audience to try their hand at it?"

"Sure. Although what the kids will do isn't really a rodeo, we should have someone here dress up as a clown and be out in the ring keeping an eye on the activities as well as acting as an emcee."

As everyone offered suggestions, Darcy grew excited about the fund-raiser. Once most of the program was agreed upon and people were put in charge of different activities, she said, "This will be a great opportunity to show everyone what the boys ranch is really all about and how people can come together to support the place. When we're through next Saturday, hopefully we'll have convinced any naysayers about why the ranch should be here. I'm personally going to invite Fletcher Phillips to the event."

"He won't come," Bea said immediately.

Howard walked into the room. "Challenge him. He usually can't resist that."

"Thanks, Howard. I'll do that. Now, some folks might not attend the outdoor event, but in the evening we could have a ladies' choice dance, possibly in the arena after it is cleaned from the show."

"I have a better idea," Pastor Andrew said. "How about we have it here at the church in our hall? There would be more room, and I have a group of women who would love to organize it, especially if it's a ladies' choice dance."

Heath held Josie's hand. "I know a Texas Ranger in my office who sometimes works as a DJ. I can see if he's free."

"If he isn't available, I can do it in a pinch," Howard said.

Darcy wrapped up the meeting once all the members had assignments. "We'll meet back here on Wednesday evening. Thanks, Carol, for volunteering to get the word out about the fund-raiser."

"I'll do that and more. Clarence will help too." Carol accompanied the pastor and Katie as they left the room.

Bea hung back and pulled Darcy to the side. "We need to make sure this fund-raiser goes off without a hitch. I got a call from the Texas Department of Family and Protective Services. They're concerned about safety at the ranch, especially after the fire. They are launching an investigation. I told them about the planned fund-raiser, and they stressed that nothing bad better happen to call more attention to the place."

"I'll let Nick and Flint know. Perhaps a call from Heath, letting them know about what the police are doing, will ease their concerns."

"Good idea, Darcy. I'll talk to Heath and the sheriff." Bea hurried out of the room.

Darcy shut her notebook and faced Lana, Flint and Nick. "I have my work cut out for me in the next week."

Lana chuckled. "She was just complaining on Friday that she wished the kids were out of school so she could help them more than she already does," Lana told Flint and Nick. "Now you have something to do, Darcy, and I'll join in where I can."

"Before I forget to tell you, I had coffee with Avery right before the meeting," Darcy said. "The woman I talked to didn't know when the real Avery's birthday was. She started to say a month other than February but stopped herself and hurried out of the café. If she went into foster care, she would know when she was born. It would be in the records. She would need it for school."

"So she isn't the real Avery. Now what?"

"Let me do some more digging and then we can confront her for answers. She should be able to get a copy of her birth certificate if she's the real Avery, so if she can't, that's an indication she's an imposter. And we can call her on it."

"Then we should start looking for the real one. The town still has to meet Cyrus's requirement for the boys to stay at the Culpepper ranch."

"I'll start looking quietly."

"What are you two plotting?" Flint asked.

"The fake Avery's downfall and we need to do it soon. Time is running out to find the real one." Lana linked her arm through his. "See you tomorrow, Darcy."

Nick put the chairs back at the tables where they belonged. "The meeting went well. I hope it generates a lot of interest in the community. The boys ranch can always use donations and volunteers."

"And Josie hopes someone will start a girls ranch. Now that's something I would love to be part of." The second she said it, she realized that it wouldn't be possible for her, but maybe she could do something similar where she lived. It wouldn't have the feel of a Western ranch, but a farm could work.

"C'mon. I'll walk you to your car."

"I didn't use my car. Today was beautiful, and I enjoyed the exercise. I'm praying this will be what next Saturday is like."

"Then I'll drive you to the Blue Bonnet Inn."

"How about taking a walk with me? Bea told me that the Lone Star Cowboy League sponsors the boys ranch. Are you a member?"

Nick opened the door for her and then followed her outside. "Yes, although not as active as Gabe Everett, the president, or Tanner Barstow, the vice president. The Lone Star Cowboy League serves the whole county."

"Even Waco?"

"Yes, the secretary of the league is Seth Jacobs. He has a prosperous ranch and lives in Waco. What I like about the meetings—" he paused, smiling "—that is, when I attend—is talking with other ranchers around McLennan County."

"I can understand that. What affects one rancher could impact another." Darcy glanced at Lila's Café and gestured toward it. "Besides having coffee with Avery there, I officially met Fletcher today."

The only response Nick gave her was a frown.

"He won't be too happy when I uncover that Avery's a fraud."

"I heard you talking to Lana. So you're sure?"

"Ninety-nine percent, but I'll do some double-checking before I say anything."

"I'd love to see Fletcher's face when that happens."

"Maybe the man really feels the boys ranch isn't good for Haven."

Nick started to reply, but Darcy stopped, faced him and touched his mouth. "We know it is. Next Saturday I intend to *show* Fletcher it is."

"You really think he'll come?"

"I'm gonna make it impossible for him to say no. Once he sees how much the ranch is helping the children, I refuse to believe the man will continue his legal battle to shut it down." Because half of her genes were his and she wanted him to be more like her adopted father.

"You'll be disappointed, Darcy." He stepped closer. "But what I like about you is your fighting spirit to the end. You don't give up easily."

His nearness sent her pulse racing. "I have a feeling you don't either." Her breaths shortened.

"No. If I did I would have walked away from my family ranch when I came home from serving in the army."

"Why? What I saw of your place was nice."

He lowered his head closer to her. "It was neglected for years, but my uncle and I have been slowly turning it around."

His scent swirled around her, mingling with the smells carried on the breeze. She wanted him to kiss her again. But then a car on Main turned onto Third Street, honking as it went by.

Nick backed away, his cheeks red.

"Who was that?" Darcy brushed her hair away from her face, her hand trembling slightly.

"Gabe Everett. Probably going to the boys ranch, which is where I need to be."

"Yeah, I have some investigating to do. I can walk the rest of the way by myself. Haven isn't big enough to get lost in." She looked both ways on Main and then crossed the street.

She should thank Gabe for honking. Kissing Nick in the middle of the town wasn't what she'd come to

Haven for. Her days here were ticking down, and she needed to find a time to tell Fletcher he was her biological father, because she still wanted to know about her biological family.

Late Monday afternoon, Nick left the stall in the old barn where Bessie was staying, expecting Corey and several others to visit after Darcy tutored them. Between his chores at the Flying Eagle, working with Flint on the animals that would be in the rodeo and instructing Corey and the other boys participating in a beginner version of barrel racing, he probably wouldn't see much of Darcy until the meeting on Wednesday.

That was a good thing. At least he was trying to convince himself it was. But for the past twenty-four hours, since he had almost kissed her again, he couldn't get her out of his mind. She lived hundreds of miles away. On several occasions she had talked about her stay in Haven ending at the end of January. He had to get through the next few weeks, and then life would get back to normal.

He headed to the entrance to wait for the younger barrel racers. Flint was working with the older group. He spied four boys walking toward him, but Corey wasn't one of them. His cell phone rang. Quickly he answered Bea's call. "Nick, I need you up at my office."

"Is something wrong? Is Corey all right?"

"Corey is fine and still with Darcy."

"I'll be there."

After letting Flint know he was going to Bea's office, Nick hastened to the main house. He knocked on Bea's door, heard her tell him to come in and then he entered, surprised to find Darcy sitting in one of two chairs in front of the director's desk. It must be about the fund-raiser. Had Fletcher caused some kind of ruckus concerning it? He took a seat, sharing a puzzled look with Darcy.

"Darcy, is Corey with Katie?"

She nodded.

"He is new here, and I don't know him well enough to tell him that his father was in a car wreck half an hour ago. He was pronounced dead at the scene of the one-car accident. I was hoping one of you would break the news to Corey."

"I will," both Nick and Darcy said at the same time.

He slanted a glance at Darcy, pleased she wanted to help. "We'll do it together."

Bea heaved a sigh. "Good. He needs people around him who he's familiar with. While you talk with him, I'm going to let his houseparents know. Abby and John will inform the other boys in Corey's wing."

"Where was the wreck?"

"A mile from here."

"So he could have been on his way here." Darcy's voice wavered.

"That's what I think." Bea rose and headed for the door. "I'll send Corey in here."

"Do you think Ned was going to cause another scene here?" Nick asked the second the director left.

"I want to think that Ned was coming to apologize."

"How do you manage to look on the bright side in the middle of all of this?"

"Because it gives me hope."

He wished he could see things her way, but knowing Ned as he did, he doubted that was the case. "Possibly unrealistic hope? You must get disappointed a lot."

"Yes, sometimes I am, but I don't want to go through life only looking at the negative in a person."

The sound of footsteps nearing the office silenced Nick's reply. He hadn't started out so pessimistic, but during the years he'd lived with an alcoholic father, he'd been disillusioned too many times when his dad had promised to do better and never did.

After Corey entered the room, Nick closed the door and pulled up a third chair while the child sank down onto his seat. Corey's teeth bit into his bottom lip. His gaze flitted from Darcy to Nick and then back. The child knew something was wrong.

Darcy leaned forward and took Corey's hand. "Corey, we have some bad news. Miss Bea was just notified that your father was in a wreck. I'm sorry to tell you, but he didn't survive."

Corey sat, silent, staring at Darcy as though he hadn't heard what she said.

"Nick and I are here for you."

The boy swung his attention to Nick. "Was he drunk?"

"I don't know. He was coming to see you." Nick shifted his gaze to Darcy briefly and decided he would believe the best of Ned. "He was only a mile away from here. He, no doubt, wanted to ask for your forgiveness."

"Why did he come last time?" Corey swallowed hard. "He embarrassed me. He was always yelling at me."

"Some people drink for courage. They think alcohol helps them to do what they need to. They haven't figured out that it actually hurts their cause. That doesn't mean he didn't love you. He yelled because he was frustrated, more with himself than with anyone." As he said those words to Corey, he began to wonder if his father had felt that way. Had Dad loved him and just hadn't known how to show it?

Corey chewed on his bottom lip, fighting the grief

sweeping over him. Nick knew that look. At his dad's funeral he'd worn the same expression, not sure how to feel. Relieved or sad or both? Corey dropped his chin, clenching his hands together in his lap.

Nick didn't know what else to say. He hadn't handled his dad's death well, so how could he counsel another kid experiencing the same thing? He connected with Darcy's gaze. Maybe she would be better at it. Her look of sympathy, which suggested she knew what Corey was going through—what Nick had gone through too— swamped him. She couldn't know. She came from a supportive family who made her feel loved.

Corey raised his head, his eyes shiny. "What's gonna happen to me?"

"You'll stay here for a while. Nothing should change right now." He didn't want the child to go into the foster care system, possibly shuffled from one home to the next. Corey already had a hard time believing anyone loved him. But, for so many reasons, Nick didn't think he would be a good father figure for the boy. Maybe there was a relative that would come forward.

Darcy clasped his upper arm. "That shouldn't concern you right now. I'm a lawyer. I'll look into it for you."

"You will?" Corey asked with wonderment.

"Sure." She smiled. "Anything for you. You've got people who care about you now." She peered at Nick and then back at Corey. "Okay?"

He nodded and threw his arms around Darcy. She held him while Corey wept quietly against her shoulder.

Nick's heart swelled with emotions—love and hope—that he'd thought had been extinguished in him. Maybe there would be a happy ending for Corey.

A few minutes later, as the child drew back, a soft rap at the door prompted Nick to say, "Come in."

Bea entered with Abby and John Garrett. "They wanted to walk with you to your wing. Dinner will be served shortly."

Corey rose and went with his houseparents.

Bea waited until he was gone before asking, "How did it go?"

"As well as could be expected." Darcy glanced at the director and Nick. "Besides Fletcher Phillips, who else is Corey's relative?"

"We'll have to investigate that. His dad was the only one listed on the paperwork. Fletcher's name wasn't even on it."

"I'd like to help you with that. I've handled cases like Corey's before."

Part of Nick wanted to say that he could fill in temporarily until a relative was found, but the phone rang and Bea answered it. The other part of him was relieved he hadn't voiced that out loud. Pausing in her conversation, Bea cupped the receiver. "This may take a while. We can talk later, but, Darcy, I'll accept your help."

Darcy stood and left with Nick. Outside Bea's office, she stopped. "I need to talk with you somewhere quiet."

"This sounds serious."

"It is. There's something I need to tell you."

Chapter Ten

This was the moment when Darcy had to tell Nick why she had come to Haven in the first place. She still didn't know if she wanted to tell Fletcher, but she would have to say something to her biological father because of her growing feelings for Corey. She could give him a mother's love.

Corey needed a home. She wanted to give him one. And from all she'd gathered concerning Fletcher, he wouldn't stand in the way. He'd be relieved he didn't have to do anything.

"Since everyone will be at dinner in a few minutes, I'm sure there'll be a spare room we can talk in." Nick led her down the hallway toward the front of the large house. He poked his head into a small room used for parent visits. "This is free."

Not sure where to start, Darcy turned to face him while he shut the door. She'd come to really care for Nick, and it felt right to share her past with him. If only she knew more about him. She wished he wasn't such a private man. Regardless, she needed to tell him because of how much he cared for Corey.

"Let's sit." She waved her hand at the couch behind

her. When she was settled and Nick sat next to her, she drew in a deep breath, held it for a few seconds and then released it. "I have wonderful parents who have loved me from the beginning. But Mom and Dad are my adoptive parents. I've known most of my life and it never made a difference. I'm their daughter in every sense except a biological one."

"I had a good friend who was adopted. He had a wonderful set of parents like you did."

"When I became sick last year and was diagnosed with celiac disease, which is hereditary, I wanted to know more about my biological parents. It's no secret I want a family and children, but what would my illness do to my kids? It's manageable, but what if there was some condition in my birth father's or mother's family that was even more serious? I needed to find that out."

His eyebrows scrunched together. "Why are you telling me this now?"

She rushed ahead and said, "Because Fletcher Phillips is my birth father and therefore Corey is my cousin."

Nick's face wore a stunned expression, from his dropped jaw to his wide eyes glued to hers. Then he turned his head, and when he peered back at her, his features were composed into a neutral look, almost a bored one, as though she'd read him her grocery list. The silence lengthened into an uncomfortable sensation.

Finally she said, "Say something."

"What am I supposed to say? Congratulations?"

"Definitely not that. I'm not even sure I'm going to tell Fletcher, but then I probably will have to because I want to apply to be Corey's guardian."

"Why? You haven't known him long."

"I know he needs a family. I'm that. I know Fletcher won't take him in. Besides him, I'm probably one of Corey's closest family members."

Nick surged to his feet. "Well, it looks like you've got everything figured out."

"I thought this would be good news."

"Is Corey your new pet project? What if he doesn't want to go with you? This is his home. Not Alabama."

Ah, he was worried about Corey's reaction and the boy being states away. Any move could be hard on Corey—and Nick—but the child needed someone who wanted to care for him. "I'd stay until everything is worked out, but yes, I would move him to my home. My parents would accept him into our family as though he were my child. Corey needs a loving family."

"You're right. I hate to cut this short, but I've got chores still to do at my ranch. Good night, Darcy." He strode from the room so fast she didn't even have time to stand before he was gone.

Leaving her to wonder what was really going on.

Did he have hopes of raising Corey now that Ned was gone?

She started after Nick, but by the time she emerged from the house, he was driving away from the boys ranch. Should she go after him?

She'd left her purse in Bea's office. She hurried back to get it and go after Nick. Her bag in hand, she stepped into the hallway and ran into Corey.

"Are you leaving?" he asked in a quavering voice.

"I was, but if you want me to stay, I can."

He nodded and then looked down at his feet.

All she wanted to do was hug him and never let him go. She'd always wanted to be a wife and mother, like her own mom was, and had never thought of adopting, but this was right. She gathered him against her, and he clung to her.

Somehow she would have to tell Fletcher the truth before she applied for guardianship as Corey's relative. And somehow she would make Nick understand how she felt.

At the fund-raising meeting on Wednesday night, Nick sat across from Darcy. He'd done a good job of avoiding her. Flint was the one who had contacted her about the details of the rodeo on Saturday.

Until he'd had to face the threat of Corey leaving the area, Nick hadn't realized how much he'd come to love the child. He saw so much of himself in Corey that it was scary. The yearning. The need. The anger. Even now he couldn't let go of his deep hurt and rage at his father, feelings much like what Corey told Nick he was experiencing. But Nick also realized how wonderful Darcy would be as a mother to Corey. It would be perfect if she adopted Corey and stayed here. Then he could see the boy and continue helping him learn to ride and whatever else he needed. But Darcy had other plans.

As Darcy wrapped up the meeting, he leaned forward, ready to leave as soon as possible.

"I sent out a news release about the fund-raiser to the papers in the area," Darcy said. "Tomorrow Carol and Josie are going to blanket the surrounding towns with flyers. Thanks, Katie, for designing it and running off hundreds of copies for us. I'll see everyone early Saturday morning."

Nick hopped to his feet to go.

"Nick, could you stay a few minutes after the meeting? I have a couple of questions about the animals, and since Flint couldn't make it, I hope you can answer them."

As the committee members filed out of the room, he stood looking everywhere but at Darcy. She was Fletcher's daughter, and now she wanted to take Corey away from Haven, from him. He'd come close to telling her why Corey was so important to him. Now he was glad he hadn't revealed his relationship with his dad. He still didn't know what he'd done to deserve a father like his. He'd tried to do everything right, but nothing he had done had pleased his old man.

Suddenly Darcy was in front of him, only a couple of feet away. Concern lit her eyes, tempting him to beg her not to take Corey. To stay instead.

"I need a horse that I can do tricks on. I know this is last minute, but the more events we have in the rodeo the better it will be. I used to trick ride as a teenager and was part of the entertainment at horse shows."

Trick riding? He knew she had ridden, but that was a skill most riders didn't have. She'd been so open with him, or so he'd thought, but now he realized she had her own secrets. What else?

"I have a horse at the Flying Eagle that would be a good one to use. You could try Rose and see if you two are compatible. I noticed on the flyer that there was mention of a surprise. Is that it?"

"Yes. But if I don't do it, I'll come up with another surprise for the audience."

"When was the last time you did any tricks?" He could see similarities between Darcy and Fletcher. The same dark blond hair and blue eyes, even down to a cleft in their chins. Why hadn't he noticed it before?

"Four years ago at a fund-raiser. Not long after that

my horse died, and I stopped doing it. We had a special bond." Her voice caught on that last sentence.

He started to reach for her but stopped. He needed to break ties, not make them deeper. As much as he cared for Corey and didn't want to see him go, he knew Darcy would make a great parent for the child—in Mobile. If only she wouldn't leave... "Is that all you want?"

"Yes, but—"

He turned to leave.

"I thought you would be happy that Corey would have a home and not end up in the foster care system."

Don't answer her. Walk out the door.

"Are you mad at me?"

Darcy's question compelled Nick to stop and twist toward her. "Disappointed."

"I'm not Fletcher. I'm nothing like him."

"Are you so sure of that? You've been in Corey's life for a short time, and now you think you know what's best for him. You want to uproot him and take him away from the only place he's lived to be with strangers. Frankly he'd be better off at the boys ranch."

"He'll finally be taken care of and not left to fend for himself."

"Throwing money at him won't solve his problems. You told me you were a workaholic. Are you going to fall back into your usual pattern of working all the time? Corey doesn't need another parent who's never there."

She winced, thrusting her shoulders back. "I'll make time for him. I wouldn't take him on otherwise, and I'm not going to throw money at Corey. I'm going to love him."

"For how long? Until you marry and have your own children?" he asked before he could stop himself. She was great with the boys at the ranch, so why wouldn't she want to start a family of her own? But it was none of his business.

Darcy gasped. "If you could say that, then you don't know me. I'll check with Gabe and Tanner. Maybe they have a horse I can ride."

For the second time, he started toward the door.

"Nick, what's really going on? Do you want to take Corey? I'm not Fletcher, and I'd never treat Corey like Ned did."

No, I wouldn't be a good father for Corey, but I could be a friend. I can't, though, if he's in Mobile.

He continued his trek into the hallway and out the door to the parking lot. His pace slowed as he neared his truck. He didn't want her to have to look elsewhere for a horse she could use for trick riding. Rose would be perfect for her.

When he settled in the driver's seat, he took out his cell phone and texted her.

Come to the ranch tomorrow morning. My uncle will help you with Rose. I know you aren't Fletcher.

As he drove to the Flying Eagle, he kept telling himself Corey would have a family and that was all that mattered. But it didn't lift his spirits. He should be ecstatic for the child. He wasn't. The sadness of losing Corey overrode all other feelings.

When Nick entered his house by the back door, he hoped he could sneak to his bedroom and wallow in his grief. But Uncle Howard came into the kitchen before Nick could escape.

"Is there anything I need to know about the fundraiser?" he asked as Nick passed.

"You and I are gonna help set up what we can on

Friday afternoon. The rest will be done Saturday morning before the fund-raiser starts at twelve."

"Are you going to Ned's funeral at the gravesite in Dry Gulch tomorrow at one?"

"Yes, I told Bea I would take Corey. I don't imagine there will be many people there. I'm only going for Corey's sake."

"Maybe it's time you forgive your dad—and Ned. You should think about doing it tomorrow while you're saying your good-byes to Ned."

"He doesn't deserve forgiveness. Corey is alone in the world now, not that the man was much of a father to him when he was here."

"Who are you talking about? Your dad or Ned?"

"Both."

He stormed down the hallway and disappeared into his bedroom. All he wanted was to be left alone. But he couldn't rest. Instead, he paced the length of his room, fluctuating between anger at himself for how he'd handled losing Corey and anger at Darcy for coming into his life, turning it upside down and then planning to leave soon with a child he'd grown to care for—a child he loved.

Darcy finished loping around the corral, performing some of her tricks. She was a little rusty, but it was coming back—the technique and the fact that she missed riding on a horse even more than she'd realized when she rode with Corey and Nick. She dismounted and headed for the gate.

Howard opened it and clapped. "You have surprised this old coot. What made you start trick riding?"

"I saw a lady doing it when I was ten. She was great and so daring. It took a while before I could convince my parents I would be all right. Rose reminds me of the horse I had as a teenager." Darcy stroked the mare's neck.

When Rose turned and nudged her, Nick's uncle laughed. "She really likes you. And she doesn't cotton to everyone. But Nick has a knack of pairing a rider with the right horse."

"Where is Nick?"

"At the feed store."

"We didn't part on good terms last night."

"Yeah, he came home from the meeting as though he were a grizzly bear denied his sleep and yet he didn't get much last night. Did something happen at the church?"

"He knows that I'm going to apply to adopt Corey and, in the meantime, seek guardianship." Darcy walked the mare into the barn and removed the saddle.

Howard took it from her and returned it to where it belonged. "Now that's a surprise. Are you gonna move here?"

"No. My family and job are in Alabama."

"So you want to take Corey away. That explains why Nick has been so upset these past few days. Nick looks at Corey as if he is his younger brother. When Doug asked him to watch out for Corey and then was killed in the war, Nick took Doug's place in every sense. And Corey feels the same way about Nick. It might not be as easy as wanting to adopt the child. I know single people are able to adopt, but why do you think the state would give you guardianship?"

"Besides Nick, no one else in Haven knows this yet. That will change soon, but until I speak to Fletcher, please don't say anything to anyone but Nick."

"You want Fletcher to be your lawyer for the adoption?"

"No. I was adopted as a baby. Fletcher is my biological father, which makes Corey my cousin. When I first came to Haven, I didn't realize I had any family members here besides Fletcher. I'm going to tell Fletcher he's my birth parent and then use the fact that I'm Corey's cousin to apply for guardianship of him."

Howard rubbed the back of his neck, grabbed the reins and started for the exit. "I need to put her in the pasture. Walk with me." As they strolled out the door, he continued, "Now everything makes sense. Over the years Nick has been so reserved about his feelings and hasn't let many people close to him. Corey is one of the few he has, and honestly, when I've seen you two together, I see his walls breaking down."

"Why the walls?"

"I wish I could tell you, but it's Nick's story. All I can say is he didn't have an easy life from a young age." Howard opened the gate to a field and released Rose.

"Because of his father?"

Howard nodded.

"Did he go to the feed store because I was coming here?"

"Yes. I'm usually the one who does it. But he'll be coming home soon to get ready for Ned's funeral. He's taking Corey."

"Bea told me this morning. I hope he'll let me tag along. There's a chance of snow later, and I'd rather not drive. Do you think I should ask?"

"Yes, I see him returning from town. If you're gonna try to adopt Corey, you need to be with him as much as you can. Nick needs to learn to accept that and decide what's best for the child in the long term."

Nick parked near the opening to the barn, the back of his truck full of hay bales.

"I'll leave you to help him. I need to make a couple of calls." Howard winked and ambled away.

"Where's my uncle going?"

"To the house so we can talk."

Nick frowned and hefted the first hay bale. "We talked last night."

"I didn't mean to come in and take over with Corey. Until you told me about him, I didn't even know I had a cousin. Now that I do, it's hard for me to ignore it. I've always been a champion for projects involving children, so it was natural for me to gravitate toward the boys ranch."

Nick took another hay bale. "The reason Corey likes being with you is because you care about him. He can feel it."

Can you feel that I care about you too?

As Nick strode into the barn to put his load on a stack, Darcy grabbed one and struggled to lift it. But she did and made her way inside. "I'm telling you what I want, but if Corey is against it, I'll definitely take that into consideration. I wouldn't move him until he's visited my home." He skirted around her, and she hurried forward and stepped into his path, clasping his upper arms. "I haven't filed yet, and I won't until I tell Fletcher. I want Corey to realize I'm a relative and accept that first."

"You're leaving at the end of the month. That's a lot to get done in a couple of weeks. So why haven't you spoken to Fletcher?"

"Frankly, I'm not sure I even like the man, but then I don't know him well. I've only been around him a couple of times. And listening to you talk about him

hasn't been encouraging that he would even acknowledge me."

"There's only one way to find out."

"I know. I thought after the fund-raiser was over
I'd pay him a visit. Between looking for information
about Avery Culpepper, volunteering at the boys ranch,
spending time online working on a few ongoing cases
and then organizing a fund-raiser in a short time, I
didn't realize how stretched I was until I fell into bed
last night, dead tired but unable to sleep. Too much was
swirling around in my mind."

"Me too. I'm sorry about what I said yesterday. I
know you have Corey's best interests at heart, and if
you adopting him is good for him, then I won't stand
in your way."

She held out her hand. "Still friends then?" Although, as she said *friends*, she realized she wanted
more.

He took her hand, tugged her close and kissed her
forehead. "I can't stay mad at you. Would you like to
go with Corey and me to Ned's funeral?"

"Yes. When?"

"I'm picking him up at school around twelve so we
can be in Dry Gulch in time. We'll pick you up at 12:10
p.m. at the Blue Bonnet."

She gave him a grin. "See you then."

After the funeral in Dry Gulch, Nick drove his truck
toward Haven with Corey sitting between Darcy and
him. Snow fell, blanketing the landscape. He reduced
his speed, but a lot of the snow wasn't sticking on the
road, only on the grass.

Remembering how Darcy felt about driving in this
kind of weather, Nick slanted a look at her. As Corey

stared silently at the dashboard, lost in thought, she had her arm around the boy, giving him her quiet support as she had done throughout the funeral.

In that moment he knew that Darcy would be a great mother for Corey, and he couldn't stand in her way if the boy wanted her to adopt him. Nick realized he could help them bond. Maybe it was better that she became Corey's guardian. He'd said for years he didn't want to be responsible for a family. He'd seen and been in the middle of one that fell apart.

If only she would stay so he could see Corey grow up.

Darcy glanced at Nick. "I should be panicking now because the fund-raiser is in two days, but the weatherman said it will be well above freezing tomorrow and Saturday will be even warmer. Do you think the snow will melt by then?"

"Yes. This isn't going to stay around long. I predict by midmorning it'll start melting." Nick sent her a reassuring smile.

Blinking, Corey perked up and looked out the windshield. "I love snow."

"Where I live in south Alabama we don't get much at all, but this is the second snowfall I've seen since I came here."

"I like playing outside and making things in the snow. Snow sngels. Forts. Snowmen." Corey's voice became more excited as he talked.

"How about a snowwoman? I've never done either one."

Corey and Nick exchanged glances and then Corey whispered into his ear, "Can we make one with Darcy?"

Nick nodded. He would have to content himself with

being a friend long-distance, but right now he would cherish every moment he could with Corey.

Corey twisted back to Darcy. "We'll show you how to build a snowman."

"And a snowwoman?" Darcy asked with a chuckle.

"Yup. And I've got a good idea," Nick added. "I'll call Miss Bea and tell her you're gonna stay for dinner at my place and then I'll bring you back to the boys ranch. Before we eat, we can make them in my front yard."

"What if it doesn't stop snowing?" Darcy asked.

"We can do it while it's snowing. You won't melt." Nick winked at her, feeling his cold heart beginning to thaw.

After drinking a cup of the hot chocolate that Howard had fixed for them, Darcy traipsed outside behind Nick and Corey, ready to build her snowwoman. "Okay, all I have to do is make a snowball and then roll it on the ground until it gets as big as I want?"

"Corey, I think she's got it. You did good explaining it to her." Nick held his hand up, and the boy high-fived him. "Now, are you sure you don't want me to help you make your snowman?"

Corey nodded. "Darcy will need your help."

She planted her fist on her waist. "I beg your pardon. I'm capable of doing this by myself."

Nick scanned the yard. "Tell you what. I think there's enough snow that we each can make one and let Uncle Howard decide which is the best."

"Y'all shouldn't even bother. I'm gonna beat you." Corey scooped up a handful of snow and packed it into a ball.

Darcy started hers. As she stooped over to roll it along the ground, a snowball struck her side. She shot straight up and whirled around. Nick bent over to make another while Corey took what he had in his hand and pelted her with it.

"I can't believe y'all are ganging up on me." Darcy launched her snowball at Nick.

Then suddenly Corey followed suit. The next ten minutes he teamed up with her. He probably felt sorry for her. But that was okay.

Nick ducked behind his truck and popped up to toss several balls quickly one after another, all at her.

She tried to dodge them but instead stumbled and went down. She was covered with snow, but so were Nick and Corey. Her laughter filled the air, her tears of joy streaking down her cold face. "I call a truce."

Nick brushed what snow he could off his coat. "I couldn't resist the chance."

Corey shook his head, loosening the white flakes. "Me neither. Do we still have time to make a snowman?"

Nick looked up at the darkening sky. "If we hurry and work together. Darcy, you make the head. I'll do the bottom and, Corey, you make the middle."

Darcy trudged across the yard. "I'll be over here away from you two. If I get any wetter, I'll freeze into an ice statue." She disappeared around the side of the house.

She wouldn't trade the past half an hour for anything. She quickly made her head ball and picked it up to carry back. But before she rounded the corner, she stopped and peeked into the front yard in case they had set up an ambush.

Instead, Corey was helping Nick roll a huge ball to a spot near the porch where a medium one was. When Corey set his middle ball on top of the base, he stepped back and grinned from ear to ear. "This is gonna be the best snowman."

Darcy glanced at her pitifully small head and hurriedly added more to it, packing it down as much as possible. She was not going to be the one to ruin their masterpiece.

"Darcy, do you need help?" Corey came around the side of the house.

"I was just coming back to put the finishing touch on the snowperson." She held up the head, not totally pleased with its size, but it was much better than it had been.

When she set it on the unfinished snowman, she made a big production out of it, hoping no one would say anything about her attempt.

Nick was barely able to keep a straight face. Finally he turned his back on them—probably so she wouldn't see his grin.

"I know. Not the best in the world," she murmured and started to take it off the snowman.

Corey stopped her. "Don't. I think it's fine. Dontcha, Nick?"

Nick pivoted and, with a solemn expression, nodded, but his eyes twinkled.

To Darcy's relief, Howard stepped out on the porch. "I'm starving, so I decided to bring out a hat, scarf, carrot and chocolate pieces for the mouth and eyes. Corey and Nick, go get two branches while Darcy decorates the face."

"Thanks, Howard. I didn't know they wanted to make a giant snowperson."

"That's Texans for you. They like to do things big." Howard plopped the black cap on top of the snowman's head while Darcy stuck on the carrot and then the pieces of chocolate.

When Nick and Corey returned and planted the

sticks in place, Howard pulled out his cell phone. "Okay, y'all stand by your work of art and smile."

Instead of grinning, Nick and Corey laughed, tried not to and couldn't stop.

Darcy watched them feed off each other. Nick didn't want a family. That was such a shame. She'd always wanted one.

Finally, the guys settled down, and Howard took a photo. "I'll make sure everyone gets a picture. Now let's go eat."

As Corey entered the house with Howard, Nick hung back with Darcy. "Thanks for being a good sport. For a little while Corey was able to forget and just be a kid."

"I know. But he'll have to deal with his past and his mixed feelings concerning his dad."

"Yeah. Too bad they don't just go away on their own."

"Are you talking about your own father or Ned?"

"Both." He slung his arm over her shoulders and headed for the entrance.

But the fun of the past hour had evaporated. When would Nick trust her to tell her about his father?

Later when Nick drove toward the boys ranch to drop off Corey, he was tired. He stifled a yawn. Today had been an emotional day for the child and, for that matter, Nick too. He wanted to be part of Corey's life. He didn't want him to leave—or Darcy either, especially after the camaraderie they'd shared while playing in the snow. He thought he had everything worked out, but then his emotions fluctuated when reality set in and Darcy commented on Corey dealing with his father's death.

When they said good-night to Corey in the entry hall

at the boys ranch, Corey gave him a hug and then so did Darcy, who also kissed the top of his head.

"We'll see you tomorrow. After school, we'll practice your barrel racing with the others." Nick tousled Corey's hair. "You're a natural at riding. If I didn't know better, I would think you've been riding for a while."

Corey beamed. As he mounted the stairs, he turned halfway up and waved at them.

When Nick slid into the driver's seat, he stared at the large ranch home. "I think today went well. Corey's gonna sleep well tonight." He wasn't sure *he* would though. If Darcy took Corey to Alabama, a part of him would go with them.

"I hope so. I could use a good night's sleep too. We have a lot to do in the next two days, even more if the snow remains. I love the open-house concept for the fund-raiser. My goal is to give Fletcher a tour of the ranch. I've sent him an invitation, and I intend to follow up on it tomorrow."

"Are you going to tell him who you are?" Nick started his truck.

"No. I need him to see the value of the ranch. I don't want to confuse the issue with that revelation."

"In other words, you're putting it off."

She chuckled. "Am I that obvious?"

"Yep, but I don't blame you."

"My preference is to never tell him, but I need to establish that Corey is a relative."

Curious about her reasons, he asked, "Why wouldn't you tell Fletcher?"

"Because I already have a dad, and frankly Fletcher isn't my idea of a father."

"What about the medical information you're seeking?" He threw her a glance as he approached Haven.

"After meeting him and seeing his stand on the boys ranch, I've been reconsidering it. I could get some of the medical information by digging deep into his family and talking to people who knew Luella Snowden Phillips. I'd love to find out all I can on her. From what I've learned she was quite a woman, who had a wonderful dream with the first boys ranch. Too bad Fletcher isn't more like his grandmother."

"Sometimes close relatives can be as different as night and day." His dad and Uncle Howard had been like that.

"True. I've seen enough of that in my job."

"Do you enjoy being a lawyer?"

"Yes. Many people need a good attorney but can't pay for one. I feel like I'm helping people who can't."

"You're definitely different from Fletcher in that respect. Too bad you can't stick around and maybe become a good influence on Fletcher."

As Nick pulled up to the Blue Bonnet Inn, she asked, "I don't know that who I am would influence him one way or another. He seems pretty set in his ways."

"Yeah, you're right. I've been trying for sixteen months to get him to do something about Ned." When Darcy pushed down on the handle, he added, "I'll walk you to the porch."

"You don't have to."

"I want to." He hurried and rounded the hood as she hopped down from the cab.

A light illuminated the porch, highlighting her beautiful features. Her eyes, a glittering blue, weren't really like Fletcher's. There was a shine in them that drew Nick every time he looked at her. And her luxurious blond hair, long and wavy, framed her face and emphasized her attributes—not just outward but inward too.

Nick turned toward Darcy. "I was dreading the funeral and how Corey would do. I'm glad we went together."

"So am I. If I drove, I'd probably be stuck somewhere between Dry Gulch and Haven. I felt you lose control of your truck a few times."

"I'm surprised you didn't say anything."

"No reason. You knew what you were doing." She sighed. "I don't know if it's really hit Corey yet that his father is gone. But the houseparents and Bea are sharp and will be quick to pick up on anything wrong."

"And let us know if we need to help."

"Yes, exactly."

Darcy had made Corey's transition to the boys ranch so much easier. She'd become so important to Nick. There were times he floundered with what to do or say, but Darcy knew the perfect thing.

Darcy moved closer to Nick, and he held his ground, enjoying her nearness. "Don't fall asleep driving home."

"I won't."

"Maybe you could call me and let me know you got to your ranch all right." She ran her palm down his jawline, her eyelids closing partway.

That was all the invitation he needed. His arms encircled her, bringing her tight against him as he dipped his head and took her mouth in a kiss.

He wanted it to last, but the sound of a car door slamming nearby parted them as they shifted to see who was coming toward the house. Avery. And Fletcher was parked behind Nick's truck.

"See you tomorrow." He gave her hand a gentle squeeze and headed for his pickup whistling, his gaze on Fletcher's glare.

* * *

"My, my. It looks like you had an interesting date," Avery said as she stopped next to Darcy.

"How about you?" Darcy curled her hands at her side, trying to remember that she still wanted to get some more information from the brash woman, who was dressed in four-inch heels and a tight skirt that stopped three inches above her knees.

Avery waved her hand in the air. "Just business."

Darcy entered the bed-and-breakfast with Avery right behind her. "Maybe you can help me. On Saturday, when the boys ranch will be open to the public for tours, I wanted to give background information about the Culpepper family, who so generously donated the land and house. What was your father's name?"

"John."

"Your mother's name?"

Avery continued toward the staircase, forcing Darcy to hurry to keep up. "Mommy is all I remember."

"Isn't it on your birth certificate?"

"I'm sure it would be if I had one. Now, if you'll excuse me, I'm tired and want to go to bed." Avery practically ran up the stairs and disappeared from view.

Darcy sank onto a step. The woman knew her father's name because it was in the will but didn't know who her mother was. Avery was definitely an impostor. She really had nothing to back up her claims.

Darcy would talk with Lana and Bea after the fundraiser was over. Something needed to be done quickly because time was running out for fulfilling the terms of Cyrus Culpepper's will.

Chapter Eleven

Nick stood at the entrance the participants were using for the boys ranch's First Annual Rodeo for Youths. The bleachers that Pastor Andrew had borrowed for the fund-raiser lined the inside of the riding arena. Flint was at the other end of the ring, making sure everything ran smoothly, and so far it had.

Hundreds of people from Haven and the surrounding towns had come out to watch the boys participate in barrel racing, team penning and showmanship. Corey was in the beginner group for barrel racing. He would be the last to perform.

"Has Corey raced yet?" Darcy asked from behind Nick.

He glanced over his shoulder and saw her holding the reins to Rose. "Nope. He's coming up now."

Darcy gave Corey a thumbs-up while Nick opened the gate and patted Rose's flank. Corey entered the arena to the cheers of the crowd. He grinned from ear to ear. Wyatt was the starter for each event, but he was also there in case there was a medical problem with one of the animals. Dr. Delgado was nearby if a boy was hurt.

Wyatt dropped his arm, indicating the start, and Corey shot forward, racing toward the red, white and blue barrel at the far end. He slowed to round it and then picked up speed to cross the finish line near Nick.

"He did good," Darcy said beside Nick.

"Yeah, but he was two seconds behind the winner."

"Enough for second place."

"Yep," he said as the first three places were announced over the loudspeaker.

Darcy shouted "Hurrah!" for each winner but louder for Corey. The biggest grin shone bright on the kid's face. "Now it's my turn. I hope I don't mess up. The boys will never let me live that down."

"If they give you any grief, challenge them to do the trick. On second thought, don't. Without training, they'd break their necks."

"Safety while riding is important. I should know— I've broken my arm and leg over the years."

"And that didn't discourage you?"

"No. It made me more determined. Both times it was because I was pushing myself beyond what I or my mount was ready to do."

Gabe Everett, the emcee for the rodeo, took the mic. "We wanted to end this with a special act from Darcy Hill, who has performed tricks on a horse countless times at various shows in the South. Let's give her a big Texas welcome."

Thunderous clapping and feet stomping resonated through the riding arena. Darcy's cheeks reddened as she swung up into her special saddle, which she'd had her father ship overnight, along with the hot-pink, sequined outfit she wore.

While Rose galloped around the ring, Darcy started off swinging out of the saddle, touching the ground and then landing in front of the horn, facing backward. She did several dismounts and then performed a reverse neck and a spritz layout. The crowd roared. She ended with a hippodrome like the Romans did thousands of years ago, where she stood up and made a complete circle around the arena, waving to the audience.

Nick didn't realize he had been holding his breath through the last trick, but finally he inhaled deeply. To a standing ovation, Darcy came to a stop in the center, dismounted and then bowed to each side. Several boys, including Corey, ran to her, pumping their arms in the air. They encircled her, all asking questions at once.

As more boys gathered around Darcy, Nick hurried to rescue Rose from the onslaught. His mare was gentle and used to people but not a crowd. When he reached the circle of children, he noticed how calm Rose was, even when the kids got close to check the special saddle. Darcy showed them the extra straps on it, fielding one question after another.

"Can I learn how?" Corey asked and then more kids chimed in.

"It takes a lot of practice to do these tricks. You have to be an accomplished rider and have the right horse." Darcy looked at Nick over the sea of kids from the ranch and town. "But more than anything, don't do these tricks without an adult. I had an uncle who taught me when I was ready."

Nick watched Darcy interacting with the children. She was patient and made sure everyone had her full attention. In that moment he knew Corey would be fine with Darcy as his guardian—even if they both lived in Alabama. But would he?

That question took him by surprise. He loved Corey, but he was willing to let him go if it was better for him.

He was struggling to make his ranch a thriving business once more. That should be where his focus was. Darcy was doing him a favor.

Yeah, right. Then why don't you believe that?

As the throng of kids dissipated to get samples of the food being offered outside in the tents, Corey remained next to Darcy.

He pointed at Rose. "Can I ride her out of the ring?"

She smiled at Corey and gave him a leg up. As he sat tall in the saddle, Fletcher approached Darcy.

Darcy spied Nick coming around the other side of Rose while she kept her attention on the man who was her birth father. "I'm glad to see you at the fund-raiser." Hope flared in her that this would lead to Fletcher changing his mind about the boys ranch.

"Well, yes, but I'm not going to stay. My secretary gave me your note and the ticket to this…event." The attorney handed Darcy a ten-dollar bill. "I appreciate the gesture of free admission, but I can pay my own way."

"Darcy, I'll take Rose and Corey out of here."

She peered at Nick, wishing he could stay but realizing she had to do this alone. "Thank you. I'll come to the barn later to get my saddle."

As Nick and Corey left with the mare, Darcy turned back to Fletcher. "I understand how you may feel about the boys ranch being moved from your family's place, where it all started. Your grandmother sounds like a forward-thinking woman who cared about the community. It was a tribute to her."

He opened his mouth to say something.

Darcy hurriedly continued, "The boys ranch will always be her idea. Even though they have expanded and moved here, she will always be the founder of the Lone Star Cowboy League Boys Ranch. You must be really proud of Luella Snowden Phillips and the good she has accomplished."

"You've been in town two weeks. I'm sure by now, especially since you're friends with Nick McGarrett, you know I'm not a fan of the boys ranch."

Darcy gritted her teeth as he spoke and then forced a smile on her face. "Have you had a tour of the place?"

"No, don't see why I should. I knew what the original one was like and I didn't like the idea of a boys ranch even then."

"Before you pass judgment, don't you think you should see it all? That way, you'll be talking from a place of knowledge." Her grin wavered as Fletcher scowled. She shored it up and finished with, "Let me show you what the boys ranch is about and then you can say you're completely informed."

"I don't have much time."

She hooked her arm through his and walked toward the exit. "Then let's get started. We'll begin with the house and the three wings where the boys live with a couple in each wing who are the houseparents for them."

As they strolled toward the ranch house, Fletcher scanned the food tents, craft tables and games for the crowd. "You're not from around here. What made you come to Haven?"

"A vacation."

His bushy eyebrows slashed downward. "Haven has never been a vacation spot. I'd think you'd go skiing in the mountains or lie on a beach somewhere."

"I live near a beach and I don't ski." Darcy wanted to tell Fletcher he was the reason that she was here, but this wasn't the right time. Today was about the boys ranch. She entered the house through the front door. "I've only been here a short time, and I've seen what this place can do for a boy who needs help."

"Isn't that what a detention center for juvenile delinquents is for?"

"The boys ranch takes children from age six to seventeen. A young child isn't a juvenile delinquent. So many need guidance and time to develop their social and emotional skills." Darcy led Fletcher through one of the wings. "Take, for example, Corey, who is the most recent boy to come here. In less than two weeks, he has improved his reading, taken care of a horse and learned to ride. He's become a valuable team player. They all have chores that they're responsible for and those rotate, so they have a lot of experience in different areas."

"Isn't that what a parent is for?" Fletcher asked as they walked to one of the other wings.

The thought that he was her biological father and had just asked that irritated her. Where was Fletcher when she was born? "Ideally, yes, but life doesn't work out that way all the time. Corey lost his dad recently, but before that he'd run away from his house because his father was drinking too much and not taking care of him."

Pressing his lips together, Fletcher glared at her. He slowed his pace.

She probably shouldn't have said that. She had let her feelings toward Fletcher get the better of her. She smiled. "In Corey's case, like so many others, there isn't a good alternative. Some come here because they need social skills or they have to learn to manage their behavior, but above all else, this is a safe environment for the children. There are no boys with psychotic disorders. That's not what this facility is for."

"You could have fooled me. One of them is most likely responsible for burning the barn down."

Stopping in her tracks, she cocked her head and asked, "Do you realize that many people in town think *you* are behind the fire?"

His eyes grew round. "Me! I'd never do something like that. I'll stop this place legally, not illegally."

Darcy strolled through the kitchen to the back door. "Let me show you the old barn, where some of the livestock is kept. There are goats, sheep, cattle and horses."

"I've seen a barn before." He pointed to the building nearby. "What's that?"

"That's the library, where the children get help with their school work. I've been tutoring them after school since I arrived. I love seeing a child's expression when he finally understands something. Not far away are the basketball and volleyball courts. Exercising in fun ways helps promote healthy growth."

"It looks like a country club to me."

Anger burst from its restraints. "And what is wrong with that? They help take care of the house and ranch. They learn responsibility and develop a good self-image that will help them become productive citizens. You were fortunate to have been born into wealth. Most are not."

"I've worked hard for what I have."

"So what do you think we should do with these twenty-four boys? Give them what they need to become good citizens or let them loose with no support and possibly lead them down the path of juvenile delinquents? Wasn't your father and his behavior the reason your grandmother started the ranch?"

Fletcher harrumphed. "That was different."

"How?"

"I—I…" He tipped his Stetson and finally said, "Good day, Ms. Hill."

As the man stormed off, she sat down on the back steps. She'd made this worse. She'd hoped showing him the ranch and the good it did would change his mind. She'd been wrong. She prayed the boys didn't pay for her mistake.

Leaving the staff and the boys to clean up after the fund-raiser, Nick strolled to his truck, intending to help set up for the ladies' choice dance and then go home. It had been a long day. When he started to climb into the cab, he stopped in midmotion.

He stepped back out and picked up the envelope lying on his seat. His name was scrawled across the front in blue ink. He opened the letter and pulled it out.

The note read, *Wanna go to the dance tonight with me? Pick me up at 8. Love, Darcy.*

For a few seconds, he stared at the word *love* and imagined them as a couple. Then his gaze slid to the first word.

Wanna? He hadn't seen Darcy's handwriting, but he was sure she didn't write this. Then he remembered what some of the others had received over the past months, and he chuckled. Someone was playing matchmaker.

He looked up and panned the yard for anyone watching. If they were, they were hiding well.

But, to be on the safe side, he needed to check with Darcy. She didn't deserve to be stood up. Darcy was on the set-up committee so she would be at the church. He hopped into his truck and drove there, trying to figure out how he would ask her about the note.

When he arrived at the reception hall where the dance would take place, he glanced around for Darcy. Her car was in the parking lot. He spied her standing on a tall ladder putting up one end of the banner while Lana tacked up the other part.

"Is that even?" Darcy asked as she leaned back to decide.

"It's even," he called out.

The ladder wobbled. Nick hurried to her in case she fell. But she immediately flattened herself against the ladder and grasped it. It wavered and then settled into place.

Slowly she descended. When she turned, he glimpsed a pink tinge across her cheeks. "I'll be the first one to tell you I know what a hammer is, but I can be lethal when I use it. This time I only hit my thumb once."

"You should have waited."

"I thought you might get stuck at the ranch dealing with the animals."

"Nope. Flint and some of the older boys were finishing up at the barn and suggested I come see if you need any help."

She pushed the hammer into his hand. "Here. Any hammering can be done by you."

He chuckled. "I didn't get to ask you about the tour you gave Fletcher."

"A disaster."

"Did you tell him who you were?"

"No, definitely not the right time."

Nick pulled the note from his back pocket. "I found this in my truck on the seat. Did you send it?"

She retrieved one exactly like his, except the wording was different. "Obviously you didn't send this."

"Nope. It's a ladies' choice dance."

She blushed. "Up until recently things were tense between us, and then today was so crazy. I'm glad I remembered to come here to set up. Nick, would you like to go to the dance with me tonight?"

He grinned. "We shouldn't encourage the matchmaker, but since it could be Corey, I wouldn't want to disappoint him. As the note says, I'll pick you up at eight."

"Which only gives us a couple of hours to decorate and get home to change."

"Yep, so what do you want me to do?"

"Help me set up the tables and chairs first. I should be okay. No hammer involved."

As they walked to the closet where the tables were stored, his earlier exhaustion seemed to lift. There was a spring to his step. Darcy brightened his day and that scared him. What was he going to do when she left Haven?

"Did you hear what happened with Pastor Andrew?" Nick asked, hoping to take Darcy's mind off dancing.

"Yes, Katie told me earlier that he showed up to pick her up for the dance. Apparently the same matchmaker left him a note in his car at the fund-raiser, but Katie didn't get one. She told me when she saw him she was speechless."

"I saw them arrive together. Pastor Andrew didn't know what else to do."

Darcy moved closer to Nick. "As Katie was telling me, she was turning ten shades of red."

When Bea joined them, she was using a paper plate as a fan. "Is it just me or is it hot in here?"

"It's comfortable to me, but then I haven't been dancing like you have," Darcy said.

"That's because all these single men have been coming up to me and telling me I asked them to the dance. They received a note to meet me here at the church."

"Who?" Nick could barely contain his laughter.

"Seth Jacobs, the grocer and Slim. I've been shuffling between them. I don't want to hurt their feelings and tell them I didn't leave a note for them. I think I'll lose five pounds tonight if this keeps up." Bea's eyes grew wide as a deputy sheriff headed toward her. "Oh, no. Not another one. See you two later. I'm ducking into the restroom." Bea scurried away in the opposite direction of the officer.

Darcy looked at Nick and chuckled. "Poor Bea. Whoever the matchmakers are, they have been busy today."

Nick grinned. "I guess they really wanted Bea to dance tonight. I don't dance. I'm glad it was her, not me."

"Speaking about dancing, shouldn't we?" she asked as one song ended and another started.

"Ah, finally a slow dance," Nick said, holding out his hand to Darcy.

She placed hers in his. "Remind me to teach you a Texas line dance in our spare time."

He laughed. "When will that be?"

"After tonight, I'll be a gal on vacation. So you can fit me into your busy schedule."

His arms wrapped around her, and he moved in close, her light fragrance flirting with his senses. The music and people surrounded them, but all Nick focused on was Darcy in his embrace. Her soft hair grazed the side of his face, and suddenly he wished they weren't in the middle of a crowded dance floor.

He attempted to shove that thought out of his mind. She wanted a family. He wasn't cut out to be a father. What if he failed like his dad? He'd finally acknowledged that when she had stated she wanted to adopt Corey. If only the boy could stay here in Haven so he could be part of his life without being a father figure. When he'd been looking out for Corey, he'd considered himself to be taking Doug's place. A big brother he could do.

Lost in thought, he stepped on Darcy's foot. She hardly missed a beat and didn't say a word. "Sorry about that."

She leaned back and looked up into his face. "You warned me. Actually you're doing fine."

"You're kind to say that, but I saw you wince."

The music wound down, and some of the couples left the floor. When a fast tune blared from the loudspeakers, he grabbed her and tugged her toward the sidelines.

She limped.

"Is your toe broken?"

She laughed and adjusted her gait. "No, but I love teasing you."

He drew her into a dimly lit corner and caged her against the wall. "You're brave, teasing me—and dancing with me."

"All you need are a few lessons. Maybe I can add slow dancing to the Texas line dancing lessons before I leave."

He tensed. "When is that happening?"

"I've started the proceedings to adopt Corey so it

might be a while. I'm trying to prove my relationship to him without including Fletcher."

"You aren't going to tell him?"

"After what happened today at the ranch, I don't know that I'm ever going to tell him he's my biological father."

Someone gasped close by.

Darcy looked around Nick and glimpsed Avery a few feet away, almost concealed by a pocket of darkness.

Chapter Twelve

Before Darcy could say anything, Avery scurried from her hidden spot and out into the crowd of dancers, weaving her way through them.

As Nick moved, Darcy moaned. "Avery overheard what I said. Leave it to her to be sneaking around."

"She might not say anything to Fletcher," Nick said as he twisted around to face the partygoers.

Fletcher made a beeline for Darcy. "On second thought, she might. I don't want a scene in here. Let's leave the reception hall." Being close to one of the exits, she hurried for it, not prepared to see Fletcher. His attitude during the tour still bothered her. What had made him so judgmental—and mean?

Out in the foyer, Fletcher caught up with Darcy. Avery followed a few paces behind him.

"We need to talk before rumors start flying around town," her birth father said in a tone that meant she didn't have a choice.

"Not here." Surprisingly, Darcy remained calm while Nick intercepted Avery and *escorted* her to the reception hall.

"Yes, here!" The fury in Fletcher's voice singed Darcy.

"Let's go into a classroom where the whole town won't hear." Darcy started walking toward the hallway off the foyer. At the door, she glanced over her shoulder at Fletcher.

He scanned the large entryway and several people leaving while a couple stood off to the side, watching him. He stormed after Darcy.

When Fletcher stepped into the room, he glared at Darcy. "You are *not* my daughter. I've never had a child. If you spread false rumors about me, I will sue you. What is your plan? To wheedle your way into my life to get my money?"

Remain calm. Anger won't make your point. "I don't need your money, and I don't want it. My father is Warren Hill, and he comes from a long line of wealth. He has a penthouse in New York City, a home in Hawaii and an estate in Alabama. Perhaps you've heard of him. He's a renowned attorney." She would not let him put down her *real* parents.

Fletcher didn't back down but moved closer. "Then why are you spreading false rumors? Is it because I'm against the boys ranch?"

She placed a hand on her waist. "Why are you really against the boys ranch? In all the years it has been operating, Haven has grown. I don't see its existence as a deterrent to the growth of the town or the value of property here. You want to take away hope and a real chance for these boys to do better. Why are you so bitter?"

Fletcher's face flushed red. "I'm not bitter. I'm trying to save the town."

"And I'm not gullible. I don't buy that. Are you in

with Avery, trying to milk as much money from the Culpepper estate as she can? Is that why you are representing a fraud?"

"Avery isn't a fraud! You are, if you think I'm buying this story of yours."

"You don't have to. I know what the truth is. You had an affair with Charlotte Myers and the result of that was me." She pointed at herself. "I have the birth certificate to prove it. Does Avery have one to prove who she is?"

His eyes narrowed, as if he were assessing Darcy and finding her lacking.

She didn't care what he thought. Charlotte had rejected her, so she really wasn't surprised that he would too. "I'm leaving. Frankly I wasn't going to say a word to you. All I wanted to do was find out about you and your family. To see if there were any heredity concerns I needed to be aware of. I love my parents who adopted me. I don't need you." She charged toward the hallway, needing to get away from her biological father.

As she left the classroom, she ran into Nick waiting for her. "I have to get out of here."

Nick put his arm around her shoulder and began walking in the direction of the exit. "I'll let Lana and Flint know we're leaving."

After he assisted Darcy into the passenger side of his truck, he made a call on his cell. At the moment she didn't want to be around others. A steamroller might as well have flattened her. She'd known her birth father would deny her. He hadn't really sought the truth, or he would have seen through the fake Avery.

As Nick started his pickup, he snuck a look at her. "Where do you want me to take you?"

"Home to Alabama." She said the first thing that

came to her mind. She sighed. "But that isn't possible right now. I'm not going to let Fletcher get in my way. Please take me to the Blue Bonnet Inn. Everyone is at the dance, so I won't have to answer any questions."

When they reached the bed-and-breakfast, Darcy intended to say good-night then hole up in her bedroom to nurse her bruised feelings. But Nick opened the front door and entered before her as if he'd known what she was going to do.

"I'm not good company right now."

"That's okay. You don't have to talk, but if you do, I'm a good listener." He took her hand, drew her into the living room and sat next to her on the couch. "For as long as I've known Fletcher, he hasn't been a happy person. Where you look for the good in people, he looks for the worst."

"Why? What happened?"

"Maybe nothing. That might be what he's like."

Like Nick being so closed off. Had he always been that way? She didn't think so, but he didn't share himself with her.

"I think there's more. My biological mother wouldn't even talk to me. She had a family and wanted nothing to do with me."

Nick slipped his arm around her shoulders. "That's her loss. You're special, and she'll never find that out."

His words washed over her, numbing some of the hurt caused by the mother who gave birth to her. She'd hoped Fletcher wouldn't reject her too. "I need to look at my blessings in all of this. I have two terrific parents who loved me as though I was their biological daughter."

"See what I mean? You're already turning it around and focusing on the good. That doesn't come naturally for a lot of people." He stared across the room, a far-off look in his eyes.

He was referring to himself. She wished she could help him, but she'd asked him about his past and he'd avoided it. Telling her required trust, and he didn't trust easily.

"I try to keep my focus on the Lord," Darcy said. "When I do, it helps me get through the hard times."

"What if He's forgotten you?"

"He doesn't forget anyone. That doesn't always mean that your life will go smoothly, but He's beside you through those tough situations. You have to choose to take His support."

"So what are you going to do next concerning Fletcher?"

"Nothing. I'm still applying for guardianship of Corey. If Fletcher chooses not to believe me, that's his problem. He was listed on my original birth certificate. My main concern is for Corey. He does have family who cares."

"When are you going to tell Corey?"

"Probably Monday when I work with him. I want him to know now that I have the process for adopting him in the works. Are you okay about this? I know we've talked about this but—"

He placed his forefinger against her lips to still the rest of her sentence. "I don't want to lose Corey. He's become important to me, but once I stopped and thought about it, I realized you are the best person to take care of him."

He shifted closer to her and combed her hair back behind her ears, and then he cradled her head. As he slowly leaned toward her, she knew he was giving her time to pull away, but that was the last thing she wanted to do.

His mouth covered hers in a kiss that stole her heart. Nick had made coming to Haven so much easier than it could have been. She surrendered to the touch of his lips.

When he finally pulled back, his gaze caressed her face as though he were memorizing her features to remember later. "I figure Carol and Clarence will be coming home soon, so I'll leave and let you go upstairs. I know Carol. She'll quiz you on the dance the first chance she gets."

"And it's hard to keep from telling her everything. At least now I can freely tell her that Fletcher is my father if I want."

He rose and offered his hand to her. She took it, and he pulled her to her feet. He didn't release his grasp until he reached the front door and opened it. After a quick kiss good-bye, he left.

Her hand on the handle, she rested the top of her head against the door. She wanted more from him, but something was eating at him and he didn't trust her enough to share it with her. He might not be capable or ready to do that. He'd quickly become important to her, but he didn't seem to return those feelings. She wanted a family. He didn't. It was that simple. Somehow she needed to start protecting herself from being crushed when she returned to her home in Alabama.

With a long sigh, Darcy headed for the staircase. The sound of someone inserting a key into the lock prodded her to go faster. But the door swung open when she put her foot on the second step. She glanced back and groaned.

"I need to talk to you." Avery's voice held a shriek to it.

"I'm tired and going to bed." Darcy continued up the stairs.

But Avery flew across the foyer and grabbed her arm, halting Darcy's escape. "I heard what you said about me being an imposter. How dare you accuse me of that. My grandfather died, and I get attacked."

Darcy shook off her hand and faced the woman, who was dressed in a rhinestone-and-sequined dress— Avery's attempt to appear as though she grew up on a ranch. It didn't work. "Do you mean, why did I state the truth?"

Carol and Clarence entered their house through the open door.

"What you said isn't true. Everyone knows it!" Avery yelled.

"Why? Because you said so? Do you have any real evidence to support that claim? Where is your birth certificate?"

"I don't have one. I was in foster care."

"I'm adopted and I have my original birth certificate. It hasn't been amended. I had to ask for it. Foster children have theirs and don't have to petition for it." In case Avery went to Fletcher, Darcy decided to add, "I know the names of my biological mother and father."

Avery's eyes became pinpoints, her forehead creased. She opened and closed her mouth, but no words came out.

"You had no idea your birth mother's name was Elizabeth and the real Avery was born on February 2."

Avery stiffened. "I knew that."

"No, you didn't. I asked those questions specifically."

The woman perched on the step below Darcy and stabbed her in the chest with her finger. "You're a liar."

"Like I said, come up with hard evidence to prove your claim or leave Haven now before I take this to the police. Come Monday morning I will. You knew facts that were easy enough to dig up if you did a search on Cyrus and John Culpepper on the internet or hired a private investigator."

Avery glared a hole through her as she shoved Darcy to one side and stormed up the staircase. When a bed-room door slammed closed, Carol and Clarence clapped.

"Thank you, Darcy. Information about your con-frontation with Avery and Fletcher zoomed around the dance so fast I was getting whiplash."

"Everyone knows about Fletcher being my father?"

"By now, even the ones who didn't come tonight probably know."

"Good night, Carol, Clarence. I need some sleep." Hoping she could actually get some rest after every-thing that had happened, Darcy climbed the rest of the steps.

She didn't care if the news concerning Avery was fuel for the gossipers, but she hadn't wanted the fact that Fletcher was her father making the rounds. If only Avery hadn't overheard her and Nick talking, she could have picked the time and place. No doubt Fletcher would hunt her down again and let her know how upset he was that everyone in town knew that he had a child out of wedlock.

When Nick thought about kissing Darcy Satur-day night, all he wanted to do was berate himself. She'd made it clear on a number of occasions that she would return to Alabama when Corey's adoption went through. The first time he saw her, she had *city gal* stamped all over her, and that hadn't changed in the few weeks she'd been here.

He'd fought hard these past sixteen months to make his family ranch a success again, and he was starting to see progress. Haven was in his blood. Ranching was his life. Being a father wasn't. He knew Darcy was disappointed in him for not sharing his past. He wanted to forget it, not dredge it up all the time. He'd wanted to please his father so much that every time he had rejected Nick, something died in him. He'd stopped hoping and didn't know how to get that hope back.

No, he was best as a bachelor like Uncle Howard. He'd failed as a son. Being a husband and father was much more difficult.

Wyatt finished examining Sunshine, a mare not in foal but one of the favorite horses at the boys ranch. "She's impacted. I'll give her something for it that should take care of the problem, but if it doesn't, let me know. Keep her in a stall and keep an eye on her progress."

Nick nodded. "Flint went into town. I'll tell him when he comes back here."

"I'll let you know when I'm finished treating her. Tell Johnny he did good picking up on something being wrong with Sunshine. It's much better when we catch it early."

"I will." Nick backed out of the stall and had turned to make his way to the tack room when he caught Gabe Everett coming into the barn. He headed toward the president of the Lone Star Cowboy League. "What's going on? Why the frown?"

"I came to let you and Flint know we're having an emergency meeting at my ranch tonight concerning

Avery. Could you tell Flint I'd like Lana there? And could you ask Darcy to come too? After what happened Saturday, we need to make a decision concerning the woman who says she's Avery. If we don't accept her claim she is Avery, then we need to find the real one."

"I'll be there. Don't know about Darcy."

"I tried her at the Blue Bonnet Inn, but she wasn't there. It's important she comes. I figured you can persuade her."

"Sure." He didn't know if he could persuade her to do anything, especially keeping Corey here.

"We'll also talk about where we stand in finding the people in Cyrus's will. I'm afraid even if we have the right Avery, I'm the one who'll let everyone down. Tanner tried to find my grandfather and couldn't. I've tried too, but he seems to have vanished." Gabe swept his arm across his body. "All of this will be for nothing. We'll have to move back to the original ranch and only serve half the boys."

"I can't imagine what that would do to the boys. For so many of them, this is the chance they needed to make something of themselves." Nick stepped outside the barn. "I have to go home, but I'll track Darcy down if I need to."

Relieved, Gabe followed him to their trucks, which were parked side by side. "I'll leave a message on Flint's phone, but if you see him, let him know."

"I'll be back later."

"Good. I'm heading to the main house to meet with Bea. We need to start thinking about what our options are if we can't fulfill the will."

As Gabe strolled away, Nick climbed into his pickup and blew out a long breath. So much for staying away from Darcy.

* * *

Darcy stood on Fletcher's porch, poised in front of the door. She curled and uncurled her hands. Part of her wanted to hear why he had asked her to come to his house. Then she remembered Saturday night, and all she wanted to do was get in her car and return to Mobile. But she couldn't leave without Corey. She hadn't even told him yet she wanted to adopt him. What if he didn't want to be part of her family?

All yesterday that one question had plagued her. She wanted to talk to Nick about it, but he never returned her call. That was for the best. She was falling in love with him and couldn't see him living anywhere else but on his ranch and in Haven.

The front door swung open. Fletcher stood in the entrance, his solemn expression slowly vanishing to be replaced with a small smile. "I'm glad you came. I wasn't sure you would, but we need to talk and I don't think we should do it where others could overhear. Yesterday at church there were enough people talking about us. Come in."

Darcy hesitated, her teeth digging into her bottom lip. Should she risk another confrontation just because she was curious about what he wanted to say?

"Please, Darcy." He moved to the side to allow her into his house.

Without a word, she entered, not surprised by the massive mahogany table in the middle of the foyer, which displayed a vase of fresh flowers in the middle of winter. The hardwood floor held a high sheen with an expensive-looking woven rug under the table—more a piece of art than carpet.

"Let's go in here." He gestured to the left.

The rich ambiance of the entry hall spilled over into

his large living room. The focal point was the huge marble fireplace with a few bronze Remington statues and a painting of an older woman above the mantle. "Who is that?"

"Luella Snowden Phillips. Would you like something to drink?" Fletcher asked so politely, his behavior different from how he'd acted the other day.

"No, I can't stay long. I tutor at the boys ranch after school."

He sat at the opposite end of the ivory-colored couch. This whole house shouted, "No children allowed."

He crossed one leg and reclined as though he had not a care in the world. "I've spent a lot of time thinking about our conversation the other night."

"So have I," she bit out, wishing she hadn't said anything. She didn't want to care, but she did.

"When I found out who you were, I was stunned. I said some things I shouldn't have. I had a knee-jerk reaction to a piece of big news I never thought I would hear. But when I got over the initial shock, I realized you could be my daughter. I did some checking. You're twenty-seven, and twenty-eight years ago I was in love with Charlotte." He looked away and swallowed several times. "I'd wanted to marry her and have a whole house full of children. She was everything to me, but then one day she disappeared, leaving me a note telling me not to look for her. She broke my heart."

As she did mine, Darcy thought. She and Fletcher had something in common besides family.

"I never let myself fall in love again. I hated the helplessness. I couldn't do anything to change the situation. I'd bought an engagement ring and was going to ask her to marry me that weekend. I never got the chance."

Loneliness dripped off each word, and Darcy hurt

for him. She tried not to. There were so many reasons to be angry with him, but she couldn't.

"I never knew she was with child and that she gave birth to you. You have my coloring, but the shape of your mouth and nose is just like hers."

Darcy slipped her hand into the side pocket of her purse and removed her birth certificate. "In Alabama, I got my original one that listed my biological parents." She placed it on the couch between them.

He glanced at it and then lifted his gaze to hers. "I've been used to people trying to get something from me, and when you first told me, that was my reaction. But you don't need my money. Your adopted family is wealthier than I am. You've stated how much you love your adopted parents, so why did you come looking for me?"

"When I was diagnosed with celiac disease last year, I decided to search for my birth parents. Celiac is hereditary, and I wanted to know what else might be a problem in the future. I've always wanted to marry and have children, but that gave me pause."

He patted his head. "Baldness and high blood pressure run in my family. Nothing else that I know of." His mouth twisted in a contemplative look. "You've been here for a while. Were you ever going to tell me who you are?"

"Honestly, at first I was going to until I found out about you."

"Ouch. Any particular reason?"

"You only think about yourself. You didn't come to Ned's and Corey's assistance. You're against the boys ranch even though there's a lot of evidence that indicates how important it is and it was a pet project your grandmother started."

"What about all the thefts and even the barn fire?"

"There's no evidence pointing to the boys at the ranch, and in this country there needs to be evidence to accuse someone of a crime. Yes, some of them do things wrong, but what child doesn't? Have you ever tried to put yourself in their shoes? Corey is your cousin. He would have been a good one for you to take an interest in."

Fletcher flinched.

"I'm not so sure if the boys' suspected misbehavior is your problem. You've been vocal for a long time about the boys ranch, even before these recent events." Darcy pointed to the portrait of Luella Snowden Phillips. "Do you think she would agree with you about shutting down the ranch when she poured so much into it?"

He frowned. "She did and so did my father. Sometimes I think they forgot all about me while they were helping the boys." He surged to his feet and turned away. "I didn't mean to say that."

"But you did. You felt neglected while all the others got their attention. I can see how that could be hard on a child."

He whirled around. "You do? You don't think I was being selfish?"

"All kids need to be reassured they're loved. That is one of the things the ranch does for the boys."

"Once when I said something to my father for not coming to school to see me in a play, he dismissed it. He said it wasn't important. One of the children at the boys ranch was scared to go home and needed consoling. I was the lead in the freshman play and had worked hard so my dad would be proud of me. He never saw it. That was only one of many instances where I came in second in both my grandmother's and father's eyes. I never could please them." He avoided eye contact with her and stared in the empty fire grate.

She hadn't grown up feeling lacking in her parents' eyes, but she'd gotten a taste of what it meant to be rejected by one when she had tried to see her birth mother. Even with positive self-esteem, she'd begun to doubt herself and wondered what could be wrong with her.

Her throat tight, Darcy covered the distance between them and laid her hand on his shoulder. "I'm sorry. I sometimes have been so focused on a mission, I forget the ones around me." She dropped her arm to her side. "I'm going to be here for a while longer. I wish you would spend some time with me at the boys ranch. They always need tutors. Helping them to learn has been so rewarding for me. At least join my group. I usually help Corey and a couple of others after school."

He didn't say anything.

"Please. You might enjoy yourself." She hesitated, not sure if she should say any more. "I want to get to know you in the time I have left in town. Come with me this afternoon. I need to be there in fifteen minutes."

"Okay. I'll follow you to the ranch. If I decide to leave, you won't have to bring me back here. You can stay."

She smiled. "Thanks, but I hope you don't leave."

On the drive to the boys ranch, Darcy kept looking at the rearview mirror to see if Fletcher was still behind her. There were boys at the ranch who had gone through what he had growing up. Corey, for one. His father didn't have time for him and the child felt neglected. She prayed that Fletcher saw some of himself in the kids and that would change how he looked at the ranch.

She parked at the house, but as she climbed from her car, Nick strode toward her, a frown on his face. Was he mad because she hadn't returned his call while she was with Fletcher today? She'd intended to later, after she saw Fletcher and told Corey about her plans. Nick hadn't returned hers yesterday, so he had no right to be upset about that.

Nick stopped a few feet from her, his glare fixed on Fletcher. "What's he doing here?"

"Visiting the ranch with me."

As Fletcher paused on the steps to the porch and waited for her, Nick focused on her. Intense. Troubled. "We need to talk."

Chapter Thirteen

After Nick informed her about the Lone Star Cowboy League's emergency meeting, he asked, "What is Fletcher doing here? Hasn't he done enough damage, trying to rally people behind his cause to shut down this ranch? Is he here looking for more to complain about concerning the boys ranch?"

"We had a nice talk today, and I persuaded him to come and see the good this place does for the boys."

"And you think he's going to change? People, especially those like him, don't." Once he'd believed what she did, but he'd been disappointed too many times to feel that way now.

"People like him?" Although she could see why Nick had said that, she became defensive.

"Set in his ways. Too proud to admit he made a mistake."

"I'm not so sure he's the only one around here like that."

"What's that supposed to mean?"

"Maybe you should…" She shook her head. "Never mind. I'm late and Corey gets anxious when I am."

He clasped her arm. "Have you told him you're seeking guardianship of him? That you want to adopt him?"

"After I tutor the boys, I will."

"And he's—" Nick glanced at Fletcher "—going to be with you?"

"No."

She spun around, marched to Fletcher and then stomped up the stairs.

"Are you dating him? I see you with him a lot." A hint of hostility echoed through Fletcher's words.

She ground her teeth and entered the main house. "He's a friend. That is all. We have a common interest in Corey." Now if only she could convince her heart that was all. "We meet in the living room."

She found Corey, Aiden and Liam Ritter, another child close to her cousin's age, sitting around the coffee table. "I brought a visitor to help me today."

Corey straightened, his shoulders thrust back. "Why?"

"Because the more help you have, the faster you'll get your homework done and then y'all can go out and do your afternoon chores at the barn. Isn't today when you take care of the goats?"

All three boys nodded.

"Then let's get busy." She gestured to Fletcher to take a place next to Corey.

Darcy helped Aiden and Corey while Fletcher attempted to explain subtraction to Liam in a creative way having to do with horses. He even drew an illustration of what he was trying to get across to Liam.

"If there are only two horses, how can you take four of them away? The rancher has to get more from the pasture with fifty. He borrows ten and adds it to his two. How many does that make now?"

Liam scrunched his forehead and squinted at the paper. "Twelve."

Fletcher grinned. "Right."

"Now you can take four horses away from twelve."

Liam quickly wrote an eight on the paper.

Corey yanked on Darcy's arm and then bent close and whispered, "What's he doing?"

"He's helping. It must be working because Liam is getting the right answers. I told Fletcher how much Liam loved horses."

"So do I. I want to learn to do tricks when I ride like you do."

"Maybe one day. First you need to become an accomplished rider."

"Nick is helping me." Corey aimed a sideways glance at her as he wrote his story about the rodeo. "Nick is a good guy. Dontcha think?"

"Sure. He does a lot for the boys ranch."

"I want to learn to be a farrier. I've been watching him take care of the horses' hooves."

"Just like us with our feet, we have to take good care of theirs."

"Yeah, we couldn't ride them otherwise." Corey bent over the paper and started to write his next word. He stopped. "How do you spell *barrel*?"

"What do you think it starts with?" Darcy said *barrel* slowly, emphasizing each letter.

"A *b*. I hear an *r* and an *l* at the end."

"Good. It's *b-a-r-r-e-l*."

The rest of the tutoring session sped by, which surprised Darcy. She didn't think Fletcher would like doing something like homework with the boys, but the more he worked with Corey and Liam, the more relaxed he seemed, and he even smiled several more times.

"Liam and Aiden, I need to talk with Corey before he helps with the goats. Will y'all show Mr. Phillips where they are?"

Fletcher went without protest, but he paused at the entrance into the living room. "You'll be joining us? I won't be able to stay much longer."

"Yes, but if you need to leave before we come, the boys are fine. Cleaning their pen and giving the goats feed are part of their chores."

When the others left, Corey asked, "Why am I staying back? Did I do something wrong?"

"Because I have something to tell you that makes me so happy and excited."

His eyebrows rose. "What? Are you gonna move here?"

"No, but the reason I came to Haven in the first place was to find members of my family. You are one of those."

"I am? How?"

"Mr. Phillips is my father. He didn't know until I told him this weekend. Some great parents adopted me when I was a baby. He never knew he had a daughter before I came."

"Then why aren't you staying here with him?"

"I have two parents in Mobile, whom I love very much. My job is there. I love helping people with their legal problems. Mobile is my home. I don't live far from a beach. My father has a boat, and he goes out fishing in the Gulf all the time."

"I love to fish. My dad…used to take me several years ago until—"

Darcy held his hand. "I love to fish too. We'll have to go sometime." The emotions she was trying to keep in check swelled in her throat. She swallowed hard and continued, "Do you know what that makes us? We're cousins. I'm so happy we are. Being a relative makes it easier for me to apply to be your guardian."

"Guardian? Is that like a parent?"

"Yes. In fact, I want to adopt you. It takes a little longer, but I want us to be a family. You are special to me." She hugged him and then looked into his face, praying he felt the same way.

He grinned from ear to ear. "I love you."

"Back at you."

He threw his arms around her and plastered his body against her. "I'm gonna have a home?"

"Yes." Her eyes misted with tears. *Thank You, Lord, for making this easy on Corey.* When she thought she could talk without choking on her happiness, she said, "We'd better go check on Aiden, Liam and Mr. Phillips."

Corey jumped to his feet, excitement brightening his features. "Wait till I tell them I'm gonna have a home." He raced from the room. The sound of the front door opening was followed by "C'mon, Darcy."

"Coming." She swiped away the tears on her eyelashes.

As she strolled to the goats' pen, Corey ran ahead. When she arrived, the boys were inside, including Corey and Fletcher. Liam was telling Fletcher the names of each of the goats. Nick stood off to the side, leaning against the four-foot fence, his arms crossed over his chest, watching everything Fletcher did.

She came up behind Nick on the other side of the enclosure and whispered, "Has Fletcher sabotaged anything yet?"

"It hasn't been ruled out that he wasn't behind the barn fire."

"Darcy is going to adopt you?" Aiden exclaimed from the goat's pen. "When will you be leaving?"

Corey cocked his head to the side. "I don't know." He whirled toward her and Nick. "When?"

Darcy smiled. "As soon as the paperwork with the state is completed and approved."

Corey turned back to his friends. "I'll still be able to come see you."

Nick glanced at her. "He doesn't know you'll be returning to Mobile for good."

"I thought he did. I told him about my home. I'll talk to him alone later."

"I've found with kids that you have to give them exact, concrete information or directions. Don't forget the meeting. It starts in half an hour." Nick pushed off the fence, tipped his hat at her and ambled to the gate.

As he walked away, she felt as if he was walking out of her life. And she guessed he would be soon when she left for home with Corey.

Nick sat in Gabe's crowded living room as the last two people arrived—Darcy and Fletcher. With Avery's companion here, this meeting might be long and hostile.

Gabe stood, and slowly the chatter among the attendees ceased with everyone looking at the president of the Lone Star Cowboy League Waco Chapter. "With the rumors flying around Haven concerning the Avery Culpepper who has been here for the past several months, I felt we needed to meet and come up with a game plan. We all have seen how well the new expanded boys ranch is doing." Gabe fixed his gaze on Fletcher, but Darcy's birth father remained quiet. "We have to stop the land from going to developers."

As members nodded and verbally agreed, Nick watched Fletcher. The man leaned toward Darcy and said something. She gave him a small smile. What was going on with him? Most people didn't change and certainly not overnight.

Gabe continued, "That's why I've requested Darcy Hill and Lana Alvarez to explain about Avery Culpepper, the one who is in town right now."

Darcy and Lana rose and joined Gabe.

"I'm going to let Darcy explain what she discovered about the real Avery." Lana shifted toward Darcy.

"I'm an attorney who has worked with the foster care system and the state in Alabama, so I've learned how to dig in the right places for information. I uncovered that John Culpepper married a woman named Elizabeth. I've even tracked down Avery Culpepper's birth certificate. The fake Avery said she didn't have her original birth certificate and couldn't get one. The thing is, even adopted children in many states can get their original birth certificates, not just the one that has their adoptive parents' names on it. That's how I located my birth parents."

"So the rumor that you are Fletcher Phillips' daughter is true," Seth Jacobs, the secretary of the Lone Star Cowboy League Chapter, said.

"Yes. Fletcher is my biological father."

Whispers filled the room.

Darcy put two fingers in her mouth, and a loud whistle shrieked from her. Suddenly the room quieted. Nick grinned in spite of his mixed-up feelings for Darcy at the moment.

"I asked Avery to produce her birth certificate, and she refuses. Before that, I asked about her birth date and the name of her mother. She got both of them wrong.

What she said doesn't match the real Avery, the one you need to fulfill Cyrus Culpepper's will. She's still at the Blue Bonnet Inn. I called and invited her to come tonight." She swept her arm across her body to indicate the whole crowd. "As you can see, she didn't show up."

Gabe stepped forward. "Which means we don't have the real Avery Culpepper, and we have less than two months to find her. That leaves three people we still need to come to the seventieth anniversary of the founding of the Lone Star Cowboy League Boys Ranch."

"No, we only have two," Bea Brewster said. "At least I hope so. I just received a letter from Carolina Mason, a grandniece of Morton Mason. She is coming back to Haven soon. I think she'll help us with Morton."

Wyatt had been lounging against a wall. When Carolina Mason's name was mentioned, he stiffened. His mouth twisted into a frown, and he dropped his gaze as he apparently struggled with the announcement that Carolina Mason would be arriving in Haven soon.

"Okay, it looks like we might have a lead on Morton Mason," Gabe said. "We still have to locate the real Avery and my grandfather, and so far I haven't been able to find a trace of him. Neither has Tanner."

Fletcher came to his feet. "I have a good private investigator I use in my practice. I'll pay for him to look for both of the missing people to fulfill Cyrus's conditions."

Silence blanketed the room full of stunned faces. Nick couldn't believe what he was hearing. What was Fletcher's scheme now? "How do we know this isn't one of your tricks to ruin the boys ranch and shut it down?"

Darcy's gaze zeroed in on Nick, stabbing through

him. "I've been showing Fletcher how important the ranch is for the boys. A person can change his mind."

Nick fisted his hands. *No, they can't. I tried and prayed so hard that my father would change.*

Fletcher grinned at Darcy. "Thank you for saying that. But I can understand why some people would be leery about this proposition. Nick has a good reason for saying that." Darcy's birth father scanned the room. "Personally I would feel the same way if I were in his shoes. If you want, I'll pay whoever you find to look for those two still missing. I came today to offer my support in fulfilling the will but also to tell you I think you're right in looking for the real Avery. She never told me, but I don't believe the woman staying at the Blue Bonnet Inn is Cyrus's granddaughter." Fletcher sat again, and Darcy laid her hand over his.

"Frankly, we need all the help we can get. I'll take you up on your offer, Fletcher. But—" Gabe made a visual sweep around the room "—I hope that Lana and Darcy will continue looking into the real Avery. Without these two, we could still be dealing with the fake one."

Several nodded while others said yes. Nick remained quiet. What happened to the woman he'd started caring for? Did Fletcher have her under his control now? He needed fresh air before he said more. Nick strode into the hallway and left Gabe's.

He was halfway to his truck when Darcy called out, "Wait, Nick."

He shouldn't. He should keep going to his pickup.

"Please."

He stopped and rotated toward Darcy, beautiful as ever. She saw only the good in people. He wished he could, but growing up with a monster for a father had killed that inside him.

How do I ignore what my dad did and move past it?

"I'm going to talk with Bea about taking Corey over a long weekend to Mobile to meet my parents and see my house. I want him to become familiar with my home before he moves there."

"When are you doing this?" He clenched his teeth so hard, his jaw hurt.

"Probably this Friday. I haven't made arrangements yet."

"Why are you telling me this?"

"I—I felt you should know where Corey is. I'll be back for Heath and Josie's wedding on Tuesday."

"Have you told Corey he'll be moving soon?"

"I want him to see my home and meet my parents first before I say anything else about moving."

"See you at the wedding then." He pivoted and marched toward his truck before he said something he would regret.

On Thursday, Darcy sat on her bed at the inn, talking to her mom. "Our plane lands at Mobile Regional Airport at 1:45 p.m. tomorrow. I want to show Corey where I work before we head for Gulf Shores and my house."

"Warren and I will be there to pick y'all up at the airport. No sense renting a car. We want to spend as much time with you and Corey as we can."

"See you then. Love you, Mom."

When she hung up, Darcy stood and slipped her phone into her jeans pocket. She wanted to talk to Carol before she met Fletcher at the boys ranch. She hated how she and Nick had parted the last time they saw each other, and Carol knew Nick. Maybe she could help her understand what was going on with him.

Darcy could sympathize with Wyatt. He'd loved Carolina, and she'd left him. Although Darcy would be the one leaving Haven, she'd stay if she thought she had a future with Nick. What if she did move here anyway? Would it even make a difference to him? She didn't think she could stay here permanently if there wasn't a future for them. Her heart would break every time she saw Nick.

Darcy found Carol downstairs in the kitchen. The aroma of coffee pervaded the house. "I hope I can get a cup before I leave."

"Of course. That's why I have it on." Carol took two mugs from the cabinet and poured coffee into them. "When do you have to go?"

"I'm meeting Fletcher in a half hour." Darcy sat at the kitchen table across from Carol. "Did Avery skip out on her bill after all?"

"Fletcher tracked down her whereabouts. She has left Texas and is heading for California. Maybe she'll be able to catch a rich man out there, but Haven is so much better off without her here causing trouble."

"You went to Fletcher about this?"

"No, he came to me early this morning to tell me she was gone for good. He even paid her bill."

"He did? Why?"

"He told me part of what happened was his fault. He encouraged her to file a lawsuit to challenge Cyrus's will. How are you two getting along?"

"Okay. He has helped me the last two days at the ranch tutoring the boys and will again today. He's determined to teach Liam how to subtract."

"That's a surprise. Is there any more talk of shutting down the boys ranch?"

"Not to me, but then, he knows where I stand on it." Darcy sipped the delicious coffee. She would miss this every day.

"How's Nick doing?" Carol ducked her head while she stirred sugar into her drink.

"I don't know. I didn't see him yesterday at the ranch. I pulled up at the main house, and he hopped into his pickup and left. He's not happy with me because I'm going to Mobile this weekend and taking Corey to see where I live."

The clang of the spoon hitting the side of the cup resonated through the kitchen. "That's not the problem. It's the fact that you'll be permanently taking Corey away from Haven. The child has been a large part of his life since he left the army. Corey has been good for Nick, but he's also been good for the boy."

"Are you telling me I shouldn't leave with Corey?"

Carol shook her head. "When you started seeing Nick, I was thrilled. I was hoping you two would get together. That would be perfect for Corey. He cares about you both. The child might not say anything to you, but he isn't gonna like leaving Haven for an unknown place."

"That's why we're going to visit."

Carol lifted her mug and took a drink. "What happened to you and Nick? I saw you and him dancing Saturday night. I haven't seen him look at another woman the way he looks at you."

"I thought we were making progress, but lately he has pulled away from me."

"Because you announced you're leaving Haven when everything is settled concerning Corey. He went into defensive mode. Don't tell anyone, but Howard told me he's sure his nephew is in love with you."

"Nick said that to Howard?"

"Well, not in so many words, but if anyone knows Nick, it's his uncle. He's the one who helped Nick with his father."

"Nick doesn't want to be a father. I have to go where I'll have family support." If Nick wanted to be that support, though, she would stay. She had no doubt Nick loved and cared about Corey. But she couldn't stay without more commitment from Nick.

Darcy closed her eyes for a few seconds, picturing Nick the last time she had talked with him on Monday. There was a finality to his look as he turned to walk to his truck—as though he had shut his emotions down and closed himself off from her. "All I know about Nick's father was that he was an alcoholic. I think that's why he bonded so well with Corey. Nick would never tell me anything else, but whatever it was, it scarred him."

"He doesn't talk to anyone about it, not even Howard."

"There can never be a relationship between us without the truth. Not that he has lied to me. There's a lot I know about him from his caring nature and kind disposition, especially to the boys at the ranch. He would be a great father for Corey, even if he doesn't think so. But I can't fall in love with someone who shuts me out and doesn't want marriage and a family. Corey and I will be a package deal." What was sad was she'd already fallen in love with Nick, but she'd find a way to get over him and move on—for Corey.

"Tell him what you just said to me."

"My example of a loving couple is my parents. They share and tell each other everything. Sometimes they can complete each other's sentences. I won't settle for anything less. I'd rather be single than marry the wrong man."

"You want him to open up to you, but have you told him how you feel?"

Darcy sighed. "I'm still trying to figure that out. He confuses me. But Nick knows I want a family."

"Then pray about it. God is always there to help us when we need it." Carol patted Darcy's hand on the table. "Go home and see your parents. Let Corey have a mini vacation. He certainly deserves it after the past few months."

Darcy rose. "I have to meet Fletcher, but I appreciate your insight and kindness. I've grown to like Haven and especially the townspeople. When I leave for good, I'll miss y'all." She hugged Carol and then hurried from the kitchen before she got misty-eyed.

Ten minutes later when she arrived at the boys ranch, she saw Nick's truck still parked at the barn. She glanced at her watch and decided she had some time to talk to Nick since she didn't see Fletcher's car yet. Nick wasn't going to avoid her yet again.

Chapter Fourteen

Nick paused in the entrance to the tack room at the old barn. Flint had set up his temporary office inside. "I'm leaving."

"You're going to miss seeing the boys today. Like you have the last two days. What's going on? You usually prefer being here when they come."

Nick hated to admit that he was avoiding Darcy. When he saw her, he wished their circumstances were different. He'd known when she came to Haven that she was only here temporarily. He didn't plan to fall in love with her. If he stayed away from her, he'd get over her and move forward. At least that had been his plan. She would be leaving soon—with Corey. A stab of pain pierced his heart when he thought about not seeing them again.

He started to turn away when Flint asked, "Lady problems?"

Instead of leaving, Nick moved closer to Flint and lowered his voice. "Is it that obvious?"

"Like a neon sign in the dead of night. If Darcy hadn't helped Lana with Avery, we could have been in a world of hurt come March when the real Avery wasn't at the celebration. So what's wrong?"

"She's leaving and taking Corey with her when the paperwork for guardianship is finalized."

"And you don't want Corey or Darcy to leave Haven?"

"Neither of them," Nick finally admitted out loud.

"Have you asked her to stay?"

"Well, not in so many words. We haven't known each other long, so how can I do that?"

"You let her know what you're feeling for her. She can't read your mind."

"She's always wanted a family. Not just one child but also more. I'd be lousy father material." Lousy husband material too.

Flint's eyebrows slashed downward. "*Lousy?* Who in the world says that?"

"Me."

"Well, you're wrong. I've seen you working with the boys countless times. You're a natural and would make a great father. Why do you feel that way?"

"My father wasn't a good example. I never want a child to feel like I did." The last sentence slipped out before Nick could censor himself.

"You're not your father. For a long time I thought I wasn't a good dad because of all the problems Logan was having. Children can go through bad times. The key is to stick with them. Like the Lord. There are times we draw away from Him, but He doesn't give up on us. Our Heavenly Father is the best example of what a father is."

Nick wanted to tell Flint He was the exception. "What if God has given up? What if your prayers aren't being answered?"

"How do you know they weren't answered?"

"Because nothing changed. I prayed for one of my combat buddies to live when he was gunned down, but he didn't. He died while I was trying to save him."

"The Lord doesn't always do what you ask because He has a better solution we might not see. Death is part of our life cycle. You may walk away from Him, but He never does from you."

"Nick, are you in here?" Darcy called out.

"I have to go to the storage barn. I'll tell her you're in here," Flint said as he exited the tack room.

For a second panic raced through Nick. He wasn't prepared to talk to her. As he frantically searched for a way to escape, Darcy appeared in the doorway and blocked his only path. Her somber expression didn't bode well for this conversation. She'd called, and he hadn't called back. They seemed to be doing a lot of that lately—not returning calls.

But seeing her only confirmed what he'd already figured out. He loved her. In a short time they had been through a lot together because of Corey and the boys ranch. If he told her, would it make a difference in her leaving Haven?

"I know you've been avoiding me, but I wanted to remind you that Corey and I will be flying to Mobile tomorrow morning."

So soon? Stunned, his emotions deflated, he sank onto a small desk Flint had brought into the tack room. When he wanted time to slow down, it sped up instead.

"We'll be back Monday evening. I thought you should know the exact times."

Before he could make a comment, she spun around and hastened away.

A jolt of energy spurred him into action. He rushed

after her and caught her before she left the barn. "Why are you taking Corey to live in Mobile? Everyone he knows lives around here." He repeated what he'd already told her, but he didn't know what else to say to her. "Corey is special to me…" He wouldn't be able to fulfill his promise to Doug.

She halted but didn't turn around. "I wanted Corey to meet my parents and for them to meet him. It might be weeks before everything is completed concerning the guardianship."

"Then you and Corey will leave for good?"

She glanced over her shoulder. "Yes. Is there a reason I shouldn't?"

"This is Corey's home. I won't see him anymore. I won't—"

"I have to go tutor. Good-bye."

"—see you anymore." He finally finished his sentence when Darcy was two yards away, but his whispered words didn't reach her. He repeated louder, "I won't see *you* anymore."

She slowed and then finally stopped, her body stiff.

He came up behind her and clasped her shoulder. The tension beneath his palm melted, and she rotated toward him. He searched her expression, but he couldn't read what she was feeling. She tilted her head back and stared into his eyes.

His throat closed at her probing gaze. Worse, though, was the silence that filled the air.

You let her know what you're feeling for her.

He scanned the yard. Surprisingly they were alone. "I'm falling in love with you, Darcy. I didn't want to. I know you want a family. I don't know if I can do that. I've been angry with my dad for most of my life. He threw his life away. Alcohol was more important to him than I was. He wouldn't stop. I wasn't enough for him to want to. When I went into the service and left home, I never wanted to see him again. And I didn't. He died before I came back home, and I was relieved." The one thing he'd held back even from his uncle spilled from his lips before he could stop.

She grasped his hand. "Why?"

"Because I can't forgive him for using me as a punching bag when he was drunk and upset."

She closed her eyes for a few seconds, and when she reopened them, tears glistened in them. "He abused you physically?"

"Yes, and mentally until I enlisted in the army and escaped. As I got bigger and stronger, the abuse was more verbal, but his words hurt every time he said them. I was the reason my mom wasted away, according to him. After having me, she never was the same."

"Did he abuse your mother?"

"He didn't hit her, but he belittled her all the time. It got worse over the years." He stepped closer. "Now you see why I have avoided any relationship that meant I had to commit to someone. I lived in a dysfunctional family and then went overseas to fight often unknown enemies. It's hard for me to trust anyone, especially with my feelings." Nick swept his arms out from his sides. "This was real hard. I want to forget the past, and each time I talk about it, I relive it."

"And I imagine that helping Corey has opened old wounds for you."

He nodded. "I didn't want you to leave without knowing how I feel. That's how much you mean to me."

Darcy cupped his face. "I'm so sorry. Thanks for telling me. That means a lot to me, but I have to have it all. I know how important a family can be."

"I wanted you to know why it wouldn't work for us. You have a good life in Mobile. Maybe Corey leaving here will be better for him in the long run. I know you'll have his best interests at heart. I trust you with him."

"Nick! Nick, you're here today." Corey raced in his direction with Aiden right behind him. "I've missed you the last couple of days." Corey threw his arms around Nick.

He embraced the child. How much longer would he be able to do this?

"Where did y'all come from?" Nick ruffled Corey's hair.

He twisted around and pointed at the school bus leaving. "Will you be here after I do my homework?"

Nick looked up at Darcy.

She mouthed the word *please*.

"Yeah, I'll even give you and Aiden a riding lesson if you do everything you need to with Darcy."

"Yay. C'mon, Aiden. Let's get our snack and do our homework."

Corey and his friend rushed toward the back of the main house.

"That's my cue to get busy. I'm glad you're going to see them later." She clasped his arm. "Go talk to Pastor Andrew. You need to deal with your anger at your father. You'll never be free if you let him control you even now. You aren't him, but I think there's a part of you that fears you are."

"C'mon, Darcy. We want to ride," Corey yelled from the back stoop, Fletcher next to the boys.

"Duty calls."

"Will you be coming down with them?"

"No, I've got to pack for the trip tomorrow morning. Y'all have guy time." She strolled away.

He watched her go into the main house. *Don't let her get away.*

He didn't move. He didn't know what to do anymore. Normally he was very decisive, but Darcy tilted his world upside down. And she was right. He had unfinished business with the Lord. When he left the ranch, he would pay Pastor Andrew a visit.

When Darcy stepped out onto her parents' back deck overlooking the water, she breathed in a deep lungful of the sea air. She loved the smell she associated with so many wonderful memories. Standing at the railing, she spied her dad and Corey on the beach walking. The past two days had been great. As she knew they would, her parents made Corey feel like he was part of the family. Corey was already calling them Papa Warren and Grandma Betty, and they loved it.

This would be a good place for Corey to grow up, and yet every time she thought that, Nick filled her thoughts, especially images of him Thursday night teaching Corey and Aiden how to ride when she snuck down to the corral for a few minutes before leaving. If only he saw what she did. He would be a terrific father, and Corey adored him—all the boys respected him and listened to him.

From the moment she had decided to adopt Corey, she'd thought of him living here where she'd grown up, in the place she had loved all her life. But then Nick had finally opened his heart to her—the one thing that had been holding her back. When he told her about his father, her heart tore as though she'd gone through the horror with him.

Thank You, God. You blessed me with wonderful parents. All children should have that. What do I do about Nick? I love him, but I love my parents and my home too. I can't live in Haven without a commitment from Nick. What is best for Corey? For me? For Nick?

Her parents were expecting her to come home. They were looking forward to being part of hers and Corey's lives. Nick didn't think he deserved that happily-ever-after.

The soft breeze off the water played with her hair as she watched Corey take off his shoes and run in the shallow water, laughing. A long sigh escaped from her.

"Honey, where are your dad and Corey?" Her mother came up behind her.

Darcy pointed in the direction of the beach. "Out there playing—again." Now her dad was shoeless and letting Corey chase him through the water.

Mom laughed. "He's having so much fun."

"Which one?"

"Both, but I was talking about your dad. When we were going to bed last night, all he talked about was Corey."

If she stayed in Haven, it would break her parents' hearts, and would Nick ever be able to make the commitment she and Corey needed? But if she lived here with Corey, how would she ever forget Nick and move on?

"You're awfully quiet, dear. Is something wrong?" Her mother leaned against the railing while she studied Darcy, as she did when she knew something wasn't right. "Something is troubling you," she added when Darcy didn't reply.

"Mom, I'm torn between two places—here and Haven."

"You are? Why? You've only been there a short time. Is it your birth father?"

When she'd talked about Haven in the past two days, she'd mentioned all the people she'd gotten to know, but she hadn't told them what she was feeling concerning Nick because she'd been sorting through her emotions. She thought when she came here that she might realize she didn't love him. But that didn't happen. He might as well be with her. She couldn't shake him from her mind. Would distance help her with that?

"No. Remember I told you about Nick, especially his relationship with Corey? Nick and I grew very close too. I love him."

Her mother's eyes grew round. "You haven't known him long."

"Sometimes, like you and Dad, you know it in here." She patted her chest over her heart. "You and Dad were only together a couple of months before you married, and look at how long and great your marriage has been."

"We've had our ups and downs. All marriages do, but we've always been able to work our problems out. Do you feel you could do that with this Nick?"

"Yes."

"What do you want to do? Would he move here?"

"His home and ranch are in Haven. For that matter, Corey has lived in that area all his life."

"So you would stay there?"

"Yes" came out of Darcy's mouth instantly before she really considered it, and the answer felt so right. She would fight for Nick—make him see what everyone else did. He was nothing like the father he'd described to her.

"Then expect us to visit a lot."

"And I'll come home a lot, especially in the summer. Corey would live on the beach if I let him." When he had seen the water for the first time, he pumped his arm in the air and grinned from ear to ear.

"What about your work?"

"I'll find something similar in Haven or Waco after I qualify to practice law in Texas. There's the boys ranch, and if they ever start a girls ranch, I'll be involved in it too. I started riding horses again and realize how much I've missed it the past few years."

Her mother hugged her. "I'm thrilled you're riding again. You were so happy when you were doing it. When Beauty died, I was worried about you. You took it hard."

"I shouldn't have pushed her that day."

"She loved jumping as much as you did, and she was quite an entertainer."

"Will you and Dad be okay with me staying in Haven?"

"We've been blessed to have you for twenty-seven years. We knew there would come a time when you'd begin your own family. And with your dad semiretiring this year, we'll have more freedom to go where we want."

When she looked into her mother's eyes, peace settled over Darcy. She was doing what she was supposed to do. She knew that now.

Darcy sat next to Corey at the wedding ceremony for Josie and Heath at the Haven Community Church. Josie's ivory-colored gown fell in soft folds to the floor while Heath had donned his Texas Rangers' dress uniform.

The couple stood holding hands before Pastor Andrew as they exchanged their own marriage vows. Flint, the best man, gave Josie's wedding band to Heath, and he slipped it onto her left hand. She smiled with tears running down her face.

When Pastor Andrew said, "You may kiss the bride," Heath leaned toward Josie and kissed her. Suddenly he stepped back, his eyes round.

Josie laughed, taking Heath's hand and laying it on her round belly. "The baby is welcoming you to the family."

The audience, full of family, friends and Texas Rangers, broke out into cheers while Heath turned to the guests with his and Josie's linked hands raised. His face radiated a smile.

"Mr. and Mrs. Heath Grayson," Pastor Andrew announced.

When the couple began their walk down the center aisle, Corey bent close to Darcy. "Why's Josie crying?"

"Those are happy tears." Darcy turned as the newly wedded pair strolled past her.

Several pews back she caught sight of Nick and Howard, cheering and clapping. Suddenly Nick stopped, and his gaze zeroed in on Darcy. Chills streaked down her body. She hadn't seen him since before she left for Mobile. She'd been at the boys ranch all day helping with the setup for the reception. She'd hoped Nick would be there and they could talk, but through the grapevine, she'd discovered he was searching for several cows that were missing from his herd.

The audience filed out of the pews. Carol and Clarence left first, followed by her and Corey.

Walking out of the sanctuary, Carol whispered, "Did you ever talk to Nick?"

"Not yet."

Carol nodded toward where Nick still sat and whispered, "I'll make sure Corey gets to the ranch. You'll never enjoy the reception until you settle things with Nick."

Howard rose and headed to the exit while Nick stayed, his head bowed. His uncle slowed, clasped Darcy's hand and gently squeezed, then continued into the foyer.

As the wedding guest emptied the sanctuary, Darcy sat in the last row of pews. He'd stayed for a reason. She wanted to give him the time he needed. Her heartbeat picked up speed while observing him. Their last conversation hadn't settled anything. He said he loved her and trusted her judgment concerning Corey. He understood why she wanted to live in Mobile and gave his blessing. Did that mean he didn't love her enough to put his past behind him?

She wanted more. She wanted him.

The silence in the church soothed Nick for the first time in a long while. After talking with Pastor Andrew the other day, he knew he would never heal until he let go of the past and forgave his father. He'd ruled Nick's life long enough.

Closing his eyes, he instantly pictured Darcy and Corey as they sat waiting for the wedding. He'd been tempted to sit in the same pew, but he and his uncle had come in late. They'd grabbed what seats they could near the back.

He'd missed her so much while she'd been in Mobile. She was all he thought about day and night. He'd hoped when she'd decided she should move to Alabama with Corey that everything would go back to normal. But she haunted him even more than she did when she was here in Haven.

That was when he knew he had to find a solution or go crazy.

Father, help me to forgive my dad. Help me find my way back to You. I'm tired of living alone. There has to be more to life than getting up every morning, working and then going to bed at night.

The memory of his last riding lesson with Corey invaded his mind. The boys ranch had answered a need deep inside Nick. Every day, especially since Corey had arrived, he'd looked forward to helping out there—even after a long day working on his own land. The boys' smiles were all the thanks he needed.

Was this contentment when he left the boys ranch—even when things didn't go well—what it felt like to be a father, nurturing and caring for a child?

He wanted more of that. He didn't have to follow in his dad's footsteps. Being so angry with him had taken over his life. Not anymore.

Dad, I forgive you. I hope you find peace. I'm not going to let you dictate my life anymore.

He drew in a deep, composing breath and released it slowly as he let go of the rage. While doing that, he also opened his heart to the Lord. He couldn't continue going through life alone. Tranquility cloaked him.

God was here with him. A smile grew from deep inside Nick and took over his solemn expression. Now he was ready to fight for the woman he loved.

He was starting to rise when he glimpsed Darcy standing at the end of pew. Warmth emanated from her. Words fled his mind as she came near him and sat beside him. Emotions he'd never thought he would experience crammed his throat.

"I missed you," she said in a soft voice that flowed over him.

He swallowed several times. "I missed you too." When he bent toward her, he grazed her lips with his. "You were gone way too long." He wanted to ask her about the trip but was afraid of what she would tell him.

She raised her hand and ran her fingertips across his mouth. "Well, I'm going to be here for quite a while now."

"What does that mean?" he asked, his heartbeat thundering in his ears.

"It means I'm staying here, unless you don't want me to."

He cradled her face and drank in her beautiful features while he murmured, "Are you sure?"

"I love you, Nick McGarrett. I'm very sure."

"Good, because I was contemplating moving to Alabama."

"You were?"

"I love you too. I realized I didn't want to live without you in my life. I took your advice and talked with Pastor Andrew. I forgave my father. He doesn't have a hold over me anymore. I choose not to dwell on the past and what he did." And he would fight to keep it that way.

Her smile grew. "Good. Now you can really live." She wound her arms around him and kissed him.

He poured all his feelings into it. He didn't want her to doubt his love for her.

When they parted, he laid his forehead against hers, his hands on her shoulders. "Where's Corey?"

"Carol took him to the ranch for the wedding reception. She was playing matchmaker, and I doubt Corey minded. In Mobile he told my parents all about you and how you were teaching him to ride horses. He loves you like a father."

"Is that why you're staying?"

"I'm staying because it's the best move for him but also for me. I can practice law anywhere. The ranch that you've poured money and a lot of time into is here. It will be a great place to raise Corey and call home."

"Does that mean you'd marry me?"

"Yes. When I think about that, it feels right."

"Then we won't have a long engagement."

"I agree. The whole time I was at home I thought about you. Absence does make the heart grow fonder."

He weaved his fingers through hers. "I never thought I wanted a family—a wife and kids—but now I know I do if it's with you. We both have a lot to give Corey, but I hope also other children."

Tears sparkled in her eyes. "I do too."

"Let's go celebrate. What's a better way to do that than with our friends?"

"And family. Will you be all right with Fletcher being in my life?"

"I'll make it work. While you were gone, he was at the boys ranch volunteering in your place. There's hope for Fletcher." And for the first time in a long while, he felt there was hope for him.

They rose together and left the church, hand in hand.

The minute Darcy entered the wedding reception at the boys ranch with Nick, Corey made a beeline for them.

"Where have you been? I thought something happened." Worry knit the boy's forehead.

"We had a few things we needed to talk about." Darcy felt Carol's gaze boring into her. She didn't want to say much at Heath and Josie's party, but she would have to tell Carol something.

Corey shifted his attention back and forth between her and Nick. "Is something wrong?"

Nick laughed and tousled his hair. "You worry too much. Nothing is wrong. In fact, everything is right."

"I told Nick that you and I are going to live here in Haven."

"Really?" Corey said so loud everyone around them stopped talking and stared at them.

Darcy pulled him away from the people nearby. "Shh. Yes, but don't say anything yet. This is a reception to celebrate Heath and Josie getting married."

Nick slung his arm around Darcy's shoulders. "But we might be the next couple to marry in Haven."

Corey's eyebrows shot up. "Yes!" He pumped his arm in the air and then turned to leave. "Wait till—"

"No." Nick pinned him with a sharp look. "I'm counting on you to keep quiet until tomorrow. Okay?"

Corey nodded. "Yes, sir."

Darcy chuckled as the ten-year-old disappeared in the crowd. "I won't be surprised if the whole town knows by the time the party is over."

Nick moved in front of Darcy, blocking her view of the reception. "With Uncle Howard, Carol and Corey, I give it half an hour. I'm so happy I'm not sure *I* can keep quiet."

"Same here." All her feelings for Nick were screaming to let the world know.

Nick stared at her mouth. "I want to kiss you. Let's get some fresh air."

"We just got here," she said with a grin as she headed for the front door.

The second Nick stepped onto the porch and closed the front door, he tugged Darcy into his embrace. "I love you. I know life with you will never be dull."

She laughed. She rose onto her tiptoes and hooked her arms around his neck. The light touch of her lips whispered against his. "I love you, Nick McGarrett, and can't wait to be a family with you."

Nick pulled her even closer and kissed her with all the emotions he'd suppressed for years.

* * * * *

THE DOCTOR'S TEXAS BABY

Deb Kastner

To the Sacred Heart of Jesus.
May Your name ever be blessed.

He has said, "I will never forsake you or abandon you."
—*Hebrews* 13:5

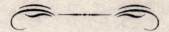

Chapter One

 What had she been thinking?

There was no question in Carolina Mason's mind that returning to her hometown, Haven, Texas, was a bad idea.

Too many complications. Too many memories. Most of all, too much heartbreak.

And yet here she was. What few household goods she owned were now unpacked in her late great-uncle's cabin, where she'd made up a room for herself and one for her two-year-old son, Matty.

If she had any sense in this head of hers, she'd ignore all the rational reasons she'd come back to Haven in the first place, pack up her sedan again and go back from whence she'd come.

If there was a *back*.

Which there wasn't.

The truth was, she had ultimately returned to Haven because, to her own shame and mortification, she had nowhere else to go.

She was facing a fairly insurmountable problem, as she saw it. No health, no home, no job and not much of an opportunity to get one. If it was just her life in the balance, she might have resisted the urge to return.

But this wasn't about her. It was about Matty. He needed the stability the small town offered, which she could not otherwise give him.

Uncle Mort's cabin was available to her rent-free. Where else would she find a deal like that? And though returning home wasn't exactly a typical fresh start, no other choices had presented themselves. She had to take what she could get.

Besides, she had important, possibly critical legal news to deliver to Bea Brewster, the director of the local boys ranch, information Carolina knew they were anxiously waiting on. The kind of news that was better delivered in person.

Since that was her first order of business after unloading all of her personal belongings, she headed to the boys ranch as soon as the moving truck had left her uncle's premises.

She paused at the door to the front office of the boys ranch and ran a palm down the denim of her jeans, considering her options for about the hundredth time that week. In one hand she clutched her purse, which contained the legal document the boys ranch director was awaiting. Matty clung tightly to her opposite arm, his hand squeezing hers.

He was usually an outgoing and curious toddler, but at the moment he was hiding behind Carolina and peeking out at his surroundings from around her leg.

Her heart clenched. She suspected her son's sudden shyness was due to his picking up on her nerves and anxiety. The poor child had had enough change, with his entire life being uprooted, without having the challenge of immediately adapting to his new surroundings.

"It's okay, little man. You and Mama are going to be just fine. You'll see." She affectionately and—she hoped—encouragingly ruffled his dark hair.

"Carolina!" Receptionist Katie Ellis exited through the front door of the office, a pink canvas lunch tote hanging from her elbow. "What a nice surprise!"

Any thoughts Carolina might have had of skipping town without being recognized dissipated into thin air as she nodded at her friend. Katie was a few years younger than Carolina but they had gotten to know each other while volunteering at community events and had become friends.

"It's good to see you," Carolina said, hoping the strain she was feeling didn't echo in her voice. "Still working for the boys ranch, I see. It's been a long time."

"Too long," Katie agreed, racing forward to envelop Carolina in an enthusiastic hug. "How many years has it been, do you think?"

"Three." Carolina sighed inwardly, the ache in her chest growing. She knew *exactly* how long it had been since she'd last been in Haven. Not just to the year, but to the month. Even to the day.

Katie grasped Carolina's elbow and turned them both back toward her office.

"I don't want to interrupt your lunch hour," Carolina protested. "I can come back later."

"Nonsense." She held up her tote. "It's only a salad, and I'm heartily tired of eating greens every day. But wouldn't you know I have to perpetually diet just to keep my figure." She shrugged and grinned. "What's a single woman to do? Anyway, lunch will wait. I want to hear all about you. What's been happening in your life since you left Haven?"

Katie dropped into her chair behind the desk and gestured for Carolina to take a seat.

"I can see at least one thing has changed," Katie said with a giggle, gesturing at Matty.

Carolina tried to pull a wiggling Matty onto her lap, but he protested loudly and tried to squirm away.

"I'm sorry," she apologized to Katie. "I promise I'll fill you in, but I need to get Matty settled first."

She set him down on the floor by her feet and fished around in her oversize purse, triumphantly retrieving two toy cars. "Here you go, buddy. One for each fist. Stay close and play quietly, please."

Matty was already distracted, his attention on the little police car and fire truck he held in his hands.

Carolina returned her attention to Katie.

Katie leaned back in her seat and smiled. "Obviously you didn't have any trouble catching a man's eye, now did you? You look exactly the same as the day you left Haven. Or prettier, even. And you had a baby? Are you and your husband planning to move back to town with your sweet little boy?" Katie stopped hammering Carolina with questions long enough to give her a once-over. "I have to say I am seriously envious of your figure right now. How do you do it?"

Carolina bit back a bitter laugh. The compliment was sincere and well meant, but she was perfectly aware that the person who'd left Haven in such a rush three years ago was not even remotely the same as the woman who'd returned. She was older now, hopefully a little wiser, and infinitely worse for the wear.

Physically, emotionally and spiritually. If she had

kept her figure, it was because she was too stressed to eat most of the time.

Life had come full circle for her, and she was back in Haven, where she'd once found her deepest peace, her grandest love and her greatest heartbreak. She'd been pregnant and troubled when she'd left town.

The biggest change in her life was that she'd become a Christian while she'd been away, living in Colorado with a friend. She was still learning what her faith entailed. Trust didn't come easy to her, and thinking about God as a loving Father was still a concept she wrestled with. Her own father hadn't exactly been a good role model.

When she'd first escaped to Colorado and had no money to buy the food she'd needed to help her have a healthy pregnancy, folks from a nearby church had reached out to help her. They'd not only shared their food but their faith, and now it was Carolina's precarious trust in God's love and mercy that kept her going, knowing He held the future, even when from her perspective it was all jumbled up.

She prayed returning home was the right decision, that she would be able to recover some of the peace she'd once had.

But love?

That was so not happening. A romantic relationship was not even a blip on the radar, and she was fairly certain it never would be. She had her hands full raising Matty.

She tensed. This was the part she had dreaded and worried about the most in coming back to town.

Breathe in, breathe out.

It was no wonder Matty was picking up on her anxiety. It was practically radiating from her.

Presenting Matty to Katie and talking about him would be relatively easy compared to what she imagined it would be like with some of the other folks in town.

It was overwhelming to realize this was the first of many times she'd have to introduce her son—to friends and acquaintances, neighbors in town, and at church. And she'd have to explain that a husband didn't come along with the package.

She anticipated a few surprised looks, maybe even a little gossip, but hopefully no one would ask about the boy's father, at least not right away. She wasn't ready to open up about Matty's parentage, to disclose her secret.

Honestly, she doubted she'd ever be ready.

"No husband," she managed to choke out.

Katie's face turned a pretty shade of pink. "Oh, I'm sorry. I just assumed—"

Carolina sighed. "It's not a big deal. You had no way of knowing. I'm sure you'll be the first of many to ask."

Actually, the question was like a jab in the stomach, but she knew she'd better get used to it.

"No worries there. Everyone is going to adore this handsome little fella," Katie assured her, clearly backtracking.

Carolina ran her palm across the cowlick in her son's dark hair, but he paid no attention to her as he busily pushed his cars across the tile floor, making vrooming and screeching noises, punctuated with the occasional fire truck or police vehicle siren.

Matty's resemblance to his father was striking, should anyone care to notice. Carolina prayed they wouldn't. If Katie didn't notice, maybe there was hope that others would miss the connection as well.

"Matty, be a gentleman and say hi to Miss Katie."

Hearing his name, Matty looked up from his toys.

"I'm Matty," he proclaimed proudly.

Katie chuckled. "Nice to meet you, Matty." Her gaze returned to Carolina, and her smile widened. "What a little sweetheart."

Carolina released the breath she hadn't even realized she'd been holding.

"Would you like to take a tour around our new ranch? It's quite an improvement over the old one. Thanks to Cyrus Culpepper, we've been able to take in twice the number of needy boys."

"That's great news. What I saw driving in looks wonderful. Actually, I've got some important information about the Culpepper will. That's why I'm here." Carolina once again fished through her purse, this time searching for the certified letter she'd received the week previously.

She really did need to buy a smaller handbag that half of her worldly possessions wouldn't get lost in. After Matty had turned two, she'd graduated from a diaper bag to her current purse, which wasn't much smaller than the enormous blue elephant bag had been. But with an active toddler, she still found it necessary to carry a lot of stuff. Toy cars, a pull-on diaper or two, wet wipes, fruit snacks…

Finally locating and retrieving the envelope, she placed it on the desk in front of her. "I need to speak to Bea. I believe it's regarding a legal matter."

"Of course. She's out to lunch right now, but I expect her back in a half an hour or so. I'll text her to let her know you're here."

Carolina shifted her gaze to Matty just as, standing on tiptoe, he reached for the stack of papers teetering on the edge of Katie's desk.

"Matty, no," Carolina barked, just barely managing to snatch him out of the way before the whole stack of invoices went flying off the desk. As it was, four or five documents fluttered to the ground around her feet.

Shaking her head in dismay, she propped Matty on her hip and turned to Katie. "I'm so sorry. Sometimes I think curiosity should have been Matty's middle name."

Heat suffused Carolina's face. She only hoped Katie would not ask what Matty's real middle name was. It would be a dead giveaway for sure.

Katie grinned and stood, moving around the desk and stooping to retrieve the errant papers. "Not a problem. No harm done."

Carolina returned her smile. "Yet. This child can get into mischief faster than you can say Jack Frost. I'm his mother and I can barely keep up with him."

"Do you like horses, Matty? I think we have just enough time before Miss Bea gets back for us to go visit the stables." She winked at Carolina. "And get him out for some fresh air? Maybe run off a bit of his energy? If only we could bottle it up and use it for ourselves, huh?" she said. "Imagine how much we could accomplish in a day."

Carolina laughed and nodded. "I'll say."

As Katie led them between outbuildings toward the stable, she regaled Carolina with funny stories about the resident boys and the animals and pointed out various buildings and working areas of the boys ranch.

Carolina was familiar with the general purpose of the ranch, which, under the guidance of the Lone Star Cowboy League, was to care for and mentor troubled boys ages six to seventeen, kids who were having difficulties at home. Most of the time their parents or caregivers, unable to deal with the boys' emotional issues on their own, placed them at the boys ranch for a time. These were the kids who were walking a fine line, and the ranch had many success stories of kids who had grown up and gone on to be model citizens and useful members of their communities.

Since Carolina wasn't personally connected to the ranch in any way, she knew very little about the specifics and had never visited. Three years ago when she'd left Haven, it had still been located at the smaller facility, which had only had the capacity to house twelve boys. Now that they'd moved, they'd been able to expand the children's options and aid them in moving forward with their lives.

As Katie talked, Carolina became increasingly impressed by the number of programs the ranch now offered to help the boys transition into public life, to become honorable, faithful and hardworking members of society. They attended the nearby public school during the week and Haven Community Church on Sundays.

The boys also had the opportunity to acquire a trade. In addition to ranch work, they could learn cooking, carpentry, welding, painting, plumbing—the impressive list went on and on.

Carolina took a deep breath of the country air and reveled in the uniquely rural aroma that assaulted her nostrils—the pungent odors of hay and horses, prairie grass, and freshly dug earth mingled with the scents of the barnyard animals they passed. Oddly, it wasn't an unpleasant sensation. After three years in the city, the ranch smelled like home.

White picket fences surrounded the property. Brown cattle dotted the rolling green hills. Matty was entranced by the squawking chickens pecking for food on the ground inside their coop. Carolina chuckled at the plump piglets rooting around in the mud, grunting to their hearts' content.

Her ears picked up on the congregational sound of bleating. A herd of hungry sheep, perhaps. Or goats.

She wondered if they might be able to take a quick detour to introduce Matty to the goats. Her son would go crazy over a cute little bleating baby with its nubby horns and curious nature. What were they called again?

Kids?

Carolina chuckled. That sounded about right, given that goats were similarly stubborn and inclined to get themselves into loads of mischief.

"I'm really excited about one of our newest projects," Katie gushed as they rounded the corner of the barn. "It's already proving to be one of the most popular programs we've ever had here on the ranch."

Carolina pulled her cell phone from her back pocket and checked the time, thinking that, although she hated to cut the visit short, she should probably suggest returning to the office so she could be waiting there to speak to Bea when the director returned from her lunch.

As much as she was enjoying the tour of the ranch, and especially watching Matty interact with the animals, it was more imperative than ever that she speak to the ranch's director as soon as possible. She'd had no idea of the length and breadth of the boys ranch activities, and now that she knew more about it, she realized just how important her information was.

It broke her heart that she was the bearer of bad news that could possibly affect the ranch's future. Hopefully not, but the sooner they got the information, the better. Her great-uncle Morton, whom the lawyer representing the ranch was seeking, had recently died of a heart attack.

A moment's grief swirled through her and she swallowed hard. She'd been especially close to her great-uncle, and his passing had been hard on her. Gritting her teeth, she stared at her boots as she mentally herded her emotions into the deepest corner of her heart and clamped them down with the strength of her will.

"Katie, I should probably—"

Blinking back tears, she looked up to find a man's dark eyes on hers. Their eyes met and locked, surprise and shock registering within his deep stare.

She gasped, her entire body stiffening like a slab of concrete.

He swallowed hard enough to make his Adam's apple bob. Clearly he was every bit as stunned as she was.

Oh, no. No, no, no, no, no.

This couldn't be happening.

Wyatt Harrow.

The man who'd won her heart and then shattered it into a million pieces.

No—that wasn't fair to him. She couldn't honestly place the blame at his door for what had happened. Not when she was the one at fault—for everything.

For not knowing better than to trust her own heart. For not having the strength to stay in control of her emotions enough not to surrender to the physical need to find comfort for their mutual grief. For not being brave enough to tell Wyatt the truth about Matty, even if she'd believed—and still believed—that it was in his best interest not to know.

She'd been the one to abruptly end their relationship, not Wyatt. She'd literally walked away from him, and from Haven, even though her heart had been breaking into smaller and smaller pieces with every step she took, for every mile of distance she put between them.

His presence was like a slap on the face.

Wyatt was here. He'd seen her. There was no turning away now. Nowhere to run or hide from the truth.

She felt as if she were drowning. She coaxed herself to breathe through the crashing waves of reality, but the air seemed to freeze in her lungs as she watched him slowly recover from his own shock.

Surrounded by a herd of goats and a motley flock of boys displaying varying degrees of interest in what he was doing, Wyatt was clearly in the middle of some kind of veterinary demonstration. He had a syringe in one hand and a goat trapped between his muscular legs.

He was every bit as handsome and rugged as she remembered, from the tip of his black Stetson to the toes of his tan cowboy boots. Jet-black hair, eyes the color of dark chocolate, powerful biceps, broad shoulders sloping to a cowboy's trim waist. A well-worn T-shirt that might once have been red, a fleece-lined denim jacket and tattered jeans that spoke of his hard manual labor as a large-animal veterinarian.

The only thing that had changed from the last time she had seen him, from the man she had left three years ago, were the lines of strain on his face and the pure icy coldness of his gaze. Her heart clenched as she remembered how his eyes used to warm when he looked at her, when his whole countenance lit up whenever she was around.

But not now.

He pulled his hat down to shadow his thoughts, but he couldn't hide the frown that curved his lips into a downward arch.

What was Wyatt doing here?

Not just here at the boys ranch. That much was fairly evident.

But why was he still in Haven?

Carolina quivered from the adrenaline still coursing through her. It hadn't even occurred to her that she might run into him. She had been so certain he would be long gone from town by now, or else she would never have even considered returning—letter or no letter.

That was the whole point, wasn't it? Why she'd left in the first place? To give Wyatt his freedom?

Wyatt stood to his full height, and Carolina's breath snagged in her throat. She'd hoped that if she ever saw him again she would feel nothing, that she would have moved beyond the long nights and emotions born of grief and loneliness.

Instead, nothing had changed, except perhaps that her feelings had grown stronger over time. It was as if every nerve in her body was attuned to his.

The brown-speckled goat Wyatt had been working on bleated and bolted away, but he didn't appear to notice. His posture was stiff and intimidating as he stared back at her, tight jawed and frowning.

"Carolina." His usually rich baritone emerged low and gritty.

"Mama?" Matty squeezed her hand.

She'd been so shocked by Wyatt's sudden appearance that she'd momentarily forgotten Matty was at her side.

Wyatt's gaze shifted to Matty and then back up to her again, his eyes widening in surprise.

Now the electricity intensified, zapping back and forth like lightning between them. Her pulse ratcheted. Her heart hammered. Her worst fear, realized.

Matty.

Oh, precious Lord, please help me.

Even as she prayed for relief, she knew there was no way out of this. It didn't matter that she hadn't intended to reveal this secret. Not to anyone, but most especially not to Wyatt.

Ever.

The whole reason she'd left Haven was to allow Wyatt to pursue the life he'd dreamed of. Ever since she'd known him, he'd spoken about his desire to help the poor and destitute in foreign countries learn how to raise animals. He wanted to provide them with a trade through which they could work themselves out of a poverty-stricken existence.

It was a noble goal, the dream of his heart, and if she had stayed, she would have ruined it for him. His parents had been foreign diplomats who'd died in an explosion, and Wyatt had never quite gotten over the loss, even if it made him more determined than ever to help those less fortunate than him. She'd known him well enough to know there was no way he would ever consider bringing a wife and child with him to a third-world country where they might be in danger.

Carolina had known and understood this, and she'd loved him enough to let him go. That was why she'd left Haven so suddenly when she'd discovered she was pregnant with Matty. Everything she'd been through since then—every struggle, every trial she'd endured, every night spent crying in her pillow, had been for Wyatt's sake.

Because if he'd known she was pregnant, he would have had no choice but to stay with her in Haven. He wasn't the kind of man who would walk away from his responsibilities. He would have given up all of his personal hopes and dreams for the sake of his son. She had no doubt whatsoever that he was the guy who would do the right thing by her and by Matty. He would have asked her to marry him.

But she'd been in love with him, and the *right thing* wasn't good enough for her—or for Matty. Their lives couldn't be built on one night's mistake.

If she'd believed Wyatt was in love with her, that would have been one thing. But before the night Matty was conceived they'd only been casually dating, and the night they'd shared had been born of sorrow, not joy. A marriage and family based only on a man's sense of decency and not true love? Her heart couldn't take it.

So she'd left.

And now she was back, only to discover Wyatt had never left at all. Why wasn't he in Uganda or deep in the Amazon jungle somewhere?

Had her sacrifice been for nothing?

"Mama?" Matty said again, yanking her arm more intently this time. "Mama. Mama."

She scooped him into her arms and gently patted his back, reassuring herself as much as him. Her fight-or-flight instinct was working overtime, and it was all she could do to stand firm and not flee.

But what good would it do her to turn away now? Wyatt had already caught sight of Matty. He was watching the toddler through narrowed eyes and pressed lips as the boy tangled his fingers into Carolina's hair.

"You're a mama?" Wyatt asked, and for one confused moment, no longer than a blink of an eye, Carolina thought…hoped…*prayed* that he wouldn't comprehend what that meant. That he wouldn't realize the truth about those identical chocolate-brown eyes that were literally staring right back at him, among the many features that mirrored his own.

"I—how could you?" he stammered, picking off his hat and threading his fingers through his hair.

Carolina cringed, waiting for him to come loose at the seams. How could he not? She wouldn't blame him. He had every right to be furious.

She held her breath, waiting for the explosion she knew was coming.

But when he spoke, it was deep, and hushed, and as hard and cold as steel.

"Tell me the truth, Carolina, for once in your life. This boy—is he my son?"

Wyatt's breath felt like icicles in his lungs, poking and puncturing his chest with each ragged gasp.

That boy, the animated, dark-haired, dark-eyed child clinging to Carolina's neck, was his *son*.

For the very first few seconds after he'd realized Carolina wasn't alone, that she had her toddler with her, there had been a flash of confusion—of anger, of *envy*—that she had been able to move on with her life so quickly after abandoning him. It had taken him months to recover enough to go on with his daily life without thinking of her with every heartbeat, and there were still days—and nights—he found difficulty putting the past behind him.

Bewilderment, uncertainty, grief, pain, fury—yet at the same time an affection and warmth unlike any he'd ever known. He had no idea where the tender feelings for Matty came from. They were just *there*.

He switched his gaze to Carolina. She looked stricken, as well she might.

How dare she keep all knowledge of his son from him for all this time?

And why had she come back now?

He guessed the boy had to be around two years of age. Had Carolina suddenly grown a conscience and decided Wyatt needed to know about the boy? It didn't seem likely, especially since Carolina appeared completely shocked to have encountered him the way she had. She certainly hadn't been seeking him out.

There were so many questions he wanted answered, so much confusion rolling through his mind and heart that he couldn't seem to form the words to voice a single one of them. He wanted to grill and interrogate Carolina on every aspect of Matty's life, but he didn't know where to begin.

And really, what did it matter anyway?

The fact was, three years ago Carolina had left him high and dry with no notice and no explanation, and now, years later, she had suddenly returned with *their* son in her arms.

He couldn't imagine any conceivable excuse or reasonable explanation that he would actually accept as a legitimate reason why she hadn't bothered to tell him about his child. There was simply nothing she could say to talk her way out of the conversation they were about to have.

"W-Wyatt?" Seventeen-year-old Johnny Drake touched his shoulder and tentatively broke into his thoughts. The teenager, whom Wyatt was personally mentoring, was reed thin, with floppy, curly brown hair and clothes that always looked like they were a size too large for him. "D-did you want me to c-catch the g-g-goat for you?"

In the shock of finding out he had a son, Wyatt had completely forgotten he was in the middle of teaching a class to a rowdy group of boys who were all gazing at him with wide-eyed curiosity and far more attention than they'd been giving him when he'd been explaining how to inoculate a goat.

"Yeah, W-W-Wyatt," said Christopher Harrington, a resentful young man who thought he was better than the others because he came from a wealthy home. Christopher hadn't yet learned the hard truth that the boys were all on equal footing here at the ranch. "What about the g-g-g-g-g-goats?"

Wyatt frowned at Christopher's exaggerated stutter as he made fun of Johnny. Poor Johnny's shoulders drooped and his bitter gaze sizzled the ground at his feet.

"Knock it off, Christopher. You boys are done for the day. Go somewhere else and find something useful to do."

The young men didn't have to be told twice before they scattered. They weren't used to receiving a sudden chunk of free time.

Only Johnny hung back and didn't follow the other boys. His stutter made him the object of ridicule, but Johnny found solace reading books and working with the ranch animals, who accepted him just the way he was.

Wyatt understood that, which was one of the main reasons he had taken Johnny under his wing, mentoring the boy with an eye to getting him into college and eventually, if Johnny excelled in his studies, veterinary school.

As much as the teenagers mercilessly teased Johnny, that was nothing close to what would happen if they got a whiff of what was happening between Wyatt and Carolina now. There was no telling what kind of havoc the boys would wreak with that kind of information.

It was time to be proactive, to deal with this situation with Carolina and Matty before anyone else found out about what had happened between them. They needed to get their stories straight and nip any rumors in the bud.

Or did everyone already know?

Was it possible that he was the only man in Haven who wasn't aware he had a son?

Fury and humiliation lapped like flames in his chest and he struggled to maintain his composure. He gritted his teeth and crossed his arms, digging his fingernails into his biceps and fighting for control of his temper.

"I know you must be angry with me." Carolina paused, her eyes uncertain. "Aren't you?"

He raised his eyebrows.

Angry?

That was the understatement of the century. He was mad enough to want to put his fist through a brick wall, just to try to transfer some of the pain in his chest to his hand. He felt like he was about to explode.

"How long were you planning on keeping this secret from me?" he snapped, jamming his hands into the pockets of his fleece-lined jeans jacket to keep from punching the air in frustration. "I can't believe you kept my own *son* from me, Carolina. How could you?"

"I never meant to hurt you."

The fire in his chest burned even hotter. How could she even consider suggesting that her motives were altruistic? Did she really think that leaving him without sharing the knowledge that she was carrying his baby wouldn't wound him?

He scoffed. "Of course not. You somehow thought I'd be better off not knowing that I have a son."

"W-W-Wyatt?"

Wyatt turned. He'd somehow forgotten—again—that Johnny was still at his side.

The boy pushed his hair off his forehead. Wyatt could see how agitated Johnny was, clenching and unclenching his fists in a silent, steady rhythm. The poor kid looked like he was about to jump out of his skin.

It struck Wyatt suddenly that *he* was the cause. Johnny was ultrasensitive and was picking up on the tension between him and Carolina. Wyatt took a deep breath and let it out slowly. No sense upsetting the young man. There was enough anger and grief in this scenario without involving the boy.

He clapped a hand on Johnny's shoulder. "Don't worry. It's all good. Carolina and I just have a few... issues to work out between us."

He pointed to the herd of goats, who were now grazing their way through another field. "Do you think you could finish vaccinating the goats?"

Wyatt nodded toward the clipboard, which contained the list of the names of all the goats. He'd dropped the clipboard in the grass earlier, when he'd had his hands full teaching the group of boys how to give a goat a subcutaneous vaccine.

"I think there are four or five of them we haven't vaccinated yet. Do you remember how to do it?"

"Y-y-yes, sir," replied Johnny, looking relieved to

have a reason to avoid being around the strained reunion between Wyatt and Carolina.

Wyatt returned his attention to Carolina and Matty, who was now wiggling and squirming in his mother's arms, pumping his chunky arms and legs in an awkward rhythm. He clearly wanted to get down, but Carolina refused, clutching the child like a lifeline.

Wyatt clenched his fists. Had his heated response affected Matty as it had Johnny?

With every ounce of his self-control, Wyatt pressed his anger—along with all of his other barely containable and ignitable emotions—to the back of his mind and heart and firmly boarded them in.

He had to get past the fact that Carolina had abruptly sprung fatherhood on him. All that mattered was taking care of Matty. His needs would always come first, no matter what.

Wyatt was going to be there for his son, and that started right now.

"Can I—" he fumbled, but his voice was husky. He cleared his throat. "May I hold him?"

"Of course." Carolina sounded surprised that he would ask—as if she hadn't expected him to step up to the plate.

What was she thinking? That he would deny the truth that was right in front of his eyes? Or maybe it was the opposite—that she feared he was going to step in and take over.

Now *that* was a thought.

He held out his arms to Matty, feeling suddenly large and ungainly. Abruptly shy, Matty tucked his head into his mother's shoulder and curled closer to her.

Wyatt's heart plummeted and he dropped his hands

to his sides, wiping his sweaty palms against the denim of his blue jeans.

Strike one.

"Wyatt, wait." Carolina held up her hand to him, gesturing for him to come closer. Then to Matty, she said, "Son, this is—" She stopped abruptly, her eyes widening in dismay as it met Wyatt's. "Um—this is Mr. Wyatt. He's a very nice man. Don't you want to say hello to him?"

Mr. Wyatt. Not Father. Not Daddy.

Talk about disheartening. But then, what did he expect from his first encounter with his son? That the years apart didn't matter? That Matty didn't know him from a stranger?

He *was* a stranger to his son.

He stuffed the anger down as quickly as it rose, afraid Matty would be able to sense it.

At least this time, when Wyatt reached for him, Matty stretched out his little arms and wrapped them tightly around Wyatt's neck.

Wyatt struggled to swallow, and not because Matty was cutting off his air. It just felt so new. So strange.

And yet somehow, so *right*.

Matty still sported the chunky arms and legs and chubby cheeks of toddlerhood, so Wyatt was surprised by how light the boy was. Wasn't he getting enough to eat?

"Where are you staying?" he asked as he mentally adjusted to the feel of Matty in his arms. He wasn't accustomed to holding children of any age. He was much more comfortable around the animals he vetted. He was only just getting used to teaching the kids at the boys ranch, and there wasn't much physical contact between them, other than the occasional encouraging pat on the back.

And all of the sudden he had a two-year-old son?

"We're lodging at my great-uncle's cabin for now," Carolina answered. An emotion Wyatt couldn't interpret flashed across her face.

For now.

What did that mean? That she wasn't planning to stick around?

Surely not. She couldn't be so coldhearted as to just waltz into town, inform Wyatt that he had a son and then disappear again.

Could she?

He didn't have the opportunity to clarify, because at that moment Bea Brewster approached, saying she'd managed to round up Gabe Everett, who was the president of the local chapter of the Lone Star Cowboy League, and attorney Harold Haverman, who was representing the Culpepper estate. They were awaiting Carolina's presence in Bea's office.

Carolina reached for Matty, and Wyatt reluctantly handed him back to her. Right when he was starting to adjust to the feel of Matty's chubby little body in his arms, the boy had been taken from him. Wyatt desperately craved more time. Much more.

He started to follow Carolina to Bea's office but then paused. If Gabe and a lawyer were involved in the meeting, it wasn't exactly his business to invite himself. Though he didn't know any of the details, he assumed the gathering had something to do with the terms of Cyrus Culpepper's will and the town's ability to retain the new boys ranch facility.

Before Carolina went anywhere, though, Wyatt intended to tell her where he stood in regard to fatherhood—in regard to Matty. He wanted to make sure his feelings on the matter were perfectly clear.

He just needed the opportunity, which would be difficult when Carolina was deep in conversation with Bea.

"You are welcome to join us, Wyatt," Bea offered, casting a grin at him.

Wyatt agreed right away, partially because he volunteered at the boys ranch and thus had some vested interest in the legal matters that would be presented, but mostly because he was determined to find the opportunity to speak to Carolina once the meeting was adjourned.

As they walked back toward Bea's office, Wyatt gave Bea an apologetic smile and snagged Carolina's elbow, urging her aside for a moment. He bent his head to whisper close to her ear so the others wouldn't hear.

Her eyes met his, large and unblinking. He'd forgotten the way those pretty golden-brown eyes, rimmed with thick, dark lashes, used to do a number on him.

Well, not this time. He ignored the tightening of his throat and the way his gut flipped over.

"We're not finished here," he warned.

"No. I didn't think we were." Her gaze broke away from his and she sighed deeply.

"Just so I know we're on the same page." His voice was low and huskier than usual.

The same *page*?

They weren't even in the same *bookstore*. The three previous years spanned behind them like a dilapidated rope bridge, and an enormous, gaping breach lay before them. From his vantage point, it seemed like an impossible chasm to cross.

But he had to try.

For his son.
For Matty.

Carolina felt very much like she'd just escaped a firing squad, if only temporarily.

How had she not planned for this contingency? Why had it not occurred to her that, free from the burden she and Matty would have been for him, Wyatt would not have taken the very first plane out of the country?

But she hadn't, and Wyatt was here in Haven, and she didn't know what she was going to do about it.

She didn't even know what her options were.

Maybe she should just take care of this legal matter and leave Haven behind her, this time for good.

Except, she reminded herself, she had nowhere else to go. No family. No friends outside Haven other than her ex-roommate and work acquaintances. Nothing.

She'd been living in Colorado since she'd left Haven, working as a nurse at a senior center and hospice. She was surviving, if not thriving, as a single mother. She'd found the Lord, and God was faithfully seeing her through, one deliberate step at a time.

But then, in a matter of weeks, her life had completely upended and fallen apart. She'd taken a bad turn on a ski slope and trashed her knee, which had required major surgery and months of physical therapy. And then her great-uncle Mort had passed away.

Between her hospital stay and recovery, combined with her doctor permanently banning her from lifting more than fifty pounds, her entire life had quickly fallen apart at the seams. Lifting fifty pounds—sometimes much more when patients slipped and fell—was required for a first responder in a nursing home, and the senior center had simply let her go, which was a nice, polite way of saying she was fired.

And then, to top it all off, her roommate, who had been Matty's primary caretaker while Carolina was in the hospital, had eloped with her boyfriend, leaving Carolina on her own without the means to cover her month-to-month rent on her apartment and nobody available to watch her son while she looked for work.

It was a catch-22 to put all others to shame.

It had frightened her beyond measure that there was a very real possibility that she and Matty might end up living in a homeless shelter. She might have grown up in the country with a single mother, where there was sometimes little left over, but there had always been a roof over her head and enough food to go around.

Now it was her responsibility to make sure Matty had the same security.

Somehow.

As devastated as she'd been about Uncle Mort's passing, when she discovered he had willed her his cabin in Haven, it had been an answer to her prayer. Owning his cabin free and clear, she would be able to live rent-free—at least until she got back on her feet and was more financially stable. Then she could make more permanent decisions about their future.

The letter from Haven's Lone Star Cowboy League arrived soon after, when she was packing up her apartment to make the move, and she felt as if the Lord was validating and confirming her plans. After the frightening time when it had felt like her whole life was going down the drain, life suddenly appeared to be on an uptick. She thought maybe everything might be turning around, falling into place for her and Matty.

And they had been.

Until she'd run smack-dab into Wyatt. Now she was wondering if her life had just taken the biggest downturn of all.

"Carolina," Bea said, her voice breaking sharply into Carolina's thoughts. With effort, she turned her attention to Bea. "First, we would all like to express our appreciation for your rapid response to our letter." Bea took a seat behind her desk and clasped her hands in front of her, her expression unusually grim. "And we appreciate the fact that you've taken the time out of your busy schedule to come see us."

Carolina bit the inside of her lip. If only Bea knew. Her schedule was, unfortunately, wide-open.

"We were concerned when we never heard directly from Morton," Bea continued politely.

Bea was a tall middle-aged woman with bobbed brown hair and dark eyes set off by horn-rimmed glasses. She definitely looked the part of the capable boys ranch director—which was the position she'd maintained for approximately the last twenty years. Her sensible jeans and well-worn boots attested to her proficiency.

Carolina was acquainted with Gabe, a muscular, dark-haired man with friendly blue eyes. He'd been a couple of years ahead of her in school. She assumed that the imposing silver-haired man who popped his leather briefcase open on the corner of Bea's desk was Harold Haverman, the lawyer representing the Culpepper estate.

Even though Wyatt hung back, leaning his broad shoulder against the door frame instead of fully entering the office, Carolina felt his presence so deeply that it filled the entire room.

Or maybe it was her own tension burdening her. Sadly, she did not come bearing good news.

Wyatt moved out of the doorway in order for Katie to enter.

"Did you want me to take care of Matty while y'all are talking?" she asked with a friendly smile.

"I would appreciate that," said Carolina, relieved not to have to worry about her loud, wiggly toddler while she worked out some of her other issues. It was going to be hard enough to get through these next few minutes without having a curious little boy trying to get into everything that wasn't tied down. "Thank you so much."

Katie held out her hand to Matty and he took it without a fuss.

"Not a problem," Katie replied brightly before turning her attention to Matty. "As I recall, we never quite made it to the stable earlier. What do you say, Matty? Do you want to come with me and see some real live horsies?"

Matty squealed in delight and everyone chuckled along with him, even Carolina. The little boy's laughter was definitely contagious.

But as soon as Katie and Matty left the room, the heaviness Carolina had earlier felt in the air reappeared. Everyone instantly became serious as all attention turned to the legal matter at hand.

Carolina let out a deep, shaky breath. No matter how many times she had rehearsed it in her head, she still couldn't say the words without trembling.

"I'm sorry I don't have better news for you. The reason you never heard from my uncle Mort is that—that is—" She cleared her throat and hiccuped a breath, struggling to finish her statement. "Unfortunately, my great-uncle passed away a month ago."

A widower, Morton had remarried at the age of seventy-five and moved in with his new wife's family in Amarillo, leaving his cabin in Haven unoccupied for a couple of years.

Compassion filled Bea's eyes. "Oh, I'm so sorry to hear that, my dear. We didn't know. My deepest condolences."

Carolina's throat grew tight and tears burned the backs of her eyes. She'd known coming into the meeting that this was going to be difficult for her to talk about, with her own grief still so fresh, but with all the added emotions brought on by encountering Wyatt, her sorrow was almost more than she could bear.

"Thank you," she scraped out, tears making a slow line down her cheeks. "He died in his sleep. His wife said it was peaceful. I—m-miss him," she stammered.

"Of course you do," said Bea. "Poor darling."

The office suddenly felt twenty degrees warmer and all the oxygen seemed to have been sucked out of the room. Her head spun and she clutched her throat, wavering.

Carolina blinked rapidly, trying to regain her equilibrium, but it felt as if she were in a narrow tunnel and darkness was edging out the light.

She gasped for breath and held out her arm, grateful when she felt a stabilizing hand at the small of her back. It was only when he pressed a handkerchief into her hand that she realized it was Wyatt by her side, silently urging her into the only other chair in the room.

She couldn't speak or even compose a smile, but she nodded her appreciation.

His eyes widened and his worried frown hardened

to rigid planes, his dark eyebrows dropping low and his lips pressing into a firm, straight line. His eyes appeared almost as black as his hair.

Her heart took a wild ride, leaping into her throat and then plunging back down again to lodge uncomfortably in her sour stomach.

Three years hadn't changed Wyatt. Not where it really counted. He was ever the gentleman, even when it went against his own better judgment. He'd taken care of her even when he was beyond furious with her, which he had every right to be. After all that had been said and done, no matter what had happened between them, he hadn't let her fall.

The attorney cleared his throat. "I don't want to sound insensitive here, but we need to address the issue of the will and Morton's part in it. Cyrus specifically indicated that all four original members of the boys ranch had to be present at the seventieth-anniversary party or the land will be forfeited."

Gabe frowned and tapped his Stetson against his thigh. "This new development certainly throws another wrench in our plans."

Another wrench? Carolina wondered what other complications they'd already encountered, but she was still too shaken up to be able to formulate any questions.

Bea steepled her fingers under her chin, clearly deep in thought. "So what do we do now, Harold? Can you tell us if Cyrus considered any such contingencies, or should we just call a halt to this whole investigation? We've already put so much effort into finding the original men that it would be a real shame if we have to end it so abruptly. Frankly, I'm terrified that we may have jumped the gun in taking on twelve extra boys, no matter how desperate the need may have been. I don't know what we're going to do if we have to give up this ranch after all we've done to expand the program. It just breaks my heart to even think about it."

Harold riffled through the files in his briefcase, at length removing one that contained several manila envelopes. He flipped through them and withdrew one near the bottom.

"Ah. Here we are."

Carolina's breath caught as she waited, although she didn't know for what. She felt nauseated. She hadn't realized in coming here that she wasn't just delivering the awful news of her great-uncle's passing, but apparently, she'd just put the final torch to the plans to expand the boys ranch. She'd assumed, when she'd read the letter requesting her great-uncle's presence in Haven for the anniversary party, that informing Bea and the other leaders of the boys ranch about Uncle Mort's death would simply put an end to any obligation he might have had in the matter. She'd never dreamed this information would create what now appeared to be an insurmountable difficulty to the whole process.

Harold picked up a letter opener from his briefcase, made a neat slice across the top of the manila envelope and then pulled out a single sheet of paper. He leaned his hip against the side of the desk and shook the paper to open it fully.

"I was instructed to open and read this letter in the case of this particular—er—contingency," he said, flashing Carolina an apologetic look. "It's addressed to next of kin. Would you like to read it, Carolina?"

Carolina shook her head. She couldn't yet find her voice, much less control her emotions. "No, thank you.

This letter involves everyone here. Please read it to all of us."

Harold nodded gravely. "Of course."

He cleared his throat and began.

I, Cyrus B. Culpepper, being of sound mind and in front of witnesses, add this addendum to my will. It occurs to me that one or the other of the four fellows I'm requiring to be at the seventieth-anniversary party might have gone to meet their maker even before I do. Should you discover that to be the case, then I hereby declare that the next of kin may represent the family legacy at the celebration, assuming the next of kin is willing to attend the party.

Yours,

Cyrus B. Culpepper

Silence shrouded the room as each person ruminated over the new contingency. Then all eyes lifted and turned expectantly to Carolina. Would she stay and represent the Mason family?

"The next of kin would be Morton's wife, yes?" Bea asked.

Carolina shook her head. "Unfortunately, my aunt Martha died just a few weeks after Morton. Since my parents have also both passed away, I believe I am all that's left of Uncle Morton's legacy."

She didn't know whether to be relieved or alarmed.

On one hand, she was pleased that she would be able to help keep the boys ranch going and that she hadn't been delivering a literal death blow.

On the other hand, that meant she had to stay in Haven. It was the beginning of February, which meant she was looking at two months, before the party in March. If things went downhill between her and Wyatt, which well they might, she wouldn't have the option to pack up and be on the next bus out of town, away from Haven and away from Wyatt, for good.

As tempting as the idea was of cutting out of town without having to deal with Wyatt at all, there was no question about her staying. Not really.

It wasn't enough that she didn't have anywhere else to go. She couldn't leave the boys ranch in the lurch. She simply couldn't. It meant too much to too many people, especially all the boys it had helped over the years—and would assist in the future, especially if they were able to keep the larger facility.

Seventy years of helping young men find a better way. She couldn't put her own needs and desires over something as amazing as that.

But more than that, when she stopped to truly examine her feelings, she knew in her heart that she couldn't leave without allowing Wyatt to get to know his son. Merely thinking about staying was more frightening than anything else she'd ever experienced—even reluctantly coming to the decision to leave town alone and pregnant three years ago.

She would have to own up to her choices. All of them, both good and bad.

She'd realized as soon as she'd seen the brokenhearted look on Wyatt's face that she'd been wrong to keep Matty's existence a secret from him. Matty was as much his son as he was hers.

He deserved to know his child. And now he would.

In a way God had made the decision for her, which was probably good, because her record in the decision-making department was deplorable of late.

She had to stay. So she would give Wyatt these two months to get to know Matty, to spend time with him and possibly build a bond as father and son. After that, only the Lord knew what would happen.

She came out of her thoughts to realize the others in Bea's office were still waiting for her answer. She took a deep, cleansing breath and dived in without knowing just how deep the water was.

"Okay. I'll stay."

Chapter Two

Wyatt let out the breath he hadn't even realized he'd been holding. Relief rushed over him like a crisp, cool waterfall.

Carolina was going to stay.

Well—at least she was going to stay for a little while. And although her reasons might have nothing to do with him, he was determined to make it be about him and Matty. Which meant he had exactly two months to convince her she ought to make her permanent home in Haven, so he could be near his son for always. He knew it wouldn't be easy for him to see Carolina on a regular basis, but he would do anything for Matty.

That his initial encounter with Carolina hadn't gone over particularly well was hardly the point. What could she possibly have expected his reaction to be? Even after having an hour to get used to the idea of her arriving in town with their son—a boy he hadn't even known existed—in tow, he still felt like he'd been run over by a freight train, but with effort he'd taken that tornado of emotions and tucked it deep into his heart and out of sight. He was still angry and frustrated, and probably would be for a long time to come, but displaying how he felt wasn't going to help anyone, least of all Matty.

Wyatt had only been half listening to the conversation going on around him. His mind kept wandering to the dark-haired little boy who was probably even now exclaiming in delight over the horses.

Despite Wyatt's hurting heart, he couldn't help but smile at the thought of his son and being a daddy now. He could teach Matty how to ride a horse and buy him his own mount as soon as he learned to balance in the saddle. He would show his precious child everything about the world, introduce him to all the different kinds of farm and domestic animals he vetted and teach him all about life in the country.

One day, when he was all grown up, Matty even might want to become a veterinarian like his father. Wyatt would be proud to pass on his business to his son.

His *son*. That one word made his chest expand until he thought he might burst.

But he was getting a little ahead of himself. Oh, who was he kidding? He was shooting off *way* ahead of himself.

First, he needed to get to know Matty, not to mention give the boy time to get comfortable with him. At some point—hopefully soon—he and Carolina would be able to explain to Matty that Wyatt was his daddy in a way a two-year-old could understand.

He was troubled by one thing. He had no idea how to go about being a good father. As a kid, he hadn't had a real male role model in his life. His parents had worked in a foreign aid office, and Wyatt had been raised solely by Gran.

He realized that while he had all of these idealistic notions about what a father should be, he didn't have a clue what was realistic and practical in everyday life.

It was unnerving to say the least, but no matter how much apprehension he felt inside, nothing would deter Wyatt from knowing his little boy and being part of Matty's life.

A big part.

He only hoped Carolina felt the same way. He was going to move forward with this either way, but it would certainly be easier if she wasn't fighting him at every turn. Did he dare assume that part of her reason for returning to Haven was that she had finally recognized that Wyatt had both the right and the responsibility to be in Matty's life? He knew she'd ostensibly come back to Haven to personally deliver the news of Morton Mason's death, but she could just as easily— actually, even more so—have sent an email to Bea. She hadn't had to come in person.

So maybe there *was* another reason she'd come back to town. Maybe it was for his sake—and Matty's.

Although that didn't explain why she had appeared so startled when she'd first seen him. Was that because he'd caught her off guard?

There were so many questions, and the only way to find the answers was to try to get along with Carolina—and cross his fingers that she would try to get along with him. At this point all he could do was hope for the best and step up for his role in this drama.

"I'm glad we got that all settled up," said the attorney, closing his briefcase with a snap that pulled Wyatt back to the present. "Thank you, Carolina, for agreeing to stay on here in Haven. I expect I speak for the Lone Star Cowboy League and the boys ranch when I say we appreciate your willingness to represent your family legacy at the seventieth-anniversary party. It may make all the difference to us and all the boys who call this place their home."

Carolina nodded. "Of course. I'm happy to do it."

Wyatt didn't think she sounded happy. He thought he still knew her well enough to distinguish the sadness in her voice. The grief.

And the stress.

Well, that made two of them.

Anyway, he really wasn't positive he knew Carolina all that well, if at all. Three years ago, he certainly hadn't anticipated that not only did she not reciprocate his feelings, but she'd run away from them, and while she was pregnant, no less.

No. He sighed inwardly. Three long years had passed between them. The truth was he probably didn't know the *real* Carolina Mason at all.

"We've still got one problem," Gabe said, cutting into Wyatt's thoughts about Carolina and their personal issues. "Even after searching extensively, I haven't been able to find my grandfather. At this point I'm not sure it's going to happen before the anniversary party."

Harold nodded gravely. "That is a problem."

Gabe planted his hat on his head and frowned. "I don't suppose you've got any enlightening letters for me in one of those file folders of yours."

"Actually, now that you mention it, there is a letter."

Gabe's eyes lit up with hope, but Harold's next words quickly doused that flame.

"It's not what you're hoping for. But it is based upon another contingency, and one that you all should know about. Especially you, Gabe. If, upon the morning of the seventieth-anniversary party, all of the men—and ladies," he said, tipping his Stetson to Carolina, "are not present and accounted for, I am to open the letter and read Cyrus's instructions on how to proceed with parceling out the land. I must caution you, it does not look promising. Obviously Cyrus had one thing and one thing only in mind when he wrote his will. So I encourage you to continue doing all you can to try to locate your grandfather before time runs out."

"Believe me, I am," Gabe said, his voice lowering in frustration. "So you're pretty much saying that the land will revert to the developer and half our boys will lose their places at the ranch."

Wyatt cringed in sympathy for his friend. Talk about a tough position to be in. He wouldn't want to be in Gabe's shoes right now, with the entire future of the boys ranch now dependent on his ability to find a man who had disappeared off the planet years ago.

Harold's steady gaze met Gabe's. "I'm not saying 'tis or 'tisn't. We won't know until I open the letter on the day of the party."

"At which point it will be too late for us to try to change things," Bea said with a groan, swiping a tired hand down her face.

"And that is exactly why we can't let that happen," Gabe said determinedly. "We've come too far to see this endeavor fall apart now. Somehow, I've got to find my grandfather and make this right."

"I know I'm new to all of this," Carolina said hesitantly, "but please feel free to call upon me if I can be of any assistance. I don't know what, if anything, I can do to help you, Gabe, but you've got my support any way you need it."

"Yeah," added Wyatt. "Same goes for me."

Wyatt's eyes met Carolina's and their eyes locked. They had their own set of problems to wade through, and the water was deep and murky.

Bea knocked her fist twice on the desk and stood, effectively ending the meeting. Folks started shuffling out of the office. Wyatt lingered so he could walk out directly after Carolina.

"I want to get to know my son," he said as soon as they cleared the building. "Spend some quality time with him."

The gaze Carolina flashed him was a combination of annoyance, frustration, hesitation and panic.

It was the hesitation that hit him hardest.

What? She didn't think he could handle Matty? That he didn't have it in him to be a father?

He frowned, all of his muscles tensing in response. He pressed his own fears aside in favor of feeling downright insulted by her attitude.

She didn't trust him with his own son? Granted, he knew nothing about children, but he'd been caring for animals all his life. He could be gentle.

If anything, *she* was the one who'd proven herself untrustworthy.

"Look. Not today," she said at last.

He clenched his fists to keep from barking out a rebuttal. At the moment, she was holding all the cards, and he felt entirely powerless.

"When, then?"

She sighed deeply, sounding bone weary. "I don't know, Wyatt. I just got into town. I haven't even set up house yet at my uncle's cabin, just a bunch of boxes in the living room and mattresses on the floor for Matty and me. It's going to take a while. And I'm still looking for a job."

"You're a registered nurse. You ought to be able to find employment around here easily enough. Have you checked at the hospital yet?"

Her eyes narrowed and she pursed her lips for a moment before answering. "Like I said—I'm looking. I'll let you know when I've found something suitable."

She sounded as if she doubted her own training and competence. Which was ridiculous. He might not be too thrilled with her personally right now, but he knew her to be an excellent nurse. She'd taken the very best care of his gran in her time of need, so much so that Gran had refused another nurse after Carolina had left.

Several other nurses, actually. No one could live up to the bar Carolina had set.

Surely any nearby medical facility would pick her up in a second. Nurses were always in shortage, especially good ones.

Maybe she was just trying to throw their conversation off track. He wasn't going to let that happen.

"Fine. I understand that you need to have the opportunity to work out all the details of your move to Haven. But I want an exact date and time when you will bring Matty to meet me, and it has to be soon."

"I said I don't know," she shot back, sounding thoroughly exasperated.

His dander rose. If she was irritated, that was all on her. He wasn't being unreasonable in asking for time to get to know his son.

Carolina blew out a breath. "I promise I'll call you just as soon as I get settled in. I suppose we can plan to set up a playdate at the park or something."

His eyebrows rose.

A *date*? Really?

If she thought he'd be going on *any* kind of date with her, she was sadly mistaken.

She looked at him questioningly and then burst into nervous laughter.

"I'm not asking you out, Wyatt. A playdate is when kids get together at the park. In this case, it will be you and your son. You can push him on the swing or play in the sandbox."

"Oh." He felt deflated, somehow. What was up with that? He knew he would have a great time with Matty, but—

"I have to go get Matty. I'm sure that Katie is rethinking her offer to watch him right about now. He can really be a handful when he gets excited, and I'm guessing he's over the moon about his first introduction to horses."

That should have been him. Yet another first that got away from him. Wyatt was determined it wouldn't happen again.

"But you'll call me, right?" Wyatt reiterated, knowing he was pushing her but beyond caring. "Soon?"

He wasn't sure *he* was ready to take on a handful of two-year-old energy any more than Katie was, but he would have to be ready. He would make himself ready.

He was a father now.

This was pointless.

Why was she even bothering to fill out an eight-page employment application at Haven's local nursing home and hospice? Carolina already knew she wasn't going to get the job. Probably not even an interview. She barely dared hope, and yet she had to try.

Thankfully, she didn't have to worry about Matty while she searched in vain for employment in the medical field. She and Katie were becoming good friends, and Katie had offered to watch Matty at the boys ranch office while Carolina went job hunting, as futile as it no doubt would be.

When had she become a cup-half-empty type of person?

Probably when her cup drained to its dregs and she hadn't seen a drop of liquid to fill it again.

No amount of previous background or additional skill sets could overcome the thorn in her side—or her knee, to be more accurate. She'd already been turned down by every other medical facility in the area, for the same reason she'd lost her job at the hospital in Colorado.

The need to be able to catch a fainting patient or respond to a slip and fall never even used to be a consideration for Carolina, much less a problem. She'd always kept herself in good shape with a gym membership that she actually used.

But then she'd made the mistake of going on a weekend ski trip with her roommate, Geena Walker. In hindsight, why she'd thought she ought to learn how to ski was beyond her comprehension. To be honest, she hadn't even really been all that interested in the sport. At the time it had seemed like a good idea, a fun way to take a short vacation and spend a weekend trying something new. She was living in Colorado, after all. Snow meant skiing, right?

She'd taken an hour's worth of quick instructional lessons, even though it was humiliating to be in a class of half-pint children who effortlessly picked up the necessary skills ten times faster than she did.

Afterward, she'd successfully skied the bunny slope

a couple of times and *thought* she was ready to tackle a beginner's run.

It was easy, Geena had assured her. Simple as pie, she'd said. All Carolina had to do was ski from one side of the hill to the other in a diagonal fashion, slowly zigzagging her way down the mountainside.

Her first clue should have been when she slipped and nearly fell getting off the lift at the top of the mountain. But she'd chalked that up to being off balance and hit the slope.

Literally.

Neither Geena nor her ski instructor had mentioned what Carolina was supposed to do when her skis became crossed in the front and she went flipping head over heels for who knew how many yards down the snow-packed ski run.

All she remembered was not being able to breathe and feeling as if she were drowning in the snow, blinded by the icy white powder that had stolen inside her supposedly leak-proof goggles.

The next thing she knew, an entire crew of very young men sporting bright red jackets with white crosses embroidered on them surrounded her, insisting that they put her on a backboard and place a brace around her neck. She'd tried to tell them that she was a nurse and it wasn't necessary to overkill the situation, but they apparently wanted to practice their rescuing skills on her.

As if that wasn't bad enough, there was the humiliating turn down the hillside with all six of her escorts, while the regular skiers—the coordinated ones who didn't make themselves into human avalanches—watched on with interest.

As it happened, her back and neck were fine. Her left knee, however, not so much.

Then had come the surgery, rehabilitation and getting summarily dismissed from her job because of her inability to lift fifty pounds. And those doctor's orders weren't going anywhere any time soon.

Nope. They were permanent.

Which meant she was in permanent trouble.

Bringing her thoughts back to the present, she sighed under her breath and scribbled her references on the employment application. Even if she already knew what the answer would be, she had to try.

Now that she had Wyatt breathing down her neck to spend time with Matty, it was more important than ever that she provide her son with a stable home, not only for his sake but to prove to Wyatt that she was able to make it on her own as a single mother.

That she didn't need his help.

Though she had started with every medical facility in the area, she didn't have time to be picky about where she worked. Even though she owned her great-uncle's cabin free and clear, she and Matty still needed to eat, and she had to pay to keep the lights on and put gas in the car.

Unfortunately for her, she wasn't really qualified for any other kind of work besides nursing. All of her education and expertise were the medical field. Retail or fast food might be an option in a pinch, but they didn't pay enough for her and Matty to subsist on in the long run. She needed a living wage, not a teenager's part-time after-school job. She supposed she could try to switch gears and become a medical receptionist, but her typing skills were atrocious and she'd never quite understood the medical filing system in the business classes she'd had to take in college.

Carolina closed her eyes and said a silent prayer. She'd been praying a lot more often recently, asking the Lord for guidance, not only in her career, but in her life. And now, more than anything, she needed direction on what she should do about her relationship—or lack of one—with Wyatt Harrow.

She was just about out of options.

Please, dear Lord, don't make me have to beg.

Carolina was handing in her application at the front desk when, to her surprise, she spotted Wyatt out of the corner of her eye. She would have recognized his long, confident gait anywhere, not to mention his handsome profile.

Though he'd come in through the main glass doors of the nursing home, he clearly hadn't seen her. He was walking down a hallway with his head down and his hands crammed into the front pockets of his jeans.

Even at a distance, and even though she couldn't see the expression on his face, Carolina could tell he was troubled from his posture alone. She'd seen that look before, when his gran had been having so much trouble.

It was none of her business. She should leave now, before he turned around and recognized her. That would be the sensible thing to do. The smart thing.

But her days of doing the sensible thing were long behind her.

Instead, curiosity got the better of her and she followed him down the hallway, taking care to stay a few steps behind him and ready to duck into a doorway if he looked back.

Happily, he didn't. He took a right, then an immediate left, and then he disappeared into a room on the right side of the hallway.

Carolina paused. What Wyatt was doing had nothing to do with her, but—

She had to look.

She just had to.

She continued down the hall straight past where Wyatt had gone, quickening her pace as she glanced into the room. She felt silly, like a teenage girl stalking her first crush around the halls in high school.

When she saw Wyatt sitting in a chair next to an old woman's bedside, her heart swelled and then melted like warm chocolate.

Of course.

Wyatt was visiting his gran. No wonder he'd looked so burdened. Eva Harrow had clearly gone downhill from when Carolina had last seen her.

Carolina was more than a little bit familiar with Wyatt's grandmother, having been the old woman's home nurse for several months three years ago, just before Carolina had left Haven.

That was how she'd gotten to know Wyatt and when she had fallen in love with him. He clearly cared so much for his grandmother—such an attractive trait in a man.

Eva had accidentally plunged down a set of porch steps and had broken her hip. At that time in her life, it had become clear that her dementia was slowly overtaking her. Wyatt had needed Carolina's round-the-clock help to keep Eva safe, but at that time he wouldn't even consider putting her in a nursing home where she could get the kind of medical assistance she needed on a more permanent basis.

Eva was also—indirectly—the reason Matty had

been conceived. One evening a few months into Carolina's work for the Harrows, Wyatt's gran had taken a sudden turn for the worse and spiked a high fever. She had ended up in the ICU with pneumonia and little chance of recovering. In his grief, Wyatt had turned to Carolina for comfort.

Carolina breathed deeply as memories flooded over her. Eva had managed to fight off a bad infection, although it was touch and go there for a while. She was one of the strongest people Carolina had ever had the privilege of knowing, but the woman had been ninety-six at the time of her injury and there was only so much recovery she could make, especially considering how quickly her dementia was changing her world for the worse.

But Wyatt hadn't been ready to let her go then—or even now, apparently. Her heart welled as she watched him interact with her. He was holding Eva's hand and speaking in a loud, animated tone of voice. Carolina was fairly certain from Eva's blank-eyed, slack-featured expression that she did not recognize Wyatt at all.

Still, she appeared to be listening to him intently and wasn't pulling away from his touch, so it was at least the semblance of a good day for her.

"Did I tell you about the donkey Johnny and I rescued? You remember I told you about Johnny, right? He's the teenager I'm mentoring. Anyway, the whole thing with the donkey was so funny. We pulled him out of the mud bog he was stuck in, and I kid you not, Gran, that animal grinned from ear to ear when we freed him. A donkey smiling. Can you imagine? And you should have heard him braying a thank-you."

Wyatt laughed at his own story, then paused, his expression drawing serious.

"Johnny really means a lot to me. I feel like I can help him, you know?" He scoffed and shook his head. "Life doesn't always work out the way we plan, huh, Gran? I thought by now I would be overseas somewhere, helping people out there, but instead I—well, there's Johnny. And you, of course. I'd never leave you. And—" Wyatt's voice caught in his throat and he paused.

And then he glanced up.

His gaze locked with Carolina's, and her adrenaline spiked, rushing through her.

She'd been made.

It was her own fault, of course, for standing in the middle of the doorway gawking at him, eavesdropping on his time with his gran. But that didn't stop embarrassment from flooding her cheeks.

"Carolina."

"Eh?" Eva said, clearly confused as she turned her head to look at Carolina.

"I—er—was just passing by and I thought I heard your voice." Carolina cringed inwardly. Now there was a lame excuse if she'd ever heard one.

"You were just strolling through the nursing home for no reason?"

"Well, no. Not exactly."

"What, then? *Exactly?*" He paused and narrowed his gaze on her, appraising her. "You weren't following me around, now, were you?"

She froze and she was sure she was gaping.

He laughed.

She let out a breath, glad he'd only been kidding about the idea of her following him around.

Even if, technically, she kind of was.

She didn't want to have to explain to him that she was still looking for work. It was so incredibly important that he perceive her as having a stable, successful life, even if in reality her existence was anything but. She didn't want to give herself away.

"Mind your manners, young man," Eva scolded. She shook a finger at Wyatt and then turned her gaze on Carolina. "Did you bring me any water?"

"I'd be happy to get you a glass of water." Her emotions overflowed with love for Eva. It broke her heart that she'd ever had to leave the woman in the first place. But what choice had she had?

And worse, she'd assumed that Eva would have passed on by now. She hadn't even asked Wyatt about her. Guilt singed her at the thought.

Wyatt caught her eyes and briefly shook his head. "I have a case of bottled water in the trunk," he explained. "I always fill up her mini fridge when I visit. I have to unscrew all the lids so she can open them herself whenever she gets thirsty."

"I'm thirsty," Eva repeated, although she didn't appear to be following Wyatt and Carolina's conversation.

"See if there's a bottle left in the fridge," Wyatt suggested. "Gran, I've brought you your favorite kind of chocolate. Dark chocolate truffles. Do you want to see?"

While Wyatt helped his grandmother unwrap a piece of candy, Carolina went to the fridge for a bottle of water. She took off the lid and handled the bottle to Eva.

"How long has she been living here?"

Wyatt's brow lowered. "Since just after you disappeared. I couldn't find a home-care nurse she liked after you left. She compared every one of them to you, and then she would scare 'em all off within the first week or so."

He wasn't pointing a finger of blame at her, although he had every right to do just that, but he appeared troubled by the memory, and Carolina was sorry she'd brought it up.

"Her one hundredth birthday is near the end of this month," he said, still looking disturbed but trying to move on. "I've been thinking about throwing her a big birthday bash so all her friends and neighbors can wish her a happy one, but I'm not sure I should. I can never anticipate if she's going to have a good day. She probably wouldn't recognize any of the guests, and it might agitate her instead of making her happy."

"Oh, you should do it," Carolina enthused, unable to help herself. "Living to be one hundred years old is an enormous accomplishment and it should be celebrated, not only by her, but by her friends. Even if she doesn't recognize anyone, I'm sure she'll enjoy knowing so many people care about her. I'll help you plan the party if you'd like."

His jaw tightened and he shook his head. "How would you know what Gran would like?" he snapped and then quickly lowered his voice when Eva frowned at him. "You left us—*her*—high and dry."

He might as well have slapped her face. His words had the same impact.

"No. You're right. I'm sorry. I'm sticking my nose where it doesn't belong. Forget I said anything."

For all she knew, he might be able to forget about what she'd said, and maybe even forget about her, Carolina thought, her gut tightening in misery.

But she wouldn't. Three years ago, when she'd left Haven, she'd walked away from her heart, her home and her life.

Now she had returned, only to find her life immeasurably more complicated.

Was there anything left for her here?

Chapter Three

Wyatt wasn't convinced he should have welcomed Carolina into the room. Maybe he should have tossed her out on her ear. He wasn't even quite clear on why she was there in the first place. He couldn't believe she would take to following him around. More likely that she was here applying for a job.

He watched her speaking to Gran, rearranging the old woman's pillows and locating the television remote for her. Carolina was good at her job. No—she was excellent. Gran was relaxed and responsive, better than she usually was around Wyatt or any of the other nurses at the facility.

Wyatt hated the disease that had eroded his precious gran's mind, leaving her perpetually confused about not only where she was, but who she was. That was the nature of the beast. It didn't seem fair that his intelligent, lively gran could be reduced to this shell of a woman.

He visited her once a week, on Monday mornings. At first, after he'd made the painful decision to place Gran in the nursing home, he'd tried to visit every other day or so. But more often than not, his appearance upset her or sent her into a flurry of mindless activity, so he'd eventually lessened his visits. It hurt his heart, but this wasn't about him.

Most of the time when he visited, Gran didn't recognize him at all. Sometimes she thought he was Grandpa George, or Wyatt's father, Ian. Occasionally, she was completely lucid and knew exactly who he was. Sometimes, like today, she had no idea what his name was but sensed he was connected to her in some way.

And then there were the times he hated the most, when his presence disturbed her, or she would beg for him to take her home with him. He didn't know whether or not to be thankful that she recognized him less and less frequently. He didn't like to see her unhappy.

Always, it was an emotional roller coaster for Wyatt. He knew he had been blessed to have his grandmother with him as long as he had, but the thought of the world without her in it still saddened and pained him.

"Does she like any specific soap operas or game shows?" Carolina asked, pointing the remote toward the television and clicking through the channels at random.

"She likes those court shows," he replied. "You know, the ones with the judges pounding their gavels, where people fight over stupid stuff?"

"Right." Carolina turned to a channel where a blackrobed judge was sitting behind a bench barking out a sentence to a miserable plaintiff and an elated defendant.

"There you go, Eva," Carolina said, her voice soft and affectionate. "How's that for you? The judges are funny, aren't they?"

Gran reached out and patted Carolina's cheek. "You are such a sweetheart."

Wyatt's stomach tightened. He used to believe that, too. It galled him to think he could be so wrong about a person, especially as close as he'd thought he'd been to Carolina.

He must be the worst judge of character ever. He should just stick to the animals. At least with them a man always knew where he stood.

Animals were loyal.

But Carolina?

She'd certainly put on a good show for him three years ago, when they'd been dating and when he'd believed he was in love with her. She was a consummate actress—he could say that about her. He'd bought her performance hook, line and sinker, believing that she was the sweetest, kindest, most beautiful woman in the world.

Believing she was the only woman in the world for him. That they were meant to be together. That he wanted to put a ring on her finger and make his love for her permanent.

That their love would last forever.

What love?

Had she ever loved him, or had it all been his imagination and a desperate need for her to feel as he did?

He still thought she was beautiful, at least on the outside. That hadn't changed. How could it?

But as for the rest of it? That woman had never existed at all, or else she wouldn't have disappeared without one word to him when she got pregnant with his child.

What kind of a person even did that?

Not the same woman who was carrying on a quiet

conversation with his gran. It was hard to reconcile what he was seeing before him.

Watching Carolina now, it was as if the years had fallen away. Sweet, sensitive Carolina had always been able to calm Gran, had always appeared to know exactly what the old woman required even when Gran couldn't voice her needs. Carolina knew how to react to any given situation without losing her composure.

Those qualities were what had made her such a good nurse, and those qualities were among those that had initially caught his eye, and eventually his heart.

He and Carolina had laughed together, cried together, and in a moment of deepest grief, they had ultimately found temporary solace in each other's arms. And while Wyatt hadn't intended for things to happen in that order, their night together had only strengthened his resolve, solidified the love between them—or at least that's what he'd thought at the time.

He had already had the ring and had been ready to propose to her. Even before that night, he'd known he wanted to spend his life with her.

He could have made it right—for all three of them—if only she would have let him. If only she would have stayed. If only she had been honest with him from the beginning.

Wyatt scoffed softly and stood abruptly, striding to the window overlooking a tree-lined greenbelt. It didn't make any sense. Not one bit of it. There wasn't anything rational about the things Carolina had done and had failed to do, before or since she had left him three years ago.

There was no way to reconcile the woman he'd thought he'd loved, the one who even now obviously cared deeply for his gran, with the woman who had callously left him in the lurch without a thought to how he would feel. Without considering that he had rights and responsibilities as a dad.

Or that Matty needed a father.

"Why are you here?" he asked without turning. He wasn't entirely certain what he was asking. Why was she here today, in Gran's room, for starters? But in truth it was so much more than one thing. Nothing was that simple anymore.

Was this visit about Gran? Had Carolina somehow discovered this was where Wyatt had placed Gran when he could no longer take care of her? Was she here to visit her? Was it purely an accident that she'd encountered Wyatt?

But no. She'd looked totally stricken—*guilty*— when he'd first spotted her in the doorway, silently observing him with Gran. Her face had turned twenty shades of red at least. She'd looked just as shocked when her gaze shifted to his grandmother as it had when their eyes had met.

But if this wasn't about Gran, then what was it, really?

"I was filling out an employment application," she replied reluctantly.

"Oh?" He swiveled on his heel, leaned his hip on the windowsill and crossed his arms. "I figured you'd probably go for a job at the hospital. I'm sure it pays better."

Color rose in her face once again, flaming her cheeks. What was she not telling him? Her unspoken words hung in the air between them until she dropped her gaze.

"I don't know why I bothered coming out here today. They won't hire me, any more than the hospital."

"What? Why not?" Whatever else Carolina was or wasn't, she was a competent, compassionate nurse. She'd been in the top of her class in college and had an outstanding résumé.

"I don't meet the physical qualifications."

Now that he *really* didn't believe. Carolina was petite, but she was in perfect physical condition. She had a runner's slim stature and she'd been a regular at the gym in all the time that he'd known her. A man couldn't be breathing and not notice her shapely form.

"I trashed my knee in a skiing accident a few months back. I had to have surgery on it, and it's still liable to give way on me at any moment. I can't trust it, and neither can a prospective employer. Doctor's orders that I don't lift too much weight. I can't blame the facilities for turning me away."

"I'm sorry to hear that," he said, and meant it. "Are you in any pain?"

She smiled, but it was sad and forlorn, matching the anguish in her eyes. "Sometimes. But more than the physical pain is not being able to do what I love to do. Nursing, not skiing," she qualified.

He chuckled, but his mind was spinning, trying to process this new information. If she couldn't find a job, then she couldn't support Matty. She wouldn't even be able to support *herself.*

Wyatt might not like what she had done to him, but she was still the mother of his child, and there was no question that he would take care of her and Matty, as much as they needed for as long as they needed.

"How can I help?"

She squared her shoulders and raised her chin. "I don't need any assistance from you."

He scrubbed a hand through his hair. There was pride, and then there was sheer stubbornness.

"Look, if you need some money or something to help you get by…"

"No." Carolina spoke so forcefully that Gran looked away from her show to eye both of them dubiously.

Carolina lowered her voice. "Thank you for offering, but I don't need your help," she repeated. "I've been taking care of Matty since he was born, and I'll do it now. I'll find a job. You don't have to worry about us. Matty and I will be just fine."

She was face-to-face with him now, close enough that he could feel her breath fanning his cheek.

He wanted to be angry at her words, at the callous way she'd dismissed him from her and Matty's lives. But despite his best efforts, his rebellious senses bolted to life, as if they'd been lying dormant for years. Every awareness amplified, from the breezy, floral scent of her perfume to the way he knew she would fit perfectly under the crook of his shoulder if he were to move forward just the tiniest bit.

He took a big step backward.

Was he *insane*?

This was the woman who had run off with his son. What he should be thinking about, what was imperative, was that Matty—and by extension, Carolina—had what they needed, not only to survive, but to thrive.

The problem was convincing Carolina he wasn't offering charity. It was his responsibility to look after them, but he was fairly certain she wouldn't see it that way.

"Promise me you won't wait too long before asking." His voice was unusually husky. "And that if you or Matty are ever in need—of anything, Carolina, and I mean that—you'll come to me first."

Her eyes widened and she pinched her lips into a tight line. She shook her head and reached for her purse, which she'd set on Gran's nightstand when she entered.

"I assure you that won't be necessary." She flashed a tense smile for Gran's sake and gave her a quick peck on the cheek. "I'll be back to visit you soon, Eva."

The next moment she was gone, without so much as another word to Wyatt.

How fittingly reminiscent of her.

"Thank you anyway, Dr. Delgado. I appreciate you calling me back." Carolina ended the call, sighed deeply and clasped her cell phone—one item she wouldn't be able to afford after the end of this month—tightly to her chest.

She squeezed her eyes closed, but tears surfaced despite her best efforts, making slow, silent streams down her cheeks. She slipped her cell phone into the back pocket of her jeans and groaned in frustration.

Thankfully Matty was absorbed in the preschool programming he was watching on television, counting along with the colorful aliens who were surreptitiously teaching him math skills in the form of entertainment.

Carolina sniffed and wiped her wet cheeks with her palm.

That was it, then. Her last hope for local employment in the medical field. Dr. Delgado had let her down kindly, but he already had two long-term employees, a registered nurse and a physician's assistant. Doc had wished Carolina well but had offered no further suggestions on where she might look for a job.

She was out of options. She was out of money.

And she was out of time.

She was grateful she owned Uncle Mort's cabin free and clear, but he hadn't had much else in the way of assets, and now was dipping into her meager savings account every time she visited the grocery store or wrote a check for utilities. Her unemployment benefits didn't begin to cover their necessities. Matty had hit another growth spurt, and all of his jeans were inches too short at the ankles. She had been looking around for viable day care options for him, but she didn't want to skimp on that expense. Matty deserved the very best care available. And next year he'd be in preschool, with a whole new set of challenges.

Not that she had a need for day care until she managed to find employment. She scoffed aloud.

Lord, what would You have me do?

She had no choice but to stay in Haven, at least for the next couple of months, and it wasn't as if she really had any better options elsewhere. She was as stuck in the mud as that donkey Wyatt had been telling his gran about.

After checking on Matty, Carolina tucked one leg under her on a kitchen chair and opened her laptop, a spiral notebook and a ballpoint pen beside her to make a record of her online applications. She was determined to check every local internet job board for postings.

At this point she was willing to consider anything. She didn't care how overqualified she might be. Beggars couldn't afford to be choosers, especially when that particular beggar had a growing boy to care for.

A half hour later, having found not a single lead or typed in a single application, she put Matty down for his afternoon nap, lingering to gaze at his sweet face, so pure and innocent in sleep.

Matty didn't deserve any of this. She had already made so many wrong choices during his young life. Carolina wanted to offer her son the world, but at this point she could barely offer him his next meal.

Promise you won't wait too long before asking.

Wyatt's words echoed through her mind, taunting her.

If Matty is ever in need, come to me first.

No.

How could she even be considering taking Wyatt up on his offer?

But then again, how could she not?

If she only had to worry about herself, she'd starve before she asked for a handout. But it wasn't her she was thinking about.

It was Matty.

Even if she went door to door among Haven businesses trying to find a job—as it appeared she would have to do, since she had found no leads online—it would take her time to connect with something, and another couple of weeks after that to get her first paycheck.

She was desperate enough to consider anything, up to and including flipping hamburgers or waitressing at the local truck stop. But she wasn't entirely convinced even the fast-food joints around town would be interested in hiring her.

Wyatt had a steady, good-paying job in Haven, and had since the day he'd graduated from veterinary school. He hadn't said anything about a wife, and he wasn't wearing a wedding ring, so presumably he didn't have a family to care for, other than his gran. He probably had plenty of extra savings to fall back on.

More than she did, anyway.

He was Matty's father.

And he had offered.

But could she do it?

The moment she'd arrived back in Haven and had come face-to-face with Wyatt, she'd been in a perpetual cycle of eating humble pie.

Choking on it, more like.

What was one more interaction in the big scheme of things? If Wyatt truly wanted to be a part of Matty's life, then providing for some of his physical needs was as good a start as any.

With a sigh, Carolina leaned over the toddler bed to brush a kiss over the soft skin of Matty's forehead.

She couldn't even believe she was seriously considering asking Wyatt for help. She was *not* a charity case—and if she was going to do this, she would make absolutely certain that Wyatt understood she wasn't asking for her own good. Nor would she take a single thing for herself.

This was all about Matty.

She slumped back into the chair at the kitchen table and wiggled her mouse to open the screen again, hoping beyond hope that in the five minutes it had taken to put Matty down for his nap, the perfect job might have somehow suddenly popped onto the top of the employment board.

It hadn't.

Which meant she had no choice but to call Wyatt.

She fished her cell phone out of the back pocket of her jeans, unlocked the screen and paused, staring at the background picture for a long moment.

It was a photo she'd taken of Matty when her previous roommate Geena's then boyfriend and now husband had given Matty his Colorado Rockies baseball hat. Matty had been grinning from ear to ear as the bill of the oversize black-and-purple cap dipped low over one eye.

After the first picture, Geena had then turned the hat backward. At that moment, Carolina remembered being struck by how much Matty looked like his father. Wyatt often wore a backward-facing baseball cap when he was out tending to the animals he vetted.

Her stomach knotted as she thumbed through her contact list to where Wyatt's cell phone number was located. Wyatt was no longer first on her quick-dial list, but though she'd considered doing it many times, she'd never quite been able to bring herself to delete his number entirely.

She was a sentimental fool.

She sniffed softly and shook her head. There was no sense putting off the inevitable.

Wyatt's phone rang four times before he picked up. Carolina was just about to end the call when she heard his voice. She figured he'd probably seen her name on his caller ID and decided he didn't want to speak with her just then. Or maybe at all. And this wasn't the sort of conversation she could leave as a message.

"Carolina?"

Hearing her name on Wyatt's lips jarred her. She gulped in surprise and nearly punched the end button.

"Yes. It's m-me." She stammered to a halt, trying to gather her thoughts.

"How are you settling in?" he asked when she didn't immediately continue.

It was a leading question in any number of ways.

She let out her breath. "Um—that's why I'm calling, actually."

There. She'd said it.

"Great. So when can I see Matty?"

It took her a moment to realize he was referring to her promise to call him once she was settled in, in order to set up a playdate.

She was *so* not ready.

"Actually, I was wondering if I could talk to you about something."

A lengthy pause followed and Carolina's throat hitched.

"Sure. Okay. What's up?"

It hurt to release the air from her lungs, like breathing frost on a cold day. "It's not really something I want to discuss over the phone. Would it be okay if I meet you at your office?"

"Well, all right. I guess so. I'm out on a house call right now, but I should be back in the office in an hour. Will that be okay for you?"

"Yes, that will actually work out great. That will give me some time to find someone to watch Matty for me while I'm visiting with you."

"You're not bringing him with you?" His clipped voice lowered.

"Not this time. Please, Wyatt. I need to speak to you alone. I promise we'll set something up with Matty, but not right now."

"In an hour, then." Wyatt ended the call without so much as a goodbye.

Carolina stared at her cell phone's orange screen flashing Call Ended and sighed.

This wasn't going to go well. He was already upset

with her, and what she was about to tell him was only going to make things worse.

If only she had any other options...

But she didn't.

She phoned Katie, who cheerfully agreed to drop by and watch Matty while Carolina conducted what she had nicknamed her *unfortunate business*. It was better than, say, *begging*. She was appreciative of her friend, who was always ready to pitch in without asking too many questions. When she got back on her feet, she'd have to buy Katie a nice bouquet of flowers or something as a thank-you gift.

Forty-five minutes later, Carolina was waiting outside Wyatt's office, rubbing her suddenly clammy palms against the denim of her blue jeans.

Wyatt opened the door before she could knock, his expression a composite of sharp planes and hard lines. He stepped out of the doorway and gestured her inside.

"Sorry about the mess," he apologized as he followed her through the door. "My administrative assistant moved away about six months ago and somehow I haven't gotten around to hiring a new one. I thought I might have—" he paused "—moved on by now. Started an office elsewhere."

So he was still planning to leave town. Carolina had interpreted his conversation with his gran to mean he still had plans abroad, but here was definite confirmation.

Which only served to complicate matters even worse. She had no idea what to do with Wyatt's relationship with Matty. She only knew she didn't want her son to be hurt, as she had been by her own father, a man who was out of her life more than he was in. He'd pop in for a weekend or two, take her out someplace fun so she'd think well of him, and then disappear for months. She often thought it would have been better for her had he simply not been there at all.

"Please, sit," he said, plucking a pile of file folders off a metal folding chair.

Wyatt's office was no more than an offshoot of the barn on his home property, where he kept not only his own animals, but any under his care who needed close observation. The L-shaped cherrywood desk fit into the back corner, flanked on one side by a metal filing cabinet and on the other by a printer.

Stacks of papers and invoices covered every flat surface in the room. It looked like he hadn't filed since his administrative assistant had left.

He lifted his Stetson and slicked a hand back through his black hair.

"I had no idea I would have to deal with so much paperwork when I became a vet. It looks like I should have minored in accounting. I keep meaning to get through this mess, but every time I try, I get called away on an emergency. Or I decide I'd rather take the day off and stream a show on television," he joked.

Her forced chuckle sounded like a witch's cackle and she cut it off short.

He took a seat on a swivel chair that looked as if it had seen better days.

"So what's up?" He leaned forward and rested his forearms on his knees, clasping his hands in front of him. "Is Matty faring all right with the move? I know it can be a little disconcerting to find yourself in new surroundings with a bunch of strangers."

"Yes, he's—" Carolina began, but then she shook her head and blew out a breath. "No. He's not fine."

Wyatt jerked to his feet, concern clouding his features. He looked ready to do—something. What? Climb aboard his trusty white steed and ride in to save the day?

Unfortunately, that was exactly what she was about to ask him to do.

"Wait. There's no cause for worry." She held up her hands and waved him back to his seat. "I'm sorry. This isn't coming out right. There's nothing wrong with Matty. That is—"

Her sentence drifted off into silence. This was *way* harder than she'd anticipated, and she'd already been certain it was going to be excruciatingly painful.

"I haven't been able to find a job," she forced out. "And it's not for want of looking."

She dropped her gaze. She just couldn't stand to look into Wyatt's eyes and admit she was a failure as a mom. To see the *I told you so* in his stare.

"I see." He leaned back and crossed his arms.

"Employment as a nurse, I mean. I'm still actively looking for something—anything, at this point, really—and I'm sure it won't be long before a job of some sort comes up, but in the meantime—"

"You'd like me to help you support Matty."

Wyatt could certainly be blunt when he wanted to be. She felt like he'd just stabbed her in the heart.

Repeatedly.

"Carolina." His voice was surprisingly tender. She didn't know what she had expected.

Anger. Frustration. Disgust, even.

Just not this.

She couldn't handle the gentleness that made him so good as a vet. It was the one emotion she had no armor strong enough to resist.

He tipped up her chin with his index finger.

"I will give Matty—and you—whatever you need."

"Don't worry about me," she said, her stubborn streak rising despite knowing that this whole meeting depended on her remaining humble and taking whatever Wyatt dished out.

"No, Carolina. That's not how this goes. I'm going to help both of you, any way I can. I have total confidence that you'll find a decent job and get back on your feet in no time."

"You do?" she asked through a dry throat.

"I do. But whether or not you're employed, I am Matty's father. I have both a right and a responsibility to contribute to his support, financially and in every other way."

"I never meant for you—"

"To find out I had a son?" he cut in brusquely.

"That's not what I was going to say."

"Good. Then it's settled."

He crouched down before the bottom drawer of the file cabinet and opened it. She couldn't see what he was doing, but there were several metallic clicks and bumps.

After a moment, he stood up and turned around, his hand now full of hundred-dollar bills. Carolina guessed he held close to two thousand dollars.

Her eyes widened, and she was fairly certain she was gaping. When she had asked for help, she hadn't meant two months of total support. A small loan was all.

"Wyatt, I can't take this."

"Of course you can. It's only a couple thousand dollars. I'm sure I'm further behind on my child support payments than that."

"No. You've got this all wrong. I don't expect you to try to make up for—"

He held up a hand and laughed drily.

"That was a joke. Not a very good one, apparently."

He reached for her hand and tucked the bills into her palm, closing her fingers around the money. When he pulled back, his elbow hit a stack of invoices, sending papers floating to the floor in every direction.

Wyatt groaned. "Oh, great. And wouldn't you know those were the ones I already had in a semblance of order."

Despite herself, Carolina chuckled.

"I think maybe you need a little help."

"More than a little," he agreed, and then his eyes lit up and he cocked his head at her.

He paused for so long that she shifted uncomfortably under his gaze.

"Can you file?"

"Can't everyone?" She raised her eyebrows. "Unless you're talking about medical filing, which is a whole other thing. But regular filing? That's just a matter of knowing your ABCs, right? And I've been consistently practicing them with Matty since the time he was six months old. I'm officially a pro."

"You're hired."

"I'm—" she sputtered. "Excuse me, what?"

"You're hired," he repeated, his grin widening. "It's the perfect solution."

"What's perfect?" She wasn't following his train of thought at *all*, and from the gratified expression on Wyatt's face, she wasn't certain she wanted to know *what* he was thinking.

"The answer to both of our dilemmas. I need help organizing my pathetic excuse for an office, and you need a job. I'll pay you the going rate for an administrative assistant and you won't be accepting charity."

"Yes, but—"

She'd been going to protest that she was thoroughly unqualified for the position, but hadn't she just this morning decided she would take whatever she could get? And really, how hard could it be?

In truth, working as his administrative assistant wasn't a half-bad idea. If it were anyone except Wyatt, she knew she would be jumping all over this opportunity.

But it *was* Wyatt who was offering.

Could she really work alongside him as if they had no past together? As if they didn't share a son?

Could she manage the emotions she knew would sneak up on her when she wasn't paying attention?

"I'll sweeten the pot." He looked enthusiastic, maybe even a little smug.

Her eyes narrowed on him. He was making this way too easy for her.

"How?"

"Have you made arrangements for Matty's day care yet?" He crossed his arms and leaned his hip against the desk, looking casually at ease.

Which was the exact opposite of how she was feeling right now. Her shoulders tightened as he pointed out yet another of her recent failings.

"I'm working on it," she admitted cautiously.

Could his grin *get* any wider?

Her frown deepened, directly mirroring the spreading of his smile.

"You can bring Matty with you to the office. You won't have child care expenses, and I'll be able to spend some time getting to know my son better. What do you say, Carolina?"

He rocked forward in anticipation of her answer. He looked as hopeful as a boy on his first fishing trip, holding his pole and waiting for a bite.

What could she say?

Wyatt deserved to know his son. She knew that. But how could she protect Matty's heart if Wyatt was ultimately going to leave him behind?

On the other hand, she needed the job and someone to watch Matty. In his determination to get to know his son, Wyatt had offered her the answer to both dilemmas. At least this way she would be in the room to supervise their interactions.

But even knowing it was the right thing to do, she still had to force the words through tight lips.

"I think we'd better set up that playdate."

Chapter Four

Wyatt had never been so nervous in his life. He'd arrived at the park fifteen minutes early so he could observe other parents on the playground interacting with their children.

Being slung so unexpectedly into fatherhood would be enough to rattle any man, but Wyatt was an only child who had been raised by his grandmother. As a boy he'd hung out with animals more than people. What he didn't know about toddlers could fill an encyclopedia set.

The only kids he'd ever spent any time with were of the baby goat variety. What if he messed up with Matty? What if he didn't have what it took to be a dad?

He watched a young father spotting his little girl down a slide. The child was giggling and her dad looked completely relaxed and carefree.

Wyatt was neither. He felt sick to his stomach and like he was about to jump out of his skin.

Ready, set, go.

Whether he was ready or not.

Carolina waved as she approached, holding a squirming Matty with her other hand. Matty had seen the playground and was clearly eager to unload some energy on it. The moment she let the boy loose, he barreled toward a spring-loaded rocket, climbed aboard and pumped back and forth with as much force as his little arms and legs could manage.

Carolina still appeared reticent about this meeting, but he supposed he should have expected that. He had no regrets about hiring her for his office, although maybe she did, after she'd returned home and had had time to think about it.

In his mind, anything that meant he would have more time with his son was a good thing, even if he was still struggling to completely wrap his mind around the idea of Carolina now also being a permanent part of his life—at least, he hoped that would be true. He still worried that she had no intention of staying in Haven permanently, that he would get to know Matty just in time for her to take him away again.

For the first few minutes, Carolina said nothing to him at all, just folded her arms as if she were chilled and silently watched Matty as he moved from the rocket to a small tower. Made for the younger children, there were no holes or gaps for them to fall into. It had steps rather than climbing bars and a small straight slide, compared to the long spiral slide the larger tower held.

For the moment, Matty appeared safe enough on his own. Wyatt thought maybe he ought to be doing something, interacting with Matty in some way like he'd seen the father of the little girl doing, but he had no idea what to do, and Carolina wasn't giving him any guidance.

After what seemed like forever, Matty dashed back in their direction.

"Swing, Mama."

Carolina glanced at Wyatt and her mouth curved into a grin. "You want to take this?"

Wyatt tried to swallow but his throat was too dry. "S-sure," he stammered.

"Come on, Matty. Mr. Wyatt is going to push you on the swing, okay?"

Matty didn't appear to care who pushed him, as long as he got to swing.

"Use one of the toddler swings—the ones that support him around the middle."

He was grateful Carolina was finally offering him a little instruction instead of leaving him to stumble his way through his first interaction with his son. Maybe this wouldn't be so difficult, after all.

"May I pick you up, little man?" he asked Matty, holding out his hands to the boy.

He half expected Matty to run in the other direction, cower behind Carolina's legs or jump into her arms and hide his head in her shoulder as he had the first time they'd met, but this time Matty didn't hesitate. He climbed right into Wyatt's arms without a protest.

Wyatt couldn't help but smile as he threaded Matty's plump legs into the seat of the swing.

He was playing with his son!

The emotions stirring in his chest were beyond imagining. Love and pride dueled for precedence at the front of the pack, but there were so many other things, too. Was this how it would always feel when he looked at Matty?

He gave the swing a little push, then another, careful not to go beyond a couple of feet in either direction.

"Higher! Higher!" Matty called impatiently, pumping his legs and rocking back and forth in the swing.

Wyatt's gaze shifted to Carolina.

She chuckled and nodded.

He pushed a little harder, but Matty continued to beg for more.

"You're going to have to do better than that," Carolina said. "He's a real daredevil. He likes to go as high as the swing will carry him."

"Isn't that dangerous?"

Her eyes widened, as if she'd never even considered the possibility. Maybe she hadn't, and he was being foolish. He didn't have the built-in daddy sensor that he assumed other men had.

"I don't think so," she responded slowly. "The chair keeps him from tipping over, and as you can see, he has a good grip on the chains. So unless you're intending to swing him in a three-hundred-sixty-degree circle, I don't think we have to worry about him falling out."

Heat traveled up Wyatt's neck and into his face. He was an idiot. Why hadn't he noticed the way the parents around him were acting? One young woman was only half paying attention as she pushed her child on a nearby swing while simultaneously texting on her cell phone.

No one looked alarmed or nervous.

Was he going to overreact to every situation in which he found himself with Matty? He didn't want to be that hovering, overprotective father, but he couldn't help the way his heart jerked into his throat when he pulled Matty out of the swing chair and the boy immediately headed toward a geometric dome made up of metal pipes. The pipes had to be slippery and the holes between the triangles were easily large enough for his two-year-old son to fall through.

"He's fine," Carolina assured Wyatt with a smile, even though he hadn't shared any of his thoughts and fears aloud. "He climbs like a monkey. Swings like one, too. And he likes bananas," she teased.

Be that as it may, Wyatt inched closer to what appeared to him to be an entirely unsafe piece of playground equipment. He wasn't about to let Matty fall.

Dads were supposed to be the ones to encourage their sons to reach higher, try harder, be strong and courageous. He was hovering over Matty like a mother hen.

Maybe—hopefully Wyatt would get to the point where he could trust himself to do the right thing, where he instinctively knew how to be a daddy. But right now he felt like he was walking over hot coals with bare feet.

"You should have seen me the first time I brought Matty to the playground." Carolina laughed and laid a hand on Wyatt's shoulder. "I was spotting him so closely that there was no way he could have fallen off anything. I was positive the other parents were laughing at me as I followed him around with inches to spare."

Wyatt shoved his hands into his pockets. Was it that easy for Carolina to read what he was thinking just from his expression alone?

Back when they were dating, she used to have an uncanny knack for guessing the emotions he was experiencing and knowing just what to say or do to make him feel better. She'd had the same gift with Gran.

Except for the part when he'd realized he was in love with her.

She hadn't gotten that at *all*.

Still, even if she had no idea what he was thinking, the compassionate way she was currently gazing at him made him feel vulnerable and uneasy.

"Worse even than the playground was my reaction the first time Matty fell down on the sidewalk and skinned his knee," she continued. "I wasn't sure my heart could take hearing him cry. I felt like the worst mother ever. It took me a long time to realize the best thing to do was not overreact. A character bandage and a kiss is usually sufficient to nurse his little-boy wounds."

"Mmm." It was all Wyatt could do to take her words in, much less give a coherent response.

"Someone once told me that they start growing away from you the moment they're born, and I guess there is some truth to that. Matty gets more independent every day. But I don't have to like it." She chuckled mildly.

"Just enjoy every moment you have with him, I guess," Wyatt agreed, his voice gravelly, thinking about all the times he'd missed.

Carolina made a choking sound. He glanced at her, but she wouldn't meet his eyes.

Was she feeling guilty over all Matty's firsts that she'd denied Wyatt? First breath, first word, the first step Matty took?

He couldn't say as he felt sorry for her. She *should* be feeling guilty. She'd made the decision to walk away. She'd created these consequences for herself, and for Wyatt, and most of all, for Matty.

But today wasn't a day for anger. Today was about spending time with his son.

"Does he like sports?" Wyatt asked.

"Well, I wouldn't say sports, exactly. He's a little young for anything organized yet. Why?"

He felt his face flushing again. He hadn't blushed this much since his senior prom, when he was a gangly youth with two left feet.

"No reason, really. I brought a couple of balls along with me, just in case."

"Oh, now that's a different thing entirely. Matty loves tossing a ball around. Let's see what you've got."

"What do you say, little man?" he asked, scooping Matty into his arms and leading Carolina to his truck. "Do you want to play ball?"

It was only as they reached his truck bed that he realized he'd just set himself up for another round of humiliation and embarrassment. Saying he'd brought a *couple* of balls was a major understatement.

"A couple means two," Matty announced proudly, holding up two fingers. "I'm two."

Wyatt laughed. His kid was super smart, as well as being the cutest boy in the whole state of Texas.

Not that he was biased or anything.

Not knowing what Matty would like, he'd pretty much loaded up every kind of sports ball imaginable— a football, a baseball, a soccer ball and a basketball. He was going to add a couple of baseball gloves, but he only had mitts for adult-size hands. A toddler-size mitt was on his ever-growing list of items he wanted to buy for his son.

Carolina didn't immediately comment when he showed her his stash.

"What? What's wrong?"

"Oh, nothing. We usually play with a big plastic bouncy ball when we're at home."

A bouncy ball.

Another item for his list.

Carolina flashed him half a smile and shrugged

apologetically. "I'm afraid I don't know much about these games beyond being able to identify which ball goes with which sport."

"That's what Matty's got a dad for."

He didn't really think about what he was saying until the words had already left his lips.

Their gazes met and locked. She was silently challenging him, but he didn't know about what. Still, he kept his gaze firmly on hers. His words might not have been premeditated, but that didn't make them any less true. He was sorry if he'd hurt her feelings, though. He wanted to keep things friendly between them.

"I think he'd probably enjoy kicking the soccer ball around with you," she said at last.

Whatever antagonism had passed between them was now gone, and he let out the breath he hadn't even realized he'd been holding.

"There's plenty of room on the green for three. What do you say? Do you want to play soccer with us?"

Shock registered in her face, but it was no more than what he was feeling. This was all so new. Untested waters.

Somehow, they had to work things out between the three of them and learn to work together, but kicking a ball around together at the park?

Why, that almost felt as if they were a *family*.

And although in a sense that was technically true, Wyatt didn't even want to go down that road.

He had every intention of being the best father he could to Matty. And in so doing, he would establish some sort of a working relationship with Carolina, some way they could both be comfortable without it getting awkward. He just couldn't bring himself to think about that right now.

Or maybe he just didn't want to.

After church the next morning, with Matty napping in his car seat, Carolina decided to take a drive out to the countryside to try to clear her head.

Too much was happening, too fast, and she couldn't begin to make sense of it all.

And to think she'd come back to Haven to find some peace and enjoy the slower pace of small-town living. So much for that daydream.

Encountering Wyatt again had changed everything. She'd been in love with him three years ago, and despite the depth of the chasm now between them, she had to acknowledge that she had once been ready to spend her life with him. But he hadn't been ready, and so she'd left. She didn't have any idea if he was ready now, but ready or not, he was a father.

Seeing him kicking the black-and-white ball around with Matty yesterday in the park had shaken her to the core. As far as she was concerned, it was a literal game changer—for all three of them.

Matty needed his father in his life.

Needed Wyatt.

And Wyatt needed him.

She supposed, deep down, she'd always known something was missing during their time in Colorado. As a single mother, she'd often overcompensated as much as she could, attempting to meet all Matty's needs.

But she couldn't be both mother and father to Matty, no matter how she tried. Only Wyatt could truly fill the role of Matty's dad in his life.

Her fists closed tightly around the steering wheel and she huffed out a frustrated breath.

Oh, why did things have to be so complicated? Choices on top of choices, and she wasn't sure any of her decisions, from the day she had walked away until the day she had returned, were right. How was she to judge?

In the best of all possible worlds, Matty wouldn't be the product of a broken home—or rather, a home that never really existed in the first place. But he was.

There were no mom and dad committed to God and each other. No brothers and sisters to play with, no dogs or cats or a family home.

Wyatt was really stepping up as a father, but the cold, hard reality was that even though they would both be in Matty's life—Carolina still wasn't certain to what extent where Wyatt was concerned—they couldn't be with each other. That ship had sailed long ago.

And the worst part was, she had no idea how she was supposed to guard Matty's heart through all of this.

She was going to be in Haven for two months. That meant Wyatt would be a part of Matty's life long enough for their son to get used to the idea of having a father. But what then?

Wyatt's gran would eventually pass on and he would finally be free to follow his dreams, aspirations that would take him far away from Haven and his son.

Matty would be heartbroken. And Carolina wasn't sure how to keep that from happening.

Already she was grieving for what could never be, the family she'd once thought she and Wyatt would eventually make together, however ridiculous the notion was in truth.

This—whatever *this* was—was a whole other thing entirely, and she didn't know what to do with it.

In the quarter hour she'd been driving, she had passed only a handful of drivers on the little-used country road, with miles and miles of Texas prairie on every side of her. Beautiful meadows waving in the wind, with waist-high grass in places.

A beat-up white pickup truck appeared ahead of her, driving well under the speed limit. The driver looked to be an old man, puttering down the highway at the slackened pace of life in the country.

Carolina checked her mirrors and prepared to pass the old codger. Suddenly, the old man slammed on his brakes and the pickup came to an abrupt stop.

Heart in her throat, Carolina swerved to the left, missing the truck by bare inches as the back of her sedan fishtailed and then came to a screeching halt.

Shaken, she pulled her car off to the left shoulder and turned to see if Matty was okay. He was awake but not crying, his startled brown eyes staring straight back at her as he sucked on his fist. Thankfully, his five-point harness had kept him out of harm's way.

"You okay, buddy?" Her voice sounded raspy even to her own ears.

In answer, Matty reached for his sippy cup and self-soothed with his apple juice.

Adrenaline was pulsing so rapidly through Carolina that she couldn't determine whether or not she had any injuries. Her shoulder was a little sore from where the seat belt had locked up, but other than that she thought she'd gotten through the accident without much physical incident.

Her next thought was about the old man who was driving the white pickup.

Why had he stopped so abruptly? Surely he had to have known she would likely rear-end him when he stomped on the brakes the way he had. Had he had some kind of physical breakdown? A heart attack, maybe? Or was he driving under the influence?

He was still sitting behind the wheel of his truck, looking straight down the road, a little dazed. But when Carolina got out of her car to cross the highway to see if he had suffered any injuries or if she needed to call an ambulance, he suddenly gunned his loud, knocking engine and swerved to the left, nearly hitting her as he drove off down the road as fast as the old truck could manage.

All righty, then.

Apparently the man wasn't hurt, although Carolina thought it was very rude of him to drive off without making sure she and her son were okay—especially since it was his fault they'd almost skidded off the road and into a ditch. Some people just didn't have a conscience.

As she returned her gaze to where his truck had been, she discovered the real reason the old man had slammed on his brakes.

A young buck with tiny nubs for antlers lay on its back on the side of the road, its legs twitching as it tried to right itself. Even from where she was standing, she could tell that the poor thing was in trouble.

She didn't want Matty to see it, but she couldn't possibly bring herself to leave the animal to suffer a slow death. She fished her cell phone out of her back pocket, intending to alert the local parks and wildlife station, which was in charge of roadkill in the area.

Except this young buck wasn't roadkill.

Not yet.

Carolina had grown up in the country and knew that often the kindest—if most difficult—thing for a person to do was to put a suffering animal out of its misery, especially a wild animal like this deer. It would never survive out here if it couldn't walk.

Something made her hesitate before making the call to the game department. Maybe it was the way the buck was valiantly, if vainly, struggling to find its feet. Maybe it was the pain and panic clouding its large brown eyes.

Whatever it was, Carolina checked her call log and dialed an entirely different number.

Wyatt's.

He would know what to do, and if it was indeed necessary to put the buck down, he would have the means to give it a quick and painless death. She trusted him to do the right thing for the poor animal.

Relief flooded through her when Wyatt's deep, warm voice answered on the second ring.

"Hey, Carolina. What's up?"

She didn't take time for pleasantries.

"Wyatt, I'm on County Road 8 about fifteen miles out of town. I was taking a Sunday drive when the pickup truck in front of me hit a young buck head-on. I don't know if he wasn't watching where he was going, or if the deer suddenly jumped into the road in front of him. I didn't see it happen. He slammed on his brakes hard and I just barely missed rear-ending him."

"What? Are you okay? Was Matty in the car? Should I call for an ambulance?"

Carolina glanced into the backseat, where Matty had fallen back into a peaceful slumber, and then addressed the issue she imagined was highest on Wyatt's list.

"Matty is in the car with me, but he's fine. I had to swerve and slam on my brakes pretty hard, but Matty is perfectly safe. His five-point car seat straps kept him from experiencing much of a jolt. I'm not sure he even noticed much of a difference from how I usually drive." She laughed unsteadily at her own joke.

"And you?"

"A little shaken up," she admitted. "But physically I'm fine."

"What about the guy driving the truck? Is he okay?" Wyatt's voice tightened.

"He's gone." Carolina couldn't help the note of anger that laced her tone. "He took off without bothering to find out if Matty or I had been injured."

Wyatt made an unintelligible growl from the back of his throat.

"Did you get his license plate number, at least?"

She shook her head, then realized Wyatt couldn't see her movement. "No. But there was really no reason for me to take it. It wasn't exactly an accident. Just a close call."

"Too close. And you're sure you and Matty are all right? No injuries?" he asked again.

"I'm sure. That's not why I'm calling. It's about the buck."

"Do you want me to call the Department of Parks and Wildlife for you?"

"If you think it's best. That's what I was about to do, but then I hesitated and called you instead. I feel kind of silly now. It's just that the buck—he's still moving. I thought maybe…"

Her voice trailed off and then picked up again when

she realized how ridiculous she sounded. She was just overemotional from the near accident.

"No. I'm sorry for bothering you. I'm being stupid. I'll call the game warden myself."

"You're not a bother, Carolina. Give me fifteen minutes to find you. And hold off on calling Parks and Wildlife. Maybe there is something I can do."

"You'll come?"

"Of course. I don't know if I can help the buck, but I can at least have a look at him."

"Thank you." She gripped the phone against her chest. Her heart swelled with gratitude. Wyatt had always been that man—the guy who dropped everything to come running when he was needed.

Whether or not he could do anything for the deer, he was making the effort.

She'd called—and he'd answered.

Chapter Five

Wyatt felt sorry for Carolina. Seeing an animal in distress was never a pleasant experience, but to see a deer hit by a truck was especially traumatic. Carolina had a good head on her shoulders and had seen many things as a nurse, but he knew she had a soft spot for animals.

He wished he could help, but he doubted even a man of his expertise could save a wild buck that had been hit by a truck. Some things were beyond him.

That was life. He'd learned not to get too attached to anyone or anything, animals and people alike. At the end of the day, they all went away, leaving a gaping hole where their presence used to be.

His mom and dad hadn't often been there for him as a child, since they were ambassadors in a third-world country and had deemed it not safe for their son. He'd begged and begged to be able to come with them, but they'd refused.

He remembered as a child he would pray every night asking God for his parents' safe return from foreign soil. And what had that gotten him?

They'd been killed. And despite the distance, and

not really knowing them very well, Wyatt had felt the void left in his heart.

And he'd never again asked God for anything.

He'd put down more farm animals and domestic pets than he could count, sharing in the family's grief at the loss of a beloved dog or cat but not letting it touch his own heart.

Letting go of people was even harder. As much as he wished it were otherwise, his gran wouldn't be around for much longer. He didn't know what he was going to do without her. She had been everything to him growing up.

Then there were the kids to whom he taught vetting skills at the boys ranch. Despite his effort to stay rational and detached in his volunteer efforts, he couldn't help but become involved, especially with Johnny Drake, the boy he was personally mentoring.

But once again, Wyatt was about to say goodbye. Johnny was seventeen and would be aging out of the program soon, and then he'd be gone, as well.

Worst of all, Wyatt had no guarantee Carolina would decide to stay in Haven after the party for the seventieth anniversary of the ranch in March.

What if she left and took Matty away?

It would be ridiculously easy for her to throw salt on that old wound and at the same time create a brand-new one by denying him his son.

He *knew* better than to care.

And yet he did.

How could he not? Matty was his son, his flesh and blood. This was one goodbye he was going to fight against.

He spotted Carolina's sedan parked on the opposite shoulder of the road, her car turned the wrong direction from the traffic. Skid marks crossed the road in a fishtail pattern and told the story all on their own.

It could easily have been a lot worse than it had been. The sedan had stopped inches from a two-foot ditch. Wyatt was thankful Carolina and Matty were safe.

He parked his truck a short distance from the buck and walked the rest of the way down the road so as not to frighten the animal further.

Carolina was leaning against the hood of her car, her arms crossed and her cell phone still in her hand. Her glassy eyes were distant as she silently stared at the young buck on the other side of the road, a frown on her lips.

Wyatt's heart went out to her.

Though she must have heard his truck pull up, she didn't appear to realize he was there. He wondered if her physical injuries were worse than she'd first imagined. Or she could be in shock.

He immediately took his denim jacket off and wrapped it around her shoulders. Her gaze shifted to him and her eyes widened.

"Are you okay?" he asked anxiously.

"What do you think?"

"I don't know, Carolina. You don't look so hot right now. Do you want to sit down?"

She chuckled drily. "No. Don't worry about me. What do you think about the buck?"

She nodded toward the yearling, which was still on its side, panting heavily. It was no longer struggling to regain its feet and flee.

"Why don't you sit down so you don't fall down and then let me see if I can get close to it."

"Thank you," she murmured in a scratchy tone.

Wyatt approached the deer slowly, speaking in a low, even tone. "No worries, buddy. I'm a vet. I'm just here to take a look at you, okay?"

He stopped when the buck's eyes rolled white and its nostrils flared. The yearling resumed its bleating and futile kicking motions for a moment, then laid its head back on the ground.

"That's right. No one is going to hurt you."

He crouched by the buck's side and tentatively reached his hand out, running a gentle palm across the deer's flank while he expertly assessed the damage.

The yearling had some deep gashes in its shoulder and flank where it must have made contact with the truck's grille. With all the blood, it was hard to say how deep the wounds were, but Wyatt guessed they were probably not as bad as they looked.

He thought he could clean the gashes against infection and patch up the deer fairly successfully, but he could not oversee its healing if he immediately let the young buck back into the wild. Yet it would never survive without treatment.

His real concern was the deer's legs. If the buck had been physically able, it would have regained its footing on its own and bounded off long ago.

As it was, it almost appeared as if the buck had lost its will to live. And if that was true, nothing Wyatt could do for the deer would help.

"What do you think?" Carolina asked softly. Wyatt hadn't heard her come up behind him. So much for her listening to his directions and sitting down. She was more worried about the deer than she was about herself. She'd always been stubborn that way.

"Can we save the poor thing?"

"Honestly? I don't know. Maybe. I think it depends a lot on how hard this guy wants to fight."

He closely examined the deer's legs but didn't immediately see any cause for alarm. Although he imagined the buck was badly bruised, nothing appeared broken.

"Where's Matty?"

"He's right here."

Wyatt glanced behind him. Matty was clinging to Carolina with one hand and clutched a toy airplane in the other. His dark brown eyes were fastened on the deer.

"Don't get too close, okay, buddy?"

Carolina moved Matty to a spot in the grass and spread out a blanket, well away from the highway and the buck, but close enough that she and Wyatt could both keep an eye on him.

"Is there anything we can do?" Carolina asked, concern lining her tone.

"Let's try to help it onto its feet," he decided. "Be careful to stay away from those hooves and make sure he doesn't try to take a nip at you."

"Okay," she agreed. "What do you need me to do?"

"You support that side of him while I support him under his belly and let's try to roll him up."

Without a second's hesitation, Carolina moved to the opposite side of the deer and carefully stroked the yearling's neck.

"Ready?"

Carolina pressed her lips together and nodded, completely intent on the task ahead of her.

Wild animals were unpredictable at best, and wounded ones even more so. He didn't want to put Carolina in any kind of danger, but he knew her well enough to know he wouldn't be able to talk her out of helping.

For some reason she had her heart set on saving this buck, and incomprehensibly, even to him, that made him want to fight for the animal's life even more, especially when she offered her appreciation once again.

He wouldn't have called it a prayer, but he hoped with his whole heart that when they helped the buck stand up, the injuries wouldn't be as bad as they looked and the deer would find its legs and bound off into the long grass.

It didn't.

Wyatt supported it under its flanks and suspended it steadily on wobbly legs, but as soon as he eased back, the deer's front left leg buckled under it. If Carolina hadn't been on the other side to offer her support, the buck would have plunged down again and would likely have really broken its leg this time.

Together, working without words, they got the yearling safely back down on its side.

"I don't think anything's broken, but it evidently has a bad sprain, enough that it can't put weight on its leg. It's not going anywhere on its own."

Carolina frowned and her eyes filled with tears. "So there's nothing we can do for him, then."

Her gaze met his, and it was as if she was transferring all her emotions to him through the golden-brown depths of her eyes.

It wasn't just that he could see her anguish and discouragement. He could actually *feel* it.

He cleared his throat and adjusted his Stetson lower over his eyes.

If he was in any other situation, he would have come

to the conclusion that the humane thing to do would be to put the suffering animal down.

But when he looked at Carolina's miserable expression, he simply couldn't.

"Let me call Johnny and have him bring us out a trailer. I'm not going to make any promises here, but if we take it back to my ranch I might be able to dress its wounds and wrap its leg."

Carolina let out a deep breath and reached for Wyatt's hand. "Thank you."

He tried to smile encouragingly. "You've said that already. Multiple times, in fact."

"Well, I am grateful. I don't know why this has shaken me up so badly. I am—I *was*—a nurse. It's not like I've never seen blood before, or serious injuries, for that matter."

Wyatt turned her gently by the shoulders and guided her to the blanket where Matty was playing.

"Sit down and try to relax for a few minutes. And please, listen to me this time. You've had quite a scare today, what with almost being in a major car accident. It's no wonder you feel a little unsettled. You're in shock."

And it was clear that she was. Despite the fact that his warm jacket was still wrapped around her, he could feel her shoulders quivering underneath his palms.

He thought she might balk at his suggestion, but she sank onto the blanket with a grateful sigh and offered him an appreciative smile.

He was glad she didn't follow that smile with another thank-you. He didn't know what to do with all her gratitude. It made him antsy and gave him the desire to do even more. He just wasn't certain what more he could do for Carolina.

He scoffed inwardly at his foolishness. It must be some kind of misguided hero complex.

What he *could* do was to take care of the yearling buck. Johnny answered his call on the first ring, and less than a half an hour later, Wyatt, Johnny and Carolina had the frightened deer loaded up in a horse trailer, cushioned by a pile of fresh hay.

"You ought to go home and rest," he urged Carolina. Her face still appeared pale and her eyes were glassy.

But no, of course she refused to listen to him. Again. Until she saw the young buck completely taken care of, she wasn't going to let this go.

He guessed he really couldn't blame her. He would have done the same thing.

And it wasn't as if he could talk Carolina into or out of anything once she had her mind set on it.

Johnny, mature for his age and always sensitive to the needs of animals, slowly drove the trailer back to Wyatt's ranch. Wyatt followed in his truck, and Carolina brought up the rear in her sedan.

Once they arrived at the ranch and loaded the deer into an empty stall, Wyatt prepared to dress its wounds.

"What do you need me to do?" Carolina asked, coming alongside him and brushing her palms across the denim of her jeans. "Do you have a list of supplies you need?"

"Uh—yes," he answered, caught off guard. He'd expected Johnny to help him vet the buck, since Carolina had their son to worry about. "Where's Matty?"

"Outside playing hide-and-seek with Johnny."

"With *Johnny*?" He couldn't hide his surprise. "How did you manage that? Johnny never interacts with anyone if he doesn't have to."

Carolina raised her eyebrows and shrugged. "How should I know? Maybe small children are his exception. I didn't even have to ask him to help. It was all his idea."

Wyatt ran a hand across the stubble on his jaw. "Hmm. Well, I'll be."

"What? Johnny is reliable, right? We can trust him to watch out for Matty?"

"Absolutely." Wyatt tried to swallow, but his throat had suddenly turned dry. Did Carolina even realize what she'd just said?

She'd said *we*, not *I*.

Whether she consciously admitted it or not, they were in this parenting thing together.

"I figure I'm invested in this animal, so I should do whatever I can to help it," Carolina said, running her palm down the quivering deer's neck. "Now, tell me, what supplies do you need?"

With Carolina's assistance, it took remarkably little time to vet the yearling. She had the same curiously calming influence on the deer as she had on his gran, and Wyatt was able to work quickly to dress the wounds.

After finishing up, they walked outside to find Matty and Johnny.

"Did you and Matty have fun?" Carolina asked as Johnny handed the boy over to her.

"Y-yes, ma'am." Johnny dropped his gaze and his face flared with color.

Carolina put her arm around the teenager and gave him a friendly hug. "Oh, gracious, no, Johnny. Just Carolina is fine. *Ma'am* makes me sound ancient."

To Wyatt's surprise, Johnny lifted his head and offered her a shy smile.

"I l-liked playing with M-Matty."

"That's great to hear. What would you say to doing a little babysitting for me every once in a while? I'm in desperate need of finding people I can trust with Matty."

Johnny's brown eyes grew as wide as his smile. He straightened his shoulders and pushed a curly lock of hair off his forehead.

"I'd really like that, ma'am. C-Carolina," he corrected.

"Wonderful. I'm sure Matty will enjoy spending more time with you."

Johnny nodded vigorously and then turned to Wyatt.

"D-did you invite her and M-Matty to the barn raising next Saturday?"

Heat crept up Wyatt's neck and into his face at Johnny's not-so-subtle attempt at matchmaking.

Matty bobbed his head and reached out for Wyatt. He took his son in his arms, his heart in his throat that Matty wanted to be with him.

Would this ever get old? Would he ever get past the emotions that rose with the strength of a tidal wave every time he held his son?

"No. I haven't asked her about it yet." It was on the tip of his tongue to say he'd been about to, but really, he hadn't. His mind was too concerned with the right here, right now to worry about next Saturday.

It was a good idea, though. Any extra time he could spend with Matty was a plus. Besides, he wanted to show off his son to the town.

He chuckled. "You beat me to it, Johnny."

Carolina raised an eyebrow. "Are you saying a whole barn needs raising?"

"At the b-boys ranch," Johnny answered before Wyatt could get a word in.

"Someone set fire to one of the barns last month, and members of the Lone Star Cowboy League, along with other volunteers, are building a new one next Saturday. I think some of the ladies in town are also gathering to plan the annual Valentine's Day ice cream social. If that's something that interests you, I'm sure they'd be glad to have you. Would you and Matty like to come?"

Carolina hesitated.

"I understand if you're too busy," he quickly added. Even though he wanted to spend more time with Matty, he didn't want to push Carolina. Not when they were just starting to get along.

Johnny looked crestfallen. Poor kid.

He couldn't blame him. Wyatt was a little down in the mouth about it, as well.

Carolina's gaze swept from Wyatt to Johnny and then back to Wyatt again.

"Too busy? No. It's not that. I'd be happy to help the community if I can. You just caught me off guard, is all. You said someone intentionally burned the barn down? It wasn't an accident?"

"It was ruled an arson by the fire chief," Wyatt said grimly. "There have been more strange things going on as well. When the incidents started, they seemed more like pranks, something a kid would do—letting calves out of their pens, petty theft, just generally creating a ruckus."

He slid his eyes toward Johnny, not wanting to give the teenager the wrong impression. He had every confidence in Johnny and didn't want him to think otherwise.

"At first everyone assumed it was one or more of the resident boys, but now whoever is causing all the problems around the ranch seems to have stepped up his game. Heath Grayson, our local Texas Ranger, now believes the crimes were perpetrated by an adult. And that it's serious business."

"Was anyone hurt in the fire?"

Matty squirmed in Wyatt's arms, and he patted the toddler's back to soothe him. It had been a long, stress-fueled day, and Matty laid his cheek against Wyatt's shoulder. After a minute, the toddler's breath became slow and even.

"No people or livestock were near the barn, thankfully. It was primarily used to store ranch equipment. But I am concerned that the arsonist is still out there somewhere, apparently holding a grudge against the boys ranch."

"That's a frightening thought." Carolina frowned, but when she glanced up at Wyatt, her frown turned into a soft smile. She laid a hand on his arm. "Matty is sound asleep. You've got the touch."

Wyatt grinned, pride welling in his chest. He would much rather not talk about the crimes being perpetrated at the boys ranch while he was enjoying the feel of his son napping in his arms.

He had the daddy touch. Carolina had just said so.

"So you'll c-come?" Johnny asked, gazing at Carolina as if she hung the moon. Wyatt couldn't blame the shy teenager. There was a time not so long ago when Carolina had had the same effect on him.

"Yes," she said, in answer to Johnny's question. But her eyes were on Wyatt. "I'll be there. I'd like the opportunity to participate in Haven community events again."

His breath hitched. Was there a deeper meaning behind her words? Could it be that she was planning to make Haven her permanent home? Would he truly have the opportunity to be a real dad to Matty?

Carolina had broken Wyatt's heart once, and he'd believed it had been beyond mending. Did he dare hope for more than just the promised two months together—or was he setting himself up for a letdown even worse than the first one?

Johnny wandered into the barn to check on the injured buck, and Matty stirred on Wyatt's shoulder.

"Goat?" asked Matty groggily, rubbing his eyes.

Carolina tittered, and Wyatt turned to see what Matty was talking about.

He joined in Carolina's laughter when he saw what Matty was all excited about. One of the baby goats had found a way out of the goat pen and was contentedly munching grass in the middle of Wyatt's yard.

"The escape artist. Guess we're going to have to call that kid Houdini. Matty, would you like to pet the goat?"

"Goat!" Matty exclaimed excitedly, suddenly wide awake.

Suddenly unsure of himself, Wyatt flashed a questioning glance at Carolina. He would keep Matty safe, of course, but he still wanted to make sure she was okay with it.

She smiled and nodded and then knelt by him as he propped Matty on the ground and helped him reach out and pet the black-and-white-spotted baby goat.

"Watch out that he doesn't get his fist clenched in the cute little thing's fur," Carolina warned.

"Gentle, gentle," Wyatt murmured, showing Matty how to run his palm across the animal's coat.

The toddler stayed calm for about two seconds, then squealed and flapped his hands in excitement. The goat balked and bounded away, kicking his legs out behind him as he headed back toward the pen where the rest of the herd was kept.

Matty frowned in disappointment.

"It's okay, sweetheart," Carolina responded tenderly. "Houdini wants to go play with his brothers and sisters now."

Wyatt stood and swung Matty around before handing him back to Carolina. "I'd better make sure our little Houdini gets back in the pen where he belongs and see if I can figure out how he made his escape in the first place."

Carolina rose and brushed off her jeans. "We need to be going anyway."

Wyatt was surprised at the sense of disappointment that swelled in his chest at her words. He had no reason to feel that way. They'd be working together now and he would see Matty often.

He supposed it was just that he'd felt like he'd had a breakthrough with the boy today, that he'd earned the toddler's trust, and Carolina's, as well.

This was just the beginning, he reminded himself. Soon he'd be comfortable being Matty's daddy, and the boy would accept and love Wyatt, as well.

He was amazed at how much his dreams had changed now that he had Matty in his life. He wanted to be where his son was—and he hoped that would be Haven. As honorable as it might have been to do missionary work in foreign countries, Matty's presence here reminded him that he could help people anywhere, even here in Haven. Take Johnny, for example.

Surely the classes he held for the boys at the ranch meant something.

And as for Carolina—today had been a good day. Wyatt had been able to help her, and that felt good. She'd needed assistance, and she'd called him.

He didn't want to put too much emphasis on her actions, but he hoped that meant they were building on the tentative trust between them. Because every day he spent with her and Matty brought them closer to the time when she might leave again, this time for good.

Now, more than ever, he realized that he couldn't handle them going away. He just couldn't. So he would work harder than ever to convince Carolina to stay.

"It's been a good day. How much longer are we going to keep this a secret?" he asked. "About me being Matty's father?"

Her eyes widened, and she captured her bottom lip between her teeth. She looked as if she were vacillating in her mind. Had she not even considered the question?

"I'm sure folks are starting to put two and two together," Carolina said hesitantly. "I don't think we ought to make a big announcement or anything, but if someone asks, I don't see a reason not to tell them the truth."

Wyatt wanted to fist pump. Finally, he could open up about the biggest blessing in his life. Carolina might not want to make a big production out of it, but he wanted to crow the news to the world.

He was Matty's daddy.

Considering that she had zero experience as a receptionist, Carolina settled into her new job at Wyatt's office with surprising efficiency and ease. Her first week of work had gone off without a hitch. It was clear she could use more education in administrative work, but she wasn't intending to make being Wyatt's assistant her permanent occupation. It was the means to an end and nothing more. She wasn't even certain she'd be staying in Haven after the seventieth-anniversary party. Her whole world was still tilted on its axis.

At least Wyatt didn't use a confusing medical filing system. The good old ABCs were satisfactory for his small practice, and as she'd mentioned when he had first offered her employment, the alphabet was a skill she excelled in. Every mother of a toddler did.

And every dad, too, for that matter.

Wyatt had been spending as much time at the office as possible, crouched down on the carpet pushing cars and trucks around and making the motor noise that seemed to be stamped somewhere deep in the male DNA.

He and Matty stacked towers of blocks that Matty delighted in knocking over every bit as much as he enjoyed building them. Wyatt wasn't frustrated by the action. He helped. And he sang endless rounds of children's songs in a deep voice that was as adorably slightly off-key as his son's higher voice was.

Wyatt never lost his patience with Matty, and his enthusiasm was contagious. Carolina couldn't push trucks around for more than five minutes without becoming bored out of her skull, although she forced herself to continue playing as long as Matty liked. She suspected she'd do much better with a daughter's baby dolls and dress up and tea parties.

If she ever had a daughter. It made her sad to think Matty might end up an only child, without brothers and sisters to play with.

Because—maybe especially because—she had been

an only child who had longed for siblings, she had always dreamed of having a large family of her own someday.

But then again, she'd never been able to envision sharing her life with anyone but Wyatt. No other man had ever measured up.

And Wyatt had had other plans. Or at least she'd thought he'd had. Now she wasn't certain about anything.

Even with as much joy as she experienced, it had been a long, awkward and sometimes painful week, watching Wyatt on the floor with his son, laughing and playing with Matty just as she'd always imagined he would do. She'd always known that when and if he ever reached that point in his life, Wyatt would be a wonderful father.

And he was. A natural.

But this wasn't how it was supposed to be.

Not knowing for sure if she was dressing for a barn raising or if she would be helping to plan a social event, Carolina dressed in layers, a lilac velour pullover over a T-shirt, an older pair of blue jeans and the comfortable cowboy boots that were now part of her daily ensemble.

It wasn't like her to fuss over an outfit. Scrubs had been her go-to clothes for many years, and there wasn't anything fancy about those. But for some reason, today she hesitated before the full-length mirror attached to her bathroom door and gave herself a critical once-over.

She clicked her tongue against her teeth and scoffed. She wasn't trying to impress Wyatt—er—*anybody*. So why had his face, and his expression as she remembered it from when they were dating, shining with admiration and affection, instantly flashed through her mind?

That wasn't simply a little harmless daydream. It was a full-blown disaster in the making. It was next to impossible not to linger on past emotions, which somehow were now starting to feel more immediate and current.

And strong. Oh, so strong.

Confusion rolled through her in waves as she struggled to tuck and file her emotions away, out of sight and mind.

Lately—as in ever since she'd come back to Haven—it seemed she had to remind herself over and over again that her life was now centered around Matty and Matty alone. No good could come from throwing bygone feelings from her past with Wyatt into what was already a precipitous situation.

Determined to shove those emotions aside, she was buckling Matty into his car seat when she noticed the red flag on her pillar mailbox was raised.

Now, that was odd. She knew she hadn't used the box for any letters to be mailed. Was someone else using her mailbox for some reason?

Curious, she opened the door to the metal mailbox and peered inside. Sure enough, there was a letter, but it wasn't outgoing as one would expect, given that the flag was up.

Instead, she found an envelope addressed to her in an unsteady script of black ink.

Clearly it hadn't come through the official postal system. For one thing, the regular mailman didn't put the flag up when he delivered the mail—he put it down after taking any letters she intended to mail out.

Just as telling, the envelope she now held in her

hand was not only devoid of a return address, but a stamp, as well.

Still, it *was* her name on the envelope.

She slid behind the wheel of her sedan, glanced in the rearview mirror to make sure Matty was happily amusing himself and used her index finger to break the seal of the envelope. She pulled out a single sheet of lined notebook paper, which had been folded at odd angles in order for it to fit into the greeting-card-size envelope.

She chewed on her bottom lip as she read the strange missive.

Deer Carolina,
Will you please go to the ice cream social with me?
    If yes, meat me there and wear red.
Your valentine,
Wyatt

What on earth?

She couldn't help it. She started giggling, and once she began, she couldn't seem to stop, not until she had tears running down her face. Maybe it was all the stress she'd been facing, or possibly a lack of sleep, but all of her emotions came pouring out in her laughter.

"Mama?" Matty was clearly concerned that his mother had completely lost her wits, but he was also laughing right along with her.

Or possibly *at* her.

She snorted and tried to gather her composure.

"I'm fine, honey. It's just that I'm reading a funny letter."

Funny letter, indeed.

And her response?

Even worse.

Because despite the fact that the mysterious missive had arrived in her mailbox without a stamp, sporting an unsteady script and riddled with more questions than answers—not to mention a couple of spectacular spelling errors that nearly set her off giggling again— her very first response had come from her heart.

Yes, she would wear red.

Yes, she would be Wyatt's valentine.

If it was really Wyatt asking. But of course, this was all stuff and nonsense, possibly even someone's idea of a cruel joke.

She hadn't a clue who would go through all the effort of creating and delivering a fake invitation, or why they would bother with her, since she had just arrived back in town.

Most of all, she couldn't imagine why they had signed Wyatt's name at the bottom.

Wyatt, of all people.

Someone certainly had their wires crossed.

She dabbed at the corner of her eyes and tossed the letter into her handbag on the passenger seat.

She was already running late because she'd taken too much time in front of the mirror. Now, having been waylaid by this silly invitation, it would be all she could do to make the official 8:00 a.m. starting time. With it being a community event, she suspected parking was going to be a bear.

She was right about that. Trucks lined the driveway from the entrance to the boys ranch onward, and some vehicles were even parked on both sides of the street that bordered the property.

Not wanting to walk a long distance with a toddler in tow, Carolina picked her way toward the main house, hoping she could find a spot that hadn't yet been taken. Her sedan was considerably smaller than most of the ranchers' trucks, and thankfully she was able to find an open location near the front of the house.

Katie Ellis met her as she was plucking a wiggling Matty out of his car seat.

"Carolina. I'm glad you could make it today. This is going to be so much fun with you here."

Carolina handed Matty off into Katie's waiting arms while she gathered the toddler's play belt and tools, which he had somehow managed to spread out all over the backseat of the car in the fifteen minutes it had taken them to get from Uncle Mort's cabin to the boys ranch. Add to that five minutes to find parking, she mentally amended.

For an active toddler like Matty, that was more than enough time to make a complete mess out of his toys, and it took her a minute to find and arrange the little plastic hammer, saw and screwdriver, as well as a jumble of other tools, onto the pint-size tool belt.

"How adorable," Katie admired as Carolina wrapped the tool belt around Matty's waist. "He'll fit right in with all the other builders."

"Right? Wyatt got this set for him."

"Daddy-son day?" Because of all the friendship and support Katie had lent her, she was one of the few to whom Carolina had admitted the truth about Wyatt and Matty.

Carolina nodded and tried to smile, though her heart dipped. Katie's words had taken her by surprise, that's all.

"Speaking of which—have you seen Wyatt? I'm not sure what Matty and I are supposed to be doing today."

"He's right—"

"Behind you," Wyatt finished for her, his voice a low rumble that simultaneously sent a skitter of electric recognition across Carolina's nerves and yet soothed something deep in her chest.

Wyatt stepped up next to her and took Matty from Katie's arms. Carolina swallowed through a dry throat, feeling his presence as if he had touched her, even though he stood several inches away.

Apparently her personal space expanded when she was around Wyatt.

"I'll take Matty with me to the building site. Johnny is going to be with me all day to help keep an eye on Matty so he doesn't get into any trouble."

Was it Carolina's imagination, or did Wyatt sound a little bit defensive?

She couldn't help but think *she* was the one who was in trouble, but of course she didn't say so. She wasn't handling this so well, emotionally speaking.

"We'll see you men at lunch." Katie threaded her arm through Carolina's and flashed Wyatt a shy smile.

This had all happened so fast that Carolina's head was reeling, but she allowed Katie to lead her into the main entrance of the boys ranch while Wyatt walked away with Matty in his arms.

"A bunch of us ladies are meeting in the dining room to plan the ice cream social," Katie explained. "We need to settle on a theme and some ideas for decorations. Lila's Café always caters the event, so we don't have to worry about hors d'oeuvres or punch."

Bea Brewster led the meeting. Carolina recognized many familiar faces. She privately admitted she'd dragged her feet in attending, wondering if people were going to judge her for the choices she'd made, coming back to town as a single mother.

But if anyone thought that way, they certainly didn't show it. Every woman in the group welcomed her openly and asked for her opinions.

When the meeting broke an hour later, plans had been set in motion for the Lady in Red–themed ice cream social. Carolina had volunteered for the decorating committee, and they had also been in charge of developing the overall idea for the social.

The theme had been Carolina's idea—or rather, it had come to her through the strange note she'd received earlier in the day. She thought it was rather clever, but only because she had no intention of being there herself, much less wearing red to the event.

She wouldn't want to give whoever had written the puzzling invitation the wrong impression about her and Wyatt.

"Whatever you were just thinking about, you have to share. Do you have a hot date for the Valentine's social?"

Carolina choked on her breath. She was glad she hadn't been sipping coffee from the mug in front of her or the hot liquid would have gone down the wrong pipe and she would have spit it halfway across the room. As it was, she couldn't catch her breath.

"Gracious, no," she managed to rasp.

Katie arched her blond eyebrows and her green eyes sparkled impishly. "I thought maybe Wyatt would have asked you."

"Absolutely not," Carolina assured her. "Wyatt and I are a thing of the past. We share a child. That's as far as it goes. He barely tolerates me, and trust me, that is only for Matty's sake."

"Is that what you think?"

"Why? Has he said something?" Her rebellious heart leaped into double time.

"No," Katie was quick to amend. "But I've seen the way he looks at you when he thinks no one is watching him. I'm good at reading other people's expressions."

"I'm sure you are, but this time you're mistaken."

Katie chuckled. "Am I?"

Carolina nodded, but the thought, even if it was erroneous, made her chest cloud with a half dozen unnamed and undesired emotions.

Whatever Wyatt thought about her, it wasn't in any way romantic. Of that much she was certain. But there was something she wanted to ask, and Katie was the perfect person to provide an answer while at the same time being discreet about it.

She dug into her handbag and withdrew the questionable invitation. "I did receive this. And to be honest, I'm completely flummoxed by it."

She slid the envelope over to Katie, who quickly scanned the contents and then promptly burst into laughter.

Carolina grinned. "Isn't that the funniest thing you've ever seen? Those spelling mistakes are to die for. It's obviously not from Wyatt."

"Obviously," Katie agreed, clearly trying to maintain her composure.

"It just randomly showed up in my mailbox this morning. No stamp or return address. Whoever stuck it in there put the flag up so I would notice. I'm assuming this is some kind of prank, but what I can't figure out is who would do this and why anyone would sign Wyatt's name to it."

"The mystery matchmakers."

"The what who?"

"They've been wreaking a bit of havoc all over town for the last few months now. No one has yet discovered who they are, although many of us suspect it may be some of the more impish residents of the boys ranch. It sounds like they are really stepping up their game for Valentine's Day. I've heard of a lot of missives being delivered. It's one of the perks of being the boys ranch secretary. I hear all the gossip."

"Fill me in."

"It's kind of cute, really. And whoever they are, they've been remarkably accurate in their predictions. Couples are coming together thanks to them. They've had quite a few more wins than losses."

"Score this one in the loss column," Carolina assured her with a laugh.

"You should wear red to the social." Again, the gleam in Katie's eyes was unmistakable.

Carolina fidgeted in her seat.

"I'm certainly not going to encourage them—whoever *they* are, with their silly matchmaking scheme. I can't imagine why they would bother with me, and I don't want them thinking Wyatt and I are an item." She paused. "What about you? Who have these mystery matchmakers paired you with?"

Katie shook her head and smiled weakly. "I'm apparently flying under their radar."

Carolina thought she heard a note of melancholy in her tone and was going to ask about it, but Katie continued before she could say a word.

"That's just as well. Really. I'm already head over heels in love with someone, although he doesn't even know I exist. There's no hope for me, and I don't think the mystery matchmakers could help."

"Who is it?" Carolina felt a little as if she were back in high school again, gossiping with a good friend. It was a light, happy feeling, and she hadn't had too many of those lately, so she embraced it.

It was much better than worrying about her own problems. It was refreshing to think about someone else's relationship status for a change, even if poor Katie seemed to be having her share of problems in the romance department.

Katie leaned in so only Carolina could hear her speak. "Can you keep a secret?" she whispered.

"Of course." Carolina's grin widened and she made a motion of locking her lips and throwing away the key.

"It's Pastor Andrew." Katie sighed dramatically. "I'm pretty sure he doesn't even know I exist, other than being one of his most devoted parishioners. I don't miss a service." Her brow scrunched over her nose and she giggled. "Oh, dear. That doesn't sound very good, does it? I really do go to church to worship God. But I can't help how I feel about Pastor Andrew. The heart wants what the heart wants, as they say. Oh, well. It's not like I would be a good minister's wife."

"I don't know about what *they* say, but I say if Pastor Andrew hasn't noticed you, then he's the one who is missing the mark. If you ask me, he ought to get his eyes checked and his head examined. You're a beautiful woman, inside and out. A man would be crazy not to notice you."

Katie's cheeks turned a pretty shade of pink. "You know what? Don't worry overmuch about keeping my secret." She highlighted the word *secret* in air quotes. "I'm fairly certain everyone in Haven knows I'm pining after the minister. Everyone except him, that is."

"Let's see what we can do about that." Carolina was

already formulating possibilities in her mind to help her friend get the pastor's attention.

Katie squeaked and laid a hand on Carolina's forearm. "No. Please don't. I'd die of embarrassment."

She laughed. "Don't worry. I was just kidding. I wouldn't want to interfere in anyone's love life. Trust me. My own track record in the romance department is a dismal failure. It wouldn't be wise of you to take any advice from me."

"Maybe we'll both find someone special at the ice cream social," Katie suggested, although her tone indicated she didn't really believe what she was saying.

"That could be problematic, since I'm not going to be there."

"What?" Katie squawked, sounding a bit like a macaw. "Oh, yes, you are. Please say you are *not* going to leave me alone as the only wallflower in the room."

"Somehow I don't think you'll be alone for long. You couldn't possibly be a wallflower."

"I will be if you aren't there to offer moral support. The whole night will be a complete disaster."

Carolina narrowed her gaze thoughtfully. "Is Pastor Andrew going to be there?"

Katie laughed. "I'm sure he will be. He never misses an opportunity to eat free food."

Carolina knew she was going to regret what she was about to say next. She had no desire to be, as Katie had called it, a wallflower at this event.

Even worse, someone out there thought she and Wyatt still belonged together, enough to take the time to write a note. What if these mystery matchmakers somehow tried to push them together at the social?

Maybe Wyatt wouldn't show up at the social at all. She could hope, couldn't she?

Because she could hardly say no to Katie's request, not when the young woman had been such a big help to her since she'd come back to town, lending an ear when Carolina needed to talk and watching Matty whenever she needed assistance or had a job interview.

Matty.

He might just be her ticket out.

Everyone in town would be at the social—Katie included. Which would mean finding Matty a babysitter would be next to impossible.

"I'll come with you," she agreed with a shrug, "as long as I can find someone to watch Matty. Although at this late date I doubt I'll be able to find anyone suitable."

Katie squealed in delight. "Yay! It's a done deal, then. You probably didn't know this, but child care will be provided right here at the social."

Carolina groaned inwardly.

What had she just been talked into? Nothing she wanted to do, that was for sure. She would have tried to find another excuse to back out, but Katie's expression looked so hopeful, flooding with joy.

Apparently, Carolina was going to the Lone Star Cowboy League's Valentine's Day ice cream social.

But she would not—*not*—wear red.

Chapter Six

Wyatt couldn't remember a day when he had ever had as much fun as he was having at this moment. Who knew that having a child—*his* child—accompany him to a community event could bring such a ray of sunshine into his life?

He'd always wanted to be a father, but it had seemed like a distant dream, especially after Carolina had disappeared from his life. To have Matty with him now seemed like more of a blessing than he deserved.

But he would take it, and be grateful for it.

Wyatt's chest burst with pride for his little guy, who, with Johnny's gentle, constant assistance, fastidiously mimicked his daddy's every move, using his little plastic tools to saw and hammer the random chunks of two-by-fours Wyatt had provided for him.

Johnny's attention was focused far more on Matty than on the construction going on around them. Wyatt couldn't have asked for better help.

He grinned at the pair. They almost looked like brothers with their heads together, animatedly working on their little project. Wyatt was still amazed at how much Johnny had come out of his shell with Matty.

The teenager's stutter wasn't as pronounced when he was around the toddler, and they looked equally excited about the little house they were making from wood scraps and some glue.

Wyatt stopped and watched them for a minute. There was something about being responsible for the welfare of his dark-haired little boy that spoke to the deepest, most protective and masculine part of Wyatt's heart. His feelings for Matty opened up a whole new world for him.

He might have missed a couple of Matty's formative years, but he was here now, and here he intended to stay.

"I can't believe how much you guys have already done on the barn."

Carolina had approached from behind him and he hadn't seen her coming, but he turned and smiled at her.

"We have plenty of help here today. It should be no problem finishing before the sun goes down."

"I hope Matty wasn't underfoot too much for you. I was worried he might get in the way."

"Not at all. You'll be happy to know that our son is a regular builder," Wyatt said, showing off the little house Matty and Johnny had constructed. He couldn't help the way his chest swelled with pride.

"How cute," Carolina exclaimed, stooping down to admire the project. "What a neat-looking house. It has a door and windows, too. Very clever."

"That was M-Matty's idea," Johnny said, pushing his hair off his forehead.

"Well, it looks to me like you've been a big help to him. I'm sure he couldn't have done it without you."

Wyatt could see how much her compliment meant

to the teenager, and the smile she flashed him had the young man grinning ear to ear. It was good to see Johnny happy. He didn't smile very often.

But it wasn't Johnny's smile that had Wyatt uncomfortably shifting his weight. When Carolina's countenance warmed, Wyatt's nerves energized and his pulse leaped. Suddenly he was having difficulty finding his voice.

After everything he and Carolina had been through, after her heartless betrayal of everything Wyatt held dear, how could her smile—and worse yet, one that was not even directed at him—make him feel giddy and light-headed?

He wondered what would happen if she looked at *him* with such happiness and joy in her eyes.

No. He did not.

Been there. Done that. Ripped up and threw away the T-shirt.

How many times did he need to remind himself that whatever feelings she evoked in him didn't count?

He sighed inwardly. He'd probably have to keep mentally giving himself the same warning until he no longer felt anything when he looked at Carolina.

Which was likely to be never.

He shook his head. There was undeniable chemistry between them. Nothing more. As long as he knew it was only the sound of her laughter and the floral scent of her perfume that was jogging his memories, he could keep a handle on it, remain in control.

And he would keep telling himself that until he believed it.

Carolina scooped Matty into her arms and swung him around until he giggled with delight. Up until that moment, Wyatt would never have imagined that a mother holding a child could be attractive to a man, but there was no doubt about it when his heart flooded with emotions.

The protectiveness and affection he felt couldn't be denied or written off, nor could the fact that it wasn't only Matty who precipitated those feelings.

No.

This had to stop. Right now.

He turned his gaze away from Carolina and picked up his hammer.

"I came to tell you lunch is ready." If she noticed his sudden aversion to her, she didn't react to it. "We're serving sandwiches buffet style in the backyard. We borrowed fold-up tables from the church for the meal."

Wyatt's stomach rumbled and Carolina laughed.

He frowned.

Stupid stomach.

Even his gut unrepentantly responded to her voice. *Nothing but trouble, Harrow.*

But he *was* hungry, so he reluctantly joined Carolina, Matty and Johnny as they walked back to the main house. Carolina kept up a lively conversation, asking Johnny about school, his veterinary work with Wyatt and how the young buck they had saved from the middle of the road was faring.

The young man's stutter increased when he spoke to her, but he seemed happy to have her attention. He stayed close even after they'd piled up their plates full of food, even though most of the other boys were already seated. Wyatt felt bad for Johnny, but Matty was pleased by the teenager's presence, and Johnny didn't seem to mind.

Wyatt could only pick out bits and pieces of the chatter, but not surprisingly, the topic of the day appeared to be the backlash the boys ranch was feeling due to the arson and thefts.

"Why do I feel as if there is more of a problem here than just the burned-down barn?" Carolina asked, sliding onto a chair opposite Wyatt, balancing Matty in one arm and two plates of food in the other. She set Matty down next to her and passed him one plate.

"The Department of Family and Protective Services has recently been taking a good, hard look at the boys ranch," he explained.

Bea Brewster took a seat next to Wyatt, and Katie sat down next to Carolina.

"We're afraid the DFPS is going to show up here unannounced," said Bea, clicking her tongue. "We're running this ranch completely by the book, of course, but you know how it is. If they're actively looking for some broken regulation, they'll probably find one. None of us is perfect."

"We'd just as soon get completely off their radar," Katie added. "And sooner rather than later."

Wyatt couldn't help but notice how Katie's gaze kept straying toward Pastor Andrew. When the pastor waved in her direction, her cheeks turned pink and she quickly looked away.

Poor woman. Unrequited love was the worst.

He should know.

"As if we needed the extra stress." Darcy Hill, along with her fiancé, Nick, joined the small group. Only recently engaged, they should have only had eyes for each other, but Wyatt could see the strain on their faces from all of the current stress. "We're having a hard enough time working out all the details of the seventieth-anniversary party. Between Gabe not being able to find his grandfather and us not having any success locating the real Avery Culpepper so she can claim her part of the will—well, let's just say things could be better."

Nick kissed Darcy's temple. "Trust in the Lord and He will direct your path," he paraphrased, his voice not a reprimand but a gentle reminder.

"I know. I know. I think I've narrowed our viable choices down to one woman, but she lives in Tennessee and won't respond to my calls and letters. Still, it looks promising. Her mother's name was Elizabeth and her birthday is February second. The facts fit together. I only wish I could get a personal confirmation from her."

"Maybe try to connect with her through social media?" Carolina suggested.

Darcy smiled, her expression full of determination. "I tried that, too, but so far I haven't heard back. Otherwise I may have to fly out to Tennessee and hunt her down in person. This reunion is far too important to the future of the boys ranch, and too many people have worked too hard on it, for us to fail now."

"Hear, hear," said Wyatt, toasting his cola can at her. He wished he could personally do more to make sure the seventieth-anniversary party went off without a hitch, but there was little he could do to help.

What he *could* do was make sure he crossed all his t's and dotted all his i's where the boys ranch animal programs were concerned. The DFPS, if they did happen to show up unannounced, would find all the ranch animals in excellent condition and his program running precisely by the book.

"Gabe's grandfather is estranged from his family?" Carolina asked no one in particular.

"Theodore Linley is not only estranged," Nick answered, running a hand through his chestnut-brown hair, "but he has vanished right off the globe. It's kind of sad, really. He abandoned his family when Gabe was about eight, and he was in prison for a while on charges of petty theft, but no one has heard from him since. The prison is officially his last known whereabouts. After he was released, he just disappeared. I don't think he wants to be found."

Wyatt cringed inwardly. He felt sorry for Gabe. If ever a man needed divine assistance, it was Gabe. This situation definitely warranted it. So many people depended on one man's success.

Wyatt's thoughts were almost a prayer.

Almost.

Feeling uncomfortable in his own skin, Wyatt broke a freshly baked chocolate chip cookie in half and showed it to Carolina.

"Is it okay for Matty to have a cookie?"

"Cookie!" Matty exclaimed.

"Oops." Wyatt grinned awkwardly.

Carolina chuckled. "No worries. He was a good boy and ate all of his sandwich. I don't think half a cookie will do him any harm. I'll make sure he brushes his teeth as soon as we get back to the cabin."

As Wyatt offered his son the cookie, a ruckus broke out near the end of the table. Wyatt glanced up to see two of the boys ranch residents—blond-haired, blue-eyed Danny McCann and brown-haired, blue-eyed Jasper Boswell—giggling and shoving each other. They were both eight years old, and they both had similar impish expressions on their faces. They were obviously looking for trouble.

Danny carried a single pink rose with a note tied to it—a sheet of typing paper folded into quarters.

The laughing boys made a lunge toward Katie Ellis, whose face had gone from pink to a flaming red as Danny thrust the rose toward her and she took the bloom in her hand.

"Oh, my," she breathed, and then giggled in delight. "This is for me?"

"Flying under their radar, huh?" Carolina teased, nudging Katie with her shoulder.

Wyatt fought to restrain a grin. He didn't have to ask who *they* were. The mystery matchmakers had struck again. And Katie seemed happy to be the recipient.

Odd, though, that the boys were delivering the message in person, in a public place, right out in the open where everyone could see. Up until now the matchmakers had acted in private, not revealing their identities as they slyly delivered their messages.

Like, for example, the note he had found on the welcome mat on his front porch just this morning. Short, sweet and to the point.

Carolina would be waiting for him at the ice cream social. And she would be wearing red.

He knew very well the note hadn't been from Carolina, and he hadn't even stopped to consider why the mystery matchmakers would choose her as his date in the first place.

So it was Jasper Boswell and Danny McCann playing Cupid, was it? Wyatt couldn't say he was completely surprised, although the fact that they were only eight years old seemed a little strange. How could such young boys manage to pull off these stunts?

Could they even write the kinds of notes folks were getting? And what did eight-year-old boys know about romance? Whoever the mystery matchmakers were had been surprisingly accurate in their pairings. He suspected some of the older boys were involved, as well, if for nothing else because someone needed to drive the younger kids around.

Conversation ceased as Katie unfolded the note and scanned its contents.

Her smile dropped from her face and tears sprang to her eyes. She stood so abruptly her silverware clattered.

"Excuse me," she said, her hand flying to her throat as she ran into the house.

Carolina's distressed gaze met Wyatt's and he arched his brow in question. Carolina had been close enough to be able to read the note. What was written on it that had sent poor Katie running off in tears?

Carolina shook her head with a brief jerk of her chin and mouthed the word *later*.

"Keep an eye on Matty?" she asked aloud.

"Of course." No question there.

Carolina took off after Katie and Wyatt switched sides of the table so he was sitting next to his son.

"Is K-Katie going to be all right?" Johnny asked. Wyatt knew Katie was one of the few people who was always kind to Johnny, so he wasn't surprised that the teenager was concerned about her.

"Oh, I imagine she'll be fine," Wyatt answered with what he hoped was a reassuring grin. "It's just girl stuff. You know how women can be. Katie's probably in the bathroom crying because she is so happy to have received a rose."

Johnny didn't look convinced. Probably because Wyatt wasn't, either.

But whatever the note had said, and whatever Katie's reaction had truly been to its contents, she was blessed to have a friend like Carolina. For all her faults, Carolina was the compassionate shoulder Katie could cry on—happy, sad or somewhere in between.

He wasn't going to be in the office much the following week, but he figured he would find out the details eventually. If not, he'd ask about Katie, make sure she was okay.

If he had to guess, he would think the note had something to do with the Valentine's social. He imagined both Carolina and Katie would be there—as, much to his dismay, would he.

As a general rule, he didn't care for dances, but he had promised to escort Gran to the event. The elderly population of Haven's nursing home would stay for the first hour to enjoy the party and then be taken back to the home by orderlies. Wyatt hoped it would do Gran good to attend a social outing, although of course that was never a sure thing, especially lately.

In the meantime, if he found the opportunity to do so, he thought he might have to have a word with Danny and Jasper. A harmless prank was one thing, but making a woman cry? That was something else entirely. If they had anything to do with it, Wyatt would see that they apologized to poor Katie.

He wondered which, if any, of the other boys were involved in the mystery matchmaking shenanigans. He briefly considered telling the boys about his own letter, but then thought better of it.

If Danny and Jasper weren't the only ones writing these notes—and Wyatt's gut told him that they weren't—then he didn't want to draw their attention to his supposed match with Carolina. That was inconsequential information.

Even if it had somehow left an indelible mark in Wyatt's heart.

The attempted matchmaking would eventually blow over on its own—although for his sake, and for Carolina's, he hoped she wouldn't be wearing red at the Valentine's social.

That could be bad.

Very bad, indeed.

Carolina stood in a corner on the far side of the church's fellowship hall, which she had helped transform into a Valentine's Day wonderland of red, pink and glittering silver hearts, bows and ribbons.

The silk blouse she was wearing was the only thing in her closet that even remotely resembled anything that would work for a Valentine's Day party. With her complexion, she couldn't pull off most shades of pink, and she hadn't had time to go shopping for anything a little less blatantly—

Red.

She'd only agreed to wear the telling color because it was part of the overall theme and she didn't want to let Katie down, not to mention the ladies who'd planned the event. She didn't want to inadvertently offend anyone.

So, limited in her choices, she had arrived in traditional Valentine's Day colors.

The Lady in Red.

Yep. That was her.

She wanted to roll her eyes. After only half an hour, she was already turning herself into the most modern definition of the word *wallflower*, and she was grateful she wasn't standing out from the crowd by wearing blue or green.

Which she had considered.

But *why* did it have to be red?

She felt as if dozens of eyes were surreptitiously upon her—she who had exactly followed the instructions of the mystery matchmakers. Were they gleefully giggling somewhere?

Not that anyone other than the kids who wrote the note—and Katie, who'd read it—would even know what was contained within. But the last thing she wanted to do was inadvertently encourage silly boys' misconceptions.

What if they left a note for Wyatt next time?

A shock of adrenaline bolted through her as it occurred to her that Wyatt might already have received a similar missive.

What if he would be looking to see if she wore red?

After that first moment of alarm, she calmed down. He hadn't said anything about having received a letter, so she was probably safe.

Katie had insisted that she and Carolina park themselves in the corner nearest the ice cream sundae bar, since dessert would presumably be the utmost thought in most of the single men's minds.

Single men, meaning Pastor Andrew, Carolina thought, amused. She didn't want to mention that she had no interest whatsoever in the single men of Haven.

At first, Katie had been taken aback and was downright indignant by the mystery matchmakers' note. With as deep as Katie's feelings ran, it was hardly a joking matter to tease her with a letter.

Unlike Carolina's awkwardly scribbled note, Katie's had been carefully typewritten. Even the signature was typeset.

Be my valentine at the ice cream social.
Pastor Andrew

Katie had regained her composure shortly after receiving the note and the rose, and, in her usually upbeat way, had overcome her initial sensitivity.

A typed signature? That was a dead giveaway for sure. There was no sense in her being a bad sport when most of the other singles in town had also received letters.

Carolina hoped Pastor Andrew hadn't heard about it. It seemed to her that the minister was as shy and awkward around Katie as she was with him. Knowing there had been an attempt at matching up the two would only serve to make things worse for both of them.

Along with Katie, Carolina was keeping her eyes trained on the door, watching laughing couples enter and mingle, and silently praying that someday, one of those happy couples would be Katie and Pastor Andrew.

A tiny flame flickered in her heart—one that she barely dared acknowledge.

The hope that she might one day have someone special to share her life with.

Her pulse jumped when Wyatt entered the room, gently escorting his gran through the crowd and to a chair near where some of her friends from the nursing home were located.

Katie nudged Carolina's shoulder with hers. "What are you waiting for? For Wyatt to notice your red blouse?"

"Ha-ha. Very funny."

Carolina was not amused.

But she did want to go speak to Eva. It was sweet of Wyatt to bring his grandmother to the social. If Eva was having a lucid day, she would welcome Carolina's familiar face. If not, Wyatt could more than likely use all the help he could get to keep her happy.

Either way…

"All right. But you're coming with me." Carolina looped her arm through Katie's, ignoring the heat rising to her face. She felt like a teenager at her first high school dance.

It wasn't a fond memory.

Eva, she reminded herself. She was doing this for Eva. There was no reason for her to feel uncomfortable.

"Eva," Carolina exclaimed as they neared. "I see you managed to talk your handsome grandson into being your date for the dance."

The older woman's eyes met hers and flashed with recognition.

"Carolina."

She crouched before the old woman and took both of her hands. Her skin felt thin and brittle to the touch, like parchment paper.

"Wyatt?"

"I'm here, Gran."

Wyatt shifted so his grandmother could see him, standing directly behind Carolina. His warm palm brushed her hair off her shoulder and electricity skittered down her spine.

Eva clucked at them. "Wyatt, take your wife out there and dance. I'll be fine here for a little while."

Carolina scrambled to make sense of the words, and it took her a while to realize Eva's gaze was resting firmly on her.

"I'm not—"

"You know I don't dance." Wyatt's laugh sounded forced as he squeezed Carolina's shoulder.

A silent reminder.

Of course. She was the registered nurse here, and yet she'd been the one to get confused. She, more than anyone, ought to know that Eva's faculties weren't working at full capacity. Her mind worked in bits and pieces. Eva probably remembered her and Wyatt together in the past and, seeing them together now, had mistakenly made more of it than it was.

Much more.

And she was embarrassed to realize how completely that connection had thrown her off.

Wyatt had done the right thing—redirecting his grandmother without correcting her misconceptions. In a short time, Eva wouldn't remember what she had said, anyway.

But Carolina would.

Eva's statement would be branded on her mind for a long time to come.

Carolina stood abruptly, her shoulders plowing into Wyatt's chest. He put out his hands to steady her.

"I'm sorry, I—" She searched for an excuse to make a speedy exit, but nothing came to mind.

She was grateful when Katie stepped in.

"Carolina and I were about to get a bowl of ice cream," Katie said cheerfully. "Wyatt, can we get you and your gran anything? A glass of punch or something?"

Wyatt shook his head, and Carolina scrambled back to the safety of the corner wall she'd originally been holding up, leaning against it and focusing on slowing her breath.

She would never, *ever* complain about being a wall-flower again.

"Well, that was interesting," Katie said with a laugh. "Mrs. Harrow."

Carolina groaned. "Please. Let's not even go there."

She needn't have worried. A moment later, Katie grabbed Carolina by the shoulders and ducked behind her.

"What now?"

"I'm so not ready for this."

Carolina spotted Pastor Andrew in the crowd and had to remind herself that Katie was still a young woman, with a young woman's hopes and dreams. It couldn't be easy for her, crushing on the town's minister—

Who looked like he was walking straight toward them.

"Katie, I think you'd better—" Carolina started to warn, but she didn't have the opportunity to complete her statement before Pastor Andrew was upon them.

He was a tall, lanky man with kind hazel eyes. He scrubbed a hand through his light brown hair as he approached.

He looked as nervous as Katie was acting. Katie made an incomprehensible squeaking sound but stepped forward, smoothing her bright pink dress with her hand.

"Katie," Pastor Andrew said, and then, almost as an afterthought, he nodded at her. "Carolina."

Carolina didn't mind at all that the minister only had eyes for the boys ranch secretary. This could be good. She sent up a silent prayer for the couple.

Pastor Andrew cleared his throat and shoved his hands into the pockets of his black slacks. He had a real gift in the pulpit and in counseling the boys at the ranch, but he looked like he was having trouble speaking to Katie. His Adam's apple bobbed and he cleared his throat a second time.

"Katie, I—I was just… How are you?"

Somehow Carolina didn't think that was the question the minister had intended to ask, but Katie, her face taking on a rosy glow that matched the color of her dress, didn't seem to notice.

"Very well, thank you," she answered shyly. "And you?"

"I'm good. Fine. That is, I just—" Pastor Andrew hesitated and rocked back on the heels of his cowboy boots. He took a deep breath and let it all out at once in a string of words. "Here's the thing. I was wondering if you read my note."

Katie's eyes went as wide as saucers. Carolina had to admit she was almost as surprised as her friend was.

The typewritten note and the rose were actually from Pastor Andrew?

He had been at the barn raising when Katie had received the letter and gift, but Carolina couldn't remember if he'd stayed to eat lunch. Had he seen her run out of the room crying?

No wonder the poor man was a bundle of nerves.

Carolina pushed Katie forward and tried to fade into the background so the couple could talk, but she didn't get far enough away that she couldn't hear what was going on between the two of them. This was just too good to miss.

And *so* romantic.

Her heart welled. She tried not to shift her gaze to Wyatt but failed miserably. She caught his eyes momentarily, gulped in a breath of air and forced herself to look away.

"That was *you*?" Katie finally found her voice.

Pastor Andrew's brow creased in confusion. "Of course it was me. I signed the note, didn't I?"

"It was typewritten."

"Yes. Well. Is—is that a problem?"

"No. It's just that I thought it must have been the mystery matchmakers at work. It wasn't handwritten, and a couple of boys delivered it."

Now it was Pastor Andrew's turn to redden. "That's the last time I try to be romantic," he mumbled under his breath.

Then, louder, he said, "I am so sorry. I can see now how you might have gotten the wrong impression. I typed the note because my handwriting is atrocious and I was afraid you wouldn't be able to read it. Worse than a doctor's script, I can promise you. I can't even read my own writing sometimes. I wanted to let you know I was interested, but instead I made you believe the exact opposite.

"I had the boys deliver the letter because—oh, never mind what I was thinking about. What matters is what you think, Katie."

"What I think?" Katie parroted, her voice still high and squeaky.

"About what I said in the note. You know—the question I asked?"

Pastor Andrew held his hand out to Katie and grinned. "Will you be my valentine?"

Carolina was happy for her friends. She really was. But she couldn't help the way her heart dipped as she considered her own circumstances.

There would be no valentine for her.

Chapter Seven

The nursing home orderlies showed up about an hour after the event started and relieved Wyatt of having to watch Gran.

No—*having* wasn't the right word. He was happy to spend time with Gran, to be her date, especially since she seemed to know who he was tonight. Granted, she'd gotten the part about his being married to Carolina wrong, but who could blame her? Past and present melded in her mind.

It was gratifying to see the joy in her eyes as she watched couples dance, and as she indulged in her own bit of perfection in the form of a bowl of chocolate ice cream smothered in hot fudge sauce. Chocolate on chocolate. The smile on her face when she looked at him was worth every bit of effort it had taken him to get her here.

But she tired easily and was more than ready when the orderlies appeared to take her away.

But now that Gran had been taken back to the nursing home, Wyatt wasn't sure what to do with himself. He probably would have left when Gran did, except

Johnny had joined him and was in the midst of a major teenage meltdown.

Wyatt did not miss being that age, when every little thing felt like the end of the world.

Did the girl he admired like him? Did he dare ask her to dance?

At least Johnny's crisis helped Wyatt not chew his cud over his grandmother's mistaken impression that Carolina was his wife.

Why couldn't he let that thought go?

Johnny fidgeted beside him, clenching and un-clenching his fists in an uneasy rhythm and mutter-ing to himself under his breath.

"You're going to have to relax, pal." Wyatt laid a hand on the boy's shoulder. "You're hyperventilating. Your girl will probably notice you if you pass out, but I think it would be better for both of you if you didn't."

Johnny didn't laugh at Wyatt's pathetic attempt at humor. From time to time, the young man would glance across the room to where a small group of teen-age girls huddled, but his gaze never lingered very long.

Wyatt conspiratorially bent his head toward Johnny. "So which one is she, again?"

Johnny had spoken of Cassie Kramer, a pretty girl he knew from the high school he attended. Johnny hadn't said much, but Wyatt had poked around a lit-tle bit and discovered Cassie was in the homecoming court and a star player on the girls' basketball team. She hadn't let her popularity go to her head, as Wyatt remembered the girls often doing when he was in high school. Rather, Johnny said she always smiled at him and sometimes stopped to talk in the hall, never belit-tling him for his stutter.

"The b-brunette," Johnny answered, shifting from one foot to another. "The p-pretty one."

Wyatt had no idea what constituted beauty in a modern teenager, so he took a guess. "The one in the pink sweater? You're right. She is pretty."

Johnny nodded so voraciously that a large lock of his curly dark hair dropped over his forehead.

"S-so is C-Carolina. She's w-wearing red."

Wyatt's eyebrows shot up and then he narrowed his eyes on his teenage protégé, He hadn't mentioned anything to Johnny about the note he had received, especially the part about Carolina wearing red.

Which meant...

He'd found his mystery matchmaker.

But why would Johnny want to set him up with Carolina? He decided to play along.

Wyatt smiled slyly and winked at Johnny. "Yeah. I noticed."

He tried not to hazard a glance at Carolina but couldn't seem to help himself. She was standing alone in the corner, her arms crossed in front of her as if she were cold, even though it was quite warm in the building. Wyatt felt a trickle of sweat run down his spine.

He turned his attention back to Johnny.

"So. This Cassie girl. Are you going to ask her to dance, or what?"

The stain on Johnny's cheeks intensified. Johnny gaped at him and shook his head.

"I could n-never—"

"Why not?" Wyatt wasn't much of a judge about such things, but despite the young man's shyness and stutter, he was a nice enough kid in both looks and personality. And he was as loyal as they came. A girl could do worse.

"C-Cassie is—" Johnny didn't finish his sentence.

"Cassie is standing right over there waiting for you to go and ask her to dance. She's glanced your way several times now."

His eyes widened. "At m-me?"

"Yes, at you. Don't sound so surprised." Wyatt nodded toward Cassie. "Go."

Johnny had always taken Wyatt's advice, so he was taken aback when the teenager shook his head.

"You aren't d-dancing. Neither is C-Carolina."

"I don't dance."

Johnny shrugged. "N-neither do I."

Wyatt could see where this was going. Johnny was continuing to play matchmaker, although after Gran's surprise statement this evening it seemed the boy would have to get in line for that particular job. Still, Wyatt was surprised at Johnny's sudden gumption. Who knew that the teenager had a stubborn streak?

"I see. So let me get this straight. The deal is that if I dance with Carolina, you will dance with Cassie?"

Johnny hesitated, then nodded.

"Okay."

"Okay?" Wyatt hadn't really expected Johnny to go for it. Now he was in a fix, but he could hardly back out now that he'd stuck his foot in his mouth. He ran a hand across his jaw. "All right, then. Let's do it."

He shook Johnny's hand to seal the deal and watched as the teen crossed the room toward his crush.

Smooth move, Harrow.

Now what was he going to do? What was Carolina going to think when he approached her with this crazy scheme? But there was no point lingering. He had to ask, even if she laughed him out of the building.

He took a deep breath and headed toward Carolina,

reminding himself that this was no more difficult than what he'd just asked Johnny to do. When he reached Carolina's side, he held out his hand to her.

"Help a guy out here, huh?"

He meant Johnny, of course, and he glanced over his shoulder to see how the boy was doing. Johnny was standing right next to Cassie, his hands shyly jammed into the front pockets of his oversized jeans. He and Cassie weren't yet headed for the dance floor, but at least she'd apparently welcomed him into the conversation with her friends.

Could be worse.

Like standing here with his arm extended when there was zero response from the woman he'd just asked to dance.

Not a positive response, at any rate. Carolina was staring at his hand as if he were holding a big, hairy spider on his palm.

She gradually met his gaze and raised an eyebrow.

"What?" he muttered.

"I think that should be my question."

"It's a simple yes or no."

"To?"

He huffed out a breath. She knew how difficult this was for him and she was going to make him ask her twice. She was enjoying this *way* too much, if the amused gleam in her eye was anything to go by.

"Dance. Do you want to dance with me, or not?"

"Dance? You want to dance? With *me*?" Her expression was so full of astonishment he would almost think she hadn't known that was what he had been asking her all along.

"Yes, with you. What else did you think I would be asking you?"

"I can't imagine. But you don't dance."

"No. I don't. But I'm making an exception just this once, for a good cause."

The lights in the fellowship hall had been turned off, replaced by the glow of several party lamps that sent soft, swirling balls of muted color—green, blue and red—swirling around the room. It was difficult for Wyatt to tell for certain, but he was fairly positive her color heightened when she placed her hand in his.

It felt right, though, somehow, when he closed his hand over hers and led her out to the dance floor, and even more when he turned and took her into his arms. Their eyes met and locked and his breath hitched in his throat.

All of a sudden, he forgot all about Johnny and the initial reason he had asked her to dance. The people around them faded away and his pulse echoed to the slow, steady beat of the music.

Her hand slid from his shoulder to his chest until her palm covered his heart. The warmth in her eyes spread through him like honey.

His gaze dropped to her full lips, which were tinted with a sparkling red gloss that perfectly matched her blouse.

She was wearing red.

Well, of course she was. Half the women in the room were wearing red. It was Valentine's Day, after all, so it wasn't a huge stretch that she'd decided to wear that color.

But was it possible she'd received a note from the mystery matchmakers similar to the one that had shown up at his door?

Was she sending him a message?

"You're wearing red," he murmured, bending his

head so he could whisper into her ear. His lips were close enough that he thought she might be able to feel him smile.

She pushed against him.

Hard.

What?

Confusion spun through him.

He leaned back enough to put space between them, but he didn't release her from his arms.

"People are watching us," she hissed in a low, scratchy voice.

He'd been so caught up in the moment that he'd completely forgotten there *were* people around them who could be watching.

He blinked, his head still fuzzy.

She was right. Whatever had been about to happen between them shouldn't be happening. This wasn't the best idea he'd ever had, particularly not in public.

But then again, he really hadn't been thinking at all.

He furtively glanced around them and was relieved to find no one was paying particular attention to them—no one except Johnny, who still stood in the midst of the group of girls. The teenager was staring right at them and grinning like a blooming madman.

Wyatt couldn't fathom why, but his being with Carolina seemed particularly important to Johnny.

Wait a minute. He was only out here on the dance floor with Carolina in the first place for Johnny's sake—or at least, that was his excuse, and he was going to stick with it.

Johnny, on the other hand, wasn't keeping his end of the bargain.

Wyatt mock frowned and nodded his head toward Cassie. Johnny looked down, clearly gathering his courage, and then tapped Cassie on the shoulder and gestured toward the dance floor.

There was a long moment when Cassie hesitated and Wyatt held his breath. If she blew Johnny off, then Wyatt would be responsible for getting his hopes up, only to see them dashed upon the ragged rocks of reality, as had happened to Wyatt. The last thing Johnny needed was another reason for him to doubt himself.

Cassie said something to the group of girls and then put her arm around Johnny's waist and smiled up at him.

Wyatt let out the breath he'd been holding in an audible whoosh of air. Relief flooded through him.

Carolina followed the direction of his gaze.

"It looks like Johnny's having fun. Is that his girlfriend?"

"Not yet." He smiled down at her. "But he'd like her to be."

"It looks like he's getting a good start, then. They are a cute couple."

"Yeah. They are. I think Johnny is still really nervous though. He's stumbling over his feet. I hope he can relax enough to enjoy his dance."

"Why aren't you?"

"Enjoying the dance?"

Oh, but he was. Too much, in fact.

"Stumbling over your feet. I thought you said you don't dance."

"I said I *don't* dance. Not that I *can't* dance. Gran made me take lessons when I was a kid. Ballroom dancing." He cringed at the memory.

"Well, the lessons paid off. You should give your gran an extra hug next time you see her."

The gap between them lessened as a new song started and their eyes once again met and held.

"You mentioned the fact that I am wearing red," she said thoughtfully.

He shrugged, not wanting to get into the whole mystery matchmaker thing if he had been the only one to receive a letter from them.

"Yeah, well, I guess that's no big surprise, is it, seeing as it's Valentine's Day and all. R-red is a good color on you, by the way."

Oh, brother. He was starting to stutter as badly as Johnny. And he was feeling just a little bit weak in the knees.

"Thank you." She smiled sweetly, then paused and pursed her lips. "But I have to be honest. The red blouse wasn't entirely my idea."

He immediately froze on the spot, a chill skittering down his spine.

She shook her head. "I got a letter—ostensibly signed by you—suggesting I should meet you here at the ice cream social wearing red, as a beacon or something."

"It wasn't from me," he felt obligated to point out, although his heart warmed with hope.

Despite, or because of, the letter, she had worn red. Was she trying to tell him there might be a chance for them? That maybe—it would take a lot of work and forgiveness on both of their parts—but maybe they could eventually be a real family together?

Wyatt, Carolina and Matty?

That notion didn't seem quite as far off as it once had been.

"No. I know it wasn't from you," she hastened to add. "Katie told me all about the mystery matchmakers and how they are trying to set up couples all over town."

"They're fairly accurate, too."

She chuckled. "So I hear. Anyway, I would have figured it out myself even without Katie's explanation. The note was presumably signed by you, but the script was too juvenile. Even after all these years, I would recognize your handwriting if I saw it. Besides, I knew you wouldn't be asking me to a Valentine's *anything*."

Well, she was right about that. He wouldn't have asked her out.

Would he?

Holding her close in his arms now, swaying gently to the music, he wasn't so sure.

"And yet you wore red. Weren't you afraid you'd be encouraging the little rascals? Or worse yet, me?" He grinned like a hyena.

"It is the only blouse I own that fits the theme."

"Lady in Red." He nodded in appreciation, his chest filling with emotion.

"Anyway, my outfit won't set nearly as many tongues wagging as people seeing you and me out on the dance floor together."

"True."

"And yet, here we are."

He arched his eyebrows and grinned even wider. "Yes, we are."

"I'm glad."

The warmth in her eyes was too much for him. He looked away.

Johnny and Cassie were dancing nearby, and the boy was beaming with delight. Wyatt didn't envy Johnny his teenage awkwardness and angst, but he remembered what dancing with his first crush felt like.

That memory didn't hold a candle to dancing with his first and only true love.

"Yeah. I'm glad, too," he said through a dry throat. "Just look at them. They can't get enough of each other."

Carolina stopped dancing. "Them?"

She turned, following his gaze.

"Johnny?" Her voice sounded stilted, somehow, as if her feelings were hurt. "Oh. I get it."

She whirled on him but didn't step back into his embrace. He felt the emptiness both in his arms and in his heart.

"You are doing this because of Johnny." Her tone and her eyes dared him to deny it.

For a moment, he considered doing just that. He was confused. Why should that matter?

But if he told her anything less than the whole truth, she would know he was lying. He'd never been good at hiding anything from her.

"Well, yes. I told Johnny I would ask you to dance if he would ask Cassie but—"

"Right. I—I should have known. I—" She paused and pressed her palms down her long, flowing black skirt. "If you'll excuse me, I need to go check on Matty."

He didn't know what to say. He wasn't sure he could have said anything if he'd tried. All he could do was watch her walk away from him, knowing he wouldn't be seeing her again any time soon.

Why couldn't he learn when to shut up? For once, things had been going well between them, and he had opened his mouth and blown it. Now, who knew what it would take for him to get back in Carolina's good graces?

He didn't have a clue how to fix this, but somehow it had to be done. His relationship with Matty depended on it.

But if he was being honest, it was more than that. Much more.

Carolina seriously considered not going to work on Monday, but thankfully Wyatt never came around the office. She didn't know whether it was because of what had happened between them at the Valentine's social or whether he just had a heavy docket of ranch calls, but either way, she was grateful for the temporary reprieve.

But when he didn't show up on Tuesday morning, she started to wonder. And worry. She might not quite be ready to face him yet, but she was just going to have to get over herself and prepare for the eventuality of being around Wyatt without it sending her into a dither every single time.

Wyatt was now a part of Matty's life. The mature, responsible thing for Carolina to do would be to seek Wyatt out and speak to him about what had happened between them at the Valentine's social, adult to adult, and clear the air about it so they could move on.

Right this second she was really tired of *adulting*.

She wanted to go hide in her room like a brokenhearted teenager.

Brokenhearted?

Where had that come from? That was impossible. She would have to be in love with Wyatt in order for him to break her heart, and she'd left that emotion behind long ago. She wasn't even certain she had a heart to break anymore.

So maybe not a broken heart, then. But she was

certainly feeling something almost as uncomfortable. Not being able to define her feelings was not helping matters any.

Despite her best efforts, she'd grown to care about Wyatt. How could she not? They were forever connected through Matty. Watching Wyatt parent their child gave a new meaning to the word *love*, one that she could accept and embrace. There was nothing in the world like the bonding that occurred between a man and his son.

Carolina fumbled for the phone on her desk and picked up the receiver, punching in Wyatt's cell phone number before she could talk herself out of it again.

He picked up on the first ring.

"We need to talk," she said without preamble.

Silence met her on the other end of the line.

"Wyatt?"

Had he hung up on her?

"Yeah. Okay. You're right." She heard him draw in a ragged breath. "I'm heading your direction. The farrier is meeting me at my stable to trim some of the horses' hooves, and one threw a shoe the other day. If I leave now, we should have a few minutes to talk before he gets there."

"I'll keep an eye out for your truck and meet you at the stable."

"You'll have Matty with you?"

"Yes. Of course."

"Great. I thought he might like to watch Nick work on the horses."

"I'm sure he will be fascinated by it. I'll see you in a few minutes."

She hung up the phone and sighed deeply.

There. That wasn't so bad.

"Come on, Matty," she said, scooping him out of the play yard she had set up for him. "Let's go see your—"

Daddy.

Her gut tightened.

It was time.

And it was the right thing to do.

If they told Matty the truth now, the toddler would most likely never remember there had been a time when Wyatt wasn't a part of his life—though however large or small a part that ended up being was still up in the air.

Instead of waiting in the office for Wyatt to arrive at the ranch, Carolina took Matty to the stable and let him pet some of the horses, moving down the lane stall by stall. She inhaled the reassuring pungency of hay, horses and something else, an unidentifiable scent that was somehow unique to Wyatt's stable. It was probably the country girl in her, but for some reason the blend of scents soothed her.

It felt like home.

The names of each of Wyatt's horses were engraved on a wooden plaque on every stall door, and Carolina introduced her son to each horse by name.

Bash the Appaloosa, Cricket the palomino, and a beautiful paint named Chief.

When they reached the end of the row, Carolina grabbed a couple of apples from a nearby bushel and they started back the way they'd come. The stalls on the opposite side were filled with various animals Wyatt was vetting and keeping for observation. In one stall they found a sow and some cute little piglets. In another, a curious llama. And in a third, a couple of bleating goats.

"Goats!" Matty announced.

"That's right, buddy."

They paused by a pretty black mare and Matty giggled in delight as Carolina showed him how to feed the horse an apple. Even Carolina chuckled as the mare crunched on the sweet fruit, smacking her lips and showing her teeth as juice ran down her muzzle. When the mare was done, she nudged Matty's outstretched hand, looking for another treat.

"I see you found Juliet," Wyatt said as he entered the barn. "She is one of the boys ranch horses. She pulled a ligament in her leg, so I've been keeping her here for a couple of weeks to monitor her progress and do some physical therapy with her."

Carolina's eyes met Wyatt's, and a long, awkward pause followed as Carolina struggled to find the right words to express the emotions she was feeling.

Wyatt held out his arms to Matty and the toddler launched himself at his daddy, his high, youthful laugh blending with Wyatt's deeper one.

Wyatt opened the stall door and stepped inside, plunking their son onto the back of the horse.

"There you go, cowboy."

A surge of anxiety flooded through Carolina. The black was a large draft horse, and a fall would be disastrous.

"Is that safe?"

Wyatt's gaze widened on her as if she'd just said something completely outrageous—which, she guessed in hindsight, she had. She was no stranger to country living. Most of the folks who'd grown up in Haven had been riding almost as long as they'd been walking. And the draft appeared gentle.

Besides, it wasn't as if Wyatt had placed Matty on the tall mount and then walked away. Wyatt's hand was still spanning Matty's waist and the toddler had his fist tightly threaded through the mare's thick mane.

"Sorry," she apologized. "I'm being a helicopter mom again. It's a bad habit of mine."

"I don't even know what that means."

"It's like we were talking about in the park. I have the tendency to hover over Matty, worry too much about him getting hurt trying new things. I guess it's just a residual response from when I was raising him all on my own—trying to be both a mother and a father to him."

Wyatt made a low, indistinguishable sound from deep in his throat, part groan, part growl.

She held up her hands to stop him before he stated the obvious.

"I know. I know. That was entirely my own fault, born of the poor decisions I personally chose to make. I hope someday you'll find it in your heart to forgive me."

She took a deep breath and let it out slowly. Her spirit felt lightened, unburdened, now that she'd finally admitted her mistakes out loud, and to Wyatt.

His gaze narrowed and he pressed his lips into a thin, hard line. Carolina could see he was trying to suppress his urge to share his own opinions on her *choices*.

She took a deep breath and bolted ahead with her thoughts before she lost her nerve.

"That was one of the things I need to talk to you about today."

She gathered her thoughts as she considered how to approach the subject, about how it was time for Matty to know Wyatt was his daddy and how they were going to work out the logistics of sharing him between them.

What they had now, with Carolina employed in Wyatt's office, was working out wonderfully. But what would happen once Wyatt took off to do service on foreign soil? What would that mean for Matty?

For her?

She coughed to remove the strangling sensation in her throat. "For starters, though, I think we need to address what happened on the dance floor the other night."

His gaze didn't waver, but his shoulders visibly tightened and a tic of strain showed at the taut corner of his whiskered jaw.

"Nothing happened." His voice was scraping as coarse as sandpaper.

"Almost happened, then," she modified.

"What are you getting at, Carolina? We don't have much more time left before Nick gets here. If you have something that you want to say to me, just spit it out."

The harshness of his tone caused her emotions to scuttle, crab-like, back into the shell of her heart.

So much for being vulnerable. Clearly she'd misread all the signals—or maybe there hadn't been any to begin with. Was her imagination running overtime? Or maybe there were unresolved emotions lingering.

"What do you want Matty to call you?" She barely got the words out. But if he wanted a change of topic, he'd just been belted with the best one she had.

"I—" He paused to lift his hat and brush a palm back through his hair. "What do you mean?"

"I think it's time to be truthful with Matty. It's not fair to him or to you to go on the way we're doing. I know that you have plans for the future, and I don't want what has happened between us to change those intentions, but I also know you want to be part of

Matty's life." She gulped for air but found none. "So what I want to know is this. Have you thought about what you'd like Matty to call you? He refers to me as Mama."

Carolina had only once in her life seen Wyatt cry. That was the night he'd been certain he was about to lose his gran. The night Matty was conceived. But now Wyatt's beautiful dark eyes turned glassy and he took a deep breath to steady himself, grasping for the stall door.

"You mean, like *Daddy*?"

His voice was shaking with emotion, and Carolina couldn't help but smile at him.

"Yes. That's exactly what I mean."

"Daddy," Wyatt breathed.

"Daddy!" Matty echoed excitedly.

Somehow the toddler had managed to tuck his legs underneath him on the horse's back, and he sprang at Wyatt without forewarning.

Carolina was grateful for Wyatt's quick reflexes. He gave an audible *oomph* as Matty slammed into his chest, but Wyatt held the boy tight and kissed the top of his head.

"What did you say, little guy?"

"Daddy." Matty beamed with pride.

Carolina marveled at the fact that their son appeared to have had no trouble at all following their conversation, nor segueing from *Mr. Wyatt* to *Daddy*. And here she'd been worried about how they could possibly explain the concept of fatherhood to a toddler.

She'd been reluctant partially because she was worried about how Matty would handle the transition, but she saw now that she shouldn't have been. Children had the amazing capacity to embrace love and to keep things simple that adults always managed to complicate. It was the other part of the equation—when the man Matty would come to depend on went away—that worried her. She and Wyatt would have to deal with that issue when the time came, but right now, it was enough that Wyatt was acknowledging his relationship with his son.

"Daddy it is, then," Wyatt choked out emotionally.

Carolina wandered down the line of stalls, intending to give Wyatt and Matty a moment of personal space for them both to adapt to this new, happy reality. She passed another llama and then paused by the stall that held the yearling buck they had rescued.

She'd asked after it a few times and Wyatt had indicated that all was going well with the deer. In fact, he had said he was planning to release the young buck back into the wild sometime during the coming week.

She'd expected to see a healthy deer, possibly suspicious of her presence and definitely eager to get out of the tiny stall and back into the grassy world in which he belonged.

Instead, the buck was lying on its side, much like when she'd first seen it, although this time it was cushioned by a light covering of hay on the floor of the stall.

She obviously wasn't an expert on animals, but there was something *off* in the way the deer was lying. Its legs were sticking straight out to the side instead of folded up underneath it, and the gash on its haunches was smeared with fresh wet blood.

"Wyatt," she called.

"What is it?" He walked toward her with Matty in his arms, the joyful light in his eyes echoed by his beaming smile.

"Is the buck still supposed to be bleeding?"

The grin dropped from Wyatt's lips as he strode forward and thrust Matty into Carolina's waiting arms. He slipped into the stall and knelt before the deer, running a comforting hand down the buck's quivering neck.

"What happened?" He sounded genuinely perplexed and, more than that, dejected.

In short order, Wyatt had wet a towel and washed out the wound. It was one of the original gashes from when the deer had been hit by the truck, but for some reason, instead of healing, there were now angry red flames of infection around the laceration.

"I don't understand. He was getting better." Carolina couldn't miss the note of discouragement in his tone.

"Could he have hit himself on something in the stall and reopened the wound?"

"I don't know. Maybe." Wyatt's voice scraped out a frustrated growl. "But I don't see how. There's nothing in the stall sharp enough to do any real damage. This gash is seriously infected. I've managed up until now to keep all of the wounds clean and covered, and now this happens."

"But he'll get better, right? Will you be able to—" her throat closed and she had difficulty finishing her sentence "—save the poor thing?"

Wyatt shook his head. "I don't know. It's bad. I may have to put it down, after all."

Seething with frustration, he planted his fist into his open palm and grumbled something unintelligible.

Carolina's heart hurt for him. Wyatt genuinely cared. That was what made him such a good veterinarian.

But this? This felt like it was more than just the typical situation with an animal Wyatt vetted, as if he had formed a special bond with the creature.

Wyatt thoroughly cleaned the wound with antiseptic and wrapped it with layers of gauze. Carolina guessed the fuzzy-antlered buck would probably make short work of the dressing, but she hoped he would ignore it so the wound would stay clean and covered.

Nick McGarrett, who often did farrier work for Wyatt, entered just as Wyatt was finishing up. Wyatt was clearly still distracted by the ailing buck, but he turned his attention to the horses.

"I thought I would spend a little time this afternoon putting together some plans for Gran's birthday party," Carolina said. "It looks like you two are going to be busy." She eyed the farrier's tools, some of which didn't look particularly safe for a curious two-year-old boy to be near. "Would you like me to take Matty back to the office with me? I'd hate for him to get underfoot and be a bother to you."

Wyatt took Matty's hand and smiled down at him. The boy beamed back at his daddy. "He won't be a bother. He's my big boy, right, Matty?"

She started to tell Wyatt to be careful but bit the inside of her lip to keep the words from tumbling out of her mouth.

There was absolutely no question that Wyatt was going to take care of Matty. He'd probably be even more attentive than she would have been.

No more helicopter mom for her. She had to let go of all her fears and worries for their son. Wyatt could handle Matty just fine for a while on his own, and they needed time to bond. There wasn't anyone else on the planet, after Carolina, who cared as much about Matty as Wyatt did. After all, he was the boy's *daddy*.

Chapter Eight

Trimming the horses' hooves was a routine procedure that every ranch had done on a regular basis, and yet Wyatt was breathing in the experience as if for the first time, seeing everything through Matty's curious eyes. As Nick worked, Wyatt explained what the farrier was doing—how he got the horse to trust him enough to lift its legs, and what he was doing with the files, hammers and nippers.

Nick even let Matty place his little hands over Nick's larger ones, allowing the toddler to "help" him file. Everything was going well at first, but then Matty got a little overexcited and his happy squeal and flapping arms set the already anxious gelding skittering to the side.

"Whoa, there," Wyatt said, pushing against the horse's flank and scooping Matty safely out of the way.

Wyatt frowned. He needed to pay closer attention to what was happening with his son. Maybe a stall with a nervous horse and a busy farrier wasn't the safest place for a toddler to be, after all.

It was bad enough that Wyatt couldn't seem to keep his mind from wandering back to where things had gone wrong with the injured buck. He couldn't toss off the idea that he could have done more to save the deer, even if rationally he knew otherwise.

But he knew his feelings came from the heart, which was what made the whole thing so devastating. He'd somehow become invested in this buck—and far more than that, so had Carolina and Matty.

He didn't want to disappoint them. They would both be brokenhearted if he had to put the buck down.

Wyatt sighed and brushed the dark hair off Matty's forehead. He had passed strike three in making mistakes as a new father a long time ago. This felt more like he was striking right out of the game, maybe even the season.

Swing, miss. Swing, miss.

He probably should have taken Carolina up on her offer to watch Matty, but he so desperately wanted to spend every waking moment with his son, to teach him all the things a boy should learn from his father.

His heart did a somersault every time he heard Matty's sweet, innocent voice calling him Daddy.

But maybe he was trying to do too much too fast. Wyatt could and would teach the boy how to care for the ranch animals, but clearly he was overcompensating for the time he had missed, and he had to remind himself that Matty was only two years old. He wouldn't be shoeing horses for a few years yet.

He had time, as long as Carolina didn't up and disappear out of his life again. Years' worth of time. Any thoughts of leaving Haven, of being separated from Matty for even one day, were long since behind him. He was Matty's father. He wouldn't disappear from the boy's life, no matter what that meant to his own prior vision of his future.

He had a new dream now, one that included his son—and even the boy's beautiful mother.

With effort, Wyatt turned back to his work. Nick had taken the mare out of the next stall and had haltered her loosely against a pole so he could replace the shoe she'd thrown.

Mercury, as her name suggested, was a bit of a bugger at times and she liked to bite—especially when people fiddled with her legs. Nick had been Wyatt's farrier for some time now and was well familiar with Mercury's bad habits, but there was only so much a man could do when a horse had sensitive legs and had been known to kick as well as use her teeth. The shoe still had to be fitted.

"Let me hold her head for you," Wyatt offered, knowing his presence would calm the mare down so the farrier could do his work with more ease.

Matty started wiggling, pumping his chunky arms and legs and pushing against Wyatt's chest so it was hard to hold the toddler in one arm.

"Down. Down," Matty insisted.

Now wasn't a good time to put the boy on the ground, but when Wyatt tried to calm him, he became even more adamant, making the calm horses in the other stalls skittish, and that was nothing to say of further agitating Mercury.

Wyatt looked around for a solution.

Just inside the barn door, framed in a ray of sunshine, was Blitzy, one of Wyatt's young goats.

Wyatt breathed a sigh of relief and dropped Matty down by Blitzy, who was just the right size for a toddler to play with, without fear that the goat would knock him over or create too much havoc. Fortunately, this particular goat was among the friendliest Wyatt owned, and he was sure the animal would be up to a little friendly petting.

Besides, Wyatt would only be a few steps away.

He stepped back to the mare's head and smoothed a hand down her neck as Nick took his position at the mare's left hind leg.

"Easy, there, girl," Wyatt soothed.

Mercury snorted her disdain and tried to toss her head when the farrier picked up her foot, but Wyatt held tight and didn't let her move. She shifted and struck out with her back legs in a half buck, but Nick was an old hand at his work and managed to avoid getting a hoof in the face.

Nick chuckled. "Stubborn old goat, isn't she?"

At the word *goat*, Wyatt's gaze slid over to Matty, expecting the boy and his new four-legged friend to be playing together, safe, sound and secure.

Instead, he discovered that Matty had somehow led the goat to the side of the barn, where a partially used bale of hay had been tossed up against the wall.

It took Wyatt just two seconds too long to figure out what Matty was trying to do.

Wyatt slipped underneath the mare's neck and darted toward Matty, just as the toddler scooted on top of the hay bale and scrambled onto the goat's back.

Wyatt and Matty's voices were simultaneous, one terrified, the other exultant.

"Matty, no!"

"Go, goat!"

At the sudden extra load wiggling on its back, the goat reared and bolted, catching Matty unaware. The toddler flipped forward off the goat's back and somersaulted twice before hitting the edge of the barn door.

Wyatt dived toward him but missed getting his hands under the boy by inches.

Matty sent up a spine-chilling wail.

This wasn't just the sound of a scared little boy. This was a pain cry. And Wyatt knew with gut-wrenching certainty that Matty was seriously injured.

"Oh, Lord, please. Not Matty," he breathed.

God had to be there. He just *had* to listen. Not because of Wyatt, who didn't deserve a moment's notice from the Almighty, but for Matty. The kid was an innocent. He didn't deserve to be hurt because of Wyatt's negligence.

He felt like throwing up as he scooped his son into his arms as gently as he could and tried to soothe him with whispered words. Matty had been injured on *his* watch.

Carolina would never forgive him.

He would never forgive himself.

But despite his own sense of humiliation and disgrace over what had just happened, he didn't pause at all before running straight for the office.

For Carolina.

She was going to be so, so angry.

But she was a nurse, and Matty's mom. She would know what to do, how to help him.

Wyatt was beyond thinking rationally. His son was hurt—his beloved son. And it was all his fault. Guilt and shame poured over him like thick, wet cement.

"What happened?" Carolina asked as Wyatt kicked the already partially open door wide with the toe of his boot.

"I goofed up," Wyatt admitted bluntly. "I goofed up, and now Matty is injured."

Carolina appeared not to have heard his words. Her eyes—and her full attention—were on Matty.

"Where does it hurt, baby?"

Matty tried to lift up his right arm and then wailed in pain, clutching his hand to his chest. "Owie!"

Wyatt cringed at the sound, and even more when he saw the little boy's face crumple. It was like a punch in his already churning gut. He wanted to try to explain what had happened and why he had let Matty down, but he knew Carolina wasn't interested in his excuses.

Not now. Maybe not ever.

Carolina took Matty's right arm and examined it from his fingertips to his shoulder.

"I think he may have fractured his wrist. It might just be a few torn ligaments, but he's having difficulty moving it. At the very least he has hyperextended his thumb. We'll have to get his hand x-rayed to know for certain." She picked up a stray board. "I'm going to stabilize his hand until we can get him to the doctor. I'll need a roll of gauze."

She sounded amazingly calm and collected, considering what she was saying, and she expertly wrapped Matty's arm within minutes.

"We need to get in to see Dr. Delgado right away." She flashed him a measured look, sizing him up. "Do you think you can drive?"

That might very well have been an insult, but she was right to ask. Wyatt still wasn't thinking clearly, and he was shaking like a leaf in a thunderstorm.

He inhaled deeply through his nose and set his jaw. He'd let Matty down once. He *would* be there for his son.

"Let's go."

"Use my sedan. Matty's car seat is already attached in the backseat and it will take us less time."

Wyatt made a mental note to buy a car seat for Matty to use in his dual-cab truck.

Carolina reached for Matty, making soothing noises as she tossed Wyatt her car keys. He slid behind the wheel while Carolina buckled Matty in the back. The boy's crying had mellowed out and he was quietly sniffling, but Carolina still rode in the back with him to reassure him and keep him from getting agitated again.

Glancing in the rearview mirror, Wyatt caught a rare glimpse of vulnerability on Carolina's face—an emotion she usually kept well hidden.

Shame filled him. He wished he could shift the blame for this particular episode onto someone or something else—the goat, or the skittish horse.

But no.

This was all on him.

They'd just today made the decision to have Matty address him as Daddy—

Just in time for him to prove definitively that he shouldn't be one at all.

Once they'd reached Dr. Delgado's office, it didn't take long for him to determine that Carolina was correct in her diagnosis of Matty's injury. Sure enough, Dr. Delgado x-rayed the toddler's wrist and found a hairline fracture. He also suspected a torn ligament or two.

Determining the need to set Matty's wrist in a soft cast, the doctor gave Matty a dose of liquid ibuprofen and left the room to gather the necessary supplies.

Matty, for the most part, already seemed to be over the trauma of his misadventure and hardly noticed his owie. Dr. Delgado had given him a toy helicopter to play with and Matty was zooming it around in the air with his uninjured hand, oblivious to the purple, swollen appendage Carolina was gently trying to keep as still and stable as possible on his lap.

Wyatt, on the other hand, looked absolutely terrible. His face was as white as a sheet and his gaze carried the glassy-eyed panic of a cornered animal. His Adam's apple was bobbing as if he were having difficulty swallowing, and more than once she saw him brush away a tear. Clearly, Matty's accident had really shaken him.

To Carolina, his tears weren't a sign of weakness, but of great strength, although she knew Wyatt wouldn't think so. He would be appalled if he thought she'd even noticed them, so she withheld the urge to reach out and take his hand to let him know that Matty would be fine, and that she didn't blame him for the injury.

Carolina remembered the first time Matty had ever had a serious accident. He'd just been learning to pull himself into a standing position, and yet the little fellow had somehow managed to leverage himself up and roll over the top edge of his playpen.

Hearing a sound, she had glanced over at him from the couch, where she had been watching television, and had recognized too late what was about to happen. From that point it had been like she was in slow motion. She'd rushed toward him when she'd realized he was going to fall, but she'd been too late to catch him. Thankfully, he hadn't landed directly on his head, and the floor was carpeted. He'd naturally tucked and rolled and his shoulder had taken the brunt of the impact. She'd watched him like a hawk for days afterward, hovering over him and looking for possible signs of concussion.

The blame she'd felt had been crippling.

She'd soon learned that mischievous little boys bumped their heads and scraped their knees on a regular basis—and yet they survived and thrived. This new tumble was just one more accident among many, past and future. She had learned not to obsess about every little thing or she would go crazy. Boys will be boys, and all that.

But for Wyatt, this was his first experience seeing his kid get hurt, and she could tell how hard he was taking it. He was gripping Matty's knee like a lifeline. His head was bowed and his lips were silently moving.

Praying?

But Wyatt had set his relationship with God aside long ago, when he was still a child and had suddenly and traumatically lost his parents.

Was it possible that something good would come from the bad, that these circumstances might drive Wyatt to his knees and remind him of his need of a Savior?

Carolina reached out her free hand and laid it over Wyatt's.

"Do you want to pray together?"

He jerked in response, and his astonished gaze burned into hers. She held her breath as the silence lingered.

"Pray?" he rasped, his voice sounding disconnected from the word. "That's what I—"

She nodded in understanding.

He paused and his eyes widened. "Yes. I'd like to pray with you. Pray for Matty. But it's been a long time and I—er, can you...?"

"Absolutely." Carolina nodded again and squeezed his hand tightly.

He bowed his head and closed his eyes, then turned his hand over and threaded his fingers through hers.

Her heartbeat quickened. Just look at the three of them. Wyatt, Carolina and the beautiful son with whom they'd been blessed. All circled together. They were a—

Family.

Her heart leaped into her throat and she wasn't sure she'd be able to speak out loud.

But Matty needed to hear Carolina's faith in God being lived out by example, and Wyatt needed to *see* it—see the strength her beliefs offered her.

"Dear Lord," she began softly, "watch after Your precious child Matty. Guide Dr. Delgado's hand as he sets the cast. And we humbly ask that Matty's wrist might come out of this even stronger than it was before."

Wyatt's hand was quivering.

She paused to gather her thoughts. "We thank You, Jesus, for Your Holy Wounds, by which we ask this blessing today. In the name of the Father, and of the Son, and of the Holy Spirit. Amen."

Wyatt tried to echo her *amen* but all that came out of his mouth was a scratchy sound scraped from the depths of his throat.

He remained silent and thoughtful and continued to hold her hand while Carolina kept Matty distracted and occupied with his little plastic airplane. She suspected motor noises were more in Wyatt's skill set than hers, but she didn't want to push him when he was clearly in an introverted and reflective mood. She sent up a silent prayer that God was working on his heart and opening him up to faith.

When Dr. Delgado returned, his arms loaded with gauze, cotton and tape, Wyatt quickly jerked back, yanking his hand from hers and crossing his arms over his chest.

She didn't know why, but his action hurt her, bruised her already fragile self-esteem.

It shouldn't. But there it was.

Any thoughts Carolina might have had about their being a family unit dissipated into thin air. Clearly Wyatt didn't want the doctor to get the wrong impression about them, that they might be a couple. Holding hands was off-limits, even if it had been for the very best of reasons.

They had been *praying* together. And there was nothing wrong with that.

When it came time to set the cast, Wyatt immediately stepped up to support Matty.

A muscle ticked in his taut jaw whenever the toddler made a distressed squeak, but his smile was encouraging and his words full of praise. He was a natural father, whether or not he thought he was.

"That's my big brave boy," Wyatt said as Dr. Delgado wrapped a cotton-like substance around his thumb and wrist that would keep it immobile and then packed it well up his forearm.

"Just like his daddy," Carolina agreed, automatically assisting the doctor with wetting the casting material and covering the cotton with it.

"We have to hold still for a few more minutes, honey," she said, knowing the cast needed time to set.

Dr. Delgado grinned. "I wish I had a place for you

in my practice, Carolina. You would most certainly be an asset to me. Your nursing skills are outstanding."

"Thank you." She wished for that, as well—or at least, she thought she did. Upon closer inspection she realized she had found a great deal of happiness working for Wyatt in his office, though of course she missed the direct interaction of helping people that nursing provided. With a little more administrative training, she thought she might actually find joy permanently working in Wyatt's office. But then, Wyatt hadn't offered her a permanent position. This was nothing more than a temporary solution to a difficult problem.

So much had changed since she'd returned to Haven. She realized she hadn't thought much about leaving. Instead, to her surprise, she was considering ways to stay.

When the cast had set, Dr. Delgado wrapped two stretch bandages over the whole area and then taped it up over the closures.

Matty was curious about his new cast and was trying out the weight of it, twisting his arm back and forth and laughing at how neat it was.

"He'll think it's really cool for about an hour, and then not so much," Dr. Delgado advised with a chuckle. "I'll need to see him back here in a week, although I suspect we may have to keep the cast on for a bit longer than that. The hard part is going to be trying to keep him out of trouble."

Carolina groaned. There was that.

Wyatt's face lost all its color.

"No goats," he muttered under his breath.

What was that about goats? Wyatt evidently had an interesting story to tell her. They'd been in such a rush to get to the doctor's office that they hadn't really had time to discuss *how* the accident had happened.

Dr. Delgado fitted Matty with a child-size sling covered with bright, primary-colored dinosaurs.

"Try to keep his arm in the sling as much as possible, but don't worry if he gets tired of wearing it sometimes. That hand is going to get heavy and the sling will help relieve the pressure on his shoulder muscles. Thankfully, he's not yet old enough for us to have to worry about it being his writing hand or him missing schoolwork."

"But he'll get better, right?" Wyatt asked, his voice lined with worry. "He won't have trouble using his hand?"

He'll get better.

It was the same question Carolina had asked about the deer, whose health had taken a major nosedive. But this wasn't the same thing at all.

"Yes, of course." Dr. Delgado smiled encouragingly. "Give him a few weeks and Matty here will be fully mended. He's so young right now that he won't even remember the time he broke his wrist."

Carolina eyed Wyatt as they walked back out to the parking lot with a sleepy Matty in Wyatt's arms. Clearly the excitement of the day was catching up with the toddler. Matty's head was tucked against Wyatt's shoulder and he was self-soothing by sucking on his fist.

Wyatt gently buckled the boy in his car seat. This time, Carolina chose to sit in the passenger seat opposite Wyatt so they could talk. Matty's eyes were already drooping and he would be sound asleep within minutes.

"You know, for a man who vets animals for a living,

you looked a little green around the gills back there," she teased, trying to lighten the moment.

"Doctoring animals is *nothing* like seeing my own son in pain." He paused and inhaled a ragged breath. "Especially when it's all my fault that it happened."

Her first impulse was to tell him that he wasn't to blame, but belittling his feelings wasn't going to help him work through the incident and reconcile himself to what had happened. Not when he believed he was at fault for it.

She reached out and took his hand.

She thought he might pull away, but instead he tightened his grip on her fingers and sighed deeply.

"Do you want to talk about it?" she asked gently.

"It was a stupid goat. I can't believe I didn't see it coming. I looked away for one second and when I looked back, Blitzy was flinging Matty into the barn door."

"It attacked him?" Carolina was horrified, picturing a mean old billy goat butting her poor, defenseless little son. "Where did it come from?"

Wyatt shook his head. "No. It was nothing like that. As you know, I have a herd of young goats. Blitzy is small and super gentle, like the one I introduced Matty to a while ago. He seemed to really like goats, so I thought he would get a kick out of petting it while I held on to one of the horses' heads for Nick. You have to believe I thought Matty would be perfectly safe, or I never would have let him near the goat."

She waited for more of an explanation, but it didn't come. Wyatt remained silent, focused on the drive. She knew he had to work through the whole story or he would never forgive himself.

"But?" she prompted.

"But Matty was too fast for me. He got it into his head to *ride* the goat. I can't imagine what he was thinking."

"He's two, Wyatt. I doubt he considered the possible consequences."

Wyatt winced. "No. That was my responsibility."

She hadn't meant to point a finger at him, but rather to show him that he couldn't anticipate every eventuality. Not when it came to an active toddler.

"He crawled up on a hay bale and climbed aboard the startled animal. I figured out what Matty was about to do a split second before the whole thing unfolded before me like a bad dream—right about the time the *goat* figured out what he was about to do."

Carolina readjusted the picture in her mind to this new scene and couldn't help but chuckle.

Wyatt looked appalled. "You think this is funny?"

She tried to wipe the smile off her face, but it popped right back up again.

"No. Yes." Her fingers brushed across the pulse in her neck as she glanced back to check on Matty, who had fallen into a sound sleep, poor little guy.

"I'm not happy that Matty fractured his wrist, of course, but you'll have to admit the circumstances are amusing. This is one of those situations that aren't funny when they happen but will make hilarious stories around the family table years down the road."

"The family table, huh?" he repeated. She felt the tension go out of his grip, and he chuckled lightly. "Yeah. I guess you're right. But I lost ten years off my life when I saw Matty climb aboard that goat."

"You're a good dad, Wyatt," she assured him.

He scoffed. "I think I've just proven conclusively that I'm not."

"Because Matty had one little spill?"

"It was more than that and we both know it. He fractured his wrist. Frankly, Carolina, I don't think I am meant to be a dad."

She heartily disagreed.

"No one is *meant* to be a dad. You just are one. God blessed you with a son. You learn and adapt and make mistakes just like every other parent out there."

"But what if I make another bad judgment call and Matty gets hurt again?"

"I think it's more a matter of *when* than *if*. Not just for you, but for me, as well. We aren't infallible. Only God is. We can't see everything. We can't be there every single second of the day. We're going to blink. We're going to miss things. And when they fall…"

His eyes caught hers and his hold on her hand tightened.

"We pick them up again. We do what we can, but ultimately we have to give our son's welfare up to God. No one loves Matty more than He does. Not even us."

A smile slowly crept up one side of his lips. "I can't imagine a love that big. Someone who cares for Matty more than I do."

"Deeper and wider." Tears sprang to her eyes and she got all choked up when Wyatt voiced how very much he loved their son.

And to think she had once believed that it would be better that Wyatt never be a part of Matty's life.

Regret filled her. How very wrong she'd been. On so many levels.

They drove in silence the rest of the way back to Wyatt's ranch, each lost in their own thoughts. Matty was snoring lightly in the backseat. As a mother, she found his snorts and snores to be one of Matty's more endearing qualities—although his future wife might not be quite so keen on the trait. She smothered a laugh at the thought.

Wyatt pulled up in front of the house and cut the engine, which surprised Carolina because she figured she would just be dropping Wyatt off at his ranch and heading straight home to put Matty to bed. It had been an adventuresome and tiring day for all of them.

Maybe Wyatt still wanted to talk.

She had to admit she was curious.

He fisted his hands on the steering wheel and glanced in the rearview mirror.

"He's out like a light, isn't he?" Wyatt's voice was rich and deep and full of affection.

Carolina chuckled. "When he is sleeping soundly, a tornado couldn't even wake him up. He gives a new meaning to *sleep like a baby*."

The corners of Wyatt's mouth rose but it wasn't his usually toothy grin, since his lips were pressed tightly together.

"I created email invitations for Gran's birthday party," she said to fill the silence. "I figured we could borrow the day room at the nursing home so she and her friends won't have to go too far out of their element."

"You were always very thoughtful."

Until she wasn't.

"Not always." Her mind darkened with the memory. This was a night for regrets.

He cleared his throat and turned toward her, his eyes a delicious dark chocolate. "I think we need to try to put the past behind us."

"For Matty's sake."

Her whole being, heart and soul, leaned in to him,

hoping beyond hope that there was something more. That he would tell her that this wasn't just about Matty.

He nodded slowly, never breaking eye contact with her. "Yes. For Matty."

Her heart dropped like lead.

"But," he continued, as a tumble of emotion squeezed the air out of her lungs, "not *just* Matty."

He paused and reached for her, framing her face with one hand. His work-worn hands were scratchy against her cheek, but Carolina thought she'd never felt anything nicer. The chemistry ricocheting between them was infinitely familiar and yet paradoxically brand-new.

They weren't the same people they had been three years ago. They had both changed. Matured.

They had a son now.

"Carolina, I—"

He stopped abruptly.

She waited. She certainly couldn't say anything. Her capacity for speech had completely deserted her the moment Wyatt touched her.

"Back at the doctor's office? When we were praying together? That felt—well, it felt like we were a family. A *real* family. I want… I need to know if…"

He didn't finish his question, or statement, or whatever it was.

Instead, he brought his lips down on hers.

At first, his kiss was soft, a bare, butterfly-winged brush of his lips over hers. But then it turned urgent, hungry, as he pulled her closer and she wrapped her arms around his neck. He was seeking answers to the questions he could not voice, and yet he was communicating to her at the very same time.

A rush of warmth flooded her heart as she realized she was *home* in Wyatt's arms.

She never should have left.

Yet there was so much still unresolved between them.

They could no more have avoided this moment than they could have stopped the sun from shining. Strong emotions burned a path between them, as they always had, together with a deep longing to make what they had between them something better. Greater.

Forever.

The sum of two parts somehow incredibly equaling three. Maybe even more, in time.

But could he ever truly forgive her for taking Matty away from him? Could they work things out and move forward with their lives together? Even if she decided to make her permanent home in Haven, that didn't mean Wyatt would. What about all the ambitions he held? Years changed a person, but some dreams never altered. He'd been so sure that was what he wanted to do.

Could his dreams have changed?

Wyatt's lips, his gentle touch and the way he whispered her name between kisses—these all gave her reasons to hope, perhaps even to start believing in the possibility of a future between them.

And yet she knew that there was still a chasm between them that was so deep she was afraid to cross it.

She had no doubt that Wyatt believed he knew what he wanted *now*. But what about the future?

His future?

Could he really give up his dreams in exchange for a staid and settled life with her and Matty? Could he stay here in Haven and truly be happy, without seeing all that was beyond the borders?

When push came to shove—would he *stay*?

Chapter Nine

Would she stay?

That had been the single most important question haunting Wyatt, a thread of doubt thrumming through his mind even at the exact moment that her soft, full lips had molded to his and a bouquet of warmth and emotion bloomed in his chest.

He'd gloried in the feel of her arms wrapped around his neck. He hadn't wanted to leave her embrace.

Not ever.

Especially when she'd burrowed her head on his chest, her ear resting next to his pounding heart. As he'd rested his chin against her hair and breathed in the scent of her, he had considered all the ways he wanted to care for her. Protect her.

Love her.

Those words frightened him. He'd been there before, and the results had been catastrophic. He was still far too vulnerable, too gun-shy, to do anything but tread lightly. Their romantic relationship, assuming they ever had one, would take a long time to come to fruition, if it ever did.

She had run away from him once. He could not and

would not risk his heart again—not until he knew for certain that she returned his love.

His heart wouldn't survive if she left again—especially because this time she had their son. He didn't want to fight for shared custody, but he couldn't be parted from his son. There was no way he would ever heal from that kind of pain.

So for now, his heart was officially on lockdown.

And he suspected she was feeling much the same way.

She hadn't said much after they'd kissed. She'd slid out of the passenger seat and walked around to the driver's side so she could take her sedan home. After he'd exited the vehicle, he'd grabbed her hand and tried to kiss her good-night, but she'd turned her head so his lips had brushed her cheek instead.

Already he could sense she was withdrawing from him. He didn't know why, but he was determined to stay the course this time—to show her all the reasons in the world why she ought to make Haven her permanent home.

And it wasn't just because of Matty.

He couldn't begin to read the woman's mind, but he was going to ask about her plans.

Flat out. No holds barred.

Was there any chance of them—all three of them—making a future together?

That, he believed, was where he'd gone wrong the last time around. They'd both known they should have waited to be together, and once it happened, he'd backed off. And so had she. So they didn't speak of it, and the gap increased between them until he hadn't known how to cross it.

He was the first to admit it would take a lot of work.

The blunder he'd made with Matty and the goat was proof of that. But he was quickly learning that God was the God of second chances. And if the Lord opened up the door for him and Carolina, he was going to walk through it.

After the shake-up on Saturday, he'd gone to Sunday services at Haven's community church for the first time in his adult life. He hadn't known what to expect, but he'd actually enjoyed singing the hymns—however off-key he might have been—and Pastor Andrew's sermon about God's love and forgiveness only made Wyatt more determined than ever to straighten out his personal life.

He'd thought maybe people would judge him, as he'd never before seen fit to darken the door of a church, but everyone had been surprisingly welcoming. Pastor Andrew had even offered to meet Wyatt in private to answer any questions he might have about being a Christian.

He'd always envied Carolina's faith. It was amazing to realize the same God Carolina talked to so openly was willing to listen to him, as well.

His mind full of future plans, he showered and shaved and prepared for his usual Monday morning rounds. The beginning of the week was usually very quiet, and most of the local ranchers called his office if they needed to set up an appointment for veterinary services, so he was surprised when his cell phone rang.

Only in an emergency did anyone call his cell phone line. A cow that had suddenly fallen ill, or a mare in foal.

He glanced at the caller ID and saw that it was the number for the boys ranch.

"Wyatt?" It was Bea Brewster's voice on the line. "I think you need to get over here as soon as possible."

Wyatt could plainly hear the tightness in her voice, the near panic of her tone.

Bea Brewster never panicked.

"Is it one of the animals?" he asked, tucking the phone to his chin while he pulled on one tan cowboy boot and then the other.

"No." Bea swept in an audible gasp of air. "Much worse. It's Johnny Drake. I knew you would want to know as soon as possible, since you mentor the boy."

"What about Johnny?" Wyatt's gut was churning like a combine. Johnny typically stayed in the trenches and avoided trouble. "Is he hurt?"

"No." Bea paused. "He's gone."

"What?" Wyatt's voice had risen an octave as his heart sprinted into gear. "What do you mean, *gone*?"

"His house parents went to find him when he didn't show up for breakfast this morning. He wasn't in his room. He didn't go to school. His duffel bag, most of his clothes and all of his books are missing."

"I'll be there in five," Wyatt said, even though the boys ranch was a good ten-minute drive away.

Panic seared his chest.

Why did it have to be Johnny?

What could have happened to the teenager that would press him to leave on the sly? Unlike many of the other boys, Johnny didn't have relatives waiting to pick him up when he was done with his time on the ranch. He was going to be aging out soon, on his eighteenth birthday—which, now that Wyatt thought about it, was coming up soon, at the beginning of April.

The ranch would allow him to finish out the school

year, but by then Johnny would have to make plans for what he was going to do next.

"Where are you, dude?" Wyatt said aloud, his voice echoing in the truck's cab.

He didn't know what prompted him to do so, but he used the Bluetooth on his dashboard to dial Carolina's cell phone number, which thankfully was on speed dial.

"Can you meet me at the boys ranch as soon as possible?"

"Wyatt? What's wrong? You sound as if you are about ready to jump out of your skin."

"I *feel* like I'm freaking out. I am about to have a major meltdown." He slammed his palm onto the steering wheel. "Johnny Drake has gone missing."

"*Missing* missing? Like he disappeared?"

"That's what Bea thinks. And I don't think he is coming back. He took his duffel bag with his clothes in it. Even more telling, he has all of his books with him."

"Oh, wow," she breathed. "Let me get Matty dressed and see if my next-door neighbor will watch him for a bit, and then I'll be right there."

Wyatt didn't know why having Carolina's presence at the ranch was so reassuring, but it was. He needed her support. He just hadn't realized until this moment how much.

Carolina's cabin was further from the boys ranch than Wyatt's own ranch, so it was to his surprise she was waiting for him when he pulled up, already deep in conversation with Bea Brewster.

"Oh, Wyatt." Carolina's beautiful golden-brown eyes were glittering with tears. She murmured his name again and pressed herself into his embrace, wrapping her quivering arms around his waist and tucking her head onto his chest.

He held her tightly as a sense of foreboding washed over him. He couldn't tell by her tone whether she was seeking his comfort or giving hers, but holding her in his arms made it easier for him to get a grip on his emotions.

Carolina cared for Johnny. She had really gotten to know the teenager over the past few weeks. She had even had him babysit Matty on several occasions.

But she also knew how important Johnny was to Wyatt. The young man was far more than merely a kid he mentored. Johnny had given him purpose when he'd been floundering, had been a lifeline when he'd needed one. He had shown Wyatt that he could make a difference right where he was, without traveling to another continent to find meaning in his life. He was an indelible part of Wyatt's world.

So why would Johnny run away? Why hadn't he come to Wyatt first? He knew the boy was often the object of ridicule because of his stutter, but that had been the case all his life.

What had changed?

What would have caused him to take such a drastic action without letting anyone know about it?

Why had he run?

"Do you have any leads on him?" Wyatt asked, gently turning Carolina so they both faced Bea. He kept Carolina within the circle of his arms, her back solid against his chest. He wasn't going to apologize for it. He didn't care who saw his actions or how they interpreted them.

She needed him right now, and in the strangest way,

he found relief for his own distress by offering her comfort, by being strong for both of them.

"We don't have a clue," said Bea. "He didn't tell anyone where he was going and he didn't leave a note."

"Maybe we're overreacting. When was the last time anyone saw him?" Wyatt ran a palm across his whiskered jaw.

"He was at dinner last evening. No one remembers seeing him afterward. He wasn't at any of the ranch's formal programs, but at the time, we didn't consider it any real cause for alarm. You know Johnny. Sometimes he gets his nose stuck in a book and forgets where he is and where he is supposed to be."

"I'm not trying to cast any kind of blame here, so please don't take this the wrong way," Carolina said with a catch in her voice. "But don't the house parents check the boys before lights-out every night?"

"Johnny's house parents, Eleanor and Edward Mack, did do a brief head count before lockdown last night."

"So then bedtime was actually the last time anyone saw him," Wyatt clarified.

"No. Unfortunately, Johnny played one of the oldest tricks in the books on us. He tucked a blanket inside his sheets to look like a body and left a hoodie propped on the pillow to create the shadow of a head. Ed didn't have any cause to take a closer look in the dark. He didn't suspect a thing. It was only this morning when Johnny didn't appear for breakfast that the Macks went back and discovered Johnny's duplicity."

As they spoke, several other folks arrived. News traveled fast in Haven. Some were employees and volunteers at the boys ranch, while others were members of the board of the Lone Star Cowboy League. Some of the older boys were also milling around, curious as to what had happened to one of their own.

Wyatt was grateful that he lived in the close-knit small town where residents looked after each other—and where folks counted the boys at the ranch in their number.

"We've got an additional problem," Bea continued, raising her voice so she could be heard by the growing crowd. "And it's a doozy."

A hush went over the people gathered in the yard.

"As most of you know, because of the recent thefts and arson, the Department of Family and Protective Services has been—" Bea paused, searching for the right words "—keeping a closer eye on us than they might otherwise be doing. And who can blame them? They have the boys' best interests at heart, just like we do."

Carolina's grip on Wyatt's forearm tightened and he laid his hand over hers. The gnawing in the pit of his stomach was turning into a sharp-toothed grind.

It didn't take a genius to figure out where Bea's concerns were taking her.

"We've had word that the DFPS is planning to make an unannounced visit soon—maybe as early as today. If they discover that one of our boys is missing—well, let's just say it will look bad for us. Of course, the most important thing is that we find Johnny and bring him back safe and sound. Then we'll deal with the authorities."

Gabe Everett stepped forward. "Okay, folks, it is obviously imperative, for both Johnny's sake and ours, that we locate the boy as soon as possible and return him to the ranch. We appreciate any help you all can give us."

There were several murmurs of agreement among the folks in the gathering.

"I think we should split into groups," Nick McGarrett suggested. "We can cover more ground that way."

"I agree," Bea said. "Gabe, Katie and I will stay in the office in case Johnny tries to make contact there, or the DFPS shows up. I will make a list of everyone's cell phone numbers and we will keep you all regularly updated via text message, so check your phones often."

"Nick and I will muster the house parents and double-check all the nooks and crannies in the main residence," Darcy Hill offered.

"Lana and I will cover the barns," Flint Rawlings added, joining hands with his fiancée.

Gabe assigned Tanner Barstow and Macy Swanson to the other outbuildings. Several members of the Lone Star Cowboy League stepped forward to offer to check on the ranch land, while a number of the town's residents planned to search in and around Haven. Pastor Andrew indicated that he would return to the church in case Johnny sought help there.

Wyatt and Carolina stood silently, still clinging together for mutual support.

Where would Johnny go?

Wyatt felt like he should know the answer to that question. He knew Johnny better than anyone else at the boys ranch. The answer fluttered in front of him like a butterfly, but when he reached for it, it eluded him, soaring just out of reach.

Carolina took his hand and led him away from the confusion of the still-forming search parties.

"What do you think?" she murmured for his ears only. "Do you have any idea where Johnny might have gone?"

Wyatt growled in frustration. "That's just it. I feel like I *do* know. I just can't quite put everything together in my mind. I've got to put this puzzle together. If I don't figure it out, I'll be the one at fault."

"Why?" Concern lined Carolina's voice and her hold on his hand tightened. "Do you think he might harm himself?"

Wyatt felt like a storm had descended over him. Clouds of black and gray settled on his shoulders, making it hard for him to think clearly.

"What? No. I mean—I don't think so. Johnny has been through a lot in his life, but he's got a solid head on his shoulders. He wouldn't do something stupid. I have no idea why he ran away, but I do think he believes he has a good reason."

"I don't understand. Why did you say you would be to blame, then?"

"I meant with the DFPS." He slid his hand from hers and grasped her shoulders, his eyes capturing hers. He needed to see that she understood what he was saying.

"Go ahead," she urged, giving him a moment to collect his thoughts and form coherent words.

"I'm not quite sure how to explain this to you, except to say that Johnny is my responsibility—my *personal* responsibility. I know he's currently a resident of the boys ranch, but our connection is special. It's more than just me being a volunteer, a teacher or even a mentor."

"You see a lot of yourself in him."

He framed her face with his hands and bent his head until their foreheads were touching. Her soft skin and unique floral scent somehow calmed his mind, and the feel of her warm breath against his cheek made his own respirations even out.

She understood.

More than that, she grounded him, kept him from drifting away in his anxiety.

She recognized his need to be the one to find Johnny. If anyone else got to the boy first, he would think he was in trouble, and then he would bolt away and disappear for good—if he hadn't already.

His heart clenched. Why did everyone and everything he loved always leave?

His parents, who had left him for foreign service and had never returned. His gran, whose mind no longer recognized his face. Carolina, who had vanished from his life once before, and he had no way of knowing whether or not she'd leave again—this time with the knowledge that she was taking Matty away from him as well.

Even the young buck he'd vetted ought to be out leaping through the waist-high Texas prairie grass, but instead was on the verge of leaving this world.

And now Johnny.

Wyatt concentrated, not on his own breathing, but on Carolina's. He lifted his mind and his heart in silent prayer, releasing all his pain and fear and allowing himself to be enveloped in the presence of God.

And then, as if the sun had finally broken through the clouds surrounding him, dissipating them into mist, his thoughts became clear, coherent and united.

Of course.

He smiled down at Carolina, but she couldn't see it because she had her eyes closed. Evidently she was praying, just as he had been.

Maybe God was answering both of their prayers. He could be wrong, but—

"Carolina, honey. I think I know where Johnny is."

* * *

Carolina trusted Wyatt's gut instinct, but she found it ironic that he suggested they return to his ranch. He'd come from there to meet with Bea and the others about Johnny's disappearance. Obviously he'd seen no trace of the teenager this morning.

Wyatt appeared deep in thought as they took his truck back to his ranch, and Carolina didn't want to disturb him. He was no doubt considering how he was going to handle the situation if Johnny was, as Wyatt suspected, somewhere on his property. It wasn't going to be an easy conversation.

Carolina was grateful it was Wyatt who had this lead and not someone else who didn't know Johnny as well. He was already going to be in a world of trouble when he was caught. He would need all of Wyatt and Carolina's help to run interference for him with the boys ranch.

Like Wyatt, Carolina had no doubt in her mind that Johnny believed he had good reasons for running away. She knew him to be a responsible young man who applied himself to his studies and his vetting work with Wyatt. She had no qualms whatsoever about leaving Johnny to babysit Matty.

She still didn't.

But she *was* worried about poor Johnny's current state of mind, and of course the impending DFPS visit to the boys ranch, which might have inadvertently been made worse by Johnny's sudden disappearance.

"I didn't get around to feeding the animals this morning," Wyatt said grimly as he pulled the truck to a stop in front of his ranch house and cut the engine. "Bea called me away before I had the chance. I think

Johnny might be in the stable. He has always drawn comfort from being around animals."

"Do you want me to stay here so you can talk to him alone first?"

Wyatt's face held genuine surprise.

"What? No. I definitely think a little feminine compassion is called for here. Johnny really responds to you." He let out a breath. "Besides, I'm not even certain that my theory is correct. He could be halfway across the state by now, for all I know."

"Or he could be in your barn."

"Right." Wyatt pressed his lips into a hard line and gave a clipped nod. "Well, there's only one way to find out."

He exited the cab and went around to open her door, giving her a hand out of the truck. It wasn't that she really needed his assistance as much as emotional support. It was a nice gesture, especially when he closed his hand over hers as they set off toward the stable.

He paused just outside the door. "Let's hope I'm right about this."

She squeezed his hand in response. She immediately noticed one obvious difference when they entered the shadowed building—the sound of a pair of antlers butting repeatedly against a stall door.

"Wyatt, look!" She pressed forward, surprised to see the injured buck not only up on its feet again, but tossing its head and bleating in annoyance over being cooped up.

Wyatt's face was beaming as he approached the stall. "Well, now. Look at you. Easy does it, big fella."

"He's better?"

"I'd say so." Wyatt picked off his hat and slicked

back his hair with the palm of his hand. "I can't believe my eyes. I really thought we were going to lose him."

As Carolina's eyes adjusted to the dimness of the interior of the barn, she noticed a brief movement in the back of the deer's stall, a scuttle toward the darkest corner.

"Wyatt," she said softly, nodding in the direction she'd seen the slight shadow of movement.

He arched his eyebrows and replaced his hat, then settled his hands on the stall door, ignoring the startled shifting of the buck.

"You can come out now, Johnny," Wyatt said, his voice low, even and gentle. "It's just Carolina and me. No one else knows you're here."

There was a long moment of silence before Johnny unfolded his lanky frame from the back corner of the stall.

Wyatt opened the stall door and Carolina distracted the buck while Johnny slipped through and Wyatt clicked the lock back into place.

Now that Carolina could see Johnny was safe, she had to bite her lip to keep from chastising him. The relief that washed through her was quickly followed by dismay. He'd put himself in danger, not only by running away, but by crawling into the buck's stall the way he had. He might not have been intentionally trying to hurt himself, but spending the night in an enclosed space with a wild animal was hardly a wise thing to do.

She knew she would come off sounding critical, or worse yet, angry, so she held her tongue. Her emotions were all the place, from the fear of not being able to find Johnny to the joy of once again seeing his unmanageable mop of curly hair. Anxiety, frustration and the realization of how much she cared for

Johnny whirled together like a cyclone, creating a perfect storm she could barely contain.

"How long have you been here?" Wyatt didn't seem to be struggling with the same stresses she was feeling, or else he was better at hiding his emotions. But that was just as well. She'd let him deal with the fallout.

"I c-came here in the middle of the n-night," Johnny answered hesitantly, his stutter amplified by the direness of the situation.

"You bunked with a wild buck?"

Johnny nodded.

"Why would you do that? Haven't I taught you anything? You had to have known how dangerous that was."

"H-he was hurt. I thought he might be d-dying. H-he was lying on his s-side and was having trouble breathing. I p-put his head on my lap and stroked his n-neck so he would know he w-wasn't alone."

Carolina's eyes pricked with tears. Johnny had such a sensitive heart, and an enormous capacity for love. He reminded her of Wyatt in so many ways.

She only hoped this incident didn't ruin his future plans. She didn't know what doors needed to open in order for him to continue his education and training, but she hoped he would find his way. She well knew how difficult life could be for a young man in Johnny's position.

"I f-fell asleep. When I woke up, the buck was standing up. I think h-he's better now."

Wyatt's eyes left Johnny long enough to inspect the deer. "I agree. I'll need your help to return him to the wild where he belongs."

Johnny's enormous, thickly lashed brown eyes grew

even bigger as he pushed that stubborn curl off his forehead.

"You're not m-mad at me?"

Wyatt's gaze flashed to Carolina before narrowing on the teenager. "What you did was wrong, but I think you already know that. There are a lot of people out looking for you right now, taking time out of their day to make sure you're safe."

"I'm s-sorry, sir."

Wyatt sighed. "I know you are. Listen. Why don't we stop by my kitchen and grab a cup of coffee before we take you back to the boys ranch? I'll text Bea to let her know we found you safe and sound and that she can call off the search."

Johnny squared his shoulders.

"I'm not going back."

Wyatt's hands briefly formed into fists. It was the first indication Carolina had seen of the frustration she knew that he had to be feeling.

"Johnny, this isn't up for discussion," Wyatt said firmly.

"You really gave us all a scare," Carolina added gently. "There are a lot of good people out there looking for you right now."

Johnny strode deeper into the stable and picked up his duffel bag from behind a bale of hay, where he'd clearly hidden it the night before. The bag was overstuffed with books. Sharp corners were sticking out everywhere at odd angles.

Johnny struggled just to sling the thing over his shoulder. He wouldn't get very far dragging that much weight around with him.

"Let's at least talk about this," Carolina suggested, holding her hands out to show she meant no harm. It was like dealing with a wild animal. There was no telling what Johnny would do if he was pressed. The teenager was every bit as likely to bolt as the young buck in the stall behind them, if given the opportunity.

"I'm n-not going back," Johnny repeated, lifting his chin in open defiance. Carolina had never seen him behave this way—more like a rebel than the sweet boy who went out of his way to help injured animals.

Wyatt shoved his hands into the pockets of his fleece-lined jeans jacket and rocked back on the heels of his boots.

"All right," he said evenly. "Why don't you tell us why you left, and explain why you don't want to come back to the boys ranch with us. Are you being bullied? Is someone threatening you?"

Johnny's anxious gaze flitted from Wyatt to Carolina and then back to Wyatt again.

"We're listening," Carolina assured him softly. "We're not here to judge."

Johnny dropped his gaze and scuffed at the dirt floor with the toe of his boot.

"I am t-turning eighteen soon," he said miserably.

"Right," Wyatt agreed. "At the end of the school year in May you will age out of the program anyway. I don't understand. Why would you want to leave now? You're going to graduate from high school soon. You've worked far too hard to miss that."

"I d-didn't want to say goodbye."

Wyatt arched his eyebrows in surprise. "Why would you have to say goodbye? Aren't you planning to stay here in Haven? I'm sure I remember you mentioning how much you like the town."

"I d-don't have a family."

Carolina could feel Johnny's desolation as if it were

her own. The sweet young man really was all alone in the world, and soon he would no longer be a member of the boys ranch, which was the only home he had.

Wyatt's head jerked as if someone had slapped him. He stepped forward and clasped the young man's shoulders, forcing him to meet his eyes.

"Yes, you do, Johnny," Wyatt said without a trace of doubt in his voice. "You do have a family, and a home—if you want it."

Carolina's heart clenched. Did that mean Wyatt was staying in Haven?

Wyatt was offering Johnny everything he'd ever wanted. A home. A family. She was genuinely happy for Johnny. It looked like there were some happy times coming for the boy, and no one deserved it more than Johnny. She didn't begrudge him any of it.

But it made her realize all that she didn't have, all that, until this moment, she hadn't even realized she wanted.

Why did it have to hurt so much?

Chapter Ten

Johnny's words had hit Wyatt like a freight train. How could the boy not see how valued—how loved—he was?

"I would be honored if you would come live with me after you age out of the boys ranch program," Wyatt said, dipping his head so the teenager could see that his words were in earnest.

"W-why?"

"Well, for one thing, Haven and the boys ranch are keeping me really busy as a veterinarian. I was hoping maybe after you finished attending college and vet school that you would join my practice."

Johnny's eyes lit up like fireworks at the mention of school, but the flame was just as quickly extinguished, doused by the reality of the situation.

"I d-don't have money for school. I thought I'd h-have to learn a trade."

"You'll learn a trade," Wyatt agreed, clapping Johnny's back. "But you have to go to college to become a veterinarian. I have money. And there are scholarships available for a bright young man such as yourself. I'm sure you must have heard that the Lone Star

Cowboy League offers a good one. I'll help you with the applications. Have you thought about which college you would like to attend?"

Johnny's mouth worked but no sound came out. He shook his head.

"No matter. We'll figure it out together. With your grades, I don't think you will have any problem being accepted wherever you apply. You may have to start spring semester, but we'll get you where you want to go."

Johnny's brows lowered over his dark, contemplative eyes. He looked far too solemn for a teenager.

Wyatt winked and smiled, trying to lighten the mood.

"W-why me?" Johnny choked out.

Why?

Wyatt had thought it would be obvious. Hadn't he already said?

Maybe not. He wasn't good with words. He hadn't meant to confuse the lad. It was important that Johnny knew exactly where he stood in Wyatt's heart.

"Because you are like a son to me."

A high-pitched squeal from beside him made him wince and he turned to find Carolina dabbing at the tears in her eyes, her breath coming in uneven hiccups.

"Don't mind me," she said between sobs. "I'm a sucker for happy endings."

Wyatt met Johnny's gaze and rolled his eyes. They both broke into laughter.

Women.

Something good happened and they cried. He offered her his handkerchief, which she took gratefully.

"D-does that mean M-Matty is my brother?"

"Of course it does," Wyatt affirmed. He grinned,

knowing how much having a sibling—even one in name only—would mean to a young man who had, up until today, experienced a very solitary youth. After the aunt who had raised Johnny had died, he had no family to call his own.

"I want to officially adopt you. You'll not only be my apprentice, you'll be my son."

Johnny beamed.

"What about C-Carolina?"

Wyatt stiffened. He'd been completely unprepared for that question.

What *about* Carolina?

How did she fit into this picture? Was he finally ready to own up to the feelings he'd been tamping down since the moment she had returned to town with Matty in her arms?

He was still sifting through his thoughts and emotions when Carolina spoke.

"Oh, Johnny, honey, I'm afraid it doesn't work that way. You know how much we both care about you, but it isn't as easy as all that. Wyatt and I are Matty's parents, but we are not a couple."

Carolina's frank denial hit Wyatt like a punch in the gut. Every emotion that had ballooned to the surface now popped, as if she were throwing darts at them.

They weren't a couple.

Of course they weren't. He knew that. And yet...

She'd spoken the words softly but firmly, with little emotion in her tone.

He had to face the hard truth.

His feelings for her were all one-sided.

Again.

"B-but you wore red." Johnny stared at Carolina, his words faltering between bemusement and accusation.

It took Wyatt a moment to piece together what Johnny was saying, but he was faster than Carolina.

"The color of her blouse at the Valentine's social didn't mean anything, Johnny. It was only a coincidence."

"What was a—" Carolina started to ask, but Johnny interrupted her.

"But you d-danced together. I saw you."

"Wait. That letter was from you?" Carolina's expression was lined with surprise, and her voice held a note of astonishment. "*You* wrote that note? Not the mystery matchmakers?"

Johnny nodded, looking unhappy.

Wyatt felt bad for Johnny, but not as regretful as he did for himself. What a terrible time to realize that history was repeating itself.

He hadn't figured out how he felt about Carolina, so he'd never spoken of his feelings. And now it was too late for them. Just like last time.

"Johnny, you know why we danced together," Wyatt reminded him, and then quickly blew out a breath and backtracked. He hadn't meant to sound so harsh.

Carolina saved him from his blunder.

"Look, sweetie. I'm well aware Wyatt only danced with me to give you the courage to dance with Cassie. It's no big deal," Carolina assured him softly. "But you can't make more of it than it actually was."

"Besides, I'm sure Carolina will be around from time to time," Wyatt added.

He wasn't *sure* of anything. Carolina could be planning to up and move to Mars the day after the seventieth-anniversary party for all he knew.

Still, he hoped. Prayed. And he held his breath until she concurred.

"Yes, of course I'll be around." Carolina was addressing Johnny, not Wyatt, but that didn't stop relief from flooding through him at the affirmation in her words.

Where there was time, there was hope. Right? Or was he just kidding himself?

Until her next words stopped him short.

"At least until the party in March. After that we'll have to see where the Lord leads. I'm thinking about going back to school, myself, and I'm really excited about it. But Wyatt and I are parenting a child together," Carolina continued. "So at least for now, we'll be seeing a lot of each other. And if you don't mind, I would appreciate being able to call on you to babysit Matty once in a while. He really loves you, you know."

Johnny beamed. "I'd l-like that."

Wyatt's gut was grinding. What was she talking about? She was leaving Haven? Going back to school somewhere?

Did she want shared custody of Matty? He would take no less than that, and he wanted so much more. The thought made him sick. Matty should be raised by both his parents.

But now wasn't the time to hash out those details. He couldn't let his feelings for Carolina take over. Not yet. There were people waiting for them to return Johnny to the ranch.

"So can we head on back to the boys ranch then?" Wyatt asked, affectionately clapping Johnny on the shoulder and doing his best to smile.

Wyatt's heart was breaking, but Johnny's was just now starting to mend. For the moment, that would have to be enough for him.

"Everyone will be so glad to see that you're safe," Carolina said with a smile.

"I'm sorry for the t-trouble I've caused."

"It's no matter now," Wyatt assured him. "As they say, all's well that ends well."

Wyatt stole a look at Carolina, but she refused to meet his eyes.

Except when it doesn't.

Carolina struggled to keep her emotions in check as Wyatt pulled up to the boys ranch office. She had offered Johnny the front passenger's seat, but he was anxious about returning to the ranch and chose to sit in the back of the cab where he could be alone with his thoughts.

Obviously, she and Wyatt couldn't have any kind of serious conversation with Johnny in the truck, but then again, what was there to say?

Wyatt had made it crystal clear where they stood in their relationship, if she could even call it that. They were in a relationship insofar as parenting Matty was concerned, but that was as far as it went.

She didn't know why it was bothering her so much. Their status hadn't changed from this morning, before they had learned that Johnny had run away.

Everything was exactly the same. For the day. The week. And the whole last month, for that matter.

So what *had* changed?

As the realization of the truth washed over her, she clasped her hands in her lap so she had something to hold on to.

She had changed.

She was not the woman who had rushed out of

Haven, pregnant and terrified and too proud to admit she couldn't do it all on her own—nor did she want to.

Wyatt was a fabulous father to Matty, just as she had known he would be. And now Wyatt's relationship with Johnny was blooming into fruition. She got choked up just thinking about what a wonderful life Wyatt had offered that young man. And having Johnny in his life would be a tremendous blessing to Wyatt, as well.

It was almost worse knowing that Wyatt intended to stay in Haven and not bound off to foreign lands. How could she ever have thought that he would put his personal dreams over a relationship with his son?

That wasn't who Wyatt was. It never had been.

Why had it taken her until now to realize that over the years, Wyatt's dreams might have changed? Since she'd been back, she had never once asked him about what he wanted out of life, but instead had made assumptions that she could now see were erroneous and maybe always had been.

It was as if her eyes were suddenly opened to the truth. Wyatt was happy living here in Haven, volunteering at the boys ranch and working as the town's veterinarian. And now he had a family to make it all worthwhile. Complete.

Except that family didn't include her.

Not really. Even though she now understood just how much she wanted to be a part of it.

Instead, she would be living on the outskirts of that family—on the outside of the house, looking in. Watching Wyatt and Johnny and Matty growing closer and closer as a family unit, while she would be all alone. Wyatt might eventually even marry, and—

She closed her eyes and willed away the thought.

She couldn't even go there. Her pulse hammered in her temple. She didn't usually get headaches, but this one was almost more than she could bear.

Still, being distracted by a headache was better than thinking about her *heartache*.

"Looks like we made it just in time." Wyatt nodded toward the black SUV that had pulled up next to the truck.

A middle-aged woman, her blond hair clipped back in a tight bun, exited the vehicle. Not only was she unfamiliar to Carolina, but she had the clipboard-holding look of an official government employee stamped all over her.

"Am I in t-trouble?" Johnny's voice wavered with anxiety. He had seen the woman, too.

Carolina glanced back and smiled reassuringly. "I can't see why you would be. Once we explain the situation to Bea, I'm sure she'll understand."

"What about that l-lady?"

"I'll talk to her," Wyatt assured him.

An official-looking woman was shaking hands with Bea as Wyatt, Carolina and Johnny entered the front office. Gabe, Katie and Pastor Andrew were also present. Katie was seated at the desk with Pastor Andrew standing directly behind her. Gabe stood casually leaning his shoulder against one wall, his arms crossed in front of him.

Bea's eyes lit up with relief the moment her gaze landed on Johnny.

"You scared ten years off my life, young man, and I can't afford to lose that much time." Even as she was scolding Johnny, she was wrapping him in a big bear hug. "Wyatt, Carolina, this is Ms. Angela White from the DFPS."

Ms. White had an openly curious expression on her face but did not ask the obvious question.

Bea turned Johnny around by the shoulders and introduced him to the government agent.

"Johnny Drake here is one of our finest success stories. Before he came to the boys ranch, he was creating a bit of havoc in the school he was attending. He was probably just standing up to the bullies, if you ask me. Anyway, since he's been here, he has turned his life around. He's gone from flunking out of school to having straight A's, and he has been specially mentored by our veterinarian, Wyatt Harrow, who volunteers here at the ranch in his free time."

Bea gestured toward Wyatt, who tipped his hat in greeting but said nothing.

Ms. White's gaze moved from Wyatt to Bea and then finally settled on Johnny.

"Why do I feel like there is a part of this story that you are not telling me?"

Carolina's anxious gaze caught Wyatt's. Without saying a word, his eyes and expression bolstered her confidence.

"It was all a misunderstanding, really," Carolina explained. "You see, Johnny is aging out of the boys ranch program soon, and he no longer has any living relatives to go home to. He wasn't sure he could handle a formal dismissal, so he decided he would leave us early and avoid the agony of saying goodbye."

"He ran away," Ms. White summed up neatly, scribbling something on the memo pad on her clipboard.

"No," Carolina exclaimed. "Well, yes, technically, but as you can see, he's here now."

"Yes, I can see that." Ms. White drummed her pen against the clipboard and turned her speculative gaze on Johnny. "And what do you have to say for yourself, young man?"

"I d-didn't mean to cause any t-trouble."

Carolina inwardly cringed at poor Johnny's stutter, made more pronounced by his anxiety.

"I'm s-sorry I r-ran away. But I'm okay now. I have a new f-family. Right, Wyatt?"

Johnny's hopeful gaze shifted to Wyatt, who stepped forward and laid a hand on his shoulder.

"That's right. He'll be coming to live with me after the end of the school year. I'm going to make sure he gets into college and vet school, and then he will join me in my practice here in Haven."

"Why, that's wonderful," Bea exclaimed. "See, Ms. White? A real success story."

Carolina was all choked up by the way the drama was unfolding, and she had to blink back the tears in her eyes. She couldn't imagine that Ms. White didn't feel the same way.

"Let me speak frankly," said the agent. "There is no doubt that the boys ranch has done and is doing good things for the residents who participate in the program. I can even understand a little…slipup like Johnny's, although I expect I won't hear of any further incidents such as this one."

She paused and her gaze swept the room.

"My concern in coming here today is that you appear to have been targeted by a person or persons who wish to do the boys ranch—and possibly the residents who live here—harm. When innocuous pranks and petty theft turn to arson, the DFPS can't help but notice. I'm here to evaluate whether the boys' safety has been compromised."

"What does that mean for the ranch?" Gabe asked the question that was on everyone's minds.

"Well—Gabe, is it? What that means is that the boys ranch might need to be, temporarily, at least, suspended from providing services. We can't risk putting the boys' lives in danger. That is simply out of the question."

"I thoroughly agree," said Bea. "But I'm not convinced closing down the ranch is the best course of action. There must be some other way we can handle it."

"There is," said a deep voice from the doorway.

Carolina turned to see Texas Ranger Heath Grayson taking up most of the doorway, none too gently shoving a man in handcuffs into the room before him.

"This is Donald Nall," Heath said grimly. "Bea, I think if you look up his name in the boys ranch records from about ten years ago or so, you will discover that his parents put in an application to have him sent here."

"Yeah, except you guys turned me down."

Nall lunged at Bea. Katie screamed. Carolina took an involuntary step backward.

It all happened in an instant, but Nall was quickly restrained again and never made contact with Bea. Heath had a good grip on his arm, and Wyatt and Gabe surrounded him. Standing about five-ten, Nall looked small compared to all the other men, and he didn't put up much of a fight.

Pastor Andrew drew Katie into his arms and smoothed her hair away from her face. "It's okay, sweetheart."

"This is all your fault," Nall accused basely, glaring at Bea. "You were supposed to fix me. You were supposed to *fix me*!"

Heath gave him a little shake. "Nall here has already done time on drug charges, and he has a history of mental health issues."

Bea nodded compassionately. "That was probably the reason why he didn't qualify for the boys ranch."

To Carolina's surprise, Bea stepped right in front of Nall and faced him squarely. "I am very sorry we were unable to assist you, Mr. Nall. Unfortunately, we have to turn down many worthy cases. I truly hope you will be able to find the help you need."

"Oh, he'll get the help he needs," Heath assured them. "He'll have plenty of time to do some soul-searching where he's going."

"Go with God's blessing," Pastor Andrew added. "We'll be praying for you."

"Are you serious?" Nall spat. "You keep away from me, preacher."

"Come on, Nall," Heath said as the sound of police sirens drew near. "Your ride is here."

Heath removed Nall from the room, and for a moment the only sound Carolina heard was the rasp of her own breath.

Bea turned to the DFPS agent. "So, Ms. White. Would you like a tour of the grounds? I can introduce you to some of the volunteers who work here."

The agent dropped the clipboard to her side. "I would really like that, but I think I will have to decline and make it another day. There is clearly no reason for me to tarry here, and I have a full caseload I need to address."

"Maybe you can come out some weekend when you're free and take some time to look around," Katie suggested.

Ms. White showed her first real smile, and Carolina thought it brightened up her whole face. "I would like that. I'll show myself out now. You all have a great day."

A knock sounded just as Ms. White was leaving.

"Please come in," Bea told an unfamiliar woman. Pretty and young with short brown hair, the lady was accompanied by four-year-old twins.

"I'm sorry to bother you, but I'm looking for Bea Brewster."

"You've found her," Bea said with a smile.

"I'm Avery Culpepper?" Her voice rose as if it were a question and not a statement of fact.

"Avery Culpepper?" Gabe repeated.

Avery looked from one of them to the other. "I'm sorry. Are you all in the middle of something?"

"Not at all," Bea assured her. "You can't imagine how happy we are to see you. Have you checked into the hotel yet? I've got a bathroom next to my office where you can freshen up. I imagine you've had a long day of travel."

"No. I mean, no thank you. It has been a long day, and my girls, Dinah and Debbie, need to rest, but if you don't mind, I'd like to talk to you now. I'm not sure how long I'll be in town."

Bea smiled. "We'd like to persuade you to stay. Your grandfather left you an inheritance in his will."

"So I understand. I think it would help me to hear the details before I start considering my options." She blew out a nervous breath and smiled.

"Of course. Shall we go back to my office?" Bea gestured her through to the other room.

"Well," said Gabe, running a hand across his jaw, "that's two problems solved, anyway."

"You still haven't found your grandfather?" Carolina asked sympathetically.

"I haven't even had a single decent lead, and time is working against me." Gabe groaned and shoved his fingers through his hair.

"Is there anything we can do to help?" Wyatt asked.

"Honestly? I've got nothing."

Carolina cringed, because that was exactly how she was feeling, too.

She had nothing.

The group dispersed. Carolina was halfway to her car when Wyatt caught up with her, reaching for her elbow and whirling her around to face him.

"You're going back to school?" he demanded, his voice low and gravelly.

"I—yes. I'm thinking about it." She hesitated. She had put in applications to a couple of business schools and had been accepted, but she hadn't yet said anything to Wyatt. In hindsight, she realized she might have been putting the cart before the horse. Just because she wanted to stay in Haven and work in Wyatt's office didn't mean he wanted her there.

He certainly didn't look happy. He lowered his brow and clamped his jaw. "You would leave? With Matty?"

"Well, yes, but—"

"I'll fight you, you know. I didn't want it to come to this, but I won't let you take my son away from me. Not this time."

Was that what he thought she was doing?

She opened her mouth to explain and then closed it again as fury washed through her, followed by a new wave of guilt. Clearly Wyatt hadn't forgiven her for the past. He believed she was the same woman she'd been back then, a woman who would take his son away from him.

He might as well have stabbed her in the heart.

And he'd turned all her plans on end. If he didn't trust her, he wouldn't want her working for him, so attending school would mean nothing. She'd only planned to be gone for the few months it took to get a certificate in administrative assisting.

Which would be worthless, now. He had taken away her last lifeline.

In planning his own life—with Matty, and with Johnny—he'd taken away hers.

She would not leave Haven. She would not do that to Wyatt, not again, no matter what he thought of her. But as to the future?

An ocean of loneliness.

Chapter Eleven

It was a good day.

It was Gran's one hundredth birthday, and she not only recognized Wyatt, but even seemed happy to see him. Much of the town had gathered to help celebrate.

It remained to be seen whether this good day would become a great day, or else would degenerate into the worst day of his entire life. There was no middle ground here.

Sink or swim. Feast or famine.

But he had to know. He couldn't just keep on with the status quo. His life had to change, one way or the other. And today was the day he would make that happen.

"Queen for the day," Carolina said, approaching Gran with a sparkling silver tiara. "For the birthday girl. Don't you look just lovely?"

"Two prettiest ladies in the room," Wyatt admired, snapping some pictures with his cell phone. He laughed when Carolina hid her face behind her hands.

He was in awe of all she had done. She had planned and executed the whole party virtually on her own. She'd allowed Wyatt and Johnny in on her secrets only when it was time to decorate the main room at the nursing home.

All the crepe paper and banners were in various colors of green, since spring was Gran's favorite season. Accents were in sparkling silver and gold. The room really did look amazingly transformed. Carolina had spent hours making sure everything was just right.

They had invited most of the staff from the boys ranch, and many of the residents of the nursing home were milling around. Most of the elderly population had no idea it was Gran's one hundredth birthday, or even who Gran was, but they were up for a party.

And so, thankfully, was Gran. She was using a wheelchair today, but that didn't matter, since she was the center of attention. Matty, sporting a navy blue suit and a red bow tie, was entranced by the wheelchair and toddling around with Gran. She, in turn, was delighted by the boy.

"Are you ready to blow out the candles on your cake?" Carolina asked, wheeling Gran toward the table with a tiered cake. "Chocolate cake with chocolate frosting, just as you like it. We've even got chocolate ice cream."

Wyatt hushed the crowd and then led off a round of "Happy Birthday." Carolina chuckled at his off-key rendition and he laughed with her. He loved to see her happy.

He loved *her*.

Enough to let her go, if that was what she truly wanted. Once he'd calmed down from learning of Carolina's plans to go back to school, he'd realized she was a different person than the one who'd left him before. He didn't know anything for certain in this crazy world his life had turned into, but he trusted Carolina. She would let him be a part of Matty's life.

But he wanted so much more than that, and there was no time like the present to tell her so. He had an engagement ring—the one he'd purchased for her three years ago—burning a hole in his pocket.

Sink or swim was an understatement.

He found his moment and pulled Carolina aside.

"When are you planning on leaving?" he asked in a ragged whisper.

She straightened her shoulders and looked him straight in the eye. "I'm not."

"You should."

"I should?" Her eyes widened and color rushed to her face. "Why? I mean, it's kind of pointless, isn't it?"

Wyatt felt like he'd lost track of the conversation. "I don't understand."

She shrugged. "All that matters is that I'm staying. So you can be with Matty." She didn't sound enthused about it.

He framed her face in his hands. "That's not all that matters, Carolina. If you need to go back to school to make yourself happy, then I want you to know I support you in that."

"You do?"

"Well, of course, if that's what you want. We've made a real success of coparenting that way."

She cringed when he mentioned coparenting.

"I had already decided to stay in town, even before you approached me just now."

Relief flooded through him, but he couldn't get past the niggling notion that something else was wrong.

"I found a business school where I can take all my classes online."

"You want to go into business?"

"I want to keep working for you."

"You do?" Now he was the one asking.

"That was always the plan. I was going to go back to school to become a certified medical office assistant. But I didn't speak to you about it first. How presumptuous of me. And I couldn't leave knowing I would disrupt your relationship with Matty."

Wyatt couldn't hold back his grin. She wasn't going to leave. It was *almost* the best news she could have given him.

So why didn't she look happy about it?

Maybe…just maybe…

His nerves were crackling and his heart was beating double time.

"The party is great. My gran is really happy."

She looked startled at the sudden change of topic, but after a moment she went with it. "I'm glad for her."

Wyatt caught Johnny's attention. The teenager was playing with Matty, and Wyatt motioned them both to join him, laughing and scooping Matty up into his arms.

"I've got to say, it looks like you've thought of just about everything where this party is concerned," he murmured close to Carolina's ear.

"Just about everything? What did I miss?" She cast her gaze around the room before her eyes returned to Wyatt.

Wyatt shoved his hand into his pocket and withdrew the diamond solitaire.

"This." His throat closed around the word.

Carolina's beautiful golden-brown eyes widened and her hand went to her neck. Matty grabbed for the shiny ring, but Wyatt laughed and held it out of his reach.

"This one is for your mama, big guy."

"I—you—"

"You're stuttering w-worse than m-me," Johnny teased.

"That's okay," Wyatt said, chuckling. Hoping. Praying. "All you have to say is yes."

"Yes," she whispered and held out her left hand so he could slide the ring on her finger. "But I thought—I thought—"

He laughed. "I can see that."

"You said we weren't a couple."

"No. *You* said we weren't a couple. And I'm fixing that little oversight right now. I realized after I had time to think about it that even if you were leaving town to return to school, you'd never leave me again. Not the way you did the first time. I trust you, Carolina. And I love you. It's not enough for us to coparent Matty. I want us to be a real family."

"I won't be on the outside looking in."

"No, sweetheart, you won't be," he assured her, his voice husky.

"C-can I call you Mom?" Johnny asked, his face turning a healthy shade of red.

Carolina kissed the teenager's cheek. "You'd better."

"Mama. Mama." Matty evidently felt he needed to add to the conversation.

"Your mama," Wyatt agreed enthusiastically. "My beloved wife."

Wow, that sounded good.

Her smile as big as the sun, Carolina wrapped one arm around Wyatt's waist and the other around Johnny's shoulder, forming a perfect circle.

A family unit.

Wyatt bent his head and softly kissed Carolina's lips, realizing his every dream had just come true.

Carolina's head was spinning. She couldn't help but flash the diamond solitaire, appreciating the glinting of the light off the cut of the stone.

This morning she had been alone, a coparent who would watch the love of her life move on with his, while she spent her heart-wrenching life alone.

Now she had Wyatt—and she had a family.

Thank You, God. Thank You, God.

She whispered the words over and over.

Katie approached and Carolina dropped her arm, but not before Katie had seen the ring. She squealed and reached for Carolina's hand.

"When did this happen? I'm so sure you didn't tell me."

Carolina laughed. "I only just learned about it a moment ago, myself."

"Wyatt just proposed?"

She nodded and put a finger over her lips. "Yes, but I don't want to make a big deal out of it. This is Gran's day. I don't want to steal her limelight."

"I'm sure she doesn't mind sharing," said Wyatt, coming up behind Carolina and wrapping his arm around her shoulders, drawing her close to him and kissing her on the cheek.

"Good thing, too. Because I see Bea headed our direction. Wyatt and Carolina are engaged," Katie spouted excitedly as Bea approached.

"I thought there might be something like that in the works," Bea said with a knowing grin. Carolina couldn't see how. *She* hadn't known anything was in the works until Wyatt had pulled that ring out of his pocket.

"Before I make a formal announcement," Bea continued, "I have another question for you, Carolina."

Carolina couldn't imagine how the day could get any better.

"I know you're working at Wyatt's office, but would you consider being a part-time nurse for the boys ranch? We can't pay as much as I imagine you were used to getting, and it's mostly going to be just scraped knees and bumped heads, but if you're willing, we'd love to have you."

Carolina couldn't speak. How could one day have gone from absolute misery to absolute bliss?

She nodded, and Wyatt gave her a reassuring squeeze.

"When God blesses, He really blesses," Wyatt murmured.

She turned toward him and lifted her face for a kiss. She was so wrapped up in Wyatt—the feel of his lips, the familiar scent of leather, animals and man that was distinctly Wyatt, his deep groan that sounded like a wildcat's purr—that she almost missed Bea's announcement.

Bea took her glass and tapped it with a spoon. "Ladies and gentlemen, I'd like to introduce the future Dr. and Mrs. Wyatt Harrow."

"Carolina Harrow," Wyatt murmured next to her ear. "That has a nice ring to it."

She turned into his embrace.

"I agree," she said between kisses that stole the breath from her. "And the sooner, the better."

* * * * *